ı

\ ...Dolphin Conservation, Campaign for Rural England, The Wildlife Trusts and We are Cycling UK.

Born in 1958, he is a baby boomer. This is his first novel.

JAKUB CICHECKI was trained to be an architect but left this industry to draw, paint and design graphics.

His main focus is environment design and landscape painting – he creates art for publishers, animation, games and the advertising industry.

He's a child of baby boomers, happy husband and father.

CULL
2031

NICK THOMAS

This paperback edition published in 2022
By Forbois Books
Frensham House, Beckford, Tewkesbury, GL207AD

Copyright © Nick Thomas 2021
Images © Jakub Cichecki 2021

The right of Nick Thomas to be identified as the author of this
work has been asserted in accordance with the Copyright,
Designs and Patents Act 1988 Sections 77 and 78.

All rights reserved. No part of this publication may be reproduced,
stored in a retrieval system, or transmitted in any form or by any means,
electronic, mechanical, photocopying, recording or otherwise,
without prior permission of the copyright holder.

This is a work of fiction. Names, characters, places and incidents either
are products of the author's imagination or are used fictitiously. Any
resemblance to actual events or locales or persons, living
or dead, is entirely coincidental.

And why not do evil that good may come?

Romans 3:8

CONTENTS

12 February 2031, Virginia, USA
Cull Day 1

John Wilkes Booth, Charles J. Guiteau, Leon Czolgosz, Lee Harvey Oswald – the president killers.

Twenty-two-year-old Todd Shears had waited inside the furnace-hot, bleach-reeking metal box all night because he wanted to add his name to that list. The list of men who had changed their world and their times with a single calculated act of violence.

Sitting, cramped and dripping inside a restroom cupboard in the National Rifle Association's headquarters in Virginia, was the only way Shears could get near the particular president he needed to kill.

William H. Jefferson had become an enemy of a cause he believed in so passionately, he would gladly commit murder for it. To Shears, Jefferson's role as Climate Change Denier-in-Chief meant he had to die. Nestled in his pocket was the tool that would help him do it – a Springfield XD-S semi-automatic pistol.

Shears could have gone for a lighter calibre gun, but had reasoned that while his target wasn't fit, he was big – six foot and two hundred and forty pounds. He would need a heavy bullet to bring him down. Testing the gun at his local club convinced him that he had made the right choice. Although the recoil felt like high-fiving a hammer, the extra punch would make it deadly at short range. He intended to be within touching distance of Jefferson when he fired.

And when the tyrant was lying lifeless on the floor in his blood and his speech notes, Shears reckoned he would be ready for the ferocious retribution that would fall on him. He was ready for his moment of destiny.

Looking down at his watch, he could just make out the faint numbers – 12.50. Jefferson should be here in ten minutes. Shears knew he liked to check himself in the nearest washroom before important speaking engagements, and this one was a big deal for him. All the media networks would be here to report on his unwavering support for the gun lobby. With an election just a year away, he needed the NRA's votes and would say whatever he had to, to remain popular with their massive membership base.

Shears tried to forget his complaining muscles by studying the mundanity around him in his gloomy hiding place. The green-handled mop near the door, leaning at a fifteen-degree angle. The wooden broom and its worn-out brush. The unopened packet of yellow sponge cloths. The five toilet cleaner bottles with the duck-shaped nozzles. The dispenser of Eazy-Kleen sink wipes. The pile of plastic wrapped toilet rolls. The inventory stuck to the door. The confederate flag bumper sticker. The graffiti scrawl proclaiming 'JED'S A FAGGOT'.

His mind wandered to what his mother might say when she saw his name on the news. All his life he'd felt he was a disappointment to her.

But when I pull this off, she'll talk about me differently. 'That's Todd, my son; the son who killed the tyrant, who created the moment, who started the revolution that saved the world.'

Suddenly, the door crashed open and two thickset men in identical dark blue suits hustled into the restroom. One of them disappeared into a cubicle and closed the door. The second man checked out the other cubicles before lumbering over to the large mirror positioned over the sinks.

'Big Bird just touched down,' the man at the mirror called out, pushing a greasy comb through greying hair.

'Everything's set for the usual in and out. He'll be back in the air in forty-five minutes' came the voice behind the cubicle door.

'Come on, dude. We've got to be in the lobby when he gets here. You know he likes a good show of muscle.'

'Ain't finished. Lousy NRA food. I'll be down in two.'

'Make it snappy. Check out those utility cupboards before you leave.' Reluctantly, the first man left the room, leaving Shears alone with the crapping agent. He started sweating again. He could feel a migraine coming. This wasn't how he had planned it, being stuck in here with an armed security agent when the president arrived.

There was a frenetic rustling from inside the cubicle, but the door still remained closed. Shears could hear sirens off in the distance. Excited chatter echoing in the corridor, and the familiar opening notes of 'The Star-Spangled Banner' starting up. The noise of walking became louder, then died down again. He despaired.

Jefferson isn't coming in. He's passed us by.
Shit, shit, shit. Weeks of planning for nothing.

Shears had moved to nearby Fairfax and managed to get a job as the general maintenance man at the building. He had performed all the low life jobs, passed all the security checks and lived alone in a pokey bedsit for a chance at his great moment. Now there would be no great moment, no starting gun for the climate revolution. And Todd Shears would not be joining the list of president killers. Not on this day at least. He'd just have to stay put, then sneak out tonight. There will be another conference and another chance soon.

But I proved I could get near the bastard.

Just as he was resigning himself to a few more hours of discomfort, a familiar booming voice sounded from outside, and he entered.

Even through the narrow letterbox of vision he had, Shears could still make out the unmistakeable, lumbering figure of the forty-seventh President of the United States, William A. Jefferson. He was as imposing as the would-be assassin had imagined, wide-shouldered, thick-necked – a bear of a man – yet he walked softly, almost gracefully, over to the mirror. Giving himself a little grin, Jefferson checked his teeth and began rearranging his thinning grey hair. To Shears, his probably once handsome face now looked like a partially deflated balloon; he was transfixed by the sight, not moving, not breathing.

Still no noise from the cubicle.

Then Shears remembered what he was here to do.

As he moved forward, no more than half an inch, the sweat that had pooled behind his knees ran down his calves. His heart pounded as he slowly, so slowly inched his hand down inside his jacket for the gun. He felt every muscle in his body tense. He paused, trying to relax, worried he might start cramping. Silently edging the green-handled mop aside, he nudged the small metal door open a fraction and braced his legs for the two-foot drop to the floor.

Shears felt he was making enough noise to wake the dead, but Jefferson seemed too preoccupied with his hair to notice. Just as he was about to leap down, the cubicle door burst open and the agent emerged wearing a face mask, black plastic smock over his jacket and holding a heavy pistol with a silencer.

Jefferson turned to face his assailant. Just as he did, a bullet hit him square in the chest and he fell backwards like a felled oak, his head striking the edge of the sink with a sickening crash. The agent was now over him, staring down at the helpless figure on the floor. Jefferson lay with his hands above his head, his legs spreadeagled like a child about to make angel shapes in the snow. He looked vulnerable and pathetic. The agent hesitated for a moment as Jefferson looked up, trying to say something, the words bubbling in his blood-filled throat. His hand came up weakly, as if reaching for something that only he could see.

'A message from Reboot, Mr President.'

Two more bullets smashed into Jefferson's distorted face. Blood spattered up the walls as his body convulsed against the shock of the impacts.

The most powerful man in the world had ceased to be. It had taken just ten savage seconds.

Shears thought he was going to throw up, but knew he had to stay silent or he would be next. The agent calmly took off his mask and blood-covered smock and threw them on the floor. Unscrewing the silencer, he slipped the gun inside his jacket, then opened the window and was gone. The revolution had sounded its starting pistol, and it had had nothing to do with Todd Shears.

20 February 1970, San Jose, California

'Honey, wish I could stay, but I can't. We're going to bury a car today, right outside the Union building!'

Sarah Homer jumped out of her lover's bed, scooped up the crumpled lime-green kaftan from the floor, pulled it over her long auburn hair and shook it down over her naked body. Perched on the edge of a frayed wicker chair, she carefully laced the knee-length brown boots she wore every day, come rain or shine. And today was a gloriously shiny early spring day in San Jose, and Sarah Homer really was going to help bury a car – a shiny new yellow Ford Maverick.

The burial was the climax of the week-long Survival Fair, organised by her State University to 'send a signal to the world that the automobile represented a grave danger to the survival of mankind.'

The fair's organising committee had wanted to use a well-known muscle car like the Dodge Charger but couldn't raise the money, so it had to be a Ford. This was just fine as far as Sarah Homer was concerned. It was still one of the cars responsible for eighty-five per cent of the nation's air pollution, and now it was about to disappear under the California dirt without its key being turned.

Homer bounded down the stairs, stepped out of the front door and was immediately swept up in a tide of people as they excitedly made their way up the hill towards the site of the big event. She picked her way across the road into the College Park and began to run. She ran because she was excited, because she was late and because she was eager to meet up with the three people who had made this week possible. The people she loved more than anybody else in the world.

The San Jose Student Union building situated near the main entrance to the college was a handsome and elegantly proportioned structure. Designed in the colonial revival style, it was built from plum-coloured brick and white marble with an extravagant colonnaded façade. Just as Homer arrived and headed for the large crowd that had gathered directly in front of it, the clock mounted into the bell tower on its roof began to chime for midday.

Pushing her way through to the centre of the ruck, she found herself on the edge of a large steep-sided rectangular hole with dirt piled high on three of its sides; at one end, a thirty-degree ramp had been created for the car to slide down. Peering down into the deep shadow of the bottom of the hole, Homer could make out the familiar stocky figure energetically smoothing its steep sides with a spade – her best friend, Mary Delaney. Her face, hair, clothes, and even her teeth were coated in soil and clay, but she was laughing.

Homer called down, 'Delaney, you wacko. Where you want to get to? Australia already?'

Delaney stopped her frenetic spade work and looked up, squinting at the sunlight. 'That you, Homer? You were supposed to be down here with me this morning. You put fucking before digging *again*. Whore.'

The students around the hole laughed, and so did Homer. Delaney was right; she had no enthusiasm for labour, but as she always pointed out when challenged by the others, 'I make up for it with brains.'

Suddenly a cry went up. 'They're coming. They're coming.'

The crowd quickly dispersed and made for the road. Homer waited for her friend and leaned down to help her up. 'C'mon. We don't want to miss the procession.'

Delaney grabbed her hand and playfully rubbed some dirt into Homer's hair. 'This should be fun.'

Along the mile length of the Plaza, students, reporters, TV crews and interested San Jose residents had lined both sides, creating a curious atmosphere of joy, anticipation and solemnity.

As they watched, an extraordinary vision moved slowly up the road towards them. A brand new, never-started, two-door, mustard-yellow Ford Maverick with blue velvet ropes draped across its bonnet, roof and trunk – being pushed along by ten students with the unhurried pace of a funeral procession. Ahead of the car, three church ministers in their fully-robed and bejewelled ecclesiastical pomp uttered prayers and thanks while a group of comely co-eds wearing emerald-green gowns walked alongside, throwing daisies into the part excited, part bemused crowd. Bringing up the rear, labouring in the noonday heat, an eight-piece brass and percussion band played a slow rhythmic dirge. They had collected the car from the dealership downtown, and for the last four hundred yards as the road steepened, the students had slowed. Now, heartened by the promise of their destination coming into view, they started to pick up the pace again.

As they approached, Homer could feel her eyes moisten with pride as she thought about what they had achieved. By her side Delaney greedily eyed the sleek lines of the gleaming coupé. 'Handsome thing. Seems a pity to total it without taking it for a blast down the coast first.'

Homer cut in quickly. 'We're not just burying just any piece of metal here. This chunk of iron is a symbol of putting dollars before the planet.'

Delaney frowned at her friend. 'True, but we could at least have started her up.'

'No way. It's important that the engine never starts. Don't you get it?'

Feeling patronised, Delaney sloped off towards the union building. 'Fuck it, I'm going to clean up and get a beer.'

Homer shouted after her. 'You'll regret not watching this!' Delaney shrugged and kept on walking.

The fervour of the crowd grew as the car finally reached the top of the hill and edged towards the side of the hole. The man who had been steering the car applied the handbrake and stepped out. With his tanned skin, muscular body, blond hair, moustache and soft Texan drawl, he had all the physical attributes of a male porn star.

Ken Driscoll got cranky when people pointed out the comparison, he took his position as the college's environmental spokesperson very seriously. Grabbing a megaphone from the back of the car, Driscoll called for quiet. He waited patiently, hands on hips, for the message to filter to those at the back.

'Great to see everyone out here today. It's been an outstanding week and the fun's not over yet!' The crowd whooped and hollered in delight as Driscoll leapt up onto the bonnet. 'As y'all know, we're not doing this for ourselves...but for our children.' More whooping as Driscoll waved his arms encouraging them to make more noise. 'We're doing this because writing to congressmen asking them to stop big corporations wrecking the planet just ain't working no more!' More hollering. Driscoll stamped his foot down hard causing the car to shake. 'People ask me why can't we rely on our congressman, Ken? And I say it's because those corrupt bastards are being paid by the likes of Ford and Exxon to turn a blind eye!' A few in the crowd murmured at the accusation, but overwhelmingly the affirmation was deafening.

Driscoll revelled in the enthusiasm for his practised rhetoric as he gleefully jumped down and pointed to the man standing to his left.

'And now folks, over to my friend Peter Trafton who will take you through the main event.'

Physically, eighteen-year-old Trafton was the antithesis of Driscoll. Thin and wiry with disproportionately long legs, he wore his dark hair military short. With large round-framed glasses perched on the tip of his nose, his high cheek bones blotched with late adolescent acne, he looked both conventional and nerdy. He was also English, his parents, both electronic engineers, had moved to California three years previously to work in nearby Silicon Valley.

'Er...thanks, Ken. And thanks ministers and thanks to the boys in the band. Not easy playing in time in this heat.' He walked over to the car and patted its roof.

'This week, San Jose has sent a clear message to Washington and corporate America. A message that will force them to rethink their priorities and policies. We don't need your cars; we don't want to be burning more fossil fuels. What we need is to live in harmony with nature and create more sustainable lives.' Trafton smiled and held his arms out wide.

'Now without further ado, I hereby commit this gasoline demon to the depths. It will never get the chance to foul our air or clog our roads. And for that we are truly grateful.'

A cry of 'Amen' went up from the crowd as Trafton continued.

'This day shall forever be known as the day we started to reclaim our planet from those who would destroy it with their greed. Bring the car forward.'

As the Maverick was slowly rolled to the edge of the ramp, the band struck up a rising single note while the marching drummer heightened the anticipation with a cacophonous drum roll. One of the church ministers came forward with a small bowl and threw splashes of holy water over the roof of the car. Trafton looked theatrically towards the sky, as if calling to a higher power. 'I declare the combustion engine dead.'

He signalled for the condemned car to be given a final push. The handbrake was released and it rolled, reluctantly at first, down the ramp. Quickly picking up speed, it hit the back wall with a resounding crash, causing it to rebound by a couple of feet before rolling forward again. As it came to a stop, one of the wing mirrors snapped off and fell with a pathetic plop into the dirt.

For a moment all was quiet, as if three hundred people were reflecting on the possible divine significance of a broken wing mirror. Then a voice shouted down from the edge of the pit.

'Rot in hell, motherfucker!'

The car's windscreen shattered as a large rock was hurled into it. Other shouts came up as more stones and missiles rained down on the hapless automobile. For a moment, it seemed the crowd was intent on smashing it to pieces before the burial. Three policemen who had been standing a few yards away impassively watching proceedings started to move towards the commotion. The sound of hundreds of clicks split the air as the assembled news photographers sensed that this was the dramatic, defining image of the event they wanted.

Driscoll ran down into the hole, waving his hands for the

students to stop. As he reached the car, he was struck in the mouth by a fist-sized piece of red brick.

Blood streaming from his lip, he screamed for order. 'Look, you fucking crazies, we want this to be reported as a peaceful ceremony! Not a riot created by a bunch of stoned hippies. The right-wing media would love that. Now for Christ's sake, let's get this thing buried with some dignity!'

As obediently as shamed children, the students put down their missiles and started to push the heaped soil over the car.

Within three hours, the hole had been filled and cut turf laid back on the topsoil. As the media, the police and students finally began to filter away, Homer, who had watched it all from fifty yards away sitting against a tree, joined Driscoll and Trafton.

'Great job, guys.' She hugged them both enthusiastically. 'This was your day to shine. We'll get a plaque made to mark this place. Maybe they'll even dig the car up in fifty years and put it in a museum.'

Homer winced at the sight of Driscoll's mouth which was still oozing blood. 'You should see a doctor. Might need stitches.'

'Make a good battle scar' said Trafton, patting him on the back.

'Dare say I'll pick up a few more before we're done, but it'll be worth it. The media's gonna make a big deal of this.' Driscoll smiled a handsome, porn star grin then looked to the union building. 'C'mon we deserve a cold beer. Bet you good money Delaney is already on her tenth.'

'J-J Joining us, Sarah?'

Trafton looked doe eyed at Homer. He harboured a massive, unrequited crush on his fellow student that had grown over the last three years into near obsession. He had convinced himself that she was perfect and that he liked virtually everything about her. Her skin, her auburn hair, her green eyes, her laugh, her easy intelligence and how close she got when she spoke to him, oblivious to the effect she was having. In fact, the only thing Trafton didn't like about Sarah Homer was that she always made him feel like a tongue-tied idiot.

'You kidding? Wouldn't miss this for the world.' To Trafton's delight she took his hand.

The three of them walked over the small rise which now marked the spot where the Maverick lay twelve feet below. They made their way under the heavy columns at the entrance to the student union building and disappeared through the ornate blue entrance door to receive the adoration of their peers.

They didn't look back once.

After leaving San Jose College, Driscoll, Trafton, Delaney and Homer abandoned their fight to save the environment. Choosing instead to join millions of other baby boomers in the quest for medical, scientific, human and economic advancement. Over the next sixty years,the achievements attributed to their generation have been remarkable:

Defeating polio, smallpox, measles, mumps, malaria and whooping cough.

Dramatically improving cancer survival rates.

Extending life expectancy in third-world countries by nearly 50 per cent.

Bringing equality of the sexes nearer than ever.

Forcing communism to its knees.

Creating the World Wide Web.

Making personal computers, smartphones and tablets available to all.

Extending our sex lives with the discovery of viagra.

Bob Dylan, The Beatles, The Beach Boys, Kate Bush, David Bowie.

Abolishing the death penalty in two-thirds of the world's countries.

Discovering DNA fingerprinting.

Inventing the implantable human heart and the portable dialysis machine.

Creating rechargeable lithium-ion batteries.

Avoiding World War Three.

Building Voyager 1, the first human-made object to leave our solar system.

Yet despite these glittering accomplishments, boomers sowed the seeds of disaster for humankind in 1970. Back then, earth was home to just 3.7 billion people, with just 250 million vehicles on the road. Now, in 2031 the world's population is over nine billion. One and a half billion vehicles clog the roads; oil consumption has tripled. Over the same period, 20 per cent of the Amazon rainforest has been destroyed.

Their generation was the first to fully appreciate the suicidal road that our species had laid down for itself and was intent on following. Yet rather than create a new age of appreciation for the natural world, they contrived an age of ignorance and self-serving falsehoods. One where misinformation and false statistics hid the catastrophic damage they were causing to the planet we live on.

Baby boomers may have kick-started environmental activism but ultimately they caused the climate change catastrophe because they declined to do more to stop it.

If they had, they could have released future generations from the abiding torment they have now become trapped in: the torment of knowing that every move they make, every journey they take, every baby they conceive, every joule of energy they burn, every mouthful of food they eat could be bringing them and their children a step closer to oblivion.

The reckless behaviour of baby boomers has endangered

the planet and the very existence of all the generations that will succeed them. Driscoll, Trafton, Delaney and Homer and their contemporaries have eaten through the earth's finite natural resources like voracious, thoughtless locusts.

Now their children had to make the hard decisions needed to save the planet. And it wouldn't be pretty.

21 November 2029, Bodø, Norway
448 days before Cull Day

Suzie Cooper walked hand in hand with her husband along the harbour front. Despite her tetchy tiredness, the legacy of a restless overnight train journey from Oslo, she had to concede this was a stunning walk.

'This is lovely, darling. But why did they have to hold the conference all the way out here?'

It was 9 am in the Norwegian town of Bodø. The Arctic sun sat low in the sky, it's dazzling white light played on the placid, deep blue water, creating millions of twinkling hotspots. Dozens of brightly-painted pleasure boats bobbed gently at the town end of the wooden wharf, patiently waiting for late season weekend trippers. At the harbour entrance, a line of fishing boats prepared to head out to sea, crew members checked engines, tidied ropes, fastened dragnets to flaking, wave-lashed hulls. Ten miles distant, a shaded headland crested by a backdrop of dark rolling hills curved round in a gentle arc. It provided the perfect breakwater against fierce chill gales that often cascaded in, unchecked from the North Sea.

The town was notoriously one of the windiest in Norway, but today those winter winds weren't troubling Bodø the Coopers or the fishermen.

Environmentalist Stephen Cooper cast his beautiful English wife of twenty- five years a sympathetic look. He was used to travelling for his job, but he knew she never slept well outside her own bed, and he felt doubly bad because he had lied to her.

He had told her that this was just another mundane technology sales convention; in reality, they had made this eleven thousand journey from their home town in Cape Town because he was a senior member of an organisation aiming to radically alter the planet – Reboot. Pre-eminent climate activists from all over the world were gathering in this remote town on the edge of the Arctic Circle to hear his and Reboot's plans to give their input, and hopefully, their blessing. The gathering had to be kept secret, so to disguise his true purpose for the trip from the South African media; he had invited his wife along as cover.

'It is remote, but isn't the air amazing, dear?' he said.

'Yes and it's a lovely view.'

'But they've had their problems, see that building site over there?' Cooper pointed to an area near the harbour entrance where bright yellow diggers and lorries were busying on the shoreline. 'The amount of storms hitting the headland has increased dramatically over the last three years, rising tide levels are threatening the North East of the town, so they're building up the sea wall. By an extra five feet I've heard.'

She tutted. 'More climate change bad news, I can't bear it.

Anyway let's forget all that, I'm ravenous for bacon and eggs.' She wagged a reproachful finger at her vegetarian husband. 'And no more rollmop herrings or gherkins Stephen.'

Cooper smiled and squeezed her hand as he led them into the harbour's Café Bar to order the nearest they could offer to a full English breakfast. 'Remember darling, the convention is only for two days. Then we'll try to see the Northern Lights as promised.'

The next day, Cooper rose at 6 am from his hotel bed and left his still sleeping wife to walk the two hundred yards to the town's largest convention venue to make the most important speech of his life.

Stormen Cultural Centre was situated in the north-west of Bodø near the harbour. Best known for its concert hall and a firm favourite with visiting orchestras and bands; its walls were lined with interwoven pine planks and compressed wool panels which meant the acoustics were outstanding. With an amphitheatre and two deep balconies, it was also big enough to seat eleven hundred people. But this wasn't where the convention was to be held. Even though Reboot had booked the entire venue, theirs was to be a more intimate gathering in the chamber hall, just large enough for ninety people.

For much of the morning, Cooper and the other delegates had watched a series of presentations on a large screen, detailing the tragic human cost of climate change from around the world. It had made for a harrowing and disturbing three hours for everyone; now they had reached the final session on the theme, simply entitled 'Delta'.

An image slowly started to appear on the screen, an image of a river's edge. The far bank, about thirty metres away, was fringed with sagging palms. The river ran by, not with the consistency of water, but of treacle. The foreground was littered with felled trees, all coated in pitch-black soot. The camera panned back to reveal more devastation. As far as the eye could see, perhaps an area of twenty square kilometres, was also saturated in the same matt black topcoat, giving the impression that the whole landscape had been drawn by a charcoal pencil. A dancing yellow flame from burning waste gas spewed from the end of a horizontal rusty pipe set low near the waterline. Nearby, another pipe vomited more gluttonous black oil into the moving slime. It was a vision of horror of nature ruined. The camera panned around to a woman standing on the bank. She slowly walked up to the camera and started to talk.

'My name is Abebi Okafor, a daughter of Bayelsa State. This place used to be green and full of life. This is the impact of oil in the Niger Delta. My village was in this place, you see. I worked the fields, and we had good harvests. My husband fished by these banks. After just an hour, he would have a lot of fish.'

She held up a picture of a smiling man, his net bulging with just caught striped bass and catfish. 'Then the oil companies arrived. Our farmland has been cloaked in oil, contaminating crops, exposing us to lead and mercury. Our waterways and mangrove swamps are destroyed. No more periwinkles to pick. No more crabs or fish in the river.' Abebi delivered her words slowly. She pointed to the flaming pipe. 'Rather than processing gas from the extraction, oil companies burn it as waste, filling our air with pollutants. Every day they say they will clean up the mess, but nothing is done. My husband dared to complain – now he is missing.'

She started to cry softly, and another younger woman stepped forward.

She said, 'My name is Chinara Mohammed, youth leader. Millions of litres of oil are spilled every year across the Delta. Three-quarters of us living here rely on fishing or farming. Our livelihoods have been devastated, so now life expectancy is very short – just forty-five years.'

This induced an audible gasp from the audience. Images of the faces of young children began to fill the screen.

'Last year alone, sixteen thousand babies died within the first month of life, because of the pollution, from terrible illnesses. This is a genocide of our people. When we complain, they call us militants and vandals. Please help us.'

The images of Abebi and Chinara faded. As they did, Stephen Cooper's sombre face replaced them on the screen. 'What you have heard this morning are just a few of the climate crimes that we are here to end. Rest assured, when we have control, we will hold those responsible to account. This afternoon's programme will outline the policies and options that Reboot will pursue to ensure that happens.'

After lunch, the delegates were shown the latest global warming figures by a team of cheerless analysts. Cooper compounded the gloomy mood by declaring that even if mankind stopped emitting carbon dioxide immediately, the problem would continue to grow. He forcefully made the point – something 'more radical' was needed.

It was 3.30 in the afternoon when along with Cooper, Reboot's de facto leaders from twelve countries gathered together at the head of the room. They sat in front of an audience now primed to consider any course of action to address the catastrophe.

Tom Stevens, co-founder of Oblivion Revolt and a prime mover in bringing together the international group which now constituted Reboot was first to rise. Taking the microphone, he surveyed the delegates without saying a word. With his grey hair swept back hard in a ponytail, scruffy goatee, long pinched face, crumpled denim shirt and ill-fitting jeans, Stevens looked as if he had just come down from a log cabin in the hills.

After an awkward minute, he finally began to speak.

'COVID-19, COVID-19. It seems so long ago, but it's just ten years in fact. What scholars of contemporary history now refer to as the "anthropause", the global-scale, temporary slowdown in human activity.' He paused for another few seconds. He had hardly said twenty words but already his audience were rapt.

'That was the last time, the last moment, when I allowed myself to think we might just save ourselves. A moment when the world hesitated, tasted fresh air, heard nature in all her glory and thought – perhaps we don't need cars and planes and money to make us happy after all. Perhaps we could get along without them. But of course, it was just an illusion. When the vaccine arrived, we simply turned the electricity, gas and oil back on and returned to our ruinous ways. We have given our governments, policymakers and businesses their opportunity to save us. They have failed. It's time to stop asking and start doing. Now is the time to turn off the old machine and reboot everything. Now is our time.'

He paused for the numerous interpreters to catch up. When they had, enthusiastic applause reverberated around the room. He looked around, picking out faces amongst the audience.

'You have come here from over sixty nations. I realise that for many of you it has been a long journey, much longer than for me.' Stevens smiled. Bodø was just a two-hour flight from his London home. 'We are here because we wanted you to experience the pure unpolluted air we want everyone to breathe again. In this part of Norway, the air is fifty times healthier than the filth ingested by the citizens of Beijing.' He inhaled theatrically.

'And we believe it is possible. It is stunning to hear how our fellow activists in over a hundred countries are galvanising such huge support from their respective populations, especially as you might expect, from the under forties. We have to thank our good friend Volodymyr Zelensky and his brilliant social media team for creating and curating so much excellent content. We have real momentum building and I understand we will be seeing many significant and high-profile actions over the next few months. Isn't that right, Volodymyr?'

The short bespectacled Zelensky stood, nodded to Stevens and acknowledged the applause.

Stevens held up both hands for quiet. 'Of course, the next critical phase is to capture the hearts and minds of your military and law enforcement leaders. What we plan, simply cannot be achieved without them. This is a global problem that requires a global solution. Again, I am delighted to tell you that we believe we have secured support at the highest chains of command.'

Stevens handed the microphone to Stephen Cooper who stood from his chair. A tall man at six feet four inches he looked striking in his dark-blue fitted suit. Renowned for being a fierce debater, his leonine head, shoulder length steel-grey hair and sharp shrewd eyes seemed to reinforce the reputation.

'The great tragedy of the climate crisis is that eight and a half billion people are paying the price, in the form of a degraded planet, so that twenty or so polluting corporations can continue to make record profits. It is the greatest moral failing of our time that the political system has allowed this to happen. We are here to put that right.' Cooper put on his glasses and walked to a lectern at the front of the room to begin his presentation.

'Now, colleagues, to the main part of today's session. We have a plan of essential actions we want to commend to you.' He looked out across the room and took a breath. 'To create the immediate impact we need, we have to implement all of them.'

Over the next hour, Cooper carefully outlined the key pillars of the Reboot plan to save the world:

To prevent further damage to the atmosphere, he demanded a phasing-out and total global ban on all fossil fuel use over the next five years.

To further reduce pollution and lessen the pressure on trees and land, a four-year phasing out of all red-meat production.

To replenish fish stocks, an immediate halt on all commercial fishing techniques – bottom trawling, drift net, long-line and sonar.

To expand global forest area by six per cent by 2035, an area of two hundred and forty million hectares – twice the size of South Africa. And to ban the sale of peat compost globally with immediate effect.

To accelerate climate solutions, a two trillion-dollar investment in geoengineering, with priorities being greenhouse gas reduction, carbon dioxide removal and solar radiation management. The research would be funded by the International Monetary Fund with a new green tax levy on large corporations and a wealth tax aimed at the ultra-rich.

To drastically reduce food waste, a limit on food production and the introduction of more efficient and high-scale recycling processes.

To fundamentally change the core values of developed societies by devising a new model where individual and societal well-being are prioritised over the accumulation of material wealth.

To reduce individual carbon footprints, an annual road and air mileage limit imposed on every individual and family for non-essential travel.

To shut down all crypto mining activities, for their obscene use of energy, digital resources and carbon dioxide emissions.

He was particularly scathing about those he felt were responsible for the climate crisis. 'We promise swift and direct action against those climate criminals who have displayed obscene over-consumption,' he brought his hand down hard on the top of the microphone causing a sharp metallic crack which reverberated through the room.

'Corporations are a modern fiction, one created to limit individual accountability. Behind the logos, the brands and the big offices, actual human beings make decisions that affect us all. These so-called citizens of the earth have decided, year after year, to put profits before all else, even as the seas rise, the fires burn, the storms swell and the ice caps melt. We are in this doomsday situation because company leaders, lobbyists, financiers, government enablers and related swindlers have enriched themselves and created a future in which we will all struggle to survive.'

Cooper was presenting the plans with a measured passion. Now he drew breath, removing his glasses and rubbing the bridge of his nose with thumb and forefinger. The room remained library quiet as he inspected his lenses and blew away a speck of dust; satisfied he had it, he put them back on and continued.

'Colleagues, what I have taken you through today is merely Plan A. We believe these measures, if fully implemented, would make an material impact on slowing climate change. However, we also believe it would still not be enough to save us. We have to go further still to allow the world to heal and recover, so we must tackle the most pressing issue we face – overpopulation. Today, the world's population is nearing nine billion. Our modelling shows that in another forty years it could reach eleven billion people, and over thirteen billion by 2100.' The mind-boggling figure flashed up on the screen – 13,000,000,000. 'It is not the rise in population by itself that is the problem, but the predicted even more rapid rise in global consumption. The situation is simply not sustainable. So what to do?'

He threw the question out into the audience. No one ventured a reply.

'It's not an easy problem, is it? We could stabilise the global population at around ten billion, then engineer a long, slow trend of decreasing population. However, it could still take centuries for significant reductions to happen. We could speed up the decline

32

in fertility rates. We know falling fertility already means virtually every country could have shrinking populations by the end of the century.' A world map flashed up on the screen. Twenty-three countries were indicated in red.

'South Korea has been seeing its population fall since 2020. Spain is expecting to see its numbers halve by 2100. Japan's population is projected to fall from one hundred and twenty-eight million to fewer than fifty-three million by the end of the century.'

A montage of the faces of women from several countries appeared.

'Much of this change will have nothing to do with sperm counts, rather by having more women in education and work, as well as greater choice and access to contraception. We will help raise the status of women further and increase efforts to enhance women's reproductive health and progress women's rights.'

Shouts of approval and applause resounded through the room.

'In many ways, this scenario is jaw-dropping, and of course good news. But even these factors would not deliver the solution we need. To save ourselves, we need a more fundamental rethink of global politics and humanity itself.' He paused again, and for the first time looked nervous – on edge. 'So, we have allowed ourselves to think the unthinkable.' He coughed and cleared his throat. 'We want you to agree to implement two measures which will seem the most radical, but are also the most important if we are to succeed.' He walked to the side of the stage, behind him the screen flickered back to life.

A large leafcutter ant darts skittishly across a forest floor, moving fast, it is perfectly adapted to range quickly and easily across its natural habitat. Scouting eagerly for food, it investigates pieces of dead twigs and other rotting detritus before finally stopping over a recently fallen leaf. The ant locates the edge of the leaf, bites hard into the outer epidermis with powerful jaws, lifts it above its head and starts back the way it came, back to the nest. It is a stunning feat of strength, in this micro world the equivalent to carrying a load twenty times its own weight. The intrepid ant won't even benefit from the leaf directly, it will be used to sustain a fungus to feed the colony. Suddenly an unexpected turn of events. From all sides, other ants appear and fall upon it with a fast clinical ferocity, quickly killing and dismembering the unfortunate insect. The camera pans back, to show hundreds of other ants being attacked in the same merciless way. Within minutes, the massacre has ceased; the swarming, murderous mob has moved on, leaving in their wake a carpet of twitching and twisted corpses.

The film stopped. Cooper returned to centre stage.

'What you have witnessed is an example of ultra-pragmatism, carried out by one of the most successful species on the planet. When an ant colony grows too large, ants kill other ants in order to maintain a sustainable population. It matters not a jot that the previous day these ants were useful members of the colony. On this day, they are surplus, they are a hindrance. They must die so others can live. When it comes to survival in nature and elsewhere, there can be no exceptions, no compassion. This is our Plan B. This is thinking the unthinkable.'

The room was silent, anticipating what was coming. Not wishing to miss a word.

'We are adding another two hundred and twenty thousand people to this planet every day. This is simply not sustainable. To address this, when we are in power, we will introduce a moratorium on any new births globally for a two-year period.'

General murmuring sounded around the room, but no dissent.

'Yet even this severe measure will still not be enough. We believe we must move more immediately to ease the unbearable pressure on the earth. Our future can only be bright if we match our numbers to the resources available – as nature intended. Thirteen billion people is simply too many. This central equation has to be tackled with brutal and extreme prejudice.' Cooper let that statement hang in the air. 'My fellow climate change champions, now it is time to grow up as a species and take the action needed to save ourselves. So it falls to our generation to evoke the greatest recalibration in human history and reduce our numbers by thirty per cent. If we agree with this analysis, then the only outstanding issue to consider is who shall perish…so we can live?'

*

It was a bitterly cold night in Kirkenes, the small town near Norway's border with Russia. The lights blazed against the immaculate coal-black backdrop of the silent sky, moving and pulsing in great swaying bands of colour like a living organism. At one moment it was a great river, in another a purple and crimson slash of fire from a raging volcano, sometimes it was great parallel lines descending to earth like the landing lights of a UFO. The colours were brilliant and pure, vibrant shades in perpetual motion, dancing, flowing, changing colour in a mesmerising kaleidoscopic swirl.

'I'll never be impressed with fireworks again.' Suzie Cooper held her husband tight as they stood together staring in awe at the incredible light show being performed over their heads.

'This really is the greatest show on earth,' he replied.

'And that's the first time I've seen you smile on the whole trip, Stephen. Are you sure the conference went well?'

Stephen Cooper held her tightly.

'Better than I could ever imagine, my darling. I am in good spirits,' he replied. 'There's just a lot of work to do when I get back, that's all.'

For now, Cooper didn't want to think about the selective slaughter of a billion people. He just wanted to stare in wonder at the aurora borealis.

23 October 2030, Latvia
112 days before Cull Day

The Leclerc Main Battle Tank AMX-56 was a formidable killing machine. Armed with a 120-millimetre smoothbore gun, the barrel was 52 calibres long instead of the normal 44 calibres specified on most modern tanks. The extra length gave the projectile a higher muzzle velocity and greater stopping power. The projectile itself was normally an armour-piercing round designed to obliterate other tanks or a high-explosive shell that could eviscerate troops or destroy buildings. A well-trained, motivated gunner could fire twelve rounds a minute and hit a target three thousand metres away, ninety per cent of the time, while firing on the move. The tank could dominate any battlefield, and in just a few minutes could unleash enough hell to wipe out a small army.

Even a lifelong pacifist like Franck Durand could appreciate it was an impressive machine, but at that moment it wasn't even the best tank in his view.

As he looked past the Leclerc from his observation bunker, he could see more than forty tanks of different types side by side, their barrels lined up in parallel formation, all eager to blast the horizon and anything on it to pieces.

To Durand, they all looked virtually identical in their standard green and brown camouflage paint and only distinguishable from each other in small ways: the length of the main gun, the shape of a turret, the number of machine guns or the position of a radio aerial. The glossy programme he had been given as a guest at NATO's Iron Spear exercise described in true enthusiast's detail the relative merits of the American M1A2 Abrams, the German Leopard 2, the Italian C1 Ariete, or the Polish PT-91, all displayed in front of him. These state-of-the-art, ultra-expensive military machines had been assembled to take part in a shooting competition to discover which nation's crew and machine was the most effective.

At the designated moment, a klaxon sounded and, a split second later, the air bent from the shock of forty high-calibre guns firing in unison. Two thousand five hundred metres away at the far end of the Adazi Camp firing range, a line of wood and cardboard targets in the shape of Russian tanks were vaporised. It had been an impressive show of marksmanship and in the observation bunker the military buyers from the UAE, Saudi Arabia, Israel and Singapore cheered in appreciation. Unlike them, Durand didn't have billions of dollars to spend on military hardware; he was there on a very different mission – on behalf of Reboot.

For months, he had been trying to make contact with senior NATO military commanders. Now, here in Latvia, eight of them had gathered together from Spain, Italy, Poland, the United Kingdom, France, Germany, Norway and the United States. To

Durand's delight, having heard he was attending, they were all keen to speak to him.

It had all changed for Durand just eight weeks previously when he received a call at his Brussels apartment at 11.30 pm.

'Hello, Franck. You need to speak with me.' The voice was clear and confident.

'Who is this?'

'Jean Baptiste.'

Durand was stunned. As NATO's deputy spokesperson, Baptiste was a major influencer on the Military Committee, the organization's highest military authority.

'Franck, listen to me. I have just had dinner with fifteen of NATO's highest ranking chiefs of defence. They want to know how they can help your movement.'

'Is this a joke?' Durand asked.

'Come to the restaurant at the Hotel Frederiksborg on Avenue Broustin, opposite the Basilica of the Sacred Heart at 7.30 tomorrow morning and judge for yourself. Be alone. Tell no one.' The caller hung up.

Durand's mind was racing. For months he had been trying to infiltrate NATO's military committee, but with little success. Now one of its most senior members had come to him. It seemed too good to be true, so possibly it was. It could be a trap and they might arrest him, but he knew it was a risk he must take.

Durand slept fitfully and left his apartment at 6.00 in drizzling rain under an iron-grey autumn sky to drive the five miles to the rendezvous point. Parking a few hundred metres away, he sat with the motor running and observed the hotel which stood at the end of the avenue just south of the city's busy ring road. The Hotel Frederiksborg was a narrow, elegant, art deco-style building with five floors. On the ground floor, its brightly lit café was already busy with customers. The restaurant located on the more ornate second floor looked dark and empty. Green painted wooden window boxes, well stocked with seasonal flowers were placed on each the window sills. Above the third-floor windows, a canvas awning proclaiming the hotel's name in large brown letters wrapped itself around the building. The scene looked typically Brussels and very innocuous, thought Durand, which is probably why it was picked.

Over the next hour, a number of people arrived who bypassed the café and walked up to the restaurant floor via a side entrance. At 7.20 Durand stepped out of his car into the now heavier rain, put up his umbrella and crossed the road towards the hotel. He entered at the side door and made his way up the highly-polished wooden stairs to the restaurant, the sharp, dry creak that accompanied every step did nothing to settle his nerves. Reaching the top of the staircase, he stepped tentatively through an open door to his right.

Despite the early hour and overcast weather, the large windows set into the rooms oak panelled walls still flooded the room with light. The space was full of neatly arranged, different-sized dining tables, each smartly set with starched white tablecloths, stainless steel cutlery and cut-crystal glasses. What it was not full of was NATO personnel. Waiting for a few seconds, he heard talking coming from the back of the room, from behind a dark brown door marked 'Privé'. He walked across, pushed the door open and was instantly hit by a thick cloud of pungent smoke. Inside, around twenty men and women dressed in casual clothes sat around two large oval tables drinking coffee. Most were smoking, even though the room's single window was wide open it couldn't clear the cloying smog. It was an unusual and nostalgic sight, smoking in Brussels' restaurants had been banned for years. Obviously, these were people used to doing exactly what they wanted, thought Durand. As he walked in, they carried on their animated conversations, hardly acknowledging his presence. Helping himself to coffee, another thought struck him – they all looked too young to be senior military commanders.

After a couple of minutes of sipping his drink and wondering what he was doing there, the door opened. Durand recognised the tall elegantly dressed man who entered as Jean Baptiste. He slowly walked to the head of the room and placed a pile of papers on the table. The room immediately fell silent.

'Good morning, everybody. Thank you for being so prompt. I appreciate how difficult it is to keep these meetings covert; however, thanks once again to Major Newton and his technology team; I believe we have been successful in doing so.' Baptiste pointed to Giles Newton who was gazing into the only laptop in the room. He looked up briefly and, staring over the top of his glasses, acknowledged the compliment.

'We don't have long so I'll get on with it,' Baptiste continued. 'As you know, since the first discussions were held at the Trident Juncture exercise last November, I have been talking further to your respective bosses about the tactical plans for this initiative. I am pleased to say that these were finalised and agreed last night.'

A murmur of approval rippled from the heart of the smog.

'The final timetable is still to be agreed, but key objectives remain intact – the removal of our respective governments, the temporary installation of a new governing council and the immediate implementation of new laws to begin the mitigation and control of climate change.' He held up the papers. 'I have here a series of documents with the signatures of most senior NATO military and defence chiefs. I ask that you get these countersigned by your superiors as soon as possible. It is an historic agreement and there is still work to do to acquire assent from a number of other NATO countries; but today, we want to put in place the next part of our strategy. I don't have to remind you how careful we still have to be.'

Durand stood transfixed by what he was hearing, realising that the people in the room weren't the commanders themselves, but their subordinates.

'I have invited Franck Durand from Reboot here today to show him the support his organisation can now expect from the military community to help enforce many of the measures that they have been advocating. We haven't included his organisation before. As you know, we have kept this a purely military initiative, but it has been decided that our movement now requires an alliance with a credible civilian entity. We have chosen Reboot to be that entity.'

Durand said nothing – and wasn't invited to speak.

The documents were distributed and after perusing the papers, individuals left at carefully regulated intervals to avoid attention.

Finally, only Durand, Baptiste and another man remained in the now smoke-free room. The man sat impassively at the opposite end of the table, dressed in an expensive-looking black suit, white shirt and black tie. He calmly regarded Durand but said nothing, as if weighing him up and deciding whether he could be trusted. In the growing tension, Durand, anxious not to seem intimidated, stared back into the man's face, making his own deductions.

Deep tan, Roman nose, thin mouth, heavy jaw, probably Mediterranean. Ragged scar stretching from his left cheek to his ear, probably military, perhaps Foreign Legion. Thick, dark brown hair with the beginnings of grey at the temples, probably mid-forties.

The man also possessed striking pale blue eyes which were looking directly at Durand; they softened as he spoke.

'Well, Franck, what do you make of what you've seen this morning?' He spoke with an Italian accent, the English perfect.

'It's very exciting. Just what we needed. It is good to know that the military establishment feels the same way as us about saving the planet.'

'We don't feel the same way as you.' The man's face hardened, stretching the scar tighter across his cheek. 'The planet is finished – anyone with a degree in science can see that.'

He got up from his chair and slowly walked over. He sat down so close that Durand could smell the pungent Gauloises tobacco on his breath.

'A handful of the younger and more idealistic among us think that we can stop this climate clusterfuck, but the majority are simply looking for a fight, before there is nothing left to fight over. An army without a war is like a singer without a song, it has no reason to exist. We are tired of firing our weapons at papier-mâché tanks. We are bored of being the playthings of mediocre politicians and having our numbers reduced year-on-year. We want to take our place at the centre of events. Your cause has come at the right time. It is simply your good fortune that we have chosen Reboot to legitimise what we want to do.'

The man pulled out a small Swiss knife from his breast pocket and started to clean his fingernails. To Durand it felt very intimidating.

'As in any war, you have to be prepared to do whatever it takes to win. There will have to be casualties, Mr Durand.' His eyes narrowed.

'Casualties?' Durand felt the hairs on his neck starting to rise.

'We have seen the numbers from your Bodø conference, and we agree with your analysis. To make the impact we need, we have to reduce the planet's headcount by at least a billion people – better still two billion. The only decisions to make are who has to die and how we will do it. We'll let Reboot decide the first question. We will find a way to answer the second.' Snapping the Swiss knife shut, the man abruptly stood. 'Jean will take you through where we are in recruiting others within NATO. As he said, we do not yet have the full support of all our partners. It will take time, but we will prevail.'

The man with the scar walked to the door, paused for a moment to check himself in a mirror, then left. His presence still hung heavily in the room. Durand turned to Baptiste.

'Who was that?'

Baptiste smiled, his small grey eyes framed by countless lines of crow's feet. 'That was Colonel Paolo Moschin, executive assistant of the Allied Joint Force Command and ex-Italian special forces. One tough bastard in possession of one extraordinary intellect. Even his boss is afraid of him. Moschin is the driving force behind this whole initiative, and right now, Mr Durand, he is the one man who can make your dreams come true.'

Baptiste lit a cigarette, took a deep drag and opened his notebook. 'Now you and I had best agree how we are going to work together.'

Following Frederiksborg, Baptiste and Durand met several times more in different hotels and safe houses across Brussels to decide the framework for negotiations. One rendezvous even taking place at NATO's own headquarters in the city. The steel interlocking buildings with their endless labyrinth of corridors and anonymous offices provided a unique location for Baptiste and Durand to speak to others who had to be kept informed of developments. This increasingly influential double act travelled around the globe to meet other Reboot members to plan how each national coup would be co-ordinated and what would be communicated to the populace on its completion.

Now, Durand was here in Latvia waiting for the tank gunnery competition to finish so he could present detailed plans to the remaining NATO alliance members who had still to sign up. He would tell them of the measures designed to bring climate change under control and precisely what the military's role would be in ending the lives of hundreds of millions of people. As radical as the plans in his briefcase were, he was confident of succeeding.

He was right to be. Just four hours later, on completion of his presentation, the armies of the entire Western alliance – Albania, Belgium, Bulgaria, Canada, Croatia, the Czech Republic, Denmark, Estonia, France, Germany, Greece, Hungary, Iceland, Italy, Luxembourg, Latvia, Lithuania, Montenegro, the Netherlands, Norway, Poland, Portugal, Romania, Slovakia, Slovenia, Spain, Turkey, the United Kingdom and the United States had all signed up to the initiative.

Over twenty million highly-trained men and women were ready to play their part in humankind's first truly global revolution.

3 December 2031, Antarctica
Cull Day 294

The roar of the straining engines filled the cramped, oily cabin as the helicopter finally wrenched itself free of the clinging ice. As it lurched into the air, the pilot kept a firm grip on the pitch lever between his legs and anxiously surveyed his array of dials, instruments and buttons.

The Sikorsky S58 was a mighty machine, but it wasn't built for comfort. The seats were thinly padded and the heating system feeble. As it gained height, the body vibrated and rattled like a washing machine on full rinse. The lack of soundproofing, removed to enable it to carry more weight, meant the noise of the twin turboshaft engines was deafening. Even so, the stripped-out interior was still only just big enough to accommodate the four passengers and their equipment. They sat in cramped contortions around a chaos of hard plastic cases, metal boxes, rucksacks and other scientific detritus.

But all that mattered little to Will Jameson and his team, because after nearly a year stuck in this godforsaken place, they were just glad to be going home.

Sixty-seven-year-old Jameson was from the UK like all his team. He was also senior geophysicist and lead partner at Jameson Hesketh Eco Engineering. With his still thick, dark brown hair, barely lined high-cheek-boned, handsome face and lean physique, he could easily have passed for someone ten years younger. Squeezed alongside him, also trying to get comfortable, was Tom Waites, a drill and exploration engineer. At twenty-eight he was the team's youngest member and tallest at six foot two. Waites' round baby face belied a strong will and combative nature.

Behind them sat thirty-one-year-old Jez Beckley, an environmentalist and qualified electrician. His unique skill set meant he had been kept busy night and day over the duration of the trip. But to his credit, he always approached his workload in good humour. Beckley loved reading and cultivated a bookish, intellectual look with with his brown tortoise shell thick-framed glasses, swept-back wavy fair hair and pale freckled skin.

Next to him, marine biologist Sarah Trevallion looked anxiously out of the windscreen as the huge machine levelled out and began to pick up speed. Thirty-eight-year-old Trevallion had put her name forward for this mission partly because she was keen to help preserve Antarctica's environment and partly because she wanted a new start after a failed marriage. Despite her excellent qualifications, Jameson had had reservations about bringing her along. He reasoned that taking a single, vulnerable and attractive female could prove a distraction.

But ultimately, he had selected Trevallion and the others because they possessed the qualities he valued most.

They were all talented, extraordinarily passionate about their work and far younger than he was – he knew he could rely on their energy and drive. And after interviewing each one of them for several hours, he was also confident they could endure the isolation and close proximity for months on end.

Now that their work was done, he could take comfort that his instincts about Waites, Beckley and Trevallion had been right. For the past three hundred and fifty-one days, they had functioned well, living and working together on the Thwaites Glacier in West Antarctica.

Their home had been Glacier Base T1, a cluster of assorted structures arranged in a semicircle, a mile inland from the Amundsen Sea. Two identical bright orange oblong buildings, constructed from repurposed shipping containers, dominated the camp's centre. One had served as their laboratory, the other their living quarters which consisted of four compact bedrooms, a kitchen-diner, lounge area and a small gym. Incredibly, neither building was heated, interior temperatures being maintained through waste heat from electrical systems and dense wall insulation which reduced heat loss to almost zero.

Adjacent to these main buildings stood a circular opaque-roofed prefabricated plastic pod for storing provisions with a separate hydroponics section for growing vegetables. Next to this was a treatment plant that filtered waste water, and a concrete-clad incinerator which burnt all other waste. On the outer edge of the site, a wind turbine and a bank of twenty-four solar panels supplied more than enough electrical power.

The only other significant piece of equipment on site was a 500 horsepower snowcat, nicknamed 'The Ice Bully'. Fallen snow accumulated faster than it melted, so any structure sitting proud of the ice quickly gained a heavy downwind tail of blown snow. The powerful machine prevented these drifts from swamping and crushing the buildings.

The base had lain empty for two months, so the team's first job had been to transport fifteen tons of equipment and supplies from the drop-off point in order to recommission the site. In poor weather, on the shifting ice shelf, the task had taken them five gruelling days.

As they were setting up their new satellite radio, disaster struck. Before they could secure the equipment properly, a brutal 150-mile-an-hour storm swept in and smashed the dish to pieces. With no chance of a replacement, it meant they would have only intermittent contact with the outside world for the majority of their stay.

Despite the setback, Jameson's team had thrown themselves enthusiastically into their task. With the exception of heavy blizzard days, they had ventured out without fail onto the pitiless, wind-scarred tundra, in temperatures as low as minus thirty-five degrees, to conduct their work.

Beckley and Trevallion were there to collect data on the health of the glacier and the creatures that relied on it. For eleven months, they collected statistics that would shock an already climate-anxious world.

Thwaites was also known as the Doomsday Glacier; if it melted completely, it would raise sea levels by at least three metres. Beckley had charted the relentlessly rising temperatures in the region and the catastrophic effect they were having on the already-fracturing ice shelf.

Trevallion had monitored the wildlife that lived around them. Wildlife that included heavyweights such as orcas, humpback whales, adelie penguins and leopard seals, as well as the more humble squid, cod, mackerel ice fish, plankton and the billions of micro-organisms. Her numbers revealed, in stark clarity, a serious decline of breeding pairs, rising mortality rates and a growing concentration of microplastics in the animals she caught and examined.

Their evidence was credible, irrefutable and terrifying. The continent which held seventy per cent of the planet's fresh water was losing mass six times faster than in the 1990s. If this rate continued, Antarctica would disappear completely in less than fifty years and the human cost would be staggering.

Will Jameson had come to this inhospitable, ice-covered continent for a different reason – to trial an approach which might prevent this catastrophe. For much of the previous two years in his laboratory in the Cotswolds he had been working on an idea to slow or prevent ice loss by creating a flexible barrier to protect ice sheets from the warming seas around them. Using a combination of polymer chains, carbon nanotubes and hydrogen bonds, he had formulated CDT-8 an insulating gel which had shown promise in tests.

Encouraged by the results, Jameson decided he needed to conduct a larger-scale experiment – much larger. Scouring the country, he found the perfect place – a disused Edwardian indoor swimming pool in Leeds.

After cladding and insulating the entire building, he filled the fifty-metre pool with pre-salted water to replicate the salinity of the oceans. Then he installed industrial freezers to lower the temperature inside to the required minus twenty-five degrees Celsius. When the pool had iced over to the thickness of a metre, Jameson gradually warmed the remaining water to begin an ice melt, then poured in his thick red miracle gel. It clung tenaciously to the ice, stopping all ice loss. Better still, after a month in place under the same conditions it showed no sign of weakening.

Jameson and his partners were ecstatic, but they also knew that the only way to prove it could really work would mean a field test in Antarctica itself. It would be impossible to shield the entire fourteen million square kilometres of the ice shelf with the gel, so they wanted to see if a layer, five kilometres wide, along a section of the continent's outer edge would be enough to prevent ice melt further in. The plan was audacious, the chances of success dubious, but if it worked it could change the future of the planet.

After five gruelling months setting up the equipment, another two months spent drilling down into the ice mantle and another four weeks mixing ninety thousand litres of CDT-8, Jameson and Waites were finally ready for the trial.

As he sat, still trying to get warm in the frigid Sikorsky, Jameson remembered every detail of that momentous day and the night that followed as he and Waites prepared to go out onto the ice.

Christ, what a day that was.

Walking around in minus thirty degrees without the right clothing would result in hyperthermia within just ten minutes, so as usual he and Waites spent time putting on the kit that would prevent such a fate. Jameson Hesketh had invested in the best weather protection money could buy.

Starting with the full-body double layer merino wool underwear they pulled on water-resistant, wind-resistant padded outer trousers, then two pairs of military issue arctic socks with reinforced toes and heels. Over these they stepped into bright yellow La Sportiva expedition boots with grippy Vibram Litebase soles that gave them purchase on the often treacherously smooth ice. Next, to protect the upper body, an inner polar fleece and an oversize 900 fill goose-down jacket.

Waites struggled to put on the heavily-padded jacket.

'Give me a hand? Starting to cook already.' Jameson helped to pull it over Waites' broad shoulders.

'Come on, let's get out there. The weather gods are with us.' Beckley and Trevallion had already been on the ice for an hour and reported that the winds had died down and conditions were good. They plodded over to the entrance of the three-door exit system like overladen astronauts. While it felt cumbersome in the confines of the cramped interior, their equipment seemed to lighten up when they got outside.

Before they pressed the large red exit switch that Trevallion had christened 'The Doomsday Button', they put on the final parts of their life-saving equipment; Merino wool hats and neck warmers, followed by neoprene face masks with built-in microphones and speakers and then the snow goggles with their special scratch-resistant polycarbonate lenses. Finally, and blessedly for the unfortunate Waites, who was now almost hyperventilating, on went the synthetic wool finger gloves and the blue nylon mitts with the fluffy tops for wiping away the snot.

Seeing his colleague's discomfort, Jameson quickly hit the switch and the inner door swung open. They stepped through, and the door closed behind them. Jameson hit another button on the next door which slid open with a satisfying hiss as the pressure equalized. They stepped through again into a small holding compartment and both immediately felt a sudden drop in temperature. The floor was suspended over a metal grid which allowed everyone to knock any compacted ice and snow off their boots before they came back in. Pausing for a moment to look through the small window at the conditions outside, Jameson turned the wheeled handle to allow them out into one of the most inhospitable places on earth.

Despite having experienced it virtually every day for the past eight months, the cold shock still made Jameson gasp. Within just two breaths, he could feel the bruising chill scraping through his nose, mouth and lungs. Even though he had taken eye drops, the ice-box air instantly dried his eyelids making every blink seem heavier. He looked across at Waites who was struggling to close the outer door.

'You OK, Tom?'

'Fucking door, gets stiffer every time. But I've done it.'

'I'll get Jez to look at the rubber seals, the warming elements might be seized. Ready to go?'

'Let's do this.'

They set off for the short walk to the trial site which lay towards the south of the base. Although the wind was light, it was blowing directly in their faces and the going was heavy across the dips, rises and hollows of Antarctica's shifting snow dunes. Within ten minutes they had reached their destination and the four pressurised interconnected CDT-8 storage tanks which ringed the area around the drill hole. Jameson started to check the valves as Waites began the procedure of starting up the pumps. The tank pressures were good and Jameson felt confident that all would function as they were designed to do. Their plan was to cover five square kilometres of ice to a thickness of 250 millimetres. If all went well, it would take around four hours to force the thick, gloopy liquid down the two-kilometre pipe and into the space where the Southern Ocean met the base ice.

After completing his checks, Jameson went to the edge of the hole and brushed away snow that had accumulated around the sides of the ten-centimetre diameter plastic pipe. As he peered down into the darkness, he wondered what might happen next.

If the gel fails, the idea will be lost to obscurity and Jameson Hesketh Eco Engineering will have to find a way to recoup the costs. If it works, maybe I'll be celebrated as one of mankind's greatest heroes. The engineer who saved us from the seas.

Waites tapped him on the shoulder, interrupting his fantasies.

'If you're up for it Will, so am I.'

They walked over to the specially designed line pump that they had shipped from England and assembled on the site; protected inside its polycarbonate shelter, it was fully warmed up and primed. Jameson passed the flow pipe leading from the first tank to Waites who carefully fitted it to the end of the pump and tightened the seals. He gave an emphatic thumbs up to Jameson; they were ready to go.

The east winds picked up strength as if heralding the historic moment, a moment which could prove a game changer for the tortured planet. Waites waited two more heartbeats, then pressed the button. With an oiled mechanical clank, the pump shook against the fixing rings that held the connectors, within seconds the pipe had expanded to twice its normal size and began to pulse as the air created the partial vacuum to start drawing down the gel. They both watched, transfixed as it started its long gelatinous descent down the hole, and for the first time in his adult life, Jameson said a little prayer. For the next hour, they concentrated on pumping out the contents of the first two tanks, before Jameson decided they should check on the results.

'Tom, turn off the power, let's have a look.'

'Aye, aye, Captain,' Waites replied cheerily.

Through the undersea cameras they could clearly see that the gel was coating the rough underbelly of the glacier and successfully isolating the fragile ice crystals from the surrounding water.

'Ha ha, it's only gone and worked,' Waites exuberantly slapped his boss hard on the shoulder.

'So far, so good. Let's pump the other two tanks through and get back.' Jameson was careful not to get Waites too hyped, but inside he was thrilled at the gel's performance.

We're going to be rich.

That evening they kept their findings secret from Beckley and Trevallion, wanting to see if the gel would survive the night. On returning to the site the next day, to their delight, they saw their immaculate barrier was still firmly in place, and despite the strong undercurrents, there was no obvious pollution or harm to wildlife from the residue. It had been a conclusive in-location test and they would still have to find a way to produce millions of tons of their wonder solution...

 ...but who knows we might, just might, have saved the world.

12 February 2031, Queensland, Australia
Cull Day 1

The route to the Carmichael Mine had been a long, dusty, throat-parching ride into the Queensland wilderness, and now it had just gone midnight.

The tarmac road that marked their route since Brisbane had long petered out into a crumbling dirt track as Sam Gubbins and his group eventually reached the barbed-wire perimeter fence they were looking for. As they drove parallel along it with dimmed headlights, neon yellow signs punched out of the gloom, warning that the mine was strictly out of bounds. But these six vigilantes with their charcoal-blackened faces weren't backing out now. They wanted to cause some carnage.

It had all changed for Sam Gubbins the previous November.

He and his wife Marie had moved the one thousand

two-hundred kilometres from their home in South Australia to the beachside town of Mallacoota to start a new life with their children. After one of the country's warmest and driest years on record they wanted to get far away from the bushfires that had threatened, and then finally devastated their small vineyard in the Adelaide Hills. The flames had ripped away their house and their livelihood and as his family settled into a new life on the beautiful Croajingolong coastline, Gubbins desperately wanted to believe they had left that nightmare far behind them.

But after just a few weeks, his local Victoria news station began showing disturbingly familiar images. Huge firestorms engulfing homes and cars, families in face masks running for their lives, koalas with severe burns drinking from their rescuers' water bottles. Since the bushfires had started in the north of the state, millions of hectares had been scorched, over fifty people killed, and an estimated one billion animals lost to the conflagration.

And on that fateful day, the fourteenth of November 2030, the apocalypse visited the family once again.

The Gubbins' had heard bushfires were nearing communities about a hundred kilometres away from Mallacoota, but were sure that with the winds blowing the other way, their home would be 'just fine'. So in denial they had decided to go fishing with their children, eight-year-old Harry and six-year-old Tom. They had just weighed anchor and cast their rods off the back of the boat when Emerson Smith, his close friend and neighbour, called.

'Sam, where are you mate?'

'Fishing with Marie and the boys just off Gabo Island. Coming over?'

'That fire is close – we're leaving. You must do the same now.'

'But it was miles away this morning.'

'It's ripped through Genoa and now it's closing in on Gypsy Point. You've got to move.'

Gypsy Point was just sixteen kilometres north of Mallacoota. Gubbins suddenly realised the seriousness of their situation.

'Shit. Marie pack it up, we're heading in,' Gubbins shouted at his wife.

'Good luck to you all. We'll see you on the other side,' Smith said before hanging up.

With just a single road into and out of the town, through heavy woodland, Gubbins knew their escape window was closing. They had to get back, and fast. On the agonisingly slow trip back, he was in turmoil. He knew the chances of being cut off and trapped in Mallacoota were high, but also that the odds of the family being caught in the firestorm while driving out were just as likely.

When they eventually got back to the house, the deep orange glow of the fire was already visible on the hills above the town. Deciding their only option was to shelter, they packed up what they could in their Holden saloon and moved down to the town's wharf, parking on the water's edge beside a low rock wall. To protect themselves from the hot embers now flying through the air, they wrapped themselves and the boys in wet woollen blankets. If the flames came too close, their only option would be to jump into the water.

As they waited, shivering and half-submerged on the water's edge, the smoke gradually thickened and the effort of breathing in the acrid air made their throats raw, even through swimming goggles, their eyes stung. Glowing ash swirled around them in a malicious and unpredictable dance, forcing Gubbins and his wife to put out numerous small fires when they landed.

The next morning, the heart of the fire had moved away and spread to the centre of the town. Across the water, they could hear the deep concussive shocks of domestic gas bottles exploding. Thirty-metre flames jumped from one neighbourhood to another, and one by one the neatly painted wooden houses caught fire and exploded. For much of the next day, they sat in deepening despair as they realised their hopes of a better life in Mallacoota had disappeared.

In the early evening, Gubbins decided it was safe to leave and to head for Canberra about three hundred and fifty kilometres south. They drove out of their ruined community and slowly made the journey through a surreal landscape of blackened bushlands, fire-blasted forests, oddly untouched emerald-green pastures and ash-covered moonscapes. Temperatures topped forty-two degrees Celsius as howling searing hot winds shook the car and filled the sky with ash, burnt leaves and bark. Smoke from nearby bushfires mixed with parched dirt that blew off overgrazed paddocks, and they had to slow to walking pace for fear of running off the road. Then, within a kilometre it would clear again and they would find themselves in a landscape of lush green fields, tall hedges, unmarked wooden farm fences and ripe fruit still abundant on the trees.

As they passed through ruined communities, where once proud houses had stood, all that remained were their skeletons. Iron roofs, split and awkwardly draped over bent steel uprights. Their walls, doors and contents completely swallowed by the fire; melted window glass laying in puddles or stuck fast to tiles. Here and there, they could see signs of former occupants; forks and spoons welded together, delicate feathers of ash that were once books, light fittings hollow and black, a garden bench split and singed from the heat. Hundreds of cars and trucks sat abandoned by the side of the road, twisted and blackened by the catastrophe that had overwhelmed them.

After twenty-four hours of multiple road closures and detours, police checkpoints and traffic controls, the Gubbins family finally arrived in Australia's capital city just as the sun was going down. It was soon apparent that while they may have survived the horrors of Mallacoota, being in Canberra did not mean they had escaped the fire.

Positioned about one hundred and fifty kilometres inland, the city was in a valley that naturally trapped smoke. Winds in the day tended to bring clearer air, but shore winds in the evenings blew waves of thick smoke from East Coast fires into the city like a noxious tide. As they drove slowly into the centre, the roads and streets were virtually deserted. Dozens of handwritten and hastily painted signs proclaimed that most amenities, public transport, tourist attractions and public pools in Canberra were closed. Gubbins wound down the window as they approached a man shuffling along, struggling to carry two bags bulging with plastic water bottles.

'Excuse me mate, where is everybody?'

The man looked up at him quizzically. He wearily put his bags on the ground. Probably only in his mid-thirties, with his blackened face and matted hair he looked much older.

'Jeez, you're obviously new to Canberra. They've all fled down the coast or are sheltering at home. Smoke will be coming in soon.'

'Anywhere near we could find some petrol or water?' Gubbins asked.

'All the stations are out of fuel. The ATMs are out of cash. The supermarkets are out of bottled water too. Most of the mains water supply has been disrupted or polluted.'

'Oh Christ, Sam, the kids are parched.' Marie Gubbins despaired at the news. On seeing her reaction, the man felt obliged to offer some hope.

'Look guys. I believe there's a freshwater bowser due outside the Dinosaur Museum in Genninderra at midnight. Better hurry, bound to be a long line.'

'Thanks mate.' Gubbins started the car and headed off for the museum.

'Don't forget to take bottles with you,' the man shouted after them.

Later, as Gubbins waited in the queue along with his water container and two hundred anxious Canberra residents, he looked over at his family waiting in the car. This wasn't the life he wanted for them. A life where being driven from your home could become a regular occurrence, where wearing filter masks was normal, where being able to leave the house in summer would be seen as a luxury. He was ashamed that his country ranked last out of fifty-seven other developed nations on climate change action. With its huge fossil fuel mining interests, Australia had become one of the world's biggest greenhouse gas emitters. Most of this had happened under Prime Minister Shaun Ashcroft's leadership. The belligerent Ashcroft had also refused to attend UN climate summits and had withdrawn from an international fund to tackle climate change.

So on that miserable day in Canberra, as he waited to collect four litres of warm water for his family, Gubbins decided to join the Reboot movement he had heard so much about and would recruit others to do the same. He vowed that he would do whatever it took to protect his loved ones from the bushfires of the future and maniacs like Ashcroft. Because he now knew that the hell of climate change was no longer on the horizon. It couldn't be outrun, it was here.

One person in particular had been the catalyst behind Reboot's initiative to seize control of the country – the Australian Army's most senior officer, Major General Dennis Curtis. Charismatic and articulate, Curtis had galvanised support within his regiments and could count on the support of over two-thirds of the regular army and all of the reserve.

Gubbins and a group of other Reboot converts met with Curtis in the desert, deep in the Northern Territory near the proposed site of what promised to be the world's largest solar farm, Sun Cable.

Gubbins still remembered the Major General's words as they sat sweltering in the open-sided canvas tent.

'I have brought you here to witness the future.' The tall, broad-shouldered Curtis spread his hands inviting his audience to take in the flat sun-roasted sand all around them. 'In just one year, all the land that you see will be covered in energy, all this land in every direction, around fifteen thousand hectares. Every square centimetre covered in ten gigawatt-capacity solar panels harvesting the one thing this part of Australia can rely on – continuous sunshine.' With a theatrical flourish, Curtis put on his sunglasses. 'Overhead transmission lines will send the electricity to Darwin and plug straight into the grid. We'll have so much, we can export the rest of it to Singapore to supply most of their needs. And that's not all, ladies and gentlemen. In Western Australia, in the Pilbara, an even bigger wind and solar hybrid plant is proposed to power and develop a green hydrogen manufacturing hub. Sounds amazing, doesn't it? Oz can make a contribution to slowing climate change.'

He smiled broadly before posing the question: 'So, what's the problem?'

Curtis looked out at the audience, took off his sunglasses and fixed his gaze on Gubbins. He noted the name on his badge and repeated the question. 'So what's the fucking problem…Sam?'

Gubbins could feel his face reddening. He felt chastened and annoyed at the same time. He had been mightily impressed by the Major General's description of the proposed projects and the promise they held, so he had no idea what the fucking problem was.

He felt he should venture a guess anyway.

'We don't have the money to develop them?'

A suppressed smile played around the corners of Curtis's mouth.

'Sam, whatever you hear from Ashcroft and his cronies, money is never the issue. They are delaying these plans because they're in bed with the fossil fuel companies. His government is putting up barriers at every turn. When we assume power, we will have these projects and more up and running within the next year.'

Relieved that the attention on him had moved on, Gubbins stood with the rest and applauded.

Curtis continued. 'Ladies and gentlemen, I can tell you that after months of covert planning with our military and law enforcement agencies, we have agreed a strategy to wrest control of Australia from this misguided and negligent government. It will be executed in three stages over the space of a week. The first will be high-profile disruption of major polluters, particularly in the oil and coal industries. The second will see us establish control of the media, the third, removal of the government and the installation of an interim ruling council.'

Curtis paused and put on his sunglasses. 'So now that you know, are you in or out?' Along with every other attendee on that day, Gubbins was in.

That was why he was here outside the Carmichael Mine in the dead of night with his wife Marie, Emerson Smith and his wife Fiona, and two highly trained commandos, Jim and Lauren Stott. Their parents had also lived in Mallacoota and on the day the inferno struck, with their son and daughter busy fighting fires in Victoria, they had decided to stay and defend the family home. Tragically they paid the ultimate price and their blackened bodies were found in the basement the following week. Now their children were here, with the blessing of their regiment, armed to the teeth and eager for revenge.

Everyone in the car had volunteered to be part of the group assigned to carry out the first stage of 'The Curtis Plan' and to break up coal production.

The new mine, which had been approved to begin production that month, would be the biggest mine in Australia and one of the largest in the world. At full capacity it would extract enough coal every year to produce one hundred and thirty million tonnes of carbon dioxide. An output exceeding the annual CO_2 emissions from fuel combustion of many developed countries. Worse, it was just the first of many extraction sites proposed for this part of Central Queensland. Australian climate scientist James Newall, on hearing about the Carmichael Mine, had declared: 'The world had better forget holding the global temperature rise to two degrees Celsius. We're all officially screwed.'

'Science tells us coal needs to stay in the ground. That's why we must do something to stop those motherfuckers,' Jim Stott had told Gubbins.

The 'something' they intended to do was risky. First, break into the mine and wreck any equipment they found. Second, capture, and hold Carmichael owner Virat Shastri to ransom. Shastri was chairman of the Indian Shiva Organization which had bought the mine and were due to open the site for production that week. Reboot wanted Shastri to reveal the impact his plans would have on the environment, including construction of a railway line that would run through precious nature reserves to allow the loading of coal into ships. They also wanted him to agree to pull his company out of Australia. To persuade him to carry out their demands, Gubbins had been given proof of Shiva's corruption of Australian government officials and evidence of Shastri's own illegal tax concessions obtained from Indian Prime Minister Rohit Vishnu.

As she sat in the back of the car, Lauren Stott slid her long hunting knife into its scabbard and then onto the army webbing belt which she slung sash-style across her shoulder. She looked menacing and powerful in her olive camouflage paint, black baseball hat, black canvas fatigues and heavy-duty boots. She was glad to be going into action at last and smiled in anticipation at the prospect of giving a serious bigwig some serious grief.

'We've got the proof to get this bastard locked up and stop the whole fucking thing. Now we just need to get him in the car.'

'What if he refuses to close the mine?' Smith had enquired.

'We cut his greedy head off and stick it on a pole as a warning to other climate killers,' replied Jim Stott who was dressed identically to his sister and sharpening his own commando-issue knife. Smith looked at the size of the weapon and then at the thickset soldier. He had no doubt that Stott would carry out his threat if he needed to.

From information obtained from sympathisers working in the huge mine complex, they knew Shastri would be spending that night in the mine manager's house. After travelling slowly around the fence for thirty minutes, they spotted the bright yellow lights of the main site entrance and security hut about two kilometres away. Parking under a small group of trees, they collected their weapons and backpacks and, with the Stotts leading, began walking along the line of the fence towards the entrance. After ten minutes the siblings signalled a halt and instructed everyone to get down.

'Guards about eight hundred metres away...they've got a mutt,' Jim Stott whispered to Gubbins. 'Stay here, we'll deal with them.' The heavily armed commandos crept off and were soon lost to the night. The group lay down on the cool dusty soil and waited.

'Why are we stopping?' Emerson Smith who was a few yards back from the leading group cried out.

'Keep it down, Emerson. It's a bloody guard dog,' Marie Gubbins replied putting her finger over her mouth.

As they waited, Sam Gubbins turned onto his back and looked up. Despite the tension, what he saw took his breath away. The absence of light in this part of the Queensland outback meant that billions of stars were visible above him. In that moment everything else ceased to exist. As he continued to stare, it seemed that he could see right into the far reaches of the cosmos. It was magnificent, uplifting and humbling.

As he lay bewitched, gazing into this epic, endless panorama of lights, it occurred to him that despite the risks they were taking and the fear he felt, they were doing the right thing. Standing up for their unique and precious home was their duty. A trillion chance events had combined with a billion biological accidents to spark life in this tiny part of the universe. Perhaps the only life there is. Planet Earth, the little oasis of blue amidst this amazing, hurtling chaos of elements was a miracle. It was beautiful; it was worth fighting for and, if necessary, killing for.

Suddenly, Gubbins noticed movement to his left, something scurrying low in the bush about twenty metres away. As he held his breath, a dingo appeared in the clearing, looking for reptiles or scraps thrown from the camp. It was small, probably a young female, probably hungry. For a split second, their eyes met. Two mammals with very different reasons to be out in the dead of night in the middle of nowhere.

A sharp noise punctured the night, a dog barking furiously. The startled dingo ran off and disappeared into the velvet black. A yelp. Then silence again.

'What's happening, Sam?' his wife asked. 'Not harming animals, are they?'

'If they have to, they will. You can't win a war without spilling some red,' he replied.

'Oh, my God'. She swallowed.

More tense minutes passed before Jim Stott appeared out of the blackness.

'OK everyone, we're through the wire. Let's go and get this Shastri cunt.'

The group followed to where Stott had cut through the

perimeter fence and one by one crawled awkwardly through the small hole, pulling their equipment after them. When the last had made their way through, Jim Stott sealed the hole with plastic ties, making a note of its position on his GPS.

Two hundred metres on, two men were sitting on the ground with their backs to each other. They had been bound and gagged. Nearby, a German shepherd dog lay on its side, a crossbow bolt lodged in its throat. Lauren Stott was pulling on the flight, trying to remove it. As it came free, a fountain of blood pulsed into the dirt. When she comprehended what Stott was doing, Marie Gubbins knelt down and vomited into the dirt.

'Come on, got to keep moving,' Jim Stott ordered, and jogged off in the direction of three buildings about eight hundred metres off to their north. The rest followed, trying to keep up with the fast-moving events.

Sam Gubbins was sweating under his thick cotton camouflage suit, feeling his pulse race with excitement and anxiety. This is what he had wanted, he thought, a chance to fight back against the bastards wrecking his children's future. It was stressful but still felt good. If they could get the mine closed down, it would prolong the life of the Great Barrier Reef too. The natural wonder was just three hundred and fifty kilometres from the mine site. Exporting coal would require new port terminals, and the seabed dredging needed to create them would damage the reef and the coral ecosystem around it. Success would be a huge early victory for their cause – and could inspire others to join.

Soon they were at the edge of a line of simple wooden buildings. The two nearest were single-storey structures with flat asphalt roofs. There were no lights or sounds of life coming from either building.

The third building was more substantial, two storeys, constructed from rendered brick with a pitched shingle roof. A light shone from one of the ground floor rooms. This had to be the one

Shastri was staying in, thought Gubbins.

Up ahead, Lauren Stott, who was a couple of inches taller than her brother, stood on her toes to see inside one of the high-set windows. After a couple of seconds, she gave a thumbs up.

'He's here alright – looks like he's on his own.' Tom Stott looked elated.

'We'll go in and get him. Why don't you cause some mayhem over there?' He pointed to a row of huge coal excavators, dump trucks and jeeps all neatly lined up about two hundred metres away. That was all the invitation that Gubbins needed. He signalled for the other three to take off their backpacks and follow him…

Two hours later, as they drove away, Gubbins looked back in satisfaction at the glow of the fire they had caused. He looked around the car at the weary but happy faces – they had all done well. Everyone had followed the explosives training the Stotts had given them, they had set and placed the Semtex properly, They had caused some mayhem and no one had killed themselves or anyone else. They had even got a slap on the back from the two professionals. Terrorism felt good.

He knew the wrecked vehicles and mangled equipment could easily be replaced, but they had made a big statement. It was time to put the climate first. Big business could go screw itself. Gubbins turned to his wife who sat beside him; she was grinning.

'How did that feel M?' he asked.

'It felt good. I found something in me today that I never realised I had.'

'What was that?' Gubbins enquired.

'Something I would kill for. When we went past those guards on the way back, I felt like cutting their throats.'

'No worries, I did it.' Emerson Smith piped up from the back.

'Man, they squealed like pigs.' The car erupted in nervous laughter, unsure if he was telling the truth.

'Shame about the dog though,' said Gubbins.

The car went quiet. It was a shame about the guard dog. A shame that innocents have to be sacrificed for the common good. It was a shame too that Shastri had not co-operated with their plan and that he had called Corporal Lauren Stott a bitch.

The Woolworths plastic bag containing his head rolled around in the footwell by Sam Gubbins' feet where Stott had dropped it. Gubbins slowly rolled down the window, picked it up and heaved it into the dark. He didn't need a billionaire's head to remind him of tonight's work. Some dingo family will make far better use of it.

12 February 2031, Geneva, Switzerland
Cull Day 1

'Hey, isn't that Jake Bryant over there?'

'Could be. Smaller than I imagined.'

Judy Crispin, the retail heiress and Laura Perry, the world's richest self-made woman had never previously met, but they were having a ball. Sharing gossip, spotting familiar faces and helping themselves to caviar blinis and chilled Barons De Rothschild Champagne. All the food and drink on offer was high-end and sumptuous, but to these billionaires it was normal; they had grown accustomed to sumptuous. In fact, Jake Bryant, the world's richest man, and everyone else assembling in the ornate conference room at Le Richemond Hotel on the shores of Lake Geneva were well versed in indulging themselves with the finest things that money could buy.

'Think with all that cash he'd invest in a hair transplant,' Crispin remarked, plucking two sea salt-seasoned quail eggs from a passing silver salver borne by one of the many handsome, over-scented young waiters.

'That looks like Don Jarvis and his latest wife.'

Before Perry could reply, the lights in the room began to dim and the forty very wealthy, very important people slowly broke away from their conversations to find a good view of the giant presentation screen at the end of the room.

A stocky short-haired man wearing a plain white T-shirt and jeans, and holding an iPad, walked to the rostrum at the side of the room and tapped a finger on the microphone. The engineer at the mixing desk gave him a thumbs up, the speaker acknowledged the gesture and was about to start when the doors at the side of the room burst open and slammed into a chair. Everyone turned to look at the source of the interruption, a slightly hunched elderly man in a dark suit shuffled in, looking flustered and hot. Muttering an apology, he found the nearest seat. Super-investor Wallace Bernard had joined the meeting.

'Hello, everyone, I'm Edgar Mills CEO of Auto X. First and foremost, I'd like to thank you all for coming. We're really delighted that all you busy people have found time to make the trip – and a massive thanks for coming here without your assistants, aides and hangers on. Believe me, it makes what I have to say to you today sooooo much easier.'

Mills slowly started to pace across the front of the room, making expansive sweeping motions with his hands as he spoke.

'You probably haven't had time to meet everybody here yet, so if you'd permit me, I'd like to run through the stunning list of attendees and some of those incredible numbers. Jake Bryant – personal worth, $190 billion. Don and Melanie Jarvis – $102 billion. Franco Baez – $76 billion. Javier Darvish – $60 billion.

Francis Sutton – another $60 billion.'

Mills read the mind-boggling net worth of all the assembled people in the room. When he had finished, Crispin and Perry, at just $7 billion each, might have been left with the feeling that in this company they were chronic underachievers.

Mills continued, 'You have come here as guests of the seventh generation of the Nexus banking dynasty on a promise – the promise of buying into a historic world-changing proposition. You have earned your right to be offered this opportunity first. After all, you are all world changers already. Over the last thirty years, you have helped shape the way mankind does its business. You employ hundreds of thousands of people across the globe. Your collective wealth is larger than the economies of some countries. You have shown extraordinarily rare leadership, courage and vision. Many in this room have also been responsible for great acts of philanthropy.'

He gazed out from his rostrum, trying to make out familiar faces.

'Don and Melanie. Don and Melanie Jarvis, please stand up so we can see you.'

The Jarvis's, who were sitting slightly apart from the rest by a window, reluctantly got to their feet.

'Don and Melanie, you have set up one of the largest private charitable foundations the world has ever seen. Used your personal wealth to enhance healthcare and reduce extreme poverty. Saved millions of lives across the third world and over the last ten years have helped to virtually eradicate malaria.'

Polite applause rippled through the room. The couple took a modest bow and quickly sat down. Mills pointed to Wallace Bernard who was sitting in the front row, now looking more composed. 'Wallace, can I call you WB?'

Bernard sheepishly nodded assent.

'WB, your generosity to good causes is also legendary. You are an inspiration. Over your career you have shown us that greed can be good after all – because it can do so much good.'

Bernard smiled weakly at the comment, not knowing if it were meant as a joke.

'Jake? Where's Jake Bryant at?'

The slim, five foot seven, casually dressed and immaculately groomed Bryant stood, acknowledged Mills with a nod and beamed his famous smile around the room.

'Now, of course, Jake has waded in with his Project Earth Fund. Let me tell you, twenty billion should do a whole lot of good, folks. But then again he can afford it!'

Bryant's smile quickly disappeared at the barbed comment.

Mills left the rostrum to walk across the room and down the main aisle between the loosely arranged rows of seats.

'Don, Melanie, Wallace and Jake are showing the way, and it's great to see these giants of our times putting something back. But they can do more, much, much more – and so can you.'

The watching billionaires began to shuffle uncomfortably in their seats. They could sense a pitch coming.

'As you probably know better than I do, because you're all so well read, that the only game in town these days, as far as philanthropic causes go, is climate change.'

Mills allowed the thought to settle into people's minds.

'Thing is folks, altruism on its lonesome is not going to get us where we need to be. Climate change is running faster than we are, way faster. You could say it's a speeding train without a driver in the cab.' Mills ran from one side of the room to the other.

'Sure, there are token initiatives like the Green Climate Fund which has another ten billion to spend. So with Jake's contribution that makes thirty billion…but as you folks already know, that's still chicken feed.' He smirked, knowing the net worth of the people in the room was at least fifty times that. 'We need much more ambition and urgency, and finance is the key – and this is where you lovely people come in.'

Mills put his hand on the shoulder of the now grim-faced travel entrepreneur, Richard Schofield. 'Ladies and gentlemen, with our combined resources, we have the power to subsume the state. We can fund projects and ideas to end this climate emergency at a level of investment that governments would never contemplate. We can implement the radical thinking that can reboot this sick little earth of ours and get it fit for the next two millennia.'

The room was still silent as the assembled plutocrats strained to fully comprehend what Mills was saying, partly because it sounded good and bad at the same time.

'So today, I am not asking you to contribute just five or ten per cent of your wealth. That's for pussies. I want you to forfeit all of it – to save the world for all of our children.' Mills held both arms in the air and stamped his foot.

'What do you say folks?'

At this, many of those seated stood or began shouting in protest. Mills returned to the rostrum and brought his fist down onto its wooden top.

'OK, I'm not here to negotiate with you. But I am going to show you why you should seriously consider signing on the dotted line today.'

As he raised his hand, the lights went out and roller blinds descended to cover the windows and darken the room further. The giant screen flicked on and was filled with the unmistakable face of another of the hyper-rich elite, Giovanni De Bourneville, the long-standing head of the confectionery empire that bore his name. He was staring into the camera with terrified eyes. His usually immaculate hair was lank and sweaty; his normally bronzed skin pallid and grey. He was shaking uncontrollably.

The camera panned back to reveal De Bourneville in a windowless room with a low ceiling, its walls painted an industrial grey. He sat stiffly upright in a metal chair bolted to the floor, his arms bound to it with heavy rope. In the back of his left hand a cannula had been sunk into a vein. On the other end was a small valve that looked like a tap. A small plastic tube wound its way from the tap to an opaque bag which contained a darkish brown liquid. De Bourneville's eyes frantically darted left and right – clearly looking at people standing out of sight behind the camera.

The film had no audio, but it was obvious that he was pleading for his life, pulling on his bonds, neck muscles straining, grimacing and sobbing with terror. As the transfixed billionaires continued to watch, a figure on his left came forward and gave the tap a half turn. De Bourneville strained harder on his ropes and looked in horror as the dark liquid slowly flowed from the bag, travelling through the winding tube and down into him. Now he was screaming, spitting, writhing, his head pulled back, seeming to want to wrench itself free of his shoulders before it slumped forward, chin resting on his chest. His arms stiffened, his upper body convulsed, his legs giving a last pathetic quiver before finally, mercifully, life appeared to leave him.

The screen went black and the lights in the room went up. A stunned silence hung heavy in the air as the audience processed what they had witnessed. Mills picked up the microphone and began to walk among the chairs again.

'Giovanni De Bourneville passed away yesterday from a heart attack brought on by the infusion of a cocktail of three chemicals – midazolam to sedate him, vecuronium bromide to paralyse his muscles, potassium chloride to stop his heart. Rest assured, he wouldn't have felt anything at the end, although it was pretty clear he was having a hard time beforehand.' Mills sneered, relishing the impact he was having.

'Now, Giovanni didn't have to die, but he refused to move with these times. You see, his birthday was 1 September 1964, making him a baby boomer – just. And all baby boomers must now pay for their role in overseeing the trashing of our planet. But Giovanni being Giovanni, he refused to pay for his crimes. So he got the brown liquid diet.'

A gasp of disgust went up from the room, followed by crying and wailing. Michael Champion, the American tycoon and politician, started shouting obscenities at Mills, demanding that those responsible be held accountable. The industrialist Steve Barker was in heated discussion with his old boss, Don Jarvis, about what to do, frantically trying to use his phone which was no longer working. Jacqueline Muller, the eighth richest woman in the world, had fainted and was being helped by the beauty empire heiress, Maria Cornwell.

'You may sound your distaste,' Mills bellowed defiantly to the room. 'I can understand why you're pissed, but you are luckier than most, because you can pay to live. Unlike most of the other one and a half billion baby boomers out there, you can afford to pay the price tag. You will by donating ninety-nine per cent of your wealth to our cause. And when you do, you'll still have plenty left over for a privileged life.'

At that, the heavy doors at either end of the room opened and armed soldiers ran in to seal off all exits. A serious-looking, slightly portly man, dressed in a sober banker's suit followed behind them – the newly-appointed chairman of the Swiss merchant bank Nexus Charterhouse, thirty-seven-year-old Justin Bollinger. He walked calmly to the front of the room.

'Ladies and gentlemen, now that you have received our proposal from Mr Mills, I trust you have found him and it suitably compelling. You will all be taken from here to your rooms to consider the logistics of transferring monies and assets with my banking staff.'

As the bewildered and shocked soon-to-be former billionaires were filed out, Mills couldn't resist a parting shot at them.

'You may have wondered why the likes of Zaborowski, Yang Hao and Kieran Johnson aren't here? Or why I am standing here telling you this instead of sweating and panicking like you are? The answer is that we're all a lot younger than you. We haven't made our money fucking up our children's home for the last five decades. Now you bastards are going to get what's coming to y—'

Mills gave a small groan and pitched forward onto his face. For a few moments, everyone in the room stopped at the sight of the crumpled figure and the blood seeping from the back of his head into the carpet's handwoven shag pile.

'You're full of shit, Mills. Have that one on me.'

Standing behind Mills's prone body, and still holding the unopened bottle of Barons De Rothschild Champagne 2019 that had delivered the blow, was a snarling Laura Perry.

She was quietly led away without protest.

Somewhere down the corridor, Jake Bryant was running the same thought over and over in his head – why couldn't he have been born in 1965?

12 February 2031, Brasilia, Brazil
Cull Day 1

The metre-long slender arrow arched gracefully up into the air escaping the shadows of the forest canopy. It caught a momentary sliver of sunlight before continuing its flight across the clearing, striking the man just behind his neck and driving down into his heart. He was dead before his body hit the moss covered forest floor with a cushioned thud. The chainsaw he was using revved wildly as it escaped his grip, spinning in the air before stopping abruptly as it too crashed into the undergrowth. The two men with him froze, mouths gaping at the sight of the twisted body in front of them, before both started frantically running down the muddy path towards their heavily laden logging truck. More of the deadly missiles whipped through the air after them. One caught the nearest man in the leg. He screamed, staggered, but kept running. Another pierced him in the arm and one more sliced into his buttock. This time he fell, writhing and grunting amongst the dead leaves. The final arrow struck him squarely in his windpipe and he fell silent.

The third man, much younger and faster, got to the lorry unscathed, lifting himself into the cab and down onto the seat in one athletic movement. As he fumbled for the keys in his panic, the axe flew through the side window and imbedded itself in the back of his head. The last thing twenty-year-old Gabriel Menino saw as his life ebbed away were the small thickset figures emerging from the rainforest shadows.

If he had lived longer, he may have seen their faces and naked bodies covered with tattoos of local plants and animals made from pigments of the jenipapo fruit. If he had lived longer still, he might have wondered who the taller men were who stood among them – these men dressed in jeans and T-shirts who watched impassively as the pygmy tribesmen stripped the skin from their victims' bodies.

Within two days, news of the killings had reached Colniza, the frontier town that stood at the edge of the Amazon in the state of Mato Grosso. By the next morning, a vigilante group of over thirty men armed with automatic rifles had been assembled and was heading back to the site of the massacre.

They came fast in a powerful convoy of trucks and cars, and they came to extract full revenge. But this time they weren't met with ancient bamboo arrows and throwing axes, but by a deadly hail of rockets, fifty-calibre machine guns and grenades. Of the two men who survived the deadly ambush, one was executed and the other sent back to give a clear message to the powers that be. There would be no more trees felled in this part of the Amazon for the foreseeable future.

President Lucas Oliveira looked out from his large office window in the Palácio do Planalto in Brasilia. He gazed idly across the main square at the Supreme Federal Court building opposite supported by its sweeping columns; to him it always gave the impression that it was floating. Its immaculate white walls looked as pristine as always in the sparkling morning light, but the sight did not improve Oliveira's foul mood. He was raging because he was under siege.

Foreign governments were berating him for allowing the Amazon to be overexploited, politicians in Brazil were on his back because the economy was in poor shape and his approval ratings were nosediving. Even Hollywood was out to nail him; he had heard that several leading actors, producers and directors were funding organisations to help drive him out of office. Even for the notoriously thick-skinned president it had been a bad morning, and it was about to get worse.

The ornate green onyx and gold inlaid phone on his desk sounded.

Chirp-chirp, chirp-chirp, chirp-chirp.

Oliveira had personally requested the ring tone as it reminded him of the mockingbirds he loved to watch as a small boy. He let it ring, contemplating the chances of the call bringing more bad news and deepening his mood further still. Tentatively, he picked up the receiver.

'Yes?'

'President? It is Antonio Varela.'

Recently, Oliveira had appointed Varela to head the office in charge of his newly created indigenous affairs agency. He sighed with relief at the prospect of a friendly voice.

'Antonio, good to hear from me. How goes plans for integration?'

'Plans will be on your desk by tomorrow morning. If you are in agreement, we can start implementation next month in time for the dry season.'

At last a piece of good news, thought Oliveira. He had vowed to integrate millions more indigenous people into the general population. If done successfully, he knew it would greatly smooth his plans for developing mining and ordering further deforestation for cattle grazing in greater Amazonia.

'Good. These tribes live like animals. Resettling them around our cities and communities, they will evolve and become more human. More Brazilian. I look forward to seeing your schedule.'

'I have to warn you, President, the migration will still take far longer than you had hoped and…'

'Yes, yes, yes. But there are always ways to speed things along, Antonio.'

Oliveira did not want to hear more negativity. He replaced the receiver and instantly felt much better. He had campaigned and been elected on his pledge to scrap indigenous people's special land and cultural rights. This had delighted the powerful mining, logging and farming communities. He was determined to keep his promise and secure the ongoing support of the National Congress.

Despite the efforts of foreign powers, the media and indigenous tribes, development in the Amazon under his presidency continued at record levels. One hundred and eight square miles of virgin forest were cleared in the previous month, a new high. The fact that every square mile resulted in more wealth for the Oliveira family was the proverbial icing on the cake.

A nervous rap sounded on his door knocking him out of his pleasant daydream.

Puta merda, he thought, *Holy Shit. What now?*

'Enter!' he bellowed to the unseen caller.

The two solid inlaid mahogany doors swung open to reveal a tall man in a heavily decorated military uniform. He carried a braided military cap under his arm. It was Admiral João Maria Otero, and as usual he looked nervous.

'Your Excellency, I have serious news.'

Oliveira despaired. 'What now? More rainforest fires spotted by American satellites? Has the price of wood pulp collapsed?'

The admiral put his hat on a coffee table and dropped into the low leather chair situated by the window. 'No, my President. Full-scale war has erupted throughout the Amazon. Loggers and insurgents are fighting in Tanaru, Rio Pardo, Mato Grosso and the Jaravi Valley. In Colniza, hundreds of loggers and our soldiers have died. Wood and pulp production has been severely disrupted. Two foreign companies have had enough and are pulling out. Walmart and Costco will no longer buy from our supply chain.'

Oliveira stood up and walked over to the Brazilian cherrywood-framed, full-length mirror he had had installed the previous week and regarded himself. He wore his usual well-cut black suit, white shirt and tie with the Brazilian green and yellow flag design. Despite his immaculate attire, he thought he looked jaded. His greying temples looked whiter than ever, the skin around his eyes darker and puffier than he remembered, the shoulders more rounded. 'Anything else, Admiral?' he asked wearily.

Otero took a deep breath before answering. 'Logging and paper mill businesses have also been attacked overnight in São Paulo, Salvador and Belo Horizonte.'

'*Puta merda*. This is the work of foreigners, climate meddlers and spies!' Oliveira spat. 'Disrupting our sovereign right to utilise the forest for the good of the Brazilian people and the economy. The Amazon may be the so-called lungs of the world, but these lungs belong to us! Can't the army do more to stop this?'

'We are doing our best, your Excellency, but there are too many sites to cover. The soldiers are also reluctant to fire on their own people. Many sympathise with the cause.'

Oliveira had spotted a mark on his jacket lapel and was vigorously wiping it with a handkerchief.

'Well, the timing couldn't be better for this environmental delegation coming here today. Do these idiots really think they can give us large enough incentives to stop deforestation?' He sneered in contempt as he recalled the last foreign attempt at moderating Brazil's use of energy. 'Remember that pittance we received from the Green Climate Fund for reducing our greenhouse gas emissions?'

'Yes, my President. But this time they say they will replace <u>all</u> the money we make from Amazonia.' Otero smiled, in hope of a positive response.

Oliveira shook his head in disbelief. 'From the rubber and the timber it's at least eight billion a year – not including taxes and kickbacks of course.' He smiled to himself. 'I hope they have deep pockets, these Europeans, Asians and Africans.'

'We should at least hear them out. The situation needs... controlling.'

Oliveira wheeled away from the mirror.

'Perhaps. But why do they have to bring those bastards from the WWF? They are liars and fraudsters. They would ruin Brazil just to save some monkeys.'

Oliveira was warming to his theme now as he strutted around his office.

'When I was a teenager, just a simple foot soldier in the Commando Vermelho in Rio, we would have pinned them to their precious trees with nails and hung their teeth round our necks.'

Otero listened with growing distaste to his commander-in-chief, blanching at the image he had conjured in his head. He had been brought up in the wealthy suburbs of São Paulo, educated at the Estadual de Campinas University, and despite his high rank and long military career had never seen fighting of any sort.

'They will be here in twenty minutes, your Excellency. I will escort them here.'

'Ok Admiral, but remember. The dogs may bark but the train will always keep rolling.'

Otero turned on his mirror-polished boot heels and softly closed the heavy doors behind him.

Oliveira slumped in his chair, reached into the solid silver box on the desk and pulled out the thing he always reached for at times like these – the Dona Flor Brasilia, a cigar specially hand-rolled to his specification. Instead of the usual twelve-centimetre length, Oliveira had insisted on a despotic fifteen centimetres. The wrapper had also been double stretched and aged for an extra three months to create a fuller flavour. He rolled the cigar under his nose and savoured the aroma acquired in the rich, dark soil of the Recôncavo Basin. Continuing his usual ritual, he sliced off the cap end with his razor-sharp monogrammed tungsten double-blade guillotine before lighting the exposed tobacco leaf folds with the solid gold lighter he had been given by Jorge Santiago, one of Brazil's richest men.

Slowly the room began to fill with aromas of coffee, cocoa and rich cedar sweetness as Oliveira leant back, put his feet on his desk, closed his eyes and reminisced about less complicated times. The tobacco was beginning to work its magic. He had burned through barely a centimetre when another sharp knock shook him out of his memories of winning the presidential election just a year previously.

'*Puta merda.*' He sat up in his chair, taking a deep drag on his cigar.

Without waiting for permission, a man had entered, immaculate and pristine in a military uniform that Oliveira didn't recognise. Following behind him came a teenage girl with a tattooed face. She wore the bright red headdress and grass skirt of a traditional Amazon tribal woman, her bare breasts streaked with yellow and black paint. Beside her was a dark-skinned man of around sixty in a light khaki suit. He looked South American, but wasn't Brazilian, thought Oliveira.

The strange trio walked straight up to the president's desk. Oliveira surveyed them carefully, most especially the powerfully built military man with the pale blue eyes and distinctive scar on his cheek. Slowly extinguishing the cigar in an ashtray, he tried not to portray the unease he was feeling.

'Who are you? Where is Admiral Otero and where is your delegation?'

Looking at Oliveira with disdain, the man in the immaculate uniform spoke.

'My name is Colonel Paolo Moschin. And you, President Oliveira, are under arrest for the following crimes – embezzling your country out of billions of dollars for your personal gain, failing to protect the Central Amazon Conservation, the Jaú National Park, the Amana Sustainable Development Reserve and all that lie within it, and failing to protect the indigenous people of the Mato Grosso from persecution and murder.'

Moschin pointed to the girl on his left. 'Maristela Uapa is fourteen years old. She is a member of the Arara-Karo indigenous group, one of the tribes which has lived peacefully for hundreds of years in the Amazon rainforest that you want to now eradicate.'

Oliveira threw his cigar onto the floor and stood up.

'This is a joke. On whose authority and on what evidence do you make these ridiculous claims, soldier?'

Another voice cut in. 'It's on my authority, which I hold implicitly by being the senior officer in charge of your armed forces and also with the full approval of the Congress.'

Fleet Admiral Otero stood by the open doors. He wasn't looking nervous, but rather like a man who knew his hour had arrived. Oliveira looked aghast, suddenly rendered speechless. A soldier walked in and tied his hands without resistance. As he was being led out, he looked towards the swarthy sixty-year-old man who hadn't said a word.

'And who is this old man?'

The man walked over to the ex-president. 'My name is Omar Tello from Ecuador. Forty years ago I gave up my job as an accountant to follow a dream. A dream to grow my own rainforest.'

He fixed the president with a hard stare and prodded him hard in the chest. 'I hated seeing the Amazon being cut down by bastards like you, so I decided to grow my own. People thought me mad, but I didn't want to see this paradise disappear to the point where seeing a wild animal was a luxury. So I bought some land, a forest that had been cleared for farming and set about replanting it. I walked away from everything to work on my fledgling forest. I found seeds and cuttings from deep in the Amazon basin and replanted them. Eventually the wildlife started returning. Butterflies, spiders, brightly coloured bees and even snakes. My forest is only a few hundred metres each way, but it proves what can be achieved. Now I will show others that we can accommodate both the forest and our needs. We will kick out Amazon's destroyers and teach farmers how to restore their land and make money. We shall turn the tide and save Amazonia for the good of all.'

Straining against his bonds, Oliveira spat out a cynical response: 'It will never work old man and I shall be back in office tomorrow.'

Oliveira was led away, mouthing obscenities. Colonel Moschin smiled and turned to his two companions.

'I think you rattled him. Now let's get busy. We have some farmers and tribal elders to convince that we really can save their rainforest.'

3 December 2031, Antarctica
Cull Day 294

As they returned that evening after the CDT-8's successful test result, Jameson and Waites were fizzing with excitement, but agreed they wouldn't say anything too soon about the momentous outcomes of their day's work. They had entered the base and gone through the long, methodical routine of storing their kit as usual; then showered and changed as they always did.

At last, both felt they were ready to share their news. In just their cotton T-shirts and underwear, they breezily walked into the kitchen area where Trevallion and Beckley were busy preparing the night's meal.

'Hey, Sarah, still got that fizz in the larder fridge?'

She looked up from her potato peeling and threw Jameson a quizzical look.

'Aren't we saving it for "going home" night?'

Waites replied, grinning like a Cheshire cat, 'We've got something bigger to celebrate. We might just have saved the planet from the fuck-ups of the past fifty years. Isn't that worth cracking open some champagne?'

Trevallion's face lit up with childlike wonder as she realised what they meant. 'OM fucking G, that's incredible. Come here you world savers!'

The four hugged, whooped and high-fived like excitable teenagers who had just received good exam grades. Now, after a tough and disciplined nine months, news of the breakthrough gave them all licence to celebrate.

Swept away by the euphoria of the occasion, they forgot about being careful with their finite food supplies and cooked up their last two chickens along with double the usual helping of vegetables. Trevallion, a passionate vegan, had been more than satisfied with her spicy bean casserole. After finishing the last of the champagne, they kept the party mood going with red wine, beer and tequila slammers and sat together on the battered brown faux leather sofa that had served them so well for the duration of their mission.

'It's been quite a year. But I couldn't have wished to spend it with anyone better than you guys.' Jameson held his glass high in salute to his team.

'Thanks Will, that really means a lot.' Trevallion leaned forward and kissed Jameson on the cheek.

That felt good.

'You've done pretty good for an old guy,' said Waites, patting his boss on the back. 'Didn't think you'd be able to keep up the pace to be honest.'

'You never get to know a person until you work with them for a few months,' Beckley piped in before taking a long drink of his beer. 'But the truth is, I've been stuck with you guys for the best part of a year and I still don't know much about you. Who says we share some secrets?'

There was a momentary silence as they contemplated the question. Beckley was right, even though they had lived virtually on top of each for nearly three hundred days, they had all been too busy or too tired for small talk.

'OK,' replied Jameson. 'I'll go first. What you want to know?'

'Anything you want to share.' Trevallion looked at him with a mischievous look in her eye, daring him to be daring.

Jameson thought for a moment, and continued to look at Trevallion as the alcohol began to help him open doors in his mind.

Come on Jameson. Think. Give them something dark.

'Can't stand heights. Anything over ten feet. I'm jelly.'

'Boring,' goaded Beckley.

'I suffer OCD, everything has to be in its right place or I freak out.'

'We know that,' Waites laughed. 'We've seen your room.'

Shit. Bastards.

Flustered, Jameson blurted out something he thought he would never tell anyone. 'I haven't had sex for five years.'

O Christ.

He looked at Trevallion; her expression hadn't changed. He wanted to goad a reaction from her so he continued.

'Not my choice. We always enjoyed sex, we enjoyed it a lot. Had it so passionately one time, nearly ripped my foreskin off.'

Beckley and Waites laughed, but not a flicker from Trevallion.

'Then Bethany my wife, started to go through the menopause, and almost overnight she just went completely off all physical contact. We don't even share a bed now.'

'That would drive me crazy. It's been driving me nuts being

here,' retorted Waites. 'My girlfriend won't be able to sit down for a week after I get back.'

Beckley roared with laughter, even Trevallion allowed herself a smile.

Jameson shrugged. 'After a while you stop missing it. But never stopped hoping it will change. I love her, so what can I do?'

Yeah. What can I do?

After Jameson's confession, they got to hear from Waites about his former gambling addiction, his love of Glasgow Celtic and his hatred of Catholic priests, his alcoholic father and Glasgow Rangers. Then they listened to Beckley's stories about his jealousy of his older cleverer brother, his love of vintage Italian cars and of his need to masturbate at least twice a day.

'We're not keeping you from your early evening wank, are we?' bellowed Waites, pretending to jerk himself off. Jameson looked at Trevallion to gauge her reaction to the raucous male banter and was glad to see her laughing along.

'Sarah, the floor is yours. Three juicy titbits please.' Beckley looked at Trevallion. For the first time that evening she looked apprehensive.

Finishing her red wine, she slowly stood up and sighed.

'I had a stalker crush on Chris Martin from Coldplay. I would stand outside his front door in London, trying to summon the courage to ring the bell.'

'Did you?' said Jameson.

'Hey, I'm not that sad.' She smiled. 'Crush only lasted a week, then I moved onto Robbie Williams which was lucky because he lived two doors up.'

Everyone laughed mightily. Waites kicked his legs out, knocking two bottles from the low table in front of him. As he crawled clumsily on the floor to retrieve them, Trevallion continued with her confessional.

'I married a man who almost killed me.' The three men fell silent, Waites forgot about the bottles.

'His name was Nigel and when I said "I do", I signed up to the promise of expanding my dreams, my possibilities, my hopes, by sharing them with someone I loved. But all he did was reduce them to ashes. His control, his paranoia, his jealously made me feel worthless. So I began cutting myself to take away the pain. To feel something else apart from the torment in my fucked-up head.' She filled her glass again and drank it all back. 'Love can blind you to a person's faults, but when I finally stopped being "in love" with this handsome, charismatic bullshitter, I saw the damage he was causing. So I left Nigel nine thousand miles away.'

Jameson, Waites and Beckley were riveted.

A huge smile creased her face. 'And it feels fucking great!'

Good for you, beautiful.

After more hard drinking and a marathon game of Perudo Dice, Beckley had passed out, leaving the rest to compare life philosophies. Waites fetched some ham from the fridge and began attacking it with his usual carnivore relish.

Trevallion shook her head as she watched. 'If we gave up eating meat, we wouldn't even need to be here.'

'How so, my pulse-loving co-worker?' retorted Waites, leaning back in his chair, hands behind his head, ready for any argument she had to offer.

'Listen up you pig-chomping asshole.' Trevallion brought her drink down hard on the table. 'The bloody hoofprint of farmed meat doesn't just cause deforestation. Methane from cows and fertilisers creates the greenhouse gas which right now is melting away the ice under our feet.'

Waites rolled his eyes and leant forward.

'Christ, I come all this way to save the planet, freezing my nuts off and I still get grief for being a meat-eating mammal doing what comes naturally.'

'What you do shouldn't be natural. See you in the morning, murderers.'

Trevallion got to her feet and walked unsteadily towards the sealed door leading to the sleeping quarters.

'If vegans like her really don't want to eat eggs, meat and fish, that's their choice, but why do they act so fucking superior?' Waites had chewed through the last of the ham, trying to swill it down with more beer. He spilt most of it down his T-shirt, but didn't seem to notice.

'Vegans are pussies. I knew one who used to walk two miles to work. He didn't want to drive just in case he splatted some insects.' Waites threw his head back and laughed, too loud and too long, like all drunks do.

'Get to bed, Tom. We've got another long day ahead.'

Waites looked at Jameson as if he wanted to argue the point, instead he just picked up his beer and took it with him to bed.

Jameson walked across to the kitchen and poured the rest of his wine down the sink. He gazed through the large triple-glazed window that gave a panoramic view out over the featureless frozen tundra. The weather had been calm that day, a lone albatross effortlessly glided on what wind there was, over the gently drifting snow that stretched away to the low mountains in the distance. Their peaks were probably no more thirty miles away but they had marked the outer limits of their world these past months. The pale sun sat low in the milky-blue sky. For months it had seemed glued to the horizon line, but in recent days had begun to rise a little. Summer was coming; the ice was on the move and soon they would have to leave.

An event I'm more than ready for.

Jameson missed being able to walk outside in his shorts and

sit in the sun. He missed walking on grass, the smells and vibrant colours around his Cotswolds home. The warm amber of the stone cottages, yellow rape fields, red dahlias, blue cornflowers, orange of the sweet peppers he grew in his greenhouse. Mired in this monochrome land, most of all he had missed the perpetual wonder of the changing seasons. It had seemed like forever, and he was aching to hold Bethany, Patrick their son, and especially his daughter Bella whom he hadn't seen for nearly a year and a half.

His eighteen-year-old daughter had begged him to attend a Reboot conference with her in London, six months before he had left for Antarctica. When he refused, she had gone anyway and never returned home. She sent just one email, stating she was going to devote her life to their cause, written as if she was simply informing an employer of her decision to quit a job, cold, detached and vague. The family were devastated and had spent days travelling around London trying to locate her. Then one night, while watching the ten o'clock news, they had seen the face of their usually timid daughter snarling at them from the television. They had watched in horrified fascination as she and six others dressed in red jumpsuits smashed their way into BP's offices in Canary Wharf and set fire to the building.

While Jameson agreed with Bella that the oil industry had a lot to answer for, he did not agree with Reboot's methods to bring them to account. He resolved that when he returned, he was going to find his daughter and persuade her to come home.

Taking a glass of water, Jameson walked wearily down the corridor, following the low-level floor lights to his bedroom. He was nearly there when a noise behind him made him stop. He turned to see Trevallion standing in her bedroom doorway silhouetted against the blue-white light of the room. Her normally swept and tied blond hair now cascaded freely onto her shoulders; her short white T-shirt barely covered the top of her thighs.

Jameson was mesmerised for a few moments. 'Are you OK?' he finally mumbled.

Without a word, she held out her hand.

Is this really happening?

13 February 2031, Beijing, China
Cull Day 2

'Hey watch out, that's my daughter.' As the train juddered to a stop, the small girl fell away from her mother and into the forest of legs.

'I have her.' The middle-aged man smiled and gently supported the girl as she got to her feet and reached out for her mother's hand.

'Thank you. Her first time on the underground?' The mother nodded her head and smiled at the good Samaritan.

'Where are you going?' the man enquired.

'To the Gate of the Nation. Along with everyone else I think.'

The man looked at the girl who was clinging hard to her mother's leg as the train started off again. 'Just one more stop little lady. Then you will see treasures like no other.'

'I'm sure she will remember this day for a long time.' As the mother gently patted her daughter's head, she had no idea just how memorable this day would turn out to be.

Despite the chill which had greeted him, Vincent Yu felt excitement as he walked up the steps of the Qianmen Subway Station which led to the south side of Tiananmen Square. At the top, he paused to wonder at the sight. Yu had been here many times, but the scale of this place always took his breath away. One hundred acres of pristine paving stretched before him, framed on four sides by huge concrete buildings and monuments. The world's largest public square, all created to showcase the grand ambitions and glorious past of the Communist Party. Yet today, even this grand promenade was struggling to hold the masses that had been pouring into it for the past three hours, and still the people came.

They streamed across the west road and found their place on the immaculate lush lawns in front of the Great Hall of the People and the Museum of the Chinese Revolution. They pushed tightly up against the walls of the Zhengyangmen Gate and the Qianmen Archery Tower which dominated the square's northern end. They grouped together to sit on the steps of Chairman Mao's mausoleum which ran across the front of the building, or to stand against its giant pillars to get a better view. Groups of children gathered under the line of flagpoles near the square's centre, laughing and pointing at the huge cotton sheets high above them as they billowed and snapped in the breeze.

Although it was usually forbidden for such crowds to gather, on this day no one was being challenged, no bags being searched, no pockets emptied. The normal security checkpoints had gone. Although state cameras continued to monitor this unusual event, the usual armed undercover policemen were nowhere to be seen. Tiananmen Square appeared once again to be in the possession of the people, as it had been once before for a few fateful days in the summer of 1989. Now, as he walked into the square on this winter morning forty-two years later, Vincent Yu recalled the terrible events of the third and fourth of June.

He had been in his final year at Beijing's University of Science, and along with thousands of students and teachers had come to China's sacred Gate of Heavenly Peace to protest against the government. They were angry at the Communist Party's newly imposed single-party system. They wanted a say in the new progressive China that beckoned with the recent collapse of the Soviet Union and the weakening grip of communism around the world. Twenty-one-year-old Yu had put himself at the epicentre of the confrontation by camping out in the most antagonistic place he could, the middle of Tiananmen Square.

One night, following weeks of occupation, the government's patience finally snapped and they ordered the army to clear the students. Like rabid animals let off a leash, hundreds of soldiers advanced on the camp and fired into it at point-blank range.

Yu bit his lip, as the horror of the first minutes of the attack returned to him. The deafening bangs, the screams, the sickening grinding as tank tracks minced flesh and bone. The sight of young men and women standing with multiple bullet wounds, unable to comprehend what had happened to them, oblivious to the fact that they were dying.

Thousands were killed or injured over the two days of carnage. Yet even before the blood had dried on the flagstones, the government were justifying their actions heralding the massacre as the heroic 'quelling of a counter-revolutionary rebellion.' State-run television proclaimed the episode a long overdue 'vaccination' for Chinese society, one that would 'provide immunity against future political turmoil'.

Despite the scale of the horror, Yu managed to escape the city without injury and took refuge in the vast dense forests of

Yesanpo nature reserve. The following months were difficult for Yu and his family. He struggled to find enough food to sustain himself and had to constantly be on the move. His parents were brutally interrogated by the security forces. When it became clear they couldn't reveal the whereabouts of their son, both mother and father were put under house arrest for a year.

When he finally came out of hiding, Yu reinvented himself to avoid persecution and certain imprisonment. Forging identity papers, he changed his name to Li Qiang and moved to Baoding, a city in the south. Over the next ten years, he worked in low-profile cleaning and labouring jobs before joining fledgling solar panel maker Yingli Solar as an engineer. Aided by fortuitous timing and generous new government subsidies for green industries, the company soon became China's largest producer of the panels. By 2029, Yu had risen to general manager, married and started a family. His transformation from radical student to benign middle-class citizen seemed complete.

But it was not to last.

When the country was booming, China had viewed environmental policies as integral to its transformation. But when the economy began to slow, that view changed. Suddenly the nation, praised as the greenest in the world, was becoming the most polluting, shifting from being the biggest advocate of wind and solar power to the largest builder of new coal plants. During this dramatic shift, the government axed its solar subsidies. Within six months, Yingli's factories were operating at a loss and Yu was without a job.

A victim once more of the Communist Party's erratic self-serving actions, Yu's political activism reawakened and he started to contact environmentalist groups to find ways of organising a new movement against the government. Travelling to Europe, he met with Erica Sandstrom and other Reboot leaders; together, they agreed the only way to succeed would be to gain a foothold in the People's Liberation Army. While the Party had relaxed control of people and the economy, its control of the PLA remained fundamental to its stranglehold on the nation. If they could weaken this grip, then Reboot might have a chance of gaining control of one and a half billion people.

After months of failed initiatives, Yu finally achieved a breakthrough when the chief of the armed forces and communist hardliner General Li Tie was killed in a military helicopter crash. His successor, Admiral Zhang Chengdong, a student at the same time as Yu, was a Reboot sympathiser and immediately made contact. Better still, Zhang knew of other high-ranking PLA officers also prepared to gamble with their lives to help turn the military against its long-time masters.

Now in Tiananmen Square, as Yu stood with hundreds of thousands of others in the very core of the communist heartland, he knew he would soon see if that brave gamble had paid off.

In a broadcast on China Central Television the previous evening, the citizens of Beijing had been invited to attend a 'historic announcement' and a 'memorable spectacle'. The presenters had not been the usual government puppets and did not give much detail, simply stating that the momentous events would commence at noon. On this Beijing Sunday morning, normally the quietest part of the quietest day in the city's week, that promise was sufficient to bring out people in their hundreds of thousands. Anticipation was already high, fuelled by vague rumours of the US president's assassination. Yu knew them to be true, but tried to concentrate on the events to come.

The square was now full to bursting, and everyone was looking towards Tiananmen Gate and the Forbidden City where Chang'an Avenue, the key approach road, was being kept clear by ranks of soldiers. Without any announcements to the contrary, people had assumed this was where the main show would take place. A million people waited, tightly packed and steaming in air that had barely risen above freezing. Children, unable to run around as they'd like, fidgeted impatiently around the legs of their parents. Souvenir sellers picked their way through the crowd selling their mass-produced wares. Mao figures carved from cow bone, Great Wall printed tea towels, T-shirts emblazoned with Red Army recruitment posters from World War Two. The Beijing classes mixed contentedly as all good communists do, and as they did, they were all asking the same questions. Why had they come here on a Sunday? What was this 'historic announcement'? Why had they only been informed the day before?

The answers were not long in coming. The square hushed, then fell silent as the approaching sound of heavy machinery coming from the west grew louder. Yu knew the sound well – tanks.

He felt his resolve weaken. His mind began to race. Had they failed? Had Zhang reneged on his promise to join them? Had the admiral been discovered and turned over to the party? Were the tanks coming to crush them again?

The fear started to grip him. It was a familiar feeling. He suffered from panic attacks and lost thousands of hours of sleep haunted by the memories of what these terror weapons could do. Slowly he inched forward, careful not to cause alarm, easing himself in and around the crush of distracted people, their bikes, their prams, stepping on bags, on feet, on pets, before mercifully, tripping out of the airless embrace of the multitude and into the welcoming light and space on the edge of the avenue. Yu took a few deep breaths and slowly calmed down, now he could get away if events turn against him.

The deep growl of heavy diesel engines became louder, and the crowd gave an enthusiastic cheer as the first clanking green and brown monster came into view. Yu recognised it as the Type

99, third generation of the battle tank that so savagely cut down his friends and his hopes. He could see that at least twenty of these sixty-ton leviathans were making their way slowly down Chang'an Avenue in single file, their tracks biting down into the tarmac and splitting paving stones as they made their imperious way along the wide promenade. They trundled slowly past in front of Yu, no more than five metres away. The ground shook, rattling his teeth; the people around him laughing in delight as in turn it did the same to them. The noise was deafening, the fumes that belched from the huge exhausts lay thick in the air, making him nauseous. Eventually, the lead tank reached the east corner of the square and stopped, the column came to a squealing, grinding halt.

To the enthralled crowd watching, this was nothing unusual. So far, this had all the hallmarks of a typical Communist Party parade, designed to showcase the country's military prowess. The only slightly unusual feature for some was that this was not October the first, National Day, the normal day for such displays.

Just as the diesel smoke cleared, an enormous whoosh filled the air as six gleaming red, white and blue jets screamed low across the square in a perfect diamond formation.

For the next five minutes all eyes turned skywards to marvel at the pride of China's air force, the Bayi aerobatic team. Twisting and turning with breath-taking precision, the elegant planes left long streams of yellow and green smoke trails in their wake which held their shape for a few moments before dissipating in the smog-hazed sky. For the enthralled crowd, this was indeed a spectacle to behold. Bayi had never performed directly over the city, and they clapped and cheered in joyous appreciation at the pilots' skill and daring. When the show finished and the planes screamed away to the east, everyone's attention once again fell on the tank column. It was only then, when they had ceased to be diverted by the air display, did they realise that something very unusual was happening.

The tanks' turrets had all turned. Turned not to face the crowd, but to level their huge guns directly at the Tiananmen Gate. An action that was strictly forbidden.

Before anyone could protest, the guns fired in unison with an ear-splitting crack, causing the scores of people nearest the tanks to stumble or fall as the huge concussive shock displaced the air around them. In a split second, the sacred monument that had stood since the Ming Dynasty was reduced to a pile of dust and smoke. The vast gathering was stunned. A clear spasm of shock swept through the crowd and out into the far corners of the square as thousands of Beijing citizens struggled to comprehend what had just happened in their city. Before anyone could react, a second volley was loosed, obliterating any remaining recognisable elements of the six-hundred-year-old structure.

For a few moments all was still, then children began crying. Here and there a cry of shock was heard or a shout of protest; scores of dogs barked furiously. Slowly, a hatch in the turret of the lead tank opened and a small portly man dressed in the uniform of a high-ranking military officer emerged.

To Yu's astonishment, he could see it was Zhang Chengdong. As the admiral scanned the square, he spotted Yu just two hundred metres away. His arms raised in triumph and his face creased into a huge grin. Climbing down from the tank, he ushered Yu over to join him at a hastily erected podium. Ascending the steps, Yu felt exultation as he looked across the mass of heads that stretched unbroken to the horizon, all of them facing towards him. Zhang gestured for quiet from the dumbfounded crowd.

'Citizens of Beijing, you have just borne witness to a most important moment in the history of the People's Republic of China. Your military will no longer be the puppets of the Party. We will no longer enforce the will of your oppressors. From this moment, we shall be the people's army, the army for you. Our new role is to help lead our great country to a new prosperity, a new era, when we shall come together with our friends in the West for the good of us all and the planet.'

The multitude were still in a state of shock, but as they slowly processed this information some began to cheer, then others started to clap. Within a few moments, as the tension finally lifted, the square erupted into a joyful cacophony of celebration.

With a contented look on his face, Zhang turned to Yu. 'It seems they like the show so far. Now…we have an important rendezvous in Meeting Room Number One.'

Instructing fifty soldiers to come with them, Zhang led Yu past the shattered remains of Tiananmen Gate and they entered the Forbidden City. As the group walked briskly through the garden at the entrance to the complex, they were joined by three other men, all dressed in dark suits. Zhang introduced them in turn as they continued further into the hallowed grounds.

'This is Feng Xiaoting, deputy head of the Publicity Bureau. He has been working on the first announcements for the country regarding the coup and also what we shall be telling the world.'

Feng nodded his head in recognition. With his long foppish hair and fashionable spectacles, Yu thought he looked young for such a senior position. He was even more surprised when Feng spoke in a clipped middle-England accent.

'This a great day for the nation and all freethinking people.'

'It is indeed,' replied Yu. 'Tell me, how did someone your age get to wear such big shoes?'

Feng grinned. 'I spent five years at Ogilvy and Mather Advertising in London. Let's just say it's given me an advantage over my stay-at-home colleagues.'

Zhang registered the surprise on Yu's face at meeting this extraordinary hybrid of east and west culture. 'The Party has always gone out of its way to pick the best students, entrepreneurs, and those who have gained experience in the West like Xiaoting. Of course, there is always a risk in recruiting intelligent people. Eventually they will want your job!'

Zhang pointed to the second man, lean with short, cropped grey hair. Squinty eyed with a jumble of buck teeth, he looked every inch the archetypal humourless Communist Party official.

'Vincent, this fine fellow is Goa Lin, our human resources genius. His organisational skills will be crucial in the coming months to mobilise China for a smooth transition. He will head up a department of over two hundred and fifty thousand people.'

Goa shook Yu's hand, bowed his head slightly, but said nothing.

The third man, muscular and middle-aged, was striding ahead at the front of the group and led them through the double doors of one of the pagoda-shaped buildings.

The doors opened up to reveal a large and well-lit reception hall. A number of salmon-coloured marble plinths, supporting large terracotta pots, framed the four corners of the space. The walls were completely covered with traditional paintings of pastoral fishing and hunting scenes. Yu wanted to pause and take in the magnificent scene, but they hurried on and exited through another set of doors which opened onto an area of lush, well-tended formal gardens. About eight hundred metres away to the west, Yu could see their ultimate destination, a tight complex of small single-storey buildings with red walls and gold and green gilt roof tiles.

Panting due to the brisk pace, Zhang pointed to the man leading them.

'The one forcing the pace up front is Wang Boashan, head of State Security. He has total control of the security forces in the complex, so we will not be prevented from going into the heart of Zhongnanhai.'

Zhongnanhai. Yu had heard so much about this place but never dreamed he would ever get into it. It was the nerve centre of operations for Premier Li Keqiang and the centre of political power in China.

It also housed Meeting Room Number One, the mythical inner sanctuary where the premier, vice-premiers, state councillors, secretaries general and ministers met in secret and made the decisions that directly affected the lives, hopes and ambitions of one-fifth of the global population. No photographs were ever taken in these meetings; no video footage existed of the way proceedings were run. A two-page news release published by the Xinhua News Agency after every meeting was the sum total of the insight and information given to the Chinese people about the government's deliberations in this room.

Now, Yu thought. On this day, in Zhongnanhai, this will change.

Yu, Zhang, Feng, Goa and the soldiers continued to scamper after Wang until he eventually stopped outside one of the single-storey buildings. Four identical black limousines were lined up neatly in front of it. Yu noticed that their registration plates numbered from 0001 to 0004.

'They are all here,' exclaimed Wang with obvious relief and delight. 'Let us give them the good news.'

He entered the building without ceremony and the others followed in his wake into a small circular reception area. Wang paused for a moment outside two large oak-faced double doors which both bore the Chinese five-star motif in their centre. On either side of the doors stood a guard armed with a bayoneted rifle. They hadn't moved from their stiff, at-attention pose, but both regarded Wang warily as he spoke.

'Faithful soldiers of Zhongnanhai. You are now relieved of your duty. Lay your rifles on the ground and leave.'

One of the soldiers thrust his rifle towards the intruder; the bayonet pressing against Wang's chest. 'Only Wang Boashan,

State Security Chief can order us from these doors,' he declared defiantly.

'I am he.' Wang slowly reached into his jacket pocket. He pulled out and showed the laminated identification card bearing his face and rank.

The soldier studied the card carefully and abruptly lowered his rifle. 'Comrade Wang. Forgive me.'

Wang waved a benevolent hand. 'You were only doing your duty. That duty is no longer needed'

The two guards bowed to their commander-in-chief, placed their rifles on the marble floor and hurried away. Pausing for a moment, Wang seemed to utter a brief prayer before pushing the doors open and entering what was known throughout China as Meeting Room Number One.

The room was about fifteen metres square and surprisingly well illuminated for a place with such a notoriously murky past. Light streamed in from large floor-to-ceiling windows on three sides, each affording excellent views of the sumptuous gardens that surrounded the complex.

On the far wall, two large paintings depicting mountain and lake scenes hung above a plain wooden fireplace. Between the windows, wooden framed hand-coloured photographs of senior members of the Party, past and present, stared into the room. In the centre of these, in a much larger silver gilt frame, the smiling face of the father of modern China, Mao Zedong beamed out. A Chinese flag stood limp at the far end of a large oval conference table which dominated the centre of the room. Around the table were twelve dark pine chairs and twelve people. Five of them sat upright, still and solemn, looking impassively at the intruders. The other seven were dead. Five had slumped forward, heads resting on the polished walnut tabletop, another had fallen and lay crumpled on the wooden floor. President Sun Jihai himself had fallen another way in his death throes. His head rested on the back of the chair, arms by his side, facing up at the ceiling, mouth open, yelling out a silent eternal scream.

Yu surveyed the grim scene and felt nothing. The events of the past thirty minutes had left him beyond comprehension and emotion. He walked to the far corner of the room, sat on a small, cushioned chair and closed his eyes.

After speaking to one of the survivors of the suicide pact, Wang relayed what had happened moments before they arrived. On hearing of the coup, and realising the hopelessness of their situation, President Sun Jihai had ordered that the ruling council should, in a 'glorious act of defiance to the imperialist savages', collectively end their lives by cyanide pill. When the pills had been distributed, he, Vice- President Wang Chao, Premier Li Keqiang, Executive Vice-Premier Han Zheng, Vice-Premier Sun Chunian, Vice-Premier Jia Delong and Vice-Premier Li Lei had all made the futile gesture. The rest of their colleagues had declined.

Presently, Goa came over and sat next to Yu.

'It's quite a sight isn't it? Seeing these famous people, all dead.'

'Very strange. They were always portrayed as superhuman.'

Goa was contemptuous. 'They are just like us – flawed, stupid, vain.'

'I'm sure, but very powerful, flawed, stupid and vain.'

'Let me tell you something about these people, and why they had to die.' Goa leaned in towards him, causing the old chair to creak. 'You remember the pandemic ten years ago Vincent?'

Yu felt his body tense. 'Did they start it? I knew they were covering something up.' He hit his fist into his palm. He had lost both his parents to COVID-19.

Goa shook his head. 'They didn't start it – we did. We created the coronavirus.'

Yu was stunned and said nothing.

Goa continued, 'We wanted something that would jolt the old economics, show nations they could adapt to life without cars, railways and planes. And we wanted to show the positive effects on the environment when they did. The numbers were impressive. Big reductions in nitrogen dioxide in every major Chinese city, and a thirty per cent drop in fine particulates, one of the most deadly air pollutants here in Beijing.'

Goa stood up and looked across the room to where Wang was gesturing for him to come over.

'But of course we know what happened when it was over,' Goa shrugged. 'Mankind went back to its old ways, so that is why we are now following Plan B.'

'Plan B?' Yu almost felt afraid to ask what that meant.

'Depopulation.' Goa's expression hardened as he walked away, pausing for a moment, he looked back. 'There is no alternative; I'm surprised Reboot hasn't told you.'

Yu stood wearily and made his way out of this place of death, past the dazed and confused guards and staff and out onto the manicured lawns that ran alongside the length of the building.

Taking a welcome deep breath of the early afternoon air, he caught the sweet taste of early-spring blossom and freshly-cut grass. Looking up over the buildings to the east, the smudge of dust and smoke from the blasted ruins of Tiananmen Gate could still be seen. Incessant car horns, excited cheers and the booming crackle of exploding fireworks sounded throughout the vast city. Beijing was celebrating, for now, the people seemed happy.

At last, he thought, the truth of the Tiananmen massacre could be revealed and the People's Republic of China could start making amends and new friends. Vincent Yu knew he should be happy too, but he felt uneasy.

Had they simply replaced one set of tyrants with another?

13 February 2031, Murmansk, Russia
Cull Day 2

Friday night in Murmansk. At the White Rabbit Bar that usually meant trouble.

Being the bar nearest to the port meant trouble usually came in the shape of merchant seamen, North Atlantic fishermen and crews from the nuclear-powered icebreaker fleet. All eager to unwind after another long week on the Barents Sea.

The temperature was minus five outside so the vodka was flowing freely inside the steamy confines of the bar's dimly-lit interior. It was only seven o'clock and already glasses were being broken and furniture smashed, but the owner, Valentin Lebedev, was relaxed about the damages. As long as his customers kept drinking his vodka and gin, continued to eat his wife's pelmeni – a greasy stew of fish and meat dumplings – and kept their hands off his twin daughters, Lebedev was happy enough. Katerina and Zoya were eighteen and with their long dark hair, flawless olive skin and slim ballerina figures, strikingly beautiful. They always attracted plenty of attention from men of the sea, starved of such delicate diversions after weeks away in the bitter Arctic oceans.

Lebedev thought the girls were safe as long as they worked at the bar together; and besides, he wanted to believe they probably had no interest in these crude drunken louts. But he was wrong. Zoya especially loved the thrill of bedding the burly plain-speaking men who frequented her father's bar, and the White Rabbit's warm cellar was the perfect place to indulge her desires.

'Lover boy, Pasha, is in tonight, Zoya.' Katerina guided her sister's eyes to the tall, handsome blond man who had entered the bar with two other men. Thirty-four-year-old Pasha Solokov wore the distinctive black uniform and peaked cap of a senior officer in the renowned Arktika-class icebreaker fleet. Zoya adored the way he filled his uniform. As he laughed freely with his crew mates, she could feel her excitement building.

'When they have been served, I'll clear the tables next to them to get his attention.' Katerina winked at her sister. 'Then I will give him his "instructions".'

'Good luck,' her sister replied.

Katerina made her way confidently through the men packed near the bar, ignoring their whistles, remarks and clumsy groping, and made her way to the table where Solokov was talking animatedly. In one skilful move, she picked up two empty glasses with one hand and pushed a note into his pocket with the other.

Satisfied that he had felt her hand, Katerina pushed her way back through the crowd to the bar. Solokov slowly turned his back and, pretending to answer his phone, read the note. It was short, hastily written but perfectly clear.

CELLAR. 5 MINUTES.

Despite the sudden pang of excitement he felt, Solokov remained composed. He turned back to his companions with a rueful expression and downed his vodka.

'It is my wife, she wants me to call her.'

'Let her wait Pasha. She always calls just as you're having some fun.' One of the men laughed, playfully turning his cap, so the peak faced backwards. 'Never jump straight away when a woman beckons. It makes them keener.'

Solokov adjusted the cap. 'I'll do it now and get it out of the way. She will just whinge about the size of our flat, the lack of heating and how much she hates me being away. I'll agree things are terrible and promise to make everything better on my return.' As he walked away, he shouted back cheerily, 'I'll be back in no time comrades. Order me one more vodka, and then it's just water for all of us. Remember we have a big day tomorrow.'

He looked forward to tasting Zoya again. She was wild but wanted nothing more than his eager cock and fifteen minutes in a warm cellar lying on some straw. With his wife thirteen hundred kilometres away in Saint Petersburg, he thought that was just fine.

Pushing his way through the thick ruck of Friday night revellers, Solokov further contemplated his good fortune. He had just been promoted to second officer on the icebreaker *Vaygach* which had been commissioned to assist shipping along the Northern Sea route in the frozen waterways north of Siberia. *Vaygach* was much more powerful than the diesel-powered ships that Solokov had trained on. He marvelled at its ability to smash through ice two and a half metres thick at speeds of up to ten knots. Now *Vaygach* was being used for scientific expeditions in the Arctic as Russia looked to exploit the region's vast mineral wealth. As a result, work for Solokov was much more interesting, as was his leisure time. The ship's normal crew had been bolstered by scientists and geologists, many of whom, like him, loved playing chess or a few hands of

Durak to pass the time during the endless sunlit Arctic evenings. Yes, life was on the up for Pasha Solokov. He was in a good mood and he was going to enjoy screwing this beautiful barmaid.

Just as he reached the top of the cellar stairs, Valentin bellowed for quiet, and Solokov, already feeling a frisson of guilt, immediately thought he was in trouble.

'Silence, you bastards. The hero who is visiting us here tomorrow is about to speak. A respectful pause, if you please. Silence for the genius who is giving Mother Russia back her pride.'

The bar went quiet as an old wall-mounted television behind the bar flickered to life. After a couple of seconds, the imposing figure of Sergei Fedorov appeared. As part of his 'everywhere man' initiative, Fedorov was due to visit Murmansk in the morning to carry out an inspection of the icebreaker fleet. Solokov had only learnt that morning that *Vaygach* had been allocated for the honour, and throughout the day he had been frantically preparing the ship. They had still not finished. But right now Fedorov was in Moscow, so they still had time to complete the painting and cleaning by working through the night.

The Russian president was standing behind a low white lectern, designed to make the six-foot-two-inch, self-proclaimed demigod appear even taller. The lectern bore the gold and red coat of arms of the Russian Federation and was flanked on both sides by the tricolour flags of Russia, one of which also bore the eagle crest. Fedorov was in full presidential mode, wearing his trademark bespoke black suit, white shirt and burgundy tie.

Cries of 'Hurrah for the Father!', 'Hurrah for the hero!' went up in the bar, but quickly died down as Fedorov began his speech. It was the usual quick-fire, wide-ranging affair that Fedorov favoured in his public addresses. Starting with the economy, he briskly moved on to an athletics doping scandal, the China peace talks, restraint of internet freedoms and the arms control treaty with the US. There seemed to be no particular logic or hierarchy to the order of the topics, making each appear as important or unimportant as the next. The customers in the bar murmured their inebriated agreement as Fedorov made the concluding comments on each of his themes.

As the loyal communist he was, Solokov respectfully listened as this peculiarly Russian ritual continued for a further ten minutes. During one especially protracted cheer and enthusiastic vodka toast, he saw his opportunity to finally slip away into the cellar. Gently closing the low painted metal door behind him, he slowly descended the old wooden stairs, treading as softly as he could manage in his heavy boots. On reaching the damp, brick floor, the sight greeting him made his heart beat faster and his blood flow considerably quicker. Zoya lay on a straw pile in the corner of the low, dark room. She had drawn up her skirt over her long slender legs to reveal that she had already removed her underwear. She smiled and opened her legs.

Fedorov's monotonous drone could still be heard clearly from the bar directly above, as Solokov walked quickly over and sat down on the straw. Just as quickly, she pushed him onto his back and started undoing his heavy leather belt.

'Allow me.'

In one practised, fluent sweep, Zoya pulled both his trousers and boxer shorts down to his boots. Panting in expectation, she pulled her skirt up and climbed on top of her lover.

'I have thought of nothing but your cock for the past two weeks. Don't keep it away so long next time.' Zoya mounted him and started to gyrate her hips. 'Now fuck me, Officer Solokov.'

As he thrust towards her, she cried out in animalistic pleasure, shaking her long hair so it fell over her face. God, I love this bar, thought Solokov. Directly above them, Fedorov started to address the concluding topic in his speech.

'On Sunday, we marked our Orthodox Christmas. As usual, the celebrations were enjoyed by millions of Russians in the traditional way.' Fedorov paused for a couple of seconds. 'What was unusual… was the temperature. Up to sixteen degrees higher than normal.'

Solokov could feel Zoya slowing her movements, just as she always did when she was about to orgasm. Good, he thought. Soon I can have my pleasure.

Above the lovers heads, Fedorov continued in a graver tone.

'Fellow Russians, I can assure you that we are taking events like this, the flooding in the Kaliningrad enclave and the recent forest fires in Siberia, very seriously. More seriously than the US, which continues to dither over its commitment to reducing carbon emissions.'

More cheers sounded from the bar above. Zoya had stopped moving. Solokov impatiently pushed upward to rouse her.

'I am pleased to tell you that we have over thirty measures in planning to address the situation. These include more state-funded dam building and use of drought-resistant crops along with emergency vaccinations and state-organised evacuations in case of disaster. We shall also prepare new educational materials to teach climate change in schools.'

Zoya was now listening intently to Fedorov. She had completely forgotten about carnal pleasures.

'Nobody knows the origins of global climate change,' Fedorov continued. 'We know previous periods of warming could depend on mysterious processes in the universe, processes such as changes in the axis in the rotation of the earth or its orbit around the sun. Both could push the planet into serious climate changes.'

Zoya looked down at her bemused and frustrated lover. 'He's lying Pasha. He's lying.'

Fedorov's voice brightened. 'Whatever the reasons for these climate variations, it could be good for us. Happy side effects of this so-called crisis could be decreased energy use in cold regions. In turn, increases in temperature could unlock and expand agricultural areas and present new sea routes in the Arctic Ocean. Warming by two or three degrees could be a good thing for Russians. We would no longer need fur coats!'

Zoya had now got off Solokov and was shouting up at the ceiling. 'He thinks we're idiots. Damn him, damn Fedorov and his fantasies.'

Solokov was appalled. 'Zoya, keep quiet. You'll get me into trouble. They could kick me off the fleet.'

Zoya ignored him as Fedorov continued his boasting. 'Moscow has exceeded its obligations under all international protocols. Russia's great efforts have already slowed global warming by almost a year. And we have been able to nearly double productivity over the same period,' he suggested, clearly lying. 'However, we must remain wary about solar and wind energy. Turbines have proven to be harmful to birds and even worms, causing them to come out of the ground because of the vibrations.'

Exasperated, Zoya screamed out in anger, banging on the floorboards above her head. 'You will ruin us with your fairy tales. We will overthrow you and tell Russia the truth about what must be done. Fedorov of the Kremlin – you self-serving son of a whore.'

Just as Solokov made to pull her down, the cellar door crashed open and Valentin lumbered down the steps carrying a double-barrelled shotgun. Panting in quick shallow breaths, he surveyed the scene before him. The man without trousers lying on the straw. His daughter standing over him.

He grunted and made towards them, shotgun at the ready.

Solokov stood with his hands out, pleading for mercy as Zoya retreated to the back of the cellar away from the impending confrontation, but said nothing to stop her father. Valentin gave a guttural roar, cocked the gun and blasted the hapless second officer with both barrels. Solokov was thrown backwards and smashed against the back of the cellar. His body slid down the wall and came to rest face up in the straw like a broken bloody marionette. Valentin waited to see if the drunks in the bar had heard anything but the laughing continued without pause. He quickly dismantled the shotgun and placed it inside a large wooden barrel before turning to his daughter, who was straightening her dress nonchalantly.

'Well done, Zoya. Now up to the bar and keep pumping drink down their throats. Once we have the codes we need from this bastard, I will inform Reboot. Our great hero will have a surprise tomorrow.'

Dmitry Tarasenko tried to calm his nerves and his coughing as the motorcade made its way into the Murmansk suburbs. This was his last assignment guarding Russia's Body Number One and he wanted it over.

For the past sixteen years, Russia's Federal Protection Service – the security agency responsible for guarding the president's life – had been headed by Tarasenko's old boss, General Alexander Ovechkin. During his leadership, Ovechkin had shaped the service into a formidable force with the right to carry out covert investigations, conduct wiretapping, detain citizens, search homes and confiscate personal possessions. Protecting the president was always the FPS's main priority, and Ovechkin dedicated enormous time, resources and creativity to the task. He had always insisted that a body double was used for Fedorov's riskier public performances – such as submersible dives into the depths of Lake Baikal or flying a fighter jet low over the Ural mountains. More than once, this policy had saved the president's life.

Being in such good favour with Moscow's political elite, it had seemed that Ovechkin's role at the agency was secure for at least another decade. But just two days previously, he had died following a heart attack and now his deputy, the coughing Tarasenko, had been promoted to the top job.

This trip to the nuclear icebreaker fleet was scheduled to be Tarasenko's last in the field before moving to the Kremlin to start his new role. Once there, his focus would expand beyond the safety of the president to include judges, officials, senior diplomats and politicians. It was the sort of high-profile role he had always wanted and was eager to get started. He also looked forward to being back in Moscow where, with his larger salary, he could indulge his love of ballet and the arts. He just had to get through this final assignment, and life would be easier, he told himself. Just one more job.

Fedorov was travelling in his favoured car, the black Aurus Senat limousine which had been airlifted the previous day into Murmansk's airport. Both bulletproof and fireproof, it ran on solid rubber tyres, and carried sophisticated communications equipment. It was further protected by the Mercedes G-Class that Tarasenko and three other agents rode in ahead and the Chevrolet support vehicle carrying another five agents behind. Four hundred metres further ahead of the convoy, six motorcycle outriders cleared traffic out of their way. They had driven the twenty-four kilometres from the airport and entered the city without incident. Murmansk's residents paused to stare as the cars speeded by, intrigued by the sirens, but there was no cheering or waving. Most were too busy going about their business, trying to keep warm in the sub-zero morning chill.

'How far to the port?' Tarasenko asked the driver.

'Five minutes at most.'

Tarasenko coughed into his handkerchief before turning to the two huge dark-suited blond-haired men sitting in the back of the car. Despite their size, both had typically snub nosed Ukrainian faces that somehow looked unfinished; they wore identical mirror sunglasses and sported small audio pickups in their ears. Denis Azarov and Boris Kalugin were men he knew well and respected. All three had trained and served in Russian Special Forces, the notorious Spetsnaz. They had fought together in the Crimea and all had killed during the conflict. They had been recruited into the FPS four years previously and worked in Fedorov's security team ever since. While Tarasenko was glad Azarov and Kalugin were here with him on this important job, today was different; this was his first assignment as their leader. Not that his recent promotion had changed their attitude to him.

'OK, Dmitry? You look worried,' said Kalugin with a knowing smirk.

'That news from America this morning, it's unsettling me,' Tarasenko replied.

'Probably not true. Jefferson has a thousand lives.' Azarov chipped in.

'You're probably right. More Yankee bullshit.'

'Anyway, nothing to worry us today, so relax, Dmitry.' Kalugin leaned forward and patted Tarasenko's shoulder.

'Just want to make a good impression…with the boss,' replied Tarasenko, pulling a grey hair off his black cashmere coat.

'What's going to happen on a freezing winter's morning in Murmansk? They love him here,' said Azarov. 'It will be a picnic. When it's done you can go and fret in your big Moscow office.'

'Can't wait…' Tarasenko erupted into another fit of coughing.

'Dmitry, lay off the cigarettes. It won't do to splutter all over Fedorov. Drink this comrade.' Kalugin passed a bottle of water to Tarasenko.

'Of all the days for this damn hacking to return.' Tarasenko took a large gulp of the lukewarm liquid, which seemed to calm his throat.

'You're right boys. What can go wrong here?' He drew in a big breath and exhaled through his nostrils as he tried to convince himself he was fretting without cause. They were approaching the harbour area, and the cars began to slow.

'Sappers been through the ship?' asked Tarasenko.

'The dogs did a thorough top to bottom last night. No bombs, no guns, not even a penknife on board,' replied Kalugin.

'Everything is in place.' Azarov smiled. 'Cheer up we're almost there.'

Tarasenko perked up as he noticed the towering shapes of the bright yellow dockside cranes to his left. Flicking down the vanity mirror in the windscreen visor, he pulled his fingers through his hair and smoothed down his bushy eyebrows. On the other side of the road, he noted a knot of people standing together outside a bar. All were wrapped in heavy winter coats and fur hats, all except for two striking looking girls with long dark hair standing in the middle of the group. They both wore white T-shirts with large bold red letters on the front. Written in English they spelled out a word unfamiliar to Tarasenko.

R-E-B-O-O-T.

The motorcade swept into the port and drove slowly along the long harbour waterfront towards the imposing *Vaygach*, moored at its far end. She was an ungainly ship, with a simplistic profile that a child might have drawn. Her shallow hull line was outlined in black and scarlet with her large square white main superstructure, sited in the first third of its length, picked out in grey. This vast edifice which housed the bridge, reception rooms and cabins dominated the upper deck, and was punctuated by six vertical rows of undersized rectangular windows, indicating the ascending deck levels of the interior. Atop the roofline stood a line of radar masts of varying heights and complexity. Set behind these and towards the middle of the ship was the huge sloping black funnel. *Vaygach* may not have been beautiful, but she was brutally effective. Her spoon-shaped bow had been designed to smash and slide over ice; along with the enormous power of her nuclear fission reactor-powered engines it made her virtually unstoppable. With an overall length of one hundred and fifty metres and a beam of twenty-eight metres, she was among the largest polar icebreakers ever built.

Standing in front of *Vaygach's* boarding platform on the quayside, a small group of officials waited apprehensively. Boris Mikhailov, the new mayor of Murmansk, stood beside his wife Irina and four city officials who would be first to greet Fedorov. Mikhailov was shaking uncontrollably, partly because he was cold – they had stood waiting for the last forty-five minutes – and partly because he was nervous.

The forty-one-year-old businessman had only been mayor for three weeks and had never met the president. For much of the previous day, he had been briefed by the FPS about what to do, what to say and as importantly, what not to say. He was left in no doubt that this was Fedorov's show and the visit should convey him in the best possible light. A man interested in every facet of Russian life, a man of the people capable of leading Russia forever. As the cars approached, Mikhailov was acutely aware of the cameras trained on him. It was 9.30 and Russian State Television wanted to broadcast footage in time for the midday news – this had to be slick and quick which made the inexperienced mayor of Murmansk even more anxious.

The first car, containing Tarasenko, Azarov and Kalugin, drove past Mikhailov's welcoming party and stopped five metres further on. Fedorov's limousine stopped directly opposite him. On impulse, Mikhailov went to open the door, but was firmly blocked by one of the agents. He had made his first mistake. As he waited, unable to move or even breathe for fear of breaking another protocol

– nothing happened. Then, slowly from the interior of the car, a tall, stocky, pale, balding man emerged, dressed in an immaculate suit, large fur coat and carrying a large bouquet of flowers.

'Good morning, Mayor. A brisk Murmansk morning.' Fedorov smiled at Mikhailov and handed the bouquet to his wife who, surprised by the gesture, smiled and curtseyed.

'Welcome, my President. This is a great honour for our city.' Mikhailov held out his hand.

Fedorov shook it but didn't reply, he simply looked past him at the towering *Vaygach*. 'Let us see more of this great ship. Come.'

With a desultory wave to the crowd, Fedorov and his entourage, including Tarasenko, Azarov and Kalugin, made their way up the ramp onto the ship. As they walked, Mikhailov outlined their itinerary and explained that Second Officer Pasha Solokov wouldn't be showing them round as planned. He had still not returned from a night in the city.

'Probably nursing a sore head. Murmansk is famous for them,' joked Fedorov, revealing a humour which took Mikhailov by surprise.

'The vodka served around the port is particularly unforgiving,' replied Mikhailov, eager to enter into any dialogue which might disarm the stifling formalities.

Fedorov looked back at his new chief. 'Tarasenko, make a note of this second officer and deal with the matter.'

Mikhailov knew enough about the unforgiving ways of the FPS to know that Solokov's career was effectively over.

After completing a tour of the radar room and the bridge, they took a break for black tea and sweet cheese pancakes, freshly baked that morning. As the odd group of politicians, businessmen and trained killers sat together in the canteen for their refreshments, Mikhailov saw another opportunity to ingratiate himself with his commander-in-chief.

'Impressive isn't she, my President?'

'Yes, but dwarfed by the *Arktika* in Saint Petersburg,' Fedorov replied.

Mikhailov had heard of the president's annoying need to be one step ahead in every conversation; he bowed his head in passive agreement.

'I love the economics,' continued Fedorov. 'For a diesel-powered ship, a full day's ice grinding would use one hundred tons of fuel. In this, three hundred grams of uranium.'

'Good news if you find yourself in the middle of nowhere,' replied Mikhailov, laughing nervously.

'And we want to make the most of that middle of nowhere, Comrade Mikhailov. We believe the Arctic Ocean holds significant oil and gas reserves. Russia should get its fair share too, don't you think?'

For a moment, Mikhailov was as thrilled as a schoolboy that this father of Russia had recalled his name, then remembered he was wearing a name badge.

'It is our right, my President,' he replied tapping the table emphatically.

Fedorov smiled then turned at the sound of a cough directly behind him.

'Sir, better keep moving. We still have to visit the power plant,' Tarasenko interrupted.

Because of the cramped confines below, it was agreed that a smaller group of Fedorov, Mikhailov, Tarasenko, Azarov and two of the ship's officers would descend to inspect the nuclear engines.

The engine room was accessed via a series of narrow descending walkways and sealed waterproof doors. Mikhailov led the way with Fedorov in close attendance. Finally, they came to a large door painted in yellow and black diagonal stripes, a plate glass window was set into it at head height.

'This is the entrance to the main engine room, my President. For extra security and safety, only two people at a time can go forward into the air-sealed compartment. From there the engine crew will allow us in. There are two codes, one that I have to get us through this door, and one for the next door which only the crew inside know.'

Fedorov nodded his approval of these prudent measures.

'It would be an honour to escort you inside,' said Mikhailov.

Tarasenko stepped forward. 'I go with you. Just in case.'

Fedorov looked at his new security chief and paused for a moment.

'It is fine, Tarasenko.' Fedorov was starting to warm to Mikhailov and was happy to allow him this small concession.

'But, my President…' Tarasenko began to protest.

'It is good. Besides I don't want to be locked in there with you spluttering all over me.' Fedorov put his hand up, his way of closing down any discussion. Tarasenko knew it was futile to argue.

'Now I put in these code numbers.' Mikhailov referred to his piece of paper and punched the buttons on the small keypad. The heavy steel door popped open with a hiss of compressed air. He folded the paper and handed it to Tarasenko.

'Take this and please close the door behind us.'

Mikhailov and Fedorov stepped forward into the space between the two doors, and Tarasenko sealed them in. It was an uncomfortably small space, and the two large men were forced together, so close that Mikhailov could smell Fedorov's aftershave. Paco Rabanne, he surmised.

As they waited in silence for the pressure to equalise, Fedorov peered into the engine compartment through the window in the second door. It was bathed in an eerie purple and blue light, generated by a bank of ultraviolet tubes suspended from the ceiling. They lit a cavernous space interspersed with a complex array of white metal pipes, brass rotary valves and matt-black, dial-covered control panels. All of these seemed to be serving or be connected to the room's main event, two huge stainless steel cylinders, which dominated the area's central portion. These were the beating hearts of the ship, simply named generator one and two.

After a few seconds, a bell sounded and the inner door opened into this engineering amphitheatre. Mikhailov stepped forward, almost tripping on the raised lip. Noting the mayor's slip, Fedorov lifted his leg higher to avoid a repeat. Just as he did, he was pushed violently to the floor by a man wearing a black balaclava, waiting to the side of the door. Another hooded man standing on the other side immediately slammed the door shut and pointed a pistol at the Russian president.

Tarasenko, watching through the glass, was stunned by the sudden turn of events. He quickly unfolded the paper Mikhailov had given him to access the door code. It had a single word written on it in blue ink – BASTARD.

Tarasenko's cough erupted as he turned the paper to look at the other side. Nothing. He turned to look at the others, the coughing had robbed him of his breath and he was barely able to speak.

'Fuck, fuck…! Give the code…? Quick!' His words seemed to disintegrate as they tumbled out of his mouth.

The ashen faced officer stepped forward. 'We don't know. It is changed every day by Second Officer Solokov. The only other person who would know it, apart from the engine room crew already in there, would be…Mikhailov.'

Tarasenko was frantic. 'There must be another way in, you cretin!'

'There is…on the other side…but it has the same code,' replied the officer, sensing that his own career might now also be over.

'Get welding gear, Azarov. We must get through this fucking door fast.'

A booming voice made them stop.

'Now hear this, now hear this.' It was coming through the public address system which ran through the ship.

'If you try to get through the door, we will shoot Fedorov now. Everyone go to the bridge. I repeat – if you want to see your president again, go the bridge. You have sixty seconds.'

Tarasenko couldn't believe this was happening. On his very last assignment.

'What do we do?' asked Azarov.

'Do as this bastard says, until we know more.'

Livid he had allowed this to happen, Tarasenko walked behind Azarov and the crew member, coughing, cursing and smashing his fist against the ship's steel bulkheads. They reached the bridge to see the rest of the group staring up at a large television monitor above the steering control panel.

The sight made Tarasenko's blood run cold.

Mikhailov was nowhere to be seen, but Fedorov was being tied to steam generator number two. One man was guarding him with a gun while the other fixed his arms and legs to the pipes that criss-crossed the structure. The generators served as a barrier between the radioactive compartment of the icebreaker's reactor, and were notoriously prone to leaking superheated water vapour. If they did, the reactors had to be shut down immediately to prevent a potential meltdown and disaster.

'What are they doing? Where is that dog, Mikhailov? How did they get onto the ship?' Kalugin was spitting his frustration at the officials and crew around him, desperate for answers, then he spotted Tarasenko.

'Boss, did you recognise either of those sons of bitches?'

'They were too quick. They must have training. Ukrainian army?'

A collective gasp went up from the group. Tarasenko watched

in fascinated dread as he realized what was going to happen. The men were sawing through two of the main pipes leading away from the generators and steam was starting to burst out in spitting boiling jets. Fedorov grimaced with effort and terror as he struggled feverishly against his bonds, and the room began to fill with the scalding mist. Within a few more seconds, the picture was completely obscured.

Everybody watched the screen transfixed, hoping to see their president emerge or waiting for the moment when it might be revealed as a cruel hoax.

Tarasenko felt a tap on his shoulder; it was Azarov. 'Boss, they might be trying to get away under cover of the vapour. We must cover the other engine door.'

Two of the ship's officers took him and Kalugin to show them where it was. Tarasenko coughed violently into his handkerchief and noticed a small patch of blood.

Two hours later, an explosives team blasted its way into the *Vaygach's* engine room to discover the burned and shrivelled corpse of Russia's longest-serving leader since Stalin. The perpetrators were long gone and the inquisition into Tarasenko's negligence and possible collusion into this national outrage was only just beginning.

Russia was not won, but on this momentous day, Reboot had removed a very significant obstacle in its way.

3 December 2031, Antarctica
Cull Day 294

As he sat still trying to get warm in the Sikorsky, Jameson thought about that night that night with Trevallion. Her body, her taste, her hunger and their sweat. He recalled the joy of feeling pure animalistic carnal lust again and the reciprocation of a willing lover. It was a feeling he had bottled up, doubted he would ever experience again. Then he remembered the morning and the days after, and suddenly didn't feel so good.

He had woken first, disorientated and dry mouthed. After slowly clearing his head and taking a drink of water, he sat on the edge of the bed looking at Trevallion's naked body as she lay sleeping on her stomach on top of the sheets. Although the light was dim, the room's small window only allowed a pale yellow glow to filter through from outside, he could still register every inch of her, and she looked beautiful. Her flawless fair skin, the graceful fall of her hair on the nape of her neck. The elegant sweep of her back as it curved upwards to meet her buttocks. Her perfectly proportioned legs, athletic but not over muscular. Her legs were slightly apart, and he remembered how he wanted her again. Then he had noticed something else, first on the tops of her thighs, and as he looked closer still, on her biceps too. Something he had not seen in the disorder of their passion a few hours previously. A series of pale red and white strips, all at least two or three inches long. Most of the scars had healed, but one on her right arm still looked an angry deep red, and another at the top of her left leg oozed a little blood. He leant forward and gently ran his finger along the raised edge of the sliced skin.

Poor Sarah.

'The pain hasn't gone away.' Trevallion spoke softly but didn't open her eyes.

'Christ I'm sorry, Sarah.'

'I'll get over it. So are we going to fuck again or not?'

For days afterwards, despite the intensity and importance of his work, Trevallion was all Jameson could think about. He had felt like a man reborn, a man given a reprieve from the inevitable decline of older age.

But she never sought his company again. She avoided being alone with him, like it had never happened, like it was an embarrassment. It hurt badly, made him feel rejected and used, but ultimately he had understood. It was just a night, a night when the stars aligned. And for them, they would never line up again. Now all he wanted to do was forget about Sarah Trevallion, forget about the data, the test results and his miracle gel, and get home.

Home was still three days' hard travel away. They would rendezvous with the polar ship, MV *Ortelius*, on the edge of the glacier; this would take them to the port of Ushuaia in Argentina, a two-day trip. From there, they would catch a four-hour flight to Buenos Aires before a thirteen-hour overnighter to Heathrow.

Jameson looked down at the shifting, glittering white carpet passing by through the thick plate glass window and sighed. From two thousand feet up, Antarctica was a truly magical sight, but he was still happy to be leaving. He thought the team would feel the same. They had all been excited as they waited for their ride home just an hour ago, but now they simply looked apprehensive and hadn't spoken. Their mood changed after the pilot had taken them aside just before take-off. Jameson had been busy loading the equipment and hadn't heard what was being talked about. But whatever the pilot said made a big impression on the others.

I've had enough of this bullshit.

An hour into the flight, Jameson was determined he had to break the silence. Waites was usually the most vocal, so he decided to speak to him.

'Everything OK, Tom? You look worried.'

'This crap heap helicopter. Sounds like it's falling apart.'

'These things are indestructible.'

Waites didn't look at Jameson, preferring to gaze out of the window. He obviously didn't want to talk.

Turning round to engage Beckley and Trevallion, Jameson was surprised to see they were staring directly at him, both with ash-white faces.

'We need to talk...' said Trevallion. 'It's not good.'

Jameson had looked at that pretty face for the past year. Noted every line, every wrinkle, every blemish. He had seen that face smile, laugh, cry and howl with rage. Seen it in the passion of lovemaking. He knew this face as well as his own, but he had never seen the concern it showed now.

She fixed him with her deep green eyes and spoke slowly. 'It's happened. They've finally done what they were threatening to do before we left.'

'Who's finally done what?' Jameson felt panic start to rise, but tried to hide it in his voice.

'They've killed President Jefferson.'

'Who killed him?'

'Reboot.'

Jameson suddenly felt sick. He knew with what had happened to Bella that Reboot had been growing in size and influence, but felt like most other wishful thinkers did, that it was simply another vocal, but essentially harmless, protest movement. He believed it had few resources and little support beyond young people. It seemed he was wrong.

Trevallion continued gravely, 'Someone got into the National Rifle Association building and literally blew his brains out. Seems it was the catalyst that millions of people were looking for. They've created uprisings everywhere and, with the military's help, they've taken down governments across the world without too much resistance. The UK, US, Canada, Australia and Germany. Most of Scandinavia. Apparently, Russia and China have fallen to Reboot too; it's mind blowing.'

Jameson couldn't believe what he was hearing.

Things like this don't happen, not in just three hundred days.

'How have they managed to do this so fast?'

'After Jefferson was killed, the vice-president was sworn in the same day. But within hours a Reboot sympathiser in an F-15 blew Air Force One, the plane he was travelling in, out of the sky. With the Republicans and Democrats running around like headless chickens, a Reboot delegation backed by the military simply walked in and took over.' Trevallion paused to look at her phone and another newsfeed. 'They've seized billionaires' funds and assets to help fund their actions…bet there's a few nervous rich people out there.'

'My heart bleeds,' Beckley replied sarcastically.

Jameson's head was spinning. They'd hardly been away a year and the political landscape, and the whole world had completely changed.

'This is crazy; what do they hope to achieve?'

Trevallion slowly handed him her phone.

'You'd better look at this.'

Jameson recognised the face staring out at him from the phone as one of the Reboot leaders, Erica Sandstrom, who he knew had driven the movement in Norway. She was standing on the steps of a parliament building, wearing a red T-shirt with RB in bold black letters emblazoned across the front. He clicked the play button and Sandstrom calmly spelt out the aims of this global revolution.

'Citizens of the new world, we have completed the first part of mankind's most important project – that of saving our home. What we have achieved this past year has been monumental and shocking for many, but it has been essential. We have only done what our forefathers should have done, but lacked the foresight and courage to do. Now to make these sacrifices meaningful, we must take the next crucial measures.' She paused, staring hard into the camera. 'Our planet remains in a critical state, our elected governments have failed to protect us as they said they would. They have ignored their promises to cut carbon emissions, and missed their own targets of limiting global increases to below two degrees Celsius. So now, we have to take the action necessary to save ourselves by reducing our consumption and our numbers.' Sandstrom took a deep breath. 'It was agreed unanimously by the Reboot Council and the elected administrations in the territories we control that those who have overseen this climate disaster should be the ones sacrificed to redress the damage. So there will be a compulsory cull, carried out over the next two years, of those born between 1946 and 1964 – those also known as baby boomers.'

That's me.

She paused for a few seconds to let her message sink in, then continued. 'Across the world, the richest ten per cent consume twenty times more energy than the poorest ten per cent, so it shall be the boomers in those countries who will be singled out first. These countries are China, United States, India, Russian Federation, Japan, Germany, South Korea, Islamic Republic of Iran, Canada, Saudi Arabia, Indonesia, Mexico, Brazil, South Africa, Australia, United Kingdom, Turkey, Italy, Poland and France. They must understand that their generation, above any other in the history of humankind, has benefitted most and contributed least to the welfare of the planet. All those who fall into this group will be given at least four weeks to put their affairs in order.'

Jameson felt nauseous again, but he still couldn't take his eyes off this mad woman.

'To all those affected, we will contact you directly, and then you must report to a designated place in the time stipulated. As I said, we shall seek to complete this cull within the next twenty-four months. After that time, a twelve-month amnesty will be granted to all citizens to allow them to report and dispose of any baby boomers who seek to avoid this decree. We have calculated that if this cull can be carried out worldwide, it will reduce the global population by at least one and a half billion people and provide a massive boost for the planet. Boomers can take comfort from the fact that where possible their remains will be recycled to enrich the soil. Let me be clear, these measures are not a choice. There will be no exception. This must happen if humans are to survive beyond the year 3000.'

Sandstrom's face faded, to be replaced by the slow motion images of eagles flying gracefully in blue skies over snow-peaked mountains. The symbolism was crass and sinister. Big Brother would have approved.

With a shaking hand, Jameson handed the phone back to Trevallion. She looked at him grimly. 'That was first broadcast nine months ago, so God knows what Reboot are up to now. The pilot has told us that there'll be people waiting for you when the ship docks in Chile.'

His mind started to race. He wasn't panicking, yet…

14 February 2031, Monaco
Cull Day 3

It was a crisp early winter's day on the French Riviera as Antoine Lauvergne walked briskly across the immaculate brick concourse of the Prince's Palace and climbed the sweeping marble staircase which led to the interior. He felt euphoric and vindicated.

Just two years previously, Lauvergne had been forced to resign in disgrace from his position as head of his country's Criminal Investigation Division. Now here he was, about to take his revenge on those responsible.

To assist him on this momentous day, he was flanked by two powerful men as determined as he was to carry out the task – the senior commander of the police force, Colonel Jérôme Toupane and his company commander, Lieutenant Philippe Beaubois. As they walked through the elegant, thickly carpeted hallway, no one tried to check their progress. The resident guards simply saluted and let them carry on unopposed into the heart of the palace. They paused as they finally reached the cream-painted and gold-leaf-patterned rococo double doors which led directly to their destination. Inside, Prince Jacques the first, 'the boss', waited for them.

The takeover of the country once referred to by Somerset Maugham as 'a sunny place for shady people' had been achieved with military precision.

At three that morning, the French army had blocked off the A8, the main route into the principality, along with all exits out of the area, effectively sealing in the twelve thousand multimillionaires and eighteen thousand other residents who called this place home. Monaco TV and Monaco Radio, already frantic with stories of Jefferson's assassination and the military coup in China, now started to broadcast news of more immediate relevance to their primary audiences. Residents were informed of the 'urgent national emergency' and told they should remain in their homes until further notice. Any citizen or tourist disobeying the order would be arrested.

Reboot's objective was to close down this symbol of mankind's gluttony that modern-day Monaco had become. To send a powerful message to other enterprises dedicated to 'reckless hedonism' such as Las Vegas, South Africa's Sun City and Dubai that they too risk being shut down.

The other thing Reboot wanted from Monaco was the one thing it had no shortage of – money. At eight o'clock, the military started to occupy the main banks. Starting with the Monte Paschi on the Avenue de Verdun, squads of armed soldiers systematically worked their way around the district's financial institutions. Where they met resistance, normally no more than a locked door; they simply drove an armoured vehicle through it and walked in. Within an hour, they had control of over twenty-five major bank buildings and their valuable contents. By ten o'clock, specially installed customer relations teams were dealing with huge numbers of enquiries from angry account holders.

In defiance of the curfew, dozens of residents emerged out onto the streets, desperate for answers. They looked for their local police force, per capita the largest in the world, with one officer for every hundred residents. They looked for the principality's famous carabinieri, the five-hundred-strong armed militia, formed to protect their sovereign and the palace. There was nothing to be seen of either force; they had ceded control to the army and melted away from the streets.

Over that morning, Lauvergne had watched the bloodless coup unfold from the wall of screens in the control room in Monaco's police headquarters building. Its system of video surveillance cameras monitored virtually every square centimetre of this tiny nation. He had enjoyed the spectacle immensely.

'Those bastards. Don't look so self-satisfied now, do they? Billionaires are just like toddlers, unable to fend for themselves,' Lauvergne had said to no one in particular, and there had been no response. The control room operatives around him were too busy relaying instructions to troop commanders to take notice.

Lauvergne continued to stare at the screens, bewitched by the sight of this bloated, overprivileged society coming apart. He could hardly contain his glee on seeing a severely overweight couple struggling outside the Edmond de Rothschild Bank in Avenue de Monte-Carlo. Wearing matching cashmere coats, fox fur hats and white trousers, each carried a small, bemused poodle under their arm. They frantically knocked, kicked and pulled on the bank's huge red main door to gain entrance, but without success. Eventually they gave up and sat, slumped and defeated on the steps outside the bank. The poodle held by the woman escaped her grasp and ran off down an adjacent alley, she didn't bother to follow.

Other screens showed more residents gathered in small groups outside banks in the Boulevard des Moulins and Avenue de la Costa. Within minutes, and despite their wailing protests, one by one they were all arrested by the troops and bundled into armoured vans. He recognised Darren Black the bitcoin billionaire trying to use his black Gucci handbag to fend off an officer; it was taken from him and thrown in a waste bin. Outside the main casino, a woman tried to flail a soldier with her pearl necklace; after being tasered, she staggered backwards and fell into the fountain. A couple tried to leave in a motorboat with a briefcase full of diamonds, without realising the harbour entrance had already been blocked with a chain boom. They were quickly rescued from their shattered boat, but the contents of the briefcase sank to the sea floor. Everywhere across the town, alarms blared, dogs barked, men raged and women screamed. In just a few hours, normally serene, self-satisfied Monte Carlo had been transformed into a disorientated war zone of pain. Around mid-afternoon, the streets gradually emptied as the army's grip tightened and the population began to realise resistance was futile.

Lauvergne took a grim satisfaction as he witnessed the principality's capitulation. Just four years earlier, the fifty-five-year-old's life had been ripped apart by some of the very people he was now destroying.

He had been charged with accepting bribes and profiting from the sale of stolen goods. Despite witness testimonies showing that evidence had been fabricated by those he was investigating, the Monegasque Council Chamber refused to drop the charges.

During his trial, he criticised the judge for being a puppet of the state, but saved most of his anger for the 'sickening corruption' of Monegasque officials. Although found guilty and sacked, Lauvergne had taken pride in the support he received from the Monaco police force. They loyally defended their former leader's reputation throughout, and now they were standing with him at this historic moment.

Satisfied that the first part of his plan had been completed, Lauvergne turned to the two men who could rubber-stamp his victory as they stood with him in the immaculate white-shirted, black-tied, black-jacketed, silver buttoned splendour of their Monaco police force uniforms. The shaven-headed Colonel Toupane wore the look of a troubled man, brow deeply furrowed, a large vein on his temple pulsed alarmingly, his lips drawn back in a half grimace. Lauvergne knew about the Colonel's hypertension and hoped he wouldn't expire before the conclusion of events. The younger, taller and dark-haired Lieutenant Beaubois looked far happier. He was due to take over from the soon-to-retire Toupane, and had the most to gain from the overthrow of the old regime. He had reckoned that a more unstable Monaco would need a more substantial police force, resulting in more status for him.

Lauvergne paused outside the rococo door, took a deep breath and felt a small pang of doubt from the dutiful, hierarchical bureaucratic still present in him. On the other side of this door, Prince Jacques, the reigning prince of Monaco and the head of the princely house of Grimaldi, waited for him. He started to wonder.

Were my shoes clean?

Colonel Toupane knocked loudly on the door, opened it without waiting for a reply, and the three men walked in. Lauvergne had only been here once before, and it looked just as impressive as he remembered. The space was modest, seven metres by five at most. The colour scheme was muted, mainly white and pale yellows; the furnishings plain and functional, no extravagant paintings or ornaments on display. It was the view that made this room special. At the far end, five windows curved round in a gentle arc, framing a magnificent view of the red roofs, green palms and honey-coloured buildings of the town below. The deep water harbour crammed with ships, cruisers, racing catamarans and superyachts. The steep sandy cliffs curling their way south as they chaperone the sparkling Mediterranean as it gently winds its way down to Nice. All topped off by the creamy white pillows hanging lazily in the azure sky, seemingly reluctant to float away and give up their place in the beguiling view. Lauvergne found it difficult to drag his eyes away and focus on the reason he was there.

The prince was sitting behind his desk, the state of which surprised Lauvergne. Numerous untidy piles of papers and files covered the green leather top. It looked chaotic, the workstation of someone with too much on their plate. Prince Jacques himself looked composed, relaxed even. Brown eyed and lightly tanned, he was blessed with a handsome, friendly face, and unlike his father he had kept his fair curly hair. He sat back in his leather chair smiling at the delegation, wearing his usual dark-blue blazer with gold buttons, light-blue shirt and red silk tie. Only his hands, which he rested on the desk, gave clues to any inner feelings. The fingers woven tightly together, his knuckles an angry white.

To his left, a beautiful woman in a striking red dress sat impassively, quietly observing the three men. With her long brown hair and startling emerald green eyes, Lauvergne recognised her immediately as Miriam Menendez, one of Monaco's richest citizens. The thirty-four-year-old granddaughter of a technology tycoon, the Argentinian-born heiress had a personal fortune of over two billion US dollars. Lauvergne wondered why she was in the room. The prince broke the silence in his soft, American east-coast accent.

'Gentlemen, would you like to take a seat?'

Out of force of habit from a lifetime of obeying their boss's orders, both Toupane and Beaubois bowed to the prince and immediately looked around for chairs. Fortified by the line of cocaine he had taken thirty minutes earlier in the toilets of the police headquarters building, Lauvergne abruptly stopped them.

'We prefer to stand, Your Highness.'

'Very well,' replied the prince curtly. 'What is it you need from me?'

Keen to belittle the man who had helped ruin his life, Lauvergne spoke as if to a small child, articulating every word slowly and deliberately.

'My Prince, we would like you to reassure your nationals and your residents that what we are doing…is necessary.'

Jacques's mouth tensed, drawing into a thin line.

'And what is it precisely that you think you are doing, apart from illegally enforcing martial law and restricting the free movement of innocent civilians?' The prince slammed the palms of his hands on the table. Menendez blinked, nervously smoothing a wrinkle from her dress. Colonel Toupane handed Lauvergne a blue folder. He retrieved two pieces of paper from inside and held them up.

'These documents state we have the full support and legal weight of France, the nation that is tasked with your security. We also have a decree signed in Paris by Reboot and the new ruling council giving us full authority to seize and freeze all assets held by residents in banks within this territory.' Lauvergne moved towards the desk, tidied a space amongst the mess and placed the papers in front of the now red-faced royal. Jacques picked them up and swivelling on his chair, carefully and precisely ran each one through the document shredder behind him. As the thin ribbons of paper dropped into the bin, Lauvergne sighed theatrically and shook his head. He had anticipated this show of defiance; he pulled out duplicates from the folder, this time keeping them both firmly in his grasp.

'My Prince, we have been authorised to take whatever action is necessary to liberate the wealth locked in Monaco to assist with our climate correction policies and to end the catastrophic greed and overconsumption as glorified by your nation.'

Newly energised by this latest hammer blow, Jacques went to stand, then a hand softly fell on his shoulder which made him hesitate.

'Gentlemen, please…perhaps there is another way.' Menendez's soothing South American accent cut through the growing tension. Momentarily diverted by the intervention, the prince sat back in his chair. Pouring herself some iced water from a jug on the desk, she took a long, slow drink. Lauvergne found it disarmingly hypnotic.

'How much is it you want from citizens here?' she enquired.

Clearing his light-headedness, Lauvergne regained his composure. 'The formulation for Monaco's subjects is simple. All those born between 1946 and 1964 will have their entire assets seized and the individuals handed over to Reboot. With no exceptions.'

The prince went pale. Being sixty-seven, he knew this could include him.

'For all others, an instant fifty per cent wealth donation and twenty per cent green tax levy per annum for remaining in the principality.'

The prince went another shade of puce. With the country's tax-free status removed, that would surely mean the end for the Grimaldi family's rule.

Menendez coolly regarded Lauvergne as if weighing up the man's resolve.

'Very well, I have a counterproposal.' She stood and walked slowly to the window. 'What if I said I would personally pay you gentlemen five million euros each to defend Monaco with your men? This would be paid every year until Reboot is overthrown and this madness is ended.'

Lauvergne was stunned; he had not anticipated this.

'Friends of mine have seen this revolution coming. They have been recruiting mercenary armies to defend themselves too,' the prince piped up. 'It is madness what has happened in the US and China. People will soon realise that this is not the solution. My people predict this will all be over within a few weeks, you'll see.' He was perspiring heavily and looked imploringly at the three men in front of him.

Lauvergne's thoughts were racing. He had been so sure, so determined when he came into this room. He wanted to humiliate Monaco's elite for what they allowed to happen to him and his family. For four years he had been exiled from the place he loved. Unable to work in the police force, he lost his lucrative pension that he worked loyally for. He had been forced to take a lower-paid job in commercial security. His health and his marriage suffered.

Then he learned about Reboot and their plans for the future and aberrations like Monaco, so had enthusiastically joined them. His unique connections within the principality made him the perfect man for this role, one he accepted readily. Now, just at the very moment he was about to take his revenge for those tortured years, he was having doubts.

What if they were right? What if Reboot and the movement were overturned? What then? There would be recriminations for all those lives that had been taken. People would be held accountable and punished. He might be seen as one of the major protagonists, even as a war criminal. 'The man who tried to close Monaco'. He could be tried again, humiliated once more, perhaps even executed.

And five million euros was a lot of money. It would serve as recompense for the torture of the past few years and set him up for life. He could bring his family back to their beloved Monte Carlo.

Lauvergne turned to Toupane and Beaubois; he could see the

doubt on their faces, their resolve melting away. He gazed out of the window once more as if looking for affirmation of his decision, then gestured for them to follow him outside.

'My Prince, Madame Menendez, please excuse us for a few moments.'

14 February 2031, Oslo, Norway
Cull Day 3

Erica Sandstrom stared idly out the tram window. It was the usual sight at this time of day, this time of year. Hunched figures rushing along the streets, bent hard against the pitiless Nordic wind and driving sleet, lost in their thoughts and eager to get home. Meandering lines of cars inching their way through the icy black slush of the previous day's snowfall. And millions of twinkling red, blue, white and yellow lights illuminating the city in a vain attempt to lend the scene some levity and warmth. For Sandstrom, this was just one more rush hour ploughing through a wintry Oslo at the end of another working day at her advertising agency in the city's business district. But in truth, she mused, it had been a good day.

Good day because she had gained approval for her new campaign for the agency's biggest client, the green energy producer,

Statkraft, and the concept she had developed was the boldest yet. Good day because she managed to hire a talented new copywriter from a rival company. Good day because she picked up three awards at the prestigious Cresta advertising festival.

But it had been an especially good day because now all these mundane pursuits were behind her. There was to be no more selling marketing ideas to clients, nurturing newly recruited copywriters or sweating for peer recognition. This time spent on a crowded, noisy tram commute through Oslo were to be the final hours of her old life.

From tomorrow, there would be a very different life beckoning for Erica Sandstrom – in a very different kind of world. Together with other appointed individuals, she would unite foreign governments and begin to implement the drastic measures necessary to ensure the survival of the planet.

Always a nature lover, Sandstrom became a committed climate activist at the tender age of fourteen and devoted most of her young adult life to campaigning against destructive human practices. Now, as leader of Reboot Norway, she was a prominent player of the worldwide organisation she had helped create. Together with Stephen Cooper, Sandstrom had drawn up the key policies and priorities for the new world order designed to give the ailing earth the massive life shock it desperately needed. But before any of that could happen, she knew that she needed to take down her own government, and that would take numbers.

It had taken her nineteen months to recruit the ten thousand activists, those 'prepared to get off their laptops and do something'. She started first on the infamous dark web, navigating its labyrinthine networks to locate the like-minded and the disaffected. One group named Black Strike called for the execution of all Norwegian politicians and for their bodies to be hung on chicken wire outside the parliament building. Another faction demanded the seizure of all bank assets and jailing of leading financial executives. Another insisted on the destruction of all motorised vehicles and commercial aircraft and a return to the plough.

But for every person or radical entity of no use, there were five more who were, the most important of whom also came with money and influence. These included wealthy young entrepreneurs, politicians, civil servants and even senior police and military officers. To add more volume, Sandstrom utilised traditional recruitment methods that appeared in plain sight of the authorities such as direct mail, posters and even radio advertising.

Her message was simple: if you wanted to save your world – join Reboot.

For thousands of ordinary Norwegians, that proposition was compelling, the pressure to act had been building to fever pitch and it needed an outlet. People were angry that their government wasn't taking climate change seriously. Exasperated that elections were still being decided on issues like the economy, health and social security rather than on curtailing the unsustainable lifestyles that their nation and all others were following.

Well, no more would this be the case. On this crisp Valentine's Day morning, that would all change. All Reboot followers had been told to meet outside Oslo's Central Station at eight o'clock to be part of 'something amazing'. The whole country had been transfixed by the incredible events unfolding in the US, China and Russia. Now Sandstrom's followers wanted to join the revolution.

Even though she arrived thirty minutes early, the square outside the Østbanehallen shopping centre next to the station was already packed with excited world changers. After allowing herself a few exuberant moments to enjoy the scene, Sandstrom made her way through the throng of well-wishers and back-patters to get to the small wooden podium hastily erected outside the centre's main entrance. Waiting for her there, were three familiar faces, Chief of Police Hans Sander Berg and General Stefan Henriksen, head of the Norwegian army. Standing between them was Markus Rossbach, the deputy mayor of Oslo and a leading Labour Party politician.

Rossbach was the first to greet Sandstrom as she carefully climbed the uneven steps.

'A beautiful morning to change the world, Erica.' He beamed, revealing a full mouth of obviously straightened and over-brightened teeth.

'Yes, it fills my heart with hope,' she replied.

Berg shook her hand warmly. 'You have given them hope; you have given us all belief too, that we can change things.'

Henriksen shook her hand, then took her to one side away from the others.

'My men are ready to shoot…if people try to stop us.'

Sandstrom looked soberly at Norway's most senior army commander. His clear skinned, blue-eyed, close-shaved angelic face belied his reputation. She had been told the Afghanistan veteran was a warmonger and could be quick to allow his troops to use their weapons..

'No killing, General. The situation is still fragile. We don't want to give cause for a violent reaction. Cameras are everywhere.'

Henriksen nodded. 'Understood. No firing…unless fired on first.'

Rossbach came over, clearly enjoying waving at the enthusiastic crowds. 'Want to say a few words to turbocharge this beautiful gathering before we go?'

'Perhaps a few, although they look pretty excited already,' Sandstrom replied.

She walked slowly to the front of the platform. The crowd, realising who it was, roared in appreciation on seeing that their leader was amongst them. For five minutes they clapped and stamped their feet before gradually falling quiet. To a man, woman and child, they looked up at this slim, athletic figure with her distinctive pink dreadlocks and pink eyepatch and waited for the stirring words they were desperate to hear.

'*God morgen,* Oslo.'

She threw her arms wide, and the multitude did the same, creating a wave of hands that raced around the square. The joyous cheering was deafening. The sight of the warm exhaled breath of five thousand people rising into the cold morning air was the most beautiful thing she had ever seen. Despite her excitement, like the practised speaker she was, Sandstrom let the noise die down again before talking.

'Never mind the cold, my friends. What you are doing should warm your hearts for the rest of your lives. Your grandchildren will speak of this day, the day that began our new relationship with the place we call home!'

More wild applause. Sandstrom thought she even heard a few lines of a Viking war chant.

'Today we are sweeping away the old order of greed, and living for the moment to welcome in a new era of planet kindness and sustainability.'

The crowd bellowed ascent. Now Sandstrom was warming to her rhetoric.

'For too long, our planet has been a shrine to good intentions. Now it needs action. We must reset and recalibrate what is important. The old laws that governed us must be set aside and new ones put in place. This will mean sacrifice, but the knowledge of what we are striving for will sustain us in difficult times. We have raped our earth enough. Now those guilty must pay, so the innocent may benefit. You know what must be done this day. Now let Norway lead the way and show the world.' Sandstrom jumped down from the podium, and along with Rossbach, Henriksen and Berg, began the short walk to the Regjeringskvartalet, the compact government quarter in central Oslo.

As they marched with the main body of the crowd, groups of soldiers and police broke off down different roads and alleyways criss-crossing their route. Their task to erect barriers to choke off the main routes into and out of the city and then capture the government-owned radio and television broadcasting companies. The Reboot Council had decided that all communication and movement must be contained within the first few hours of the coup. When controls were in place, the desired narrative would be conveyed to the nation's five and a half million citizens. Norway was to be used as the model for future takeovers. If the strategy was successful, it would be rolled out across Europe, and eventually everywhere else.

'I love it when a plan comes together,' the smiling Rossbach exclaimed, baring his blue-white teeth.

'Who do you think you are? Hannibal Smith in The A-Team?' replied Berg, who clearly disliked the extrovert deputy mayor. Rossbach ignored him and continued to wring his hands in glee, chuckling to himself. As the leading politician in the group, he fully expected to be given a senior role in the new administration.

Sandstrom wasn't thinking about new administrations or even about a new tomorrow. She was enjoying herself too much, being borne along the paved and cobbled streets of Oslo on a wave of pure adrenalin and optimism. She moved without effort, as if lifted on a serene cushion of air. To Sandstrom, the flow of the multitude felt like a single organism, a beautiful flowing oneness working together with one purpose – to save the planet.

She looked at the excited faces around her, young and old alike, all filled with the fire of optimism. It felt like all her life had led to this moment, her childhood marked by joy and dismay in equal measure at the wonder and decline of nature, her teenage years spent perfecting her arguments, learning how to best put them across in the face of fierce opposition, her formative years as a young marketer discovering exciting new channels to showcase her ideas. And now the last two years spent working with Reboot, deciding on the unpalatable actions that needed to be taken.

She had been bullied, ridiculed, shunned by friends and family, even her parents. She had been beaten at a protest in Trondheim so savagely it cost her the sight in her right eye. It had been a difficult journey, but this gathering in the centre of Sandstrom's home city showed it had all been worth it.

'Having a good time?'

Sandstrom looked around at the source of the gentle voice to her right, turning eighty degrees so her good eye could focus. Walking alongside was an elderly woman with long silver hair, dressed in a long white woollen coat and light grey seal-skin boots. The woman, at least four inches shorter than Sandstrom, looked up with kind brown eyes.

'You've done very well to get here Erica. Events like today don't happen without a lot of work.' The woman smiled and gently touched Sandstrom's arm.

'There is still much to do *frøken*.' Sandstrom replied.

'You still have time to stop this you know, before it goes to far.' The woman's eyes narrowed. She was speaking quietly, almost a whisper, yet Sandstrom could clearly hear every word. The noise of the crowd had hushed, as if someone had turned a volume control. 'You've made your point, they have listened. This pact with Reboot will only bring disaster.' She squeezed Sandstrom's arm harder, the pressure almost painful.

Sandstrom began to be intrigued by this strange interlude. 'What is your name?'

'My name is not important. This must now stop.'

'But the die is cast *frøken*. As you can see, the will of the people is now irresistible.' Sandstrom looked at the joyous faces around her.

'As you insist on following your course Erica, I wonder if I can give a little advice for a particular happening along your journey?'

'Happening?'

'You will meet many people in the coming months, but when you meet the man with the secret of eternal ice, be sure to treat him like no other.' The old woman drew Sandstrom in. 'Remember, the man of eternal ice is special. He can change everything. He must be treated accordingly.'

Abruptly, the woman let go and stopped walking; within seconds she had disappeared into the mass of movement. Sandstrom called after her as the full chatter of the crowd suddenly returned.

'Secret of eternal ice? Wait. What do you mean?'

Sandstrom was carried further away by the sea of people surrounding her, further from the silver-haired old woman and knew she would not get her answer on this day. Perhaps she would understand what this encounter meant in the months to come. Or maybe the woman was simply drunk or even a little mad. Either way, right now Sandstrom had more pressing things on her mind.

The main group had arrived at their destination – the fifteen-storey tower block that housed the prime minister's office.

Only twenty-five years previously, the building had borne witness to another seismic event when neo-Nazi Anders Behring Breivik detonated a car bomb outside its entrance, killing eight people and injuring scores more. Like millions of Norwegians, Sandstrom had been appalled by the senseless act. She knew big crowds could be unpredictable, but hoped that there would be no more casualties at this place on this historic day.

Thousands of civil servants worked in the collection of

government buildings, and Reboot had many allies among them. Some had promised to help them gain access through the various barriers and checkpoints, even so, there were still many armed security guards to contend with. Sandstrom could not predict how they would respond to a mob demanding the removal of their leaders. Suddenly a scream silenced the excited drone of the marchers. Everyone looked towards the main concourse in front of Government House. As Sandstrom finally focussed her eyes on where the noise was coming from, her blood ran cold. A woman who had climbed a twenty-metre pole to remove the national flag had lost her footing. In falling, she had been caught around her neck and shoulder by the heavy rope as it whipped and coiled in the air; friends were frantically trying to cut her down. On seeing that the unfortunate woman was being helped, the crowd's fervour returned and the stampede into the building continued.

Much to Sandstrom's relief, after weighing up the size of the force weighed against them, most of the security guards stationed around the buildings decided to do nothing or simply walk away. Unopposed, she confidently led the advance party up the grey and black marble steps, through the rotating doors and into the vast reception area. The mature poplar trees, which had been planted to impress foreign visitors, towered above them, haughtily regarding this unusual delegation. The regulated air inside the atrium was warm and its thick glass windows damped most of the noise outside, lending a surreal calm to the momentous proceedings.

Sitting alone at the large reception desk, just one brave receptionist remained at her post. The fair-haired, bespectacled woman seemed blissfully unaware of the scores of uninvited guests surrounding her.

'Can I help you?' she asked without looking up.

'Where is Therese Bjorgen, you bitch?'

Rossbach had swept past Sandstrom and slammed his hands down on the black marble desk top.

The receptionist calmly looked up, saying nothing.

'You pompous fool. There is no need for that.' Berg grabbed Rossbach's shoulders and pushed him to one side. 'Sorry about this idiot, my dear. Where might we find Prime Minister Bjorgen please?'

'On the ninth floor, but she is in session. She can't see you.'

'The ninth floor, thank you,' Berg replied, as he, Sandstrom, Henriksen and the chastened Rossbach made towards one of the eight lifts.

Sandstrom smiled to herself as the doors shut and the lift began to rise. So now at last she was going to meet Sylvi Bjorgen, the Ice Warrior. In truth, the fifty-five-year-old prime minister was not a bad person, and in many ways Sandstrom admired her.

Bjorgen had been the successful leader of a prosperous country for over ten years. Under her leadership, Norway enjoyed the highest standard of living in the world. In Europe, it had the lowest unemployment, longest life expectancy and biggest output per capita. Its long and well-managed land border with Sweden and Finland was the envy of the European Union, of which it was not a part.

She had helped to achieve all this despite a lifelong struggle with dyslexia, a condition that also hindered Sandstrom. She remembered something Bjorgen said in a television interview that resonated with her: 'Having dyslexia means we learn early on in life that you have setbacks and you don't stop because of them.'

One of Bjorgen's main political passions was for the better treatment of the oceans and cleaning up the sea. She campaigned vigorously to diminish plastic use, calling out neighbours like Britain and Ireland, stating that most of the plastic Norway got on its western shores came from those countries.

Sandstrom admired her willingness to stand up to others. Perhaps in another life and another time, Bjorgen could have remained as a leader under Reboot, but ultimately she was a right-wing leader of an oil-rich country so she had to go.

The ping of the lift released Sandstrom from her thoughts. As the doors opened, she was surprised to see the rather portly, short-haired figure of the incumbent prime minister waiting for them.

Bjorgen handed over a small dossier to Sandstrom and pointed to the first page.

'These are all the numbers of the people you'll need to contact over the next few days. I hear Zoom conferencing is a good way to get them all in one place. They seemed to have fixed their security issues. The rest of my senior ministers are inside that room waiting for you…'

With that, Bjorgen threw Rossbach a look of utter contempt, walked slowly to the lift and left public life for good. Sandstrom mused that if all the other planned coups were this smooth, they might – just might – have a chance.

3 December 2031, Antarctica
Cull Day 294

Jameson's mind started to race. He wasn't panicking – yet…

'Sarah, it's crazy. This isn't the way to tackle the issue. It's barbaric and totally out of proportion. I can't believe people are buying this crap.'

Waites turned to him with a scowl.

'It's not crap, Will. You of all people should appreciate the state this planet is in.'

'No matter how bad it is, you can't just put billions of people against a wall and kill them off. Think of the impact on their families. These people aren't guilty of any crime except ignorance.'

'You would say that. You're a baby boomer.'

Jameson stunned by the coldness in Waites's voice, continued his argument.

'Look, the people they want to get rid of are the very ones with the answers to tackle the problem. It'll put climate change knowledge back years – years we don't have. Look at me. I've potentially got the solution to stop the ice melt. CDT-8 is a game changer.'

Trevallion broke in. 'Whatever you two think, it doesn't matter. This Reboot thing is real, and it's waiting for us tomorrow.'

The high-pitched whine of the Sikorsky's motor deepened and they started to descend. Through wispy low cloud, Jameson could make out the icy blue waters of the Weddell Sea below and the unmistakable polar white and red hull of the MV *Ortelius*. For months, he had looked forward to the reunion with this ship, but now it just filled him with dread. Strong sea winds shook the helicopter as they slowly inched towards the landing deck. They virtually free-fell the last three metres and hit the steel helipad with a bone-jarring smack. The pilot cut the engines and the blades started to wind down to a reluctant stop.

Jameson looked at Trevallion. 'What now, Sarah?' He could feel his heart beating like a hammer against his ribs.

'Let's see what the crew are like. Just act normal,' she replied.

Easy for you to say. You're not the one who's had a bullseye painted on his forehead.

The pilot jumped down, secured the skids to the rolling deck and disappeared inside the ship without waiting. The four of them grabbed their personal kit and made their way to the main briefing area under the bridge. Two stony faced crew members looked down from an observation level. They didn't wave or acknowledge them in any way. Jameson pushed open the heavy steel door, stepped over the water lip and entered the warm, stuffy room.

He had been in here before at the end of a previous expedition. On that occasion the room had been filled with happy faces and the tables laden with honeyed ham, roast beef, salmon, buttered potatoes, fruit, cakes and even chilled champagne to celebrate their safe homecoming. Now the tables were empty, save for one with a stack of official-looking papers. The only person present was familiar, the unmistakable square-shouldered, white-haired, white-bearded six-foot mountain that was Mike Appel, the ship's captain.

Appel's weathered face, tanned by exposure to Arctic winds and a thin ozone layer, wasn't smiling. The normally jovial captain sat stiffly upright in his chair, nursing a half-full bottle of vodka, looking like a man under great strain. When Appel spoke, his voice was deep and precise, his accent a curious mix of Finnish and Spanish.

'Welcome back on board, Mr Jameson. I trust you and your team had a productive time on the ice. If you can just complete these papers, you will be allowed into your cabins. You must be tired.'

Jameson looked at him and the piles of bureaucracy curiously. 'Thank you, Captain, but what are these? We've never had to fill any papers in before.'

'It's just a new formality brought in by The Reboot Council. I assume you've heard about them and the events that have occurred since you've been away?'

'Our satellite radio has been out for almost the whole year. We've only just learnt.'

Appel gave him a sympathetic look. 'Then it must have come as quite a shock. Please complete the papers, then perhaps you and I can catch up on a few things.'

The papers seemed innocuous enough, but were obviously designed to ascertain one singularly important piece of information. *My date of birth.*

Jameson entered his as 1966 rather than the correct 1964, temporarily taking him off the condemned list. He looked young for his years and it would buy him some time, but he also knew it wouldn't be long before they discovered the truth. They all completed the forms in silence.

After going through them individually, Appel scooped them up and handed out cabin access cards. When Trevallion, Waites and Beckley had left, he invited Jameson to sit with him and poured them both a vodka.

Jameson sat down and shook his head. 'No thanks.'

'Take it. You'll need it when I've told you this story.' He held out the glass until Jameson reluctantly took it from him.

Over the next hour the veteran sea captain relayed in vivid detail the apocalyptic events of the past few months.

It was clear that Reboot was now firmly in control. Ninety countries were directly implementing the drastic measures outlined by Cooper in Bodø. Appel estimated that well over two hundred million baby boomers had already been executed.

'You know what?' said Appel, now clearly the worse for alcohol. 'The logic of what they are doing really stacks up.'

Fuck the logic. The methods are barbaric.

Jameson had only drunk one glass of the strong vodka, but it was already amplifying his emotions. 'I have only ever known humankind striving to extend life and improve the quality of a longer life. This goes against all those principles Captain.'

Appel stood and walked unsteadily to a metal cabinet on the wall and pulled out another bottle of Argentinian vodka.

'Can you think of a better way, Will?' He took a gulp direct from the bottle. 'Perhaps as a species we need to think more like… more like insects. More like…bees…like one big colony. To them, individuals don't matter in a crisis. If a hornet attacks the nest, scores of bees will attack the far bigger invader without hesitation, even though it is suicidal.' He took another large swig and wagged his finger at Jameson.

'They will sacrifice themselves for the good of the hive, knowing that if they can buy some time, other bees will arrive to overwhelm the hornet and kill it. It's the basic law of nature…to sacrifice for the common good. Perhaps if we saw things the same way they do, we wouldn't be in this shitstorm.'

'There must be a better way.' Jameson began to feel depressed by the conversation.

Appel slumped down in his chair and poured more vodka into Jameson's glass.

'Look, the way things stand, you and I are not long for this world anyway. I'm sixty-eight. When we dock, the authorities will have me deported back to Finland. There I'll be turned into fertiliser and spread around some new pine nursery.' He put his hands behind his head and smiled wistfully.

'Hopefully near Lake Paijanne. It's very beautiful. I met my wife there you know…on holiday eight years ago.'

Jameson was surprised. It had not occurred to him that Appel was vulnerable too.

'I also know you lied on your embarkation form,' Appel continued. 'You forgot that I have a photocopy of your passport from when you boarded last year.'

If he reports me, I'm dead.

'Don't worry, none will know. We are of far more value to each other if we stick together.' Appel seemed to have sobered up for an instant. He leaned forward towards Jameson.

'I have been giving it much thought. I need to get back to Finland with my wife, Helga. She is in Ushuaia waiting for me.' Appel smiled at the startled look on Jameson's face. They would reach the Argentinian port of Ushuaia in two days.

'She has been there for two weeks. Helga is twenty years younger than me; she's not attracting any attention. Our plan is to get home where we have a place deep in Repovesi National Park.

They will never find us. We can hunt and fish and live there for years until this slaughter is over. Perhaps in time, they will think they have removed enough people and we will be safe. Come with us. If we stay together, we can survive. We can say we are all family.'

Jameson thought for a few moments. 'I want to get home too, but for me that means the UK. I can travel with you up to there, then we'll go our separate ways.' Appel nodded in agreement.

'But Captain, that still means travelling thousands of miles and avoiding virtually every other person along the route. Thought how we might do that?'

Appel poured himself another drink. 'Pull up your chair. I'll tell you exactly how...'

Jameson finally got to his cabin two hours later. His head throbbed from the tension of the day, the strength of the vodka and the effort of trying to absorb the details of Appel's escape plan. Dumping his kit on the floor, he collapsed on the creaking, under-sprung bed and was asleep in seconds.

When he woke, it was still dark outside. Sitting up, he rested his head on the gently vibrating bulkhead. The powerful engines reverberated throughout the ship; they were obviously under way but only going around half speed. He reasoned they had probably entered an area of shifting sea ice. The *Ortelius* had an ice-strengthened hull, but she still had to be wary of icebergs five times her size. Jameson made himself a coffee, took off his quilted jacket, padded trousers and thermal underclothes and had a long, tepid shower.

He gave his hair a much-needed trim with clippers but kept his six-month beard. There wasn't too much grey in it so could help disguise his true age. Putting on a fresh T-shirt, jumper and jeans he left his room and knocked on the cabin next door, the one Trevallion had been given.

No answer.

He continued to the stairs and walked up into the ship's lounge area. It was an unpromising sight. The carpet was threadbare, the soft furnishings worn and faded. Grey metal chairs and tables were arranged in rows along one side of the room, all firmly bolted to the floor. A solitary faded picture of a polar bear hung lopsided and pathetic on the far wall, its glass broken but somehow it remained in its frame. A vase full of stagnant water and long-dead flowers sat on a sagging shelf. Old magazines spilled from an overstuffed rack and out onto the floor. It was another reminder to Jameson that the *Ortelius* was designed to smash through ice and survive sub-zero storms; it was not designed for luxury cruising.

Not that it mattered to him. Because he had been diverted by an irresistible force emanating from the canteen, an intoxicating aroma that he had missed for over a year.

A cooked breakfast.

At that moment, in spite of everything else going on in his head, the promise of bacon, eggs, tomatoes and mushrooms became his main priority.

He grabbed a tray and eagerly piled his plate high. After filling a large mug with fresh coffee, he went to find a seat. The restaurant was quiet, two off-duty crew chatted at one table and a group of three blue-overalled mechanics sat quietly poring over some drawings at another. They looked over but said nothing.

Feeling conspicuously old, he chose an empty bench near a window and sat to eat what seemed to him like the final meal of a condemned man. Staring out through the salt-sprayed glass at the rolling Weddell Sea, he went over the details of Appel's plan once more in his mind...

In two-nights' time we enter the Beagle Channel and reach the outskirts of Ushuaia. Appel will commandeer one of the Ortelius's lifeboats. Together we'll leave the ship. We'll make our way to the shoreline at Tierra del Fuego National Park. Appel's wife will meet us. She'll drive to the town, leave us in her apartment, then take the passports to a forger to get the birthdates changed.

From there we'll board the cruise ship, Magellan Explorer, as tourists. This will take us north to the Falkland Islands, a seven-day sail. Once there, we'll buy tickets for one of the MOD flights to Brize Norton in Oxfordshire.

It sounded straightforward, but would be fraught with danger. But then again, he decided, they had no other choice. Jameson was still lost in thought when a familiar voice brought him back to earth.

'This seat free?' It was Trevallion; he'd never been so glad to see her. 'How did you sleep?'

'Like a log. A log that's taken four temazepam.' Jameson had used the powerful sedative to help him sleep during long summer days at their base; it usually knocked him out cold. 'How about you?'

'Just a couple of hours. Tom woke me up and has been bending my ear about what we're going to do with you.'

'With me?'

'He's been keeping up with Reboot's demands on the web. Apparently, it's illegal to keep the whereabouts of baby boomers secret. He's saying we must report you to the captain so that he can radio the port authorities.'

'What do you want to do?' Jameson asked.

Disappear from this nightmare with you.

Trevallion was wearing her hair down as she did on their one night of passion. For a fleeting second, Jameson was transported back to that magical time and place which now seemed literally a world away. He took her hand and gently drew her closer, she didn't resist.

'I think this entire Reboot initiative is insane, and what you said is right Will. We're getting so close to some big answers. If they saw the success we've had with the isolating gel, they would surely want it...wouldn't they?'

Jameson was heartened that Trevallion had agreed with his analysis. 'And if they kill me, it would be lost.'

'Well, that's just it.' She frowned. 'Tom reckons he can just take your laptop and create the CDT-8 without you.' Jameson felt an icy chill. Not only did Waites want him out of the way, he also wanted the credit and profits for his work.

'Listen to me Sarah. I'm going to transfer the data onto an encrypted memory stick minus some key formulations for manufacture which I'll memorise. If I die, then all the other data will be useless.'

Trevallion fixed him with her large green eyes. 'How can I help?'

19 February 2031, The Vatican, Vatican City
Cull Day 8

Gabriele Rossi followed Stefano D'Antoni down the narrow dark corridor towards the lift. He was thrilled, he was nervous, he was off to meet God's right-hand man.

It was two days before the first Sunday of Lent, and Rossi had an appointment with Pope Nicholas VI at four o'clock. He had, however, inherited from his father the habit of arriving at least twenty minutes early for everything. The Vatican staff who had welcomed him were understanding and told him to make himself comfortable in one of the reception parlours. The pope would not be ready a minute before the appointed time.

With high mullioned windows and ornate stained glass, the parlour had an air of restrained opulence. Gold-framed paintings of former popes covered the red walls from ceiling to floor, and

Rossi's feet sank easily into the luxuriously thick scarlet-and-gold-patterned carpets. So thick and luxurious, they almost impeded progress. The room had numerous soft leather club chairs dotted around randomly, not unlike, Rossi thought, the ones in the members lounge at his father's private club in Milan. He recalled going there as a small child, the cigar smoke, the subdued light, the laughing, the head-patting, and later in the ebbing afternoon, the snoring. This room housed no sleeping pensioners, and appeared to be far better equipped with a Tassimo coffee machine and choice of biscuits. It was a help yourself arrangement; double espresso four euros, café latte three euros. Rossi pressed the requisite chrome buttons on the impressive machine and it started to gurgle and hiss. He chuckled inwardly when he noticed the basket for extra donations. The Catholic Church is always ready to receive gifts, even inside this gilded testament to its vast wealth.

At one minute to four, a man dressed in the black robes of a senior Vatican official walked in and made himself known to Rossi.

'Morning, Il Signor Rossi, I am Stefano D'Antoni, director of the Holy See press office. I will escort you to His Holiness.' D'Antoni was a tall, slim handsome man with a soft Christ-like beard. Probably in his fifties, he possessed the serene countenance of a man totally at ease with himself and these extraordinary surroundings. He was part of an expanding team of well-paid professionals who increasingly controlled every facet of the Vatican's administration, finances and communications.

'I will also remain for the duration of your interview. Nothing will be released into the public domain unless I expressly agree to it.'

'Of course, of course.' Rossi felt a sudden tightness in his gut as he realised he was at the very heart of one of the most secretive institutions in the world.

'These seem like very modest apartments for a pope,' Rossi

commented, as they left the parlour.

D'Antoni smiled. 'At first he was just experimenting with this simple type of living arrangement. Seeing how he liked it, now he stays here permanently.'

Pope Nicholas had moved into the Casa Santa Marta guest-house when it hosted him and other cardinals during the conclave before his election. It was meant only as a temporary arrangement. Like all popes before him, he was expected to move into the more commodious comforts of the Apostolic Palace to reflect his status.

'His Holiness dislikes pomp and majesty. He decided that being here allowed him to live in a community with others. He likes being with his priests.'

'Perhaps he also had a playing cards foursome he didn't want to break up,' joked Rossi, trying to lighten the mood.

D'Antoni ignored the comment as they got into the small lift and he pulled the brass scissor gates shut with a clatter.

'I hope this isn't the one he got stuck in.'

Media reports recently revealed that the pope needed to be rescued from a Vatican lift as he was on his way to celebrate Sunday Mass. Again, there was no reaction from the stoic D'Antoni. As the lift started, he continued to give more background about the building.

'This guesthouse was built twenty-five years ago on the site of an ancient hospice for the poor and sits on the edge of the city. Normally, it is inhabited by just a few dozen priests and bishops who work in the Vatican. Half the rooms are made available for those wanting an audience or other official occasions. From here, visitors can reach the Sistine Chapel by bus or via a short walk inside the Vatican gardens.'

'You should be a guide,' quipped Rossi. When D'Antoni again made no comment, he immediately regretted his remark. The ancient lift shuddered to a stop and Rossi followed his guide down another corridor with numbered doors set at two-metre intervals. Only the ecclesiastical pictures on the walls prevented it from looking like any generic three-star hotel in Rome.

'His Holiness resides in Suite 201. It has a more generous living room where he can receive guests.'

'Thank you. Reboot really appreciate His Holiness giving us this time.'

D'Antoni stopped and turned on Rossi. He looked down at him as if he was regarding a parasite.

'Know this Milanese, the pope will never give you animals his blessing. Your methods go against all teachings of the Catholic Church. This bloodbath that you propose is obscene.'

Rossi was shaken momentarily but quickly retorted, 'I am a Catholic. I know the Church has always done what it needed to do to survive, Signor D'Antoni. This place has plenty of blood on its hands too.'

They fell quiet on hearing a small cough. The pope was waiting for them at his door. D'Antoni smiled, shook his boss's hand and went inside. Rossi was not introduced to the pope, which he knew would happen. 'After all,' said the priest who had brokered the meeting, 'he is the one man who needs no introduction.'

'Your Holiness,' Rossi blurted out, immediately finding himself in dumbstruck awe of this man in white robes, the figurehead of the institution that had dominated his life. Even though the pope was only five feet two, and wasn't wearing his usual large cross or distinctive skullcap, his presence still dominated the room.

He smiled, shook Rossi's hand and invited him to sit in an elegant but tired floral-patterned chair; Rossi settled rather awkwardly into its sagging cushion. Pope Nicholas sat in a chair that was higher and better bolstered. He noted the emissary's rather forlorn look.

'This not a power play, young man. I have back problems. Now, please excuse me for a few moments,' he said.

As the pope handed some papers to D'Antoni, Rossi took in the scene carefully. He wanted to remember details to enthral his family and especially his devout mother. The setting was surprisingly plain, even austere – three soft chairs, a small pine desk, whitewashed walls and waxed wooden floorboards. A single plain cream woollen rug lay in the centre. The room was blessed with good natural light and the sun flooded in through two generously-sized windows. Both were flanked by heavy white silk curtains hanging from sturdy wooden poles, their material deliberately cut oversize so that the silk gathered in generous bunches on the floor to eliminate drafts. There were few other objects in the room – an icon of St Francis, a statue of Our Lady of Luján, a crucifix and a statue of St Joseph sleeping.

After a minute, Pope Nicholas had finished with his press officer and turned his attention to Rossi.

'D'Antoni brings good news. My approval ratings are going in the right direction. Did you know I am regarded favourably by sixty-five per cent of Jews, fifty-three per cent of Protestants, and even fifty-one per cent of atheists?' The pope smiled at the thought.

Rossi was transfixed by that face. In many regards it was an unremarkable face. If it was a face that belonged to a farmer or a banker; it would be deemed run of the mill, ordinary even. But what set it apart, thought Rossi, was the smile. The smile that travelled all around the world, the smile that opened hearts and won minds. The smile that transmitted love and hope to millions.

But the reason Rossi was there was no smiling matter, and he was momentarily sad at having to explain the reason for his visit.

'Your Holiness, thank you for permitting me this audience. As you probably know, I come to you as a mandated representative from my organisation.'

'Reboot, yes. An interesting name.'

'I am here to ask your help in a matter of great urgency for an issue that I know is very close to your heart.'

Nicholas listened intently. His legs stretched out in front of him, neatly crossed at the ankles.

'You recently declared that destroying the environment is a sin. You have continually stated that humans are turning God's creation into "a wasteland full of debris, desolation and filth".'

Nicholas nodded in agreement, but said nothing.

'Holy Father, you have called for decisive action on climate change and even proposed that caring for the environment be added to traditional Christian works of mercy.' More affirmative nods encouraged Rossi to continue. 'You have consistently welcomed environmental accords and encouraged voters to take action to ensure their governments do not backtrack on their pledges.' Rossi almost pointed his finger at the pope's face to accentuate his point, but thought better of it. 'And finally, Your Holiness, you spoke of the critical need to establish a new world political authority and a stronger more organised international institution to protect the planet.' Rossi leaned forward. 'Well, Holy Father, Reboot is that world authority. We have the people's mandate and we are prepared to do what is necessary to carry out your wishes for the good of all mankind.'

Nicholas said nothing for a few seconds, then shrugged, 'All very good, Signor Rossi. But what do you want from me?'

Rossi breathed deeply, trying to drag air down his suddenly very dry throat.

'We want your blessing for the necessary population reduction we must undertake.'

Nicholas looked gravely at Rossi and gave a deep careworn sigh. 'I see.'

He paused to look at the crucifix on the wall, then crossed his fingers together.

'Signor Rossi, let me tell you about the day I was elected. When I began to realise that I might be chosen...' He paused at the sound of voices outside in the corridor. As their chatter faded he began again.

'During lunch, I felt a deep and inexplicable peace come over me. But it also came with a great darkness, a deep obscurity about everything else. And those feelings accompanied me until my election and for every day since then. Because I knew this day would come and so would someone like you.' He fixed Rossi with his deep brown eyes. 'Climate change is one of the great evils of our time. If not addressed, it has the potential to destroy us all. Right now, the worst impacts are felt by those least responsible – refugees and the poor.'

Rossi could see tears welling in the pope's eyes.

'Our selfish system, motivated by the mantra of profit at any price, is responsible for this disaster. We must not be indifferent to the loss of biodiversity and destruction of ecosystems. Because of us, thousands of species will no longer give glory to God by their very existence. We have no such right. The faithful should ask forgiveness for sins committed against the environment.'

He stopped speaking and wiped away the tear that had run onto his cheek. Rossi instinctively thought to offer his handkerchief.

'Your Holiness, we believe those responsible should be offered more than forgiveness. They should be held to account with their lives. They who have caused this catastrophe that will affect all God's children. Their self-seeking actions must bear a consequence. Their passing will mean a new, glorious, fruitful beginning for their progeny.'

If the pope was shocked, he hid it well. He looked impassively at Rossi, stood stiffly and walked over to the window. Undoing the brass latch, he opened it a few inches. The room was instantly filled with the familiar city soundtrack of cars, buses, scooters and voices followed by a less recognisable sound of whooshing air.

It was early evening and getting gloomy. Nicholas looked down at the square below; he could still make out the scores of Romans as they entered and exited from all directions, skirting around each other without losing a step of their forward motion, like a well-rehearsed dance. Bankers, teachers, doctors, lawyers, salesmen, bakers, clerks, children, tourists – all oblivious to the drama playing out above their heads.

He looked up at the treeline just visible on Pincian Hill to the north, and saw the emerald-green laser beams playing on the branches as civil workers sought to prevent millions of starlings from roosting in the city. An enormous swirling flock of the birds in the darkening sky swooped low, unfolded and regrouped again as the pope closed the window.

'With what you propose, at least one in five of the people I have just seen will be swept away. It is not a solution.' He walked slowly back to his chair, lowering himself down stiffly. He tilted his head slightly to the right and looked directly at Rossi. 'To blame population growth instead of extreme consumerism is one way of refusing to face the issues. We are in this mess because a minority believed it had the right to consume in a way which could never be universalised. The climate is a common good, belonging to all and meant for all. We must call for first-world consumers to modify their lifestyle by reducing waste, planting more trees, separating rubbish, making better use of carpooling.'

'The time when carpooling could make a difference is over.' Rossi sighed. 'Your Holiness, ask yourself…what would God do? He saw how wicked and destructive people had become and sought to destroy them with the great flood.'

Nicholas put his hand up to stop him.

'I am well aware of the book of Genesis, thank you.'

Rossi regretted his use of the Old Testament to make his point, but continued his argument.

'So as God sent down the floodwaters as a judgment on humanity's wickedness that rose out of the grief of his heart, then so shall we…' Rossi could see his words were having little effect. He looked over at D'Antoni who was writing and smiling. 'Holy Father, forgive my bluntness. This Sunday, we need you – and the unborn children of the next generations need you to do something very important. To appear at your palace window, recite the Angelus prayer and tell the pilgrims in St Peter's Square and the billions of Catholics watching around the world that what we are doing is essential and that we have your blessing.'

Nicholas leaned forward in his chair.

'What you ask is impossible. All life is sacred. What you plan is the euthanasia of billions, a way of treating the human person as an object or a burden.' Nicholas looked at D'Antoni for approval who promptly gave an enthusiastic nod of his head. 'Fathers shall not be put to death because of their children, nor shall children be put to death because of their fathers. Each one shall be put to death for his own sin.' This was rewarded with an appreciative smile from D'Antoni who recognised the passage from Deuteronomy 24:16.

'There is no right to dispose arbitrarily of another's life, so no executioner can become an executive guardian of a non-existent right. What you propose is a grave violation of the law of God, since it is the deliberate, unacceptable killing of a human being.' Nicholas was treading familiar ground and felt he was winning the argument. 'In this time of great uncertainty, it's a time for inventing, for creativity. The creativity of the Christian needs to show forth in opening up new horizons, opening windows, opening transcendence towards God and towards people…'

'Enough!' Cooper rose to his feet so forcefully he knocked the side table which in turn caused the small statue of Our Lady of Luján to topple off and smash on the marble-veneered floor.

The three looked at the shattered remnants of the

four-hundred-year-old artefact. Momentarily struck dumb, each experienced different and powerful emotions. Cooper still angry but glad he had finally cracked the self-satisfied façade of these so called agents of God. D'Antoni stupefied by the destruction of the statue, yet already calculating the odds of a successful insurance claim against the cost of repair. Pope Nicholas, sorrowful that in his custodianship the precious object has been lost.

D'Antoni quickly rose to his feet, scattering his notes. 'You arrogant fool. That statue was priceless.'

Rossi ignored him and made towards the door. He stopped at the entrance and turned. 'While the world burns, all you worry about are trinkets and outdated doctrines. You see the agonies of the planet, but you do nothing. Just when your followers need guidance most, you stay silent. You have the influence to change the course of humankind but you refuse to bring it to bear. If you spurn this opportunity to align yourself to the new world order, the Church will be doomed. God will be seen by more people for what he really is. Simply the law of cause and effect.'

Pope Nicholas looked at Rossi and smiled. 'I think, Signor Rossi, perhaps you are in the wrong place. This is not a religious issue – it's a human rights issue.'

'Where were human rights during the Papal Inquisition when an innocent person could be burnt at the stake because they would not repent or submit to the will of this church?'

D'Antoni sat down and answered with the surety of someone who had responded to such accusations before. 'Pope John Paul asked for forgiveness for the sins of Roman Catholics through the ages. We have moved on.'

Rossi rolled his eyes in frustration. 'Then why can't you move on with this issue? If we fail, then there will be no more Catholics. No Vatican City. No pope.'

Nicholas held up both hands and shook his head. 'We must

find another way, my son. You and your Reboot cannot play God. There is only one who may do that.'

Rossi saw that he had lost the argument, so he played the card he'd hoped he wouldn't have to.

'You leave me no choice. Tomorrow I will begin the process of removing your papal rule and the dismissal of the Secretariat of State.'

Nicholas looked shocked. D'Antoni got to his feet again.

'You cannot depose the pope. This is absurd. We terminate this meeting.'

Rossi stepped aggressively towards D'Antoni, who quickly backed away, fearing violence. From his jacket pocket, Rossi produced some papers.

'We have many allies within this church who are sympathetic to our mission and willing to put a case forward that you, Pope Nicholas, are unfit for this office. On this paper are the signatures of one hundred and sixty-five of your cardinals representing fifty-eight countries. They include eighty-one of the one hundred and twenty cardinal electors. We have all the authority we need. We can have another conclave organised within a week.'

'Let me see that,' demanded D'Antoni. He perused the paper with incredulity and handed it to Nicholas who gave another weary sigh and looked at Rossi.

'Ah yes, the conservatives. I can never please them.'

'The endless rise of the antipopes, Your Holiness. They are nothing,' D'Antoni said dismissively.

Nicholas waved his hand at Rossi.

'You will have your answer in the morning.'

So it came to pass that on the following Sunday, Pope Nicholas VI addressed the thousands of worshippers in St Peter's Square to tell them of a new dawn of hope for mankind and also of the grave sacrifices some would have to make to achieve it. He delivered the fine words he had been given. He invited his congregation to understand the jeopardy mankind was in and to envision the more just world which all God's followers wanted. He stated his conviction that if the Church could break down old conventions and summon the courage to embrace new beginnings, then everything was possible. And he shocked with his call for all Catholics to embrace contraception and cease procreation.

He gave no further details other than to give Reboot's plans his blessing and the imperative to obey them.

Immediately after, Stefano D'Antoni relayed the main points of his boss's speech through hundreds of communiques to Catholic leaders and their communities across the world.

There would be protests, there would be riots, there would be bloodshed, but for Gabriele Rossi it was mission accomplished. Reboot could now start playing God.

20 February 2031, London, England
Cull Day 9

'Where's O'Brien? Where's the little shit sloped off to now?'

Dressed in his expensive yet untidily worn black suit, former Prime Minister John Kirklees lurched through the corridor that linked number 10 to number 11 Downing Street, throwing open doors as he went, looking for his chief advisor. He was annoyed.

'Please calm down, sir. He'll turn up, probably in the toilet.' Trudy Potter, Kirklees' Parliamentary Private Secretary scurried after her boss, trying to placate him.

'Well, find him Potter. He can't be too hard to spot. There's hardly anyone else here. I don't care if he's got his pants down. Those bastards from Reboot are due in thirty minutes and I want to go through this fucking presentation with my fucking communications director.'

Potter darted down an adjacent corridor to see if she could locate the hapless Dan O'Brien. Kirklees went back to his study, sat at his desk and took a sip of whisky from the hip flask he kept in his jacket pocket. He caught a glimpse of himself in the ornate Georgian mirror on the opposite wall. He was not a vain man, but even he despaired at the sight of his unruly mess of ginger hair. Kirklees was in a high state of anxiety because this was an important day. It had been suggested to him that he might be given a key role in the new Reboot administration representing the UK. His communication skills had been recognised by the selection panel tasked with putting together the new executive; particularly for the way he'd run his re-election campaign the previous year, winning with a record-breaking landslide majority.

They had asked him and O'Brien to create a simple and engaging campaign to sell Reboot's new vision for the world – no easy task as it had to put a positive spin on the idea that the planned genocide of an entire generation was the right way to go.

With both men effectively out of a job if their ideas weren't accepted, they had been working on it solidly for the past two days. O'Brien had pulled the brief together, and together they had called in some of the UK's best marketing brains to pitch their thinking.

At a heated meeting that had gone on until the early morning, they finally settled on their favourite and were now ready to put it to Reboot's selection panel.

Kirklees was certain they had a first-class concept but still wanted to rehearse the main points again with his most trusted advisor.

'Where the hell is he?' Kirklees muttered to himself as he sat stewing. He'd been loyal to O'Brien these past few years, hadn't he? Especially after the idiot was caught in flagrante with two call girls at the Tory Conference and the media had screamed for his blood. He had done no less than staked his reputation, put his government on the line and risked undermining his entire public political strategy in order to preserve him.

It was true that since that incident O'Brien had been sidelined and only given low-profile work, but now Kirklees was putting faith in his communications genius once again, giving him a chance to redeem himself and help deliver the 'most important advertising campaign in the history of mankind'.

Kirklees heard a creak and looked up to see a sheepish-looking Trudy Potter at the door. 'We know where Dan is…'

'Well, where the blazing balls of Hades is he?' replied Kirklees impatiently.

'In his car travelling to the south-west.'

'He's what?' Kirklees stood up abruptly causing his shirt to flop out of his trousers for the tenth time that day.

'He said he had to take his children down to Cornwall… He thinks his wife might have the…er…flu.'

Kirklees couldn't believe what he was hearing. They were about to give the most important presentation of their lives and the person responsible for creating it wasn't going to be there to contribute.

He slumped wearily into his chair and looked out of the window into the Downing Street rose garden. A fine mist of saturating drizzle was falling. A gentle breeze coaxed one of the last poplar leaves from its branch and it dropped onto the yellowing, mossy lawn. A lone robin sat on the wooden handle of a spade before darting onto a stone bird bath and taking a quick drink. A black cat walked slowly across the lawn, imperiously regarding the red-breasted bird, but doing nothing. A good omen, Kirklees thought, and he immediately perked up.

'Right. Think. What would Winnie do?'

Kirklees sat in his favourite place in all Downing Street, the cabinet meeting room. The room where he had chaired so many meetings in his glory days as the UK's chief executive. Every Thursday, behind its soundproofed doors with his team around him, he discussed policy and the state of the nation, and shared a little Westminster gossip.

Its tall Georgian ceiling, generous windows, lemony yellow wallpaper and carpets. The honeyed-walnut bookcases containing hundreds of black leather-bound encyclopaedias and other learned journals, every one of them bursting with the promise of new knowledge, exotic animals, medical advances and scientific wonders. The portrait of Churchill in his famous Blood, Sweat and Tears pose that Kirklees had had brought in from the corridor, and deliberately positioned to look over the middle of the polished oak meeting table. The elegantly proportioned marble fireplace which dominated the far wall and the French Louis XV-style clock that stood on the mantel, reputedly taken from Napoleon's apartment in Paris just after he was exiled. They all combined to lend the room a unique, almost magical atmosphere.

He had chosen this as the venue for the Reboot meeting and was going to sell the campaign with all he had, just as Winnie would have done. The concept was good; it had intellectual rigour, hit the right emotional pitch. Moreover, the slogan was every bit as catchy as the one that helped drag the UK out of Europe. Winston Leonard Spencer Churchill would have sold this with aplomb and so will John Miles Thomas Albert Kirklees. There would be no doubts or wavering, just pure conviction that this was the right approach and that he was the man to sell it across the world.

As he waited for the delegation to arrive, he straightened the green felt cloth that covered the long table and checked himself out once more in the room's only mirror. His favoured red silk tie was arrow straight, the dark suit freshly dry cleaned, the shirt tucked tightly in his underpants. Even his fiercely independent hair had been temporarily tamed.

He checked the computer to make sure his PowerPoint was on full view with slide notes visible. All good – he was ready for the tough cross-examination that was bound to come. He had only met with a Reboot delegation twice, the first with the 'distinctly lightweight' Tommy Speake from Global Revolt and 'the decidedly more able' Erica Sandstrom to inform him that his government was being suspended; the second just four days previously with the more formidable pairing of Colonel Paolo Moschin and Franck Durand. In a humiliating meeting at Chequers, his country estate in Buckinghamshire, they had given Kirklees and the first ministers of Scotland, Wales and Northern Ireland notice to quit. He had been allowed to stay in Downing Street until further notice as UK figurehead, but the nation had effectively been put under military rule, pending the new governing council and new constitution being introduced.

Kirklees had not been informed of who would be attending the meeting today, so the small, wooden nameplate holders on the table remained empty. He picked one up and examined it. For objects of such modest utility, they were beautifully made. Probably handcrafted by some lowly Victorian carpenter in a sawdust covered workshop for a farthing apiece, he mused. Yet these small oak pieces had held upright the names of hundreds of kings, queens, presidents and prime ministers.

A knock on the door interrupted his thoughts. It was Potter.

'The…er…delegation from Reboot are here.'

'Well, show them in, show them in.'

The door opened and six children dressed in school uniforms bounded in, followed by a plump, short-haired Indian woman dressed in a tweed skirt and jacket.

'Right, children, please take your seats and remember no questions until the man has finished, and don't forget to write what you'd like to ask as we go along.' The children, all chattering excitedly, sat down together at the far end of the table, opened their backpacks and took out notepads and pencils. The teacher sat opposite Kirklees, took out her iPad and peered at him over her glasses.

'Good morning Mister Kirklees. Children?'

The children looked up from their pads. 'Good morning Mister Kirklees.'

Kirklees, stunned, said nothing.

'Now, if we could please keep this down to fifteen minutes. I'd like to get the children back on the bus for eleven.'

'But where's the Reboot delegation?' asked Kirklees.

'This is the delegation.' She pointed out the individual children. 'This is Barney, Megan, Florence, Lucy, Ishan and Lucas. They are all from Year Six at Westminster Primary School. I'm Mrs Sidhu, their teacher.'

'But...er...um...surely there must be...um.' Kirklees was completely flummoxed by the turn of events.

'Chop-chop, Mister Kirklees,' Mrs Sidhu replied curtly.

Kirklees decided he had no choice but to plough on with the show. Sixteen minutes later he was finished, but with only half his audience intact. He'd lost the attention of Megan and Florence within two minutes. They spent their time drawing the cat, which stood outside the window waiting to be let in. Lucy had gone to the toilet halfway through and not returned.

Kirklees looked imploringly at the remaining three children and Mrs Sidhu.

'Any questions?'

Ishan put her hand up. 'Where's Lucy gone?'

There was another knock on the door and Trudy Potter walked in, holding a little fair-haired girl's hand.

'Found her in the basement kitchen helping herself to a glass of milk.'

'Lucy!' shouted Ishan in glee. 'Come and sit with me.'

Kirklees was beginning to despair.

'I have a question.' It was Mrs Sidhu.

'Yes, yes, anything at all.'

'Well first I have to say that I liked your central assertion that the campaign needs to be clear, impactful and simple enough to be understood in all languages and by all colours and creeds. I also think the way you used graphics to demonstrate the immediate gains for reducing the population was inspired. But I have to know. How will you manage to get lions, giraffes and zebras to dance in such harmony?'

'Computer generated wizardry. Everything is possible these days,' replied Kirklees, grateful for the generally positive feedback.

'Look, I drew the giraffe!' shouted Lucas.

'Giraffe, I missed that. Can we play it again Miss?' said Lucy.

'Perhaps later, Lucy.' Mrs Sidhu looked at her notes, turned back to Kirklees and smiled. 'And one more thing. I must say Walt Disney himself would have been pleased with the powerful symbolism of children ascending Mount Everest in a blizzard to erect the Reboot flag on its summit.'

Kirklees, who had a weakness for praise, was pleased. Using the world's highest mountain to illustrate the optimism of a new dawn of mankind was his idea.

'So many things about your presentation former prime minister, that I really loved. My concern is around the main message. It seemed…familiar. Could you get that slide back up, please?'

'Yes, of course. We're very pleased with its…er…punch. Its memorable directness.' Kirklees returned to the laptop and found the slide which showcased the campaign slogan.

SEIZE CONTROL. CULL BOOMERS. SAVE THE WORLD.

*

The next day, Kirklees was anxiously pacing around his study. He had heard no further word about the success or otherwise of his presentation. Mrs Sidhu had simply gathered up her pupils and given a vague promise of 'getting back in touch soon'.

He turned to Potter who was looking out at the courtyard for signs of activity. Apart from the usual gaggle of reporters, nothing seemed to be happening.

'Any word from that bastard O'Brien?'

'Not a word sir.'

'Take it from me, even if we win this pitch, he's not going to be part of it. He's finished.' Kirklees slammed his fist into the palm of his other hand.

Potter knew well that this wasn't the first time her boss had made this assertion about his chief advisor, but ultimately he had always given O'Brien the benefit of the doubt. She felt that now wasn't the time to remind him of the fact.

Kirklees finally sat down behind his desk and relaxed his shoulders.

'Trudy, can you make me a coffee please? Some of those dark chocolate gingers would be nice too.'

Potter smiled at another one of Kirklees' idiosyncrasies, his ability to change from raging bull to twinkle-eyed charmer in an instant.

'The ones from Fortnum?'

'Smashing.'

As Potter left the room, Kirklees allowed himself to luxuriate momentarily in the thought of Colombian dark chocolate melting into Colombian coffee.

As he did, a ping indicated that an email had arrived.

He looked at the header to decide whether he wanted to open it:

RESULT OF PITCH.

Caught in a mixture of excitement and trepidation, he hesitated. Why hadn't they rung? This was not usually a good sign. But these Reboot people loved to keep you off guard. This was just the way they did business. No fuss, no travel, no room to negotiate. He steeled himself and clicked on the header:

Dear Mr Kirklees,

Thank you for your very interesting proposal. Class Six enjoyed it very much – Lucy says thank you for the milk! ☺

You may have wondered why did we bring along some ten-year-olds to view your presentation?

The answer is simple.

This was the level Daniel O'Brien told us you wanted to pitch it. He said that you insisted on 'dumbing it down' to primary school level. That you wanted to display the numbers as 'Sesame Street would do' and to sweeten the pill as 'only Hollywood could have done'.

We are delighted to tell you that you accomplished your objective with your target audience.

Barney, Megan and Ishan were all happy and clear on your central proposal – that baby boomers must go to heaven to save the world – I'm thrilled that they even understood the verb 'to cull'. Florence and Lucas could recall some of your story, but were understandably fuzzy on some of the details. Lucy would like your presentation on a USB so that she can watch it with her mummy.

But despite the enthusiasm of Class Six, we do not however concur with your analysis or your concepts or your targeting strategy. We believe that we have to engage our adult audience in a considered, logical and intelligent way to convince them of the need to sacrifice their loved ones.

We cannot dumb this down to the lowest common emotional denominator and build our case on half-truths and slick sound bites. You may have fooled enough of the British people enough of the time Mr Kirklees, but we are firmly of the view that it won't work for the rest of the world.

In conclusion, I regret to have to inform you that we will not be going forward with your proposal, but rather will be working on another with Mr O'Brien who gave his excellent presentation yesterday afternoon.

On another issue, we have become aware of your real birthdate, which is not 19 June 1965 as you indicated, but in fact 19 June 1964.

I am sure you are well aware of the implications of this. We will be sending a team to collect you this morning. 😵

Thanks again for your time,

Yours,
Mrs R Sidhu
Form teacher, Year Six
Westminster Primary School

A knock came on the door. It was Potter.

'Reboot are here, sir. Fingers crossed it's good news.'

4 December 2031, Drake Passage, Atlantic Ocean
Cull Day 295

'Can you keep the memory stick safe? Feel free to say no.' Jameson looked into Trevallion's beautiful green eyes. He wanted to tell her how much she meant to him, how much the night they had spent together had been one of the most beautiful, most intense of his life. But he couldn't, he was afraid of hearing her answer. And as he looked, he thought he saw doubt in her eyes too.

She smiled and squeezed his hand. 'I'll do it.'

That night, Jameson transferred the data and went over the key formulations in his head until they were committed to memory. He passed the memory stick to Trevallion in the corridor, and with a sense of foreboding and sadness returned to his room to wipe away the last two years of his life. Walking to the oval-shaped window he undid the two fastening catches and opened it. An icy blast blew into his face and the cacophony of the wind-lashed sea filled the room.

Hope I'm doing the right thing.

With a lump in his throat, he picked up the silver coloured laptop containing so many hard-won equations, formulas and specifications; ground-breaking work he hoped might save the world and bring him renown. Giving it a kiss, he tossed it out into the half-light. The computer spun through the air, quickly losing its momentum at the top of its arc in the fierce gale, it landed no more than five metres from the ship and sank into the foam. Clipping the window shut, Jameson tried to reassure himself he had done the right thing.

It is gone, it is over. Now a new chapter with a new goal –survival.

The next morning, he was jolted awake by the sound of shouting outside his room. He opened the door just as one of the ship's crew ran past.

'What's the noise about?'

The crew member kept running but shouted back. 'Someone's overboard. We've only got a few minutes to get them out of the water.'

Pulling on his clothes, Jameson ran along the corridor and up the steep flight of stairs that led to the stern of the ship. As he stepped out of the heavy door that led outside, the cold took his breath away. He turned to go back for more clothes but was drawn to a group of people standing by the railings staring down at the sea. The ship shook as the engines were put into reverse and it slowed, having lost propulsion it started to rise and fall to the swell of the waves. There was shouting from two decks down and Jameson saw three crewmen frantically working to lower a lifeboat.

'Who is it?' he asked a crewman who was leaning over the rails to get a better look as the drama unfolded.

'Looks like a woman,' he replied. 'Whoever it is may be gone already. No one can survive in these waters for long.'

Jameson strained his eyes in the direction they were all looking. For a few moments he couldn't make out anything, then among the cresting waves he saw a shape. A head, bobbing barely above the surface about four hundred metres away, just beyond the ship's long white wake. The head sank again, then came back up, an arm flailing weakly then slipping from view. Whoever this person was, thought Jameson, they were dying. The lifeboat looked pathetically small in the huge swell as it made its way slowly forward on its forlorn rescue mission. Finally, it reached the limp body and dragged it on board.

Jameson looked around at the people watching. He recognised Waites and Beckley who were standing together, but he couldn't see Sarah.

Then he was overcome by a feeling of complete and utter dread.

The ship's doctor pulled the sheet back and Jameson looked down at Trevallion. Her eyes were closed, her lips were blue, her skin was white and her hair was lank. But she still looked beautiful.

'She wouldn't have suffered too much...with the shock of the water...she would have begun to lose consciousness almost immediately.' Jameson could hear the doctor's voice mumbling in a deep monotonous drone off in some other part of his head. He wasn't processing the words; he was too lost in his anguish.

My poor, sweet beautiful Sarah. What have they done?

'Will, I'm so sorry. You must have been close, working together for so long.'

It was Appel; Jameson looked at him hard.

This was no fucking accident.

'I think she was murdered.'

Appel looked surprised. 'Most likely an accident. She must have leant over the rails too far. It's rough out there.'

'She was the most careful person I knew and never took risks.'

'The ship can pitch over at steep angles without warning. If she was on the edge...'

'Christ, she even hated going to the edge of the ice. She'd never have done that.'

'We live in strange times Will, but really...who would want her dead?' He put his hand on Jameson's shoulder.

'Tom and maybe Jez too. They must have found out she was going to help me. Perhaps they tried to persuade her not to and she refused. Christ, I don't know.' Jameson was starting to lose control. The strain of the last couple of days had tipped him over and he wanted to kick back. Sarah hadn't done anything wrong, and now she was dead. *Someone was going to pay.*

'I'm going to kick the truth out of them.'

'No,' replied Appel firmly. 'We go in the lifeboat tonight. Until then, you stay in your cabin and out of sight. I will have Waites and Beckley watched.' He patted Jameson's shoulder reassuringly. 'Okay?'

Jameson looked past him but nodded his assent. 'Could you leave me for a few minutes please Captain?'

Appel left the room, and Jameson looked down at the woman he had been falling in love with.

'I'm so sorry Sarah. Sorry I picked you for this mission. Sorry I couldn't save you. Sorry that your brilliant life had to end here... in this godforsaken place.'

Jameson was crying now as he gently touched her forehead. 'I'm not sorry that I met you. Not sorry that your light shone on me. Not sorry that I was the last person to make love to you.'

He gently placed the sheet over her face. 'I will find who did this and make them pay. I will make sure your work finds an audience and that people remember Sarah Trevallion.'

For the rest of the day Jameson stewed in his room, vowing that he would take vengeance on Sarah's killers. He tried to rest, knowing that the next few days would be exhausting; all he could do was lie on his small lumpy bed and worry.

Worry for him used to be about simple things. Can I pay the mortgage? Does my wife still love me? What will the kids do when they leave home? What's for tea tonight? Now worry was about life or death. Will I get caught? Will they execute me? Will my wife be killed? Has she been executed already? Will Jason and Bella survive this madness? Did they get the memory stick from Sarah?

It was approaching midnight when Jameson felt the ship slowing and there was a knock on his cabin door. Before he could open it, Waites entered, pointing a pistol directly at his face.

'Going somewhere?'

He thought about pushing Waites aside, but Beckley was standing in the doorway, holding a heavy monkey wrench. 'Sit down Will.'

Jameson hesitated for a few moments, weighing up his chances of escape, then sat down on the bed.

Waites smiled. 'Good man.'

'Tom, why are you doing this? This won't work, millions will die for nothing.' He looked in Waites's eyes, searching for any flicker of anxiety, searching for a corner of the young man's psyche that may harbour doubts.

'Reboot have achieved more in one year than you boomers achieved in a lifetime. I'm just helping them to keep up the good work,' Waites sneered.

'Look, I'm not saying that some of their ideas aren't valid.'

'Valid? They are building a beautiful new world,' Beckley replied. Emboldened by Jameson's seeming capitulation, he stepped into the room, tapping the wrench against the palm of his hand.

'A new world built on the genocide of an entire generation, how can that be justified?' Jameson argued.

'I grant you it will make interesting reading in the history book.' Beckley laughed. 'But people will see that what we did was necessary. The price paid by a few to guarantee a future for the many.'

'Catchy. Joseph Goebbels would have approved.' Jameson could see that comment stung Beckley and Waites. The three of them spent hours talking about the tyranny of the Nazis and had all agreed they were the epitome of evil.

'We know you've totalled your laptop, so now we've got to beat the data out of you.' Waites pressed his gun against Jameson's forehead.

'Did you beat that information out of Sarah? If you didn't have that gun, I'd rip your head off.'

'That had nothing to do with us,' protested Waites.

'Lying cunt'.

A familiar voice cut in from behind Beckley.

'They didn't kill her Will...I did.'

22 February 2031, Dallas, USA
Cull Day 11

The clock on the dashboard indicated it was just ten o'clock in the morning, yet the sun had already reached a high point for the day in the milky-blue Texas sky.

Police trooper Ben Norton chatted amiably to his patrol buddy, bespectacled, auburn-haired Ted Grimes as they drove up the pristine palm tree-lined boulevard. The road was marble smooth and three-car wide, bordered on either side by generous grass verges, high whitewashed boundary walls and electronic security gates. The huge houses they protected were barely visible behind them.

The dazzling light of the day amplified the vivid lime green of the tightly cut Bermuda lawns, the burnt terracotta of the flawless tiled roofs, the rippling azure of the bug cleaned swimming pools and the blue-white smiles of the fussing, territorial Mexican housemaids.

'It's like Million Dollar Listing, but on steroids,' remarked Norton. 'This truly is the land of the American dream. There can't be a house worth less than five million bucks.'

'Well outta salary range of a Texas lawman, for sure,' Grimes replied in his home-grown Texan drawl.

'Invested in a couple a Powerball tickets last night. I could be looking at buying some real estate up here by the weekend.' Norton laughed to himself. The most he'd ever won from any Lottery was twenty dollars.

Grimes moved over to the middle of the road as a water sprinkler burst into life and sprayed the windscreen. 'Mary, me and the kids wouldn't live up here, even if we had the money,' he said. 'It's all phoney. They spend half their time chasing eternal youth with new faces, tits and teeth and the other half worrying themselves into an early grave.'

Norton smiled ruefully as he thought of his own wife. 'That's not how it is for my Abigail. She'd love it up here breathing in all this money. Showing off the house, throwing dinner parties and stuff. Even the sight of gold gets her horny.'

'Glad she's not with us now then,' replied Grimes.

He slowed as a low-slung, gold-coloured Lamborghini pulled out of a drive on their right. The driver, a balding overweight man and his blonde, plump-lipped, much younger passenger gave their tinted windowed black Dodge Charger an anxious look.

'They don't take the sight of us crawling around too kindly up here,' commented Grimes. 'This Reboot thing's got the neighbourhood spooked; must be a few more freaked out people than usual behind these walls.'

'Guess that'll go for the guy we have to pick up too,' replied Norton grimly.

Norton had been an officer in Dallas for five years, but his patch had always been downtown. He'd never been called up to the rarefied heights of the Texas elite, up to the Southlake area and into Continental Boulevard where the high achievers lived. Not that he was worried; nothing much worried him.

Benjamin Edward Theodore Norton was a big man in every sense – square jawed, dark-haired, fearless, honest, and a born leader. He had commendations for bravery, and the previous year won the Medal of Valour, the department's highest award for disarming a drug-fuelled gunman. Standing six feet five inches, weighing two hundred and eighty pounds, he could have played professional football for the Dallas Cowboys but had chosen a police career instead. 'Football was a college pursuit. Law and order was for grown-ups,' Norton had told his proud parents.

In his dark Texan tan uniform, bulletproof vest and with his nine-millimetre handgun, he looked formidable. Wearing his cream Resistol Western style hat and sporting a Texas trooper regulation haircut, tapered at the neck, trimmed off at the ears above the collar, he looked immaculate too.

This suited Norton just fine, because the job they had been given was high profile. He wanted to look his best.

To the experienced trooper, the task itself seemed straightforward: Go to the house of ex-chief of staff of the White House, Daryl Aikman. Read him his rights. Put him in the car. Transport him to Police Department Headquarters in downtown Dallas. Hand him over at the desk. Mission completed.

What Norton didn't know was that theirs was one of hundreds of similar tasks ordered by Reboot that day, all with the objective of arresting prominent individuals who had 'in deed or word increased the impact of human-caused climate change'. TV stations across the world had been given prior notice of the arrests and were preparing to broadcast the seizures of other corporate leaders, politicians, journalists and scientists, a list that read like a rogues' gallery of climate villainy. People such as Michael K. Wittman, ex-CEO of Unity Fuels, a company responsible for more carbon emissions than any other private entity.

Lynn Steinberg, executive director of Saudi Aramco, the world's largest oil exporter, and responsible for five per cent of all carbon pumped into the atmosphere since 1965.

Ken Toleman, owner of the Alaska Delta Pipeline. His pipelines leaked more than five thousand gallons of oil into the grasslands of the Katmai Preserve.

Brian Livermore, former minister and founder of a climate change denial group that promoted junk science and fracking.

Edgar Begley, CEO of Hydra, who had led the charge for fracking in the UK. The firm's first efforts caused two earthquakes.

Stig Brandt, the EU climate commissioner and former oil mogul. Records showed that eighty per cent of his meetings were with business lobbyists and just one per cent with renewable energy companies.

Aikman was on the list because he had run Ipcress Gas during the seventies and eighties, when under his leadership it had become the most polluting oil firm in the world. Ipcress had spent millions funding climate denial groups, despite its own scientific research, revealing the real dangers and causes of global warming as early as 1974.

Norton and Grimes had been given the low-down on the seventy-one-year-old 'climate criminal' they were to bring in, along with details of Aikman's property at a briefing two hours earlier. They were pleased to hear that Aikman was normally a calm rational man, and although his arrest might come as a shock, they should expect him to come quietly. In case of trouble, there would be a helicopter in attendance overhead. The house itself was big, over sixteen-thousand square feet, sitting in two acres of garden. Aikman and his wife, Dolly, had bought it from baseball star Jackson Wilson two years earlier; the police planners had used the agent's details from the sale to work out the layout of the rooms and any potential escape routes.

'It's got a spa wing, games room, cinema, wine cellar, gym and an indoor batting cage. If Aikman does want to hide, he's got plenty of places to do it,' Norton's boss, Captain Ted Jackson, had told them.

Now as they cruised up the hill, passed the gated entrance to the exclusive Timarron Country Club and turned into Continental Boulevard, Norton and Grimes knew this wasn't going to be the usual quiet house arrest.

Lining the road on both sides were dozens of TV and radio broadcast trailers. Armies of technicians in overalls scurried around frantically, setting up satellite dishes, laying cables, checking sound and signal levels. Around them in the industrious mayhem, station correspondents in two-thousand-dollar suits were being briefed, reading scripts, recording reports or having make-up applied. Two mobile fast-food vans looked to be doing good business, one in cheeseburgers, the other in Texas corn dogs. Further ahead, an agitated scrum of journalists, protesters and interested bystanders had gathered at the entrance gates to Aikman's home. They jockeyed for the best view as they waited for the Continental Boulevard showdown to kick off.

As Norton and Grimes slowly approached, everyone began to focus their attention and cameras on them. Reporters approached the squad car, microphones outstretched. Grimes tensed at the sight.

'Jeezus. What do we do, Ben?'

'Keep driving slow. They'll get out of the way. Remember, we don't speak to anyone unless it's to give a direct instruction not to impede our job.'

The reporters banged on the car calling on them to stop and give an interview. Norton and Grimes kept their windows firmly shut. Finally, they reached the mansion's gates. To Norton's surprise, he found they were open. He thought for a couple of moments, then opened his door, climbed onto the bonnet and stretched up to his full height.

'Listen up, y'all.' The scrum continued to bellow up at him demanding answers, someone began tugging at his trouser leg.

'I said shut the hell up!'

His booming voice did the trick. Everyone fell silent at the sight of this giant towering above them.

'Look. I know you've got a job to do – so have we. We're here to take Aikman down to Central without any dramas. He will not. Repeat not. Be stopping for interviews.' Norton stared down at the tightly bunched gaggle of reporters and camera operators, all anxious to make the most of the moment.

'No one must come through these gates. If you do, we'll take you in as well.'

With that, he jumped down, pushed a cameraman out of the way and got back into the squad car just as the next volley of questions flew after him.

As he closed the door to shut out their pleading, Trooper Norton's world went weird.

Suddenly, the windshield shattered with a brutal cracking thud. As if lifted by a giant unseen hand, the car jumped and lurched backwards, throwing Norton up into the roof. Slamming back down into his seat, he bit through his tongue, instantly tasting blood. The car was vibrating, screaming, trying to tear itself apart, moving in reverse. To his left, a head struck the side window, leaving a smudge of grey gore. People were running in all directions, bent over, seeking safety, faces contorted with fear and panic. Although they were screaming, to Norton the shouts were

196

muted, faint.

What the hell just happened?

Still dazed, he cautiously put his hand up to his face, apprehensive about what he might feel.

Nose busted for sure, probably caused by the dashboard airbag.

His shoulder throbbed, but he could still move his arm.

Good no broken bones there.

He picked up the radio microphone, but it was shattered and useless. As he sat waiting for his training to tell him what to do, oily smoke started to billow into the car.

Shit. Have to move. Fast.

'Ted, we're on fire. Gotta go.'

Norton looked across at Grimes and recoiled at the sight. His long-time partner's face was virtually gone beneath the nose. His chest heaving in short shallow breaths as he strained to take in air through the ruined pulp that had been his mouth and jawbone. Blood bubbled and gurgled in his windpipe. He was quietly sobbing.

Numb with shock, Norton tried to open his door, it wouldn't budge. Bracing his powerful frame against the back of his twisted seat, he pushed with his legs and felt it move. The smoke was thickening and he felt himself starting to panic. He could hear Grimes trying to suck in air and retching. Bringing his knees up to his chin, he kicked against the door panel as hard as he could. Once, twice three times. With a wrench of tortured metal, the door opened a couple of inches allowing the smoke to dissipate a little. With one more heavy kick, the door finally opened enough for the giant trooper to squeeze through and Norton started to crawl around to the other side of the car. Suddenly, he was aware of objects cutting through the air all around him, some striking the car, causing it to shake.

Bastard's still firing at us.

Staying low, he reached up to the driver's door, immediately attracting another volley of fire. Crouching down, he could see that the smoke was coming from grass that had been set alight around the car. Wondering how he might get into the car's trunk to retrieve the extinguisher, he heard a whoosh and it started to rain.

Water? What the fuck?

The sprinkler system on the verge had decided to activate; for three minutes it soaked him, the car, and the smouldering grass under gallons of water.

Seeing that the immediate danger from the fire was over, Norton reckoned if he was going to save his buddy, he would have to draw the gunman's attention away from the squad car. Despite the confusion and his terrible wounds, after the initial attack, Grimes had somehow managed to reverse the charger across the road from the house and into an adjacent wall, but it was still clearly in the gunman's line of sight.

Norton lay dripping on the grass, surveying the carnage. Several people were sprawled out in the road ahead of him. At least six clearly dead, many others wounded, crying out for help. Three cars blazed and a cluster of shattered palm trees had fallen across the road. Those who had escaped the first attack sheltered behind and under vehicles that lined the road, too frightened to move. Incredibly one cameraman stood on the top of his van still trying to film the chaos. Norton looked to the sky, he couldn't see or hear the helicopter, maybe that had been hit too.

The wall that bordered Aikman's property was about ten yards away. It could give him cover from the shooter who obviously had a heavy weapon. Norton would have liked his own semi-automatic, but knew it would be too dangerous to fetch the weapon and its ammunition from the car. He'd have to make do with his Smith & Wesson handgun and the eighteen bullets in his belt.

The familiar sound of an M16 rifle sounded from behind the

wall, like fireworks but not as chaotic, just a steady crack-crack-crack. The gunman was still firing in long steady bursts, emptying his magazine out each time.

Whoever this is, is inexperienced or just scared.

Anyone from a gun club or with military or police training would never run his gun out so freely. Norton decided he would make a break for it after the next burst and hoped to time it when the madman was reloading.

Another salvo of bullets whistled overhead and thudded into the trees behind him. Then the firing stopped, and he was on his feet, sprinting – running as fast as he had ever done. But to Norton it still felt like slow motion. His legs were heavy, and the dense grass sucked like treacle on his boots. For every step he took, the wall seemed to move another two steps further away, like a nightmare. Something clawed at his ankle – he kicked it away. A moan of pain. His head was spinning. He felt nausea, then blessed relief. Heart pounding, and gasping for air, somehow he had reached the safety of the wall. His sprint had not gone unnoticed. A sweeping arc of heavy-calibre bullets chewed the air above him, tearing off fist-sized chunks of plaster, showering him in dry, choking cement dust. More bullets hit the bodies on the road, causing them to jerk. Mincing them into ever more grotesque mangles of limbs, flesh and shredded clothes.

Sick shit.

Realising he was safe under the shelter of the wall, Norton edged towards the entrance to the property, crawling on his belly. Reaching the first gate pillar, he stopped to consider his next move. Just inside the entrance to his right, he spied a mature cedar ten yards away which would provide his next point of cover. Crouching low on all fours, keeping the tree between himself and the house, he covered the distance without drawing any further fire. His broken nose had gummed up with dried blood and his breathing was becoming laboured. As he sat panting on the grass, he looked around to see where he might go next.

The house was still fifty yards away. At around half that distance, he noticed the next worthwhile piece of cover, a small red-brick building with a blue-tiled roof. Probably the pool's pump house, thought Norton. The ground to get there had no trees or shrubs to obscure his movements. Anxiously, he strained his eyes to see where the gunman was firing from. The front of the building had a first-floor balcony which ran along most of its length. Norton discerned a shape of a man moving at the far end of it.

Young guy, no more than thirty years old. Dark hair, white Caucasian.

He considered shooting, but knew the range was too great. He was also still shaking too much from the shock and exertion of the previous ten minutes to fire straight.

So he decided to wait for a couple of minutes, and as he sat there on the grass, he heard a distinctive sound.

Chuff-chuff-chuff. Chuff-chuff-chuff. Chuff-chuff-chuff.

That is beautiful.

It was the unmistakeable sound of his eye in the sky. The helicopter hadn't been hit after all. Through the tree canopy to the north, Norton could see it approaching about five hundred yards up, on a line directly above the entrance gates. The next instant, more gunfire erupted from the house as the shooter turned his attention to this new threat. He knew this could be his opportunity.

Taking his gun out of its holster, he checked the magazine, flicked off the safety and got to his feet. Within a moment he was in the open and hurtling over the ground. Norton felt exposed and vulnerable on this sunlit patch of Texas – everything was too bright, too sharp, too dangerous. Surely the gunman must see him, but he was still alive, still gasping, still running. Perhaps he was too busy trying to bring down the chopper. The pump house was rushing up to him, almost close enough to touch. It looked welcoming – safe. He was going to make it. Norton was no more than two paces away from sanctuary when the air was sucked from his lungs and he was sent airborne along with the earth around him and under him in a rush of superheated gas.

Whooooah.

He fell, deafened and winded against the pump-house door, his arm trapped under his body. As he lay there, Norton lifted his head to try to orientate himself and felt the ground begin to shake. His vision was hazy but he was still aware of a blur of dark shapes thundering past him, and he knew everything would be OK.

He rolled over and wearily rested his head down on the thick, soft, cushioning short-cut Bermuda grass that normally looked so good up here on Continental Boulevard, and shut his eyes.

'That crazy bastard. That stupid crazy bastard.'

Norton was lying on the stretcher in the back of the ambulance, a drip hooked up into each arm. Captain Ted Jackson had just been told what had happened.

Aikman's youngest son, Billy Joe, had visited the house the previous night and been told about the fate that awaited his father. In a drunken rage of indignation and madness at the 'affront to the family's good name', he had shot his parents and vowed revenge on the authorities.

Arming himself with an arsenal of weapons, including a World War Two bazooka which had come close to killing Norton, he had turned the road outside into a killing zone. The Texas National Guard had been called in and stormed the house with their armoured trucks. Seeing the weight of forces ranged against him, Aikman Junior had surrendered. Now he would be charged with the murder of nine people, including Trooper Ted Grimes.

'I hope not all these goddam Reboot seizures are going to be as big a clusterfuck as this one,' remarked Jackson as he stepped down out of the ambulance. 'Sorry about Grimes too, Ben. He was a good man.'

'One of the best, sir,' replied Norton. 'Does his family know?'

'Just off to tell her. Hope I get there before these newshounds do.'

'Anything I can do?' Norton raised his head and winced in pain.

'You get some rest and tell them to straighten that nose. We want you looking like our poster boy again. There'll be another medal coming your way after this shitstorm. And that means plenty of pictures in the *Dallas Morning News*.'

Norton lay back and felt his twisted nose.

Million Dollar Listing never had days like this, he thought.

3 May 2031, Western Sudan
Cull Day 81

Ibrahim Abdalla was tired. Tired of working this dusty, infertile soil under a pitiless, baking sun. Of patching the dam and watching it collapse. Of digging irrigation ditches all day and seeing them fill again with sand overnight. Most of all, he was tired of waiting for the rains to fall. His back and arms ached, his hands were bloody and raw, and he was hungry. He was thirty-five but felt twice that. And in North Darfur, where a man can only expect to live sixty-three years, that was troubling.

But even that wasn't the worst of it for Ibrahim because today, as he stood with his eldest son, he knew that the pastoralists from Khartoum were coming. Coming to drive them from this place and probably to kill them both.

Six weeks ago, it had been so different for Ibrahim, his wife

Samiya and their six children. They were living happily as part of a thriving community of subsistence farmers near the town of Kusti. They worked productively and grew enough crops to feed the family well, and surplus enough to sell in the town. With the village bordering the abundant clean waters of the White Nile, Ibrahim was even able to establish a stand of acacia trees whose gum bought additional income into the family. Peace, good health, stability. This had been the happy status quo for Ibrahim and his family for the last eight years.

Then one terrible day, the war came.

It was around midnight when Samiya heard what sounded like faraway thunder, just as they were settling to sleep.

'Are the rains coming? It seems very early,' she said to her husband.

'It doesn't sound like the roar that brings the rainfall,' Ibrahim replied. Curious, he pulled on his robe and went outside.

Samiya followed, pushing aside the thin mosquito screen hung above the door.

Walking a few paces from the tent, they both looked towards the north and saw the intermittent white flashes on the horizon. They realised it could only mean one thing – the SLM rebels were attacking Kusti.

Ibrahim knew that the drylands, three hundred miles to the south, offered the best chance of survival. If they kept moving, stayed off the roads and avoided villages, they might reach them within a month. They decided to rest during the day and walk in the cool of the night. Even in the thin shade they could find, the heat was blistering. For extra cover from the midday sun, they spread a ten-foot-square sand coloured tarpaulin over a tree or bush.

One day as they lay underneath the sheet, which bore the logo of the United States Agency for International Development,

Samiya ruefully commented to Ibrahim, 'The children used this as their play thing, now it is saving our lives.'

While Samiya looked after the youngest children and the animals, Ibrahim and their two eldest boys, Suliman and Jamal, scavenged for water and fire fuel. They usually had good success locating water around dried-up riverbeds and groundwater reserves. Scrub and brushwood were much harder to find, too many refugees had passed this way before them.

Keeping constant vigilance meant fractured sleep. Several times they had to move on seeing lights of approaching jeeps or trucks. Packs of wild dogs tracked them constantly too, looking to grab easy food. Through luck and determination, for the first fourteen days the family managed to survive on what they foraged, and the pulses, seeds and fruit they had brought with them. In the third week, the privations began to take their toll.

Their two youngest children had developed diarrhoea and were becoming dehydrated. Eventually they could no longer walk and had to be carried on the donkeys. With no water or food to spare, there was little their parents could do. Worse, along with their obvious weight loss, the children's hair was reddening and growing wispy, signs Ibrahim recognised as the early onset of malnutrition.

On the twenty-eighth day of their ordeal, Ibrahim returned from a long foraging trip to discover his wife crying outside their makeshift shelter. He was almost too afraid to ask the question of her.

'Who is it?'

'Both our little angels. They died within the same hour.'

That night, four-year-old Eli and three-year-old Omar were buried together in a shallow gully under the shade of a palm tree grove.

With heavy hearts the family moved on, travelling quicker,

they covered fifteen miles in the night. The next morning after stopping in an area of low dunes and patchy scrub, Jamal discovered two abandoned mud-and-brush huts. Nearby, his brother found a shallow stream that was almost hidden by the low bushes and young trees that ran along its borders. Tired of travelling and seeing the location had promise, Ibrahim and Samiya decided to try to make this isolated tract in the Sudanese drylands their new home.

As Jamal and his mother made good the huts, Ibrahim and Suliman set to work to clear the land of rocks and encourage the thin soil back to life. The ground had been worked before, and they found sporadic green shoots of sugar millet and sorghum from previous plantings. Their most important task was to re-establish the old irrigation canals to make more of the available water.

Over the following days, to their anguish, the gusting desert winds continually undid their work, but they knew they had to persist with their labours or perish.

They soon found that the scarcity of fertile land brought with it another problem – conflict with local pastoralists who grazed their animals freely across the area. One evening, Ibrahim came across a goatherd who had led his animals onto an area he had laboured hard on for two days. The goats had already destroyed a dam and trampled down most of the carefully laid rows of shallow seed channels.

'What are you doing? Can't you see this land has been cultivated?' Ibrahim raged as he approached the intruder.

The young herder, who looked no older than sixteen, looked at him, first with bemusement and then defiance.

'I have grazed here all my life. It is Allah's desert, not yours.'

Ibrahim was tired and in no mood for the boy's arrogance. 'I have claimed this land for my family. You will not come here again.'

The boy stood his ground and produced a small pearl handled

knife from inside his kaftan. He pointed the blade menacingly towards Ibrahim.

'And…if I do?'

In a blur of movement, Ibrahim had closed the gap between them and kicked the knife from the boy's hand. He retrieved it from the sand and walked over to the nearest goat. Pulling the creatures head back, he drew the razor sharp blade across its taut neck. For a moment, the goat seemed oblivious to the gush of its blood pouring into the sand. Then slowly it sank to its knees, gave a pathetic bleat and rolled over onto its side. As it lay twitching on the sand, Ibrahim turned back to the boy.

'If I see you again, I will do this to all your herd.'

He threw the blade at the boy's feet, who stood open-mouthed.

'By killing my goat, you have condemned your family.'

The boy picked up his knife, threw the dying animal over his shoulders and walked away with the rest of his herd. When he had gone one hundred paces, he stopped and turned back to look at Ibrahim. The blood of the goat had soaked the top half of his kaftan with dark scarlet streaks and was now dripping down his bare legs.

'We will come for you tomorrow,' he shouted angrily, emboldened by the distance between them, he pointed his finger at Ibrahim then up to the sky.

'Say your prayers farmer. You shall meet your God soon.'

Now it was the next day, and Ibrahim waited with his fifteen-year-old son to defend what they had. Together they had knelt on a small rise for hours, squinting at the shimmering horizon, waiting for men with spears to appear.

Ibrahim knew they would have little chance if there were more than four of them. Suliman was a good fighter, strong for a boy of his age, but he had never fought skilled men. If they were lucky, he thought, they might survive the attack and be given time to leave. More likely they would be killed and their bodies left for the night animals. They both knew this, but both father and son were tired of running.

'Perhaps they won't come today,' Suliman said forlornly. 'Perhaps they have forgotten us and won't come at all.'

'They will come. They will want blood for blood. Do not fear. If God is on our side, we will prevail.' Ibrahim doubted his words but wanted to shield his son from imagining the probable outcome. Suliman smiled at his father and continued to sharpen his hunting knife.

'It is their blood that will stain this dirt, Father.'

The sun was starting to dip in the sky when they first noticed the thick dust cloud coming from the west, from the direction of Khartoum. They strained to flesh out the detail of what was causing it.

The portentous cloud grew larger, and as it did, Ibrahim began to despair. A dust storm that dense could only mean one thing – camels, and lots of them. The pastoralists meant business, thought Ibrahim. By tonight they will all be dead.

As they stood side by side on the small rise, Ibrahim grasped his long tamarind-wood hunting spear to him, and Suliman held his long curved knife defiantly across his chest, both trying to look as intimidating as possible.

Soon, they realised that it wasn't camels making the cloud; it was a convoy of large jeeps. Was it the SLM? Had the pastoralists simply hired them to do the job? Would they be cut down in a hail of bullets from a Kalashnikov?

As they watched, several jeeps started to peel away from the convoy to the east and west, all throwing up more towering clouds of dust and sand as they sped to their different destinations.

One jeep kept coming directly towards them. Its diesel

engine could be heard now, deep and rumbling. It was travelling fast, leaping and crashing over the rutted sand roads, jolting its occupants. Ibrahim could make out a heavy-calibre machine gun mounted on a welded frame above the cab. Two years previously in Khartoum, he had seen the damage these devil guns could do when government troops high on drink and drugs had fired into a crowded market for no apparent reason.

But today, no one stood by this gun waiting to shoot, which he thought strange. The vehicle was strange too, painted a canary yellow with the letters RB stencilled in black on its flanks. It was only twenty metres away from them when it came to a juddering stop, throwing up an enormous spray of sand, dust and stones as it did so. For a few anxious moments, it was completely obscured by the choking smog.

Ibrahim grasped his spear tight, and waited. He could feel the blood thumping in his neck, the sweat dripping down his back. He resolved that he was ready to die.

'To God we belong and to God we shall return,' he muttered to himself. He was sad that his sons and daughters would not see more of this life. He felt heartsick that he had not said a goodbye to his beloved Samiya.

Finally, after what seemed an age, the doors of the jeep opened and two men stepped out. Neither was armed. They walked confidently over to the father and son, who waited tensely and climbed up to them. The first man, of about thirty, was a pale European, his skin smothered in white cream. Wearing a long-sleeved green cotton shirt, khaki knee-length shorts, tan desert boots, white baseball cap and mirror aviator sunglasses, he looked disconcertingly other-worldly to Ibrahim and Suliman; his companion much less so.

He looked Sudanese, wearing just a white and blue linen jalabiya robe and a huge grin.

'Ibrahim? Ibrahim Abdalla?'

Ibrahim was stunned that he knew his name.

'I am Abdalla,' he replied. 'Have you come to kill us?'

Two hours later, Ibrahim was still trying to comprehend all that he had been told. He was told that there was to be no fight with the pastoralists from Khartoum this day, because the European and the Sudanese had paid them to go away. He was told that he and his family would be allowed to stay on the land – told that he would be given help to hold back the creeping sands and improve the soil's fertility.

So he had told his wife too, and after reassuring her that the danger had passed, he and Suliman had travelled with the men to their camp situated on the banks of Wadi El Ku. Now as he sat with Suliman in the cool tent, sipping cold melon juice remembering the mixture of relief and anxiety on his wife Samiya's face he waited. Waited with hundreds of other displaced and confused farmers for further explanations from these strange men.

The man in the baseball cap, whose name was Ben, stood on the makeshift stage and spoke to them slowly and with reverence.

'Welcome to you all. We welcome you, the farmers of the new Darfur, of the new Africa. You have endured for too long this civil war and the pain it has caused your families. We are here to help you rise again and bring abundant life back to your lands.'

The farmers, who sat cross-legged on the floor, surveyed him with world weary suspicion. They had been given promises before from both government and rebels. Over time, they were all broken and swept away by guns and greed and lust.

The man whose name was Ben detected their cynicism. He made a signal to someone behind him, and other men came forward and climbed up onto the stage. They came in pairs, each pair carrying a weighty hessian bag between them. Soon, four bags had been dropped onto the wooden floorboards. The man whose name was Ben came forward, walked down the line of bags and sliced through the material of each with a knife. As the contents slithered out, it became clear that each of the bags contained a battered, bloody body, three men and a woman.

Now that he had the farmers' full attention, he went down the line of bodies, pulling up the head of each so they could see. The first body was dressed in a khaki military uniform. The eyes had been gouged out and the throat slashed.

'This dog is Ramadan El Salim, leader of the government-backed Janjaweed. I have to tell you he screamed like a girl before we killed him.' The Janjaweed were feared and hated by all Darfuri men and women, and news of his death brought a cheer.

'We have also killed Amir Bashir, the militia leader. We left his bloated body in the desert.' The farmers were beginning to stand to get a better view.

The man whose name was Sam went next to the twisted corpse of a heavyset man dressed in a grey suit made ragged by bullet holes. 'This is Walaa Bakhet Hamid, prime minister of Sudan, who has been funding the terrorists. We tried to blow him up two years ago in his car, so it was satisfying to catch up with the dog.'

Next to Hamid was the woman, her dress was torn, her bare breasts had been slashed. 'This is his wife, Samir. Her bank account was full of your money. We let the women deal with her.'

The last body was that of a thin Sudanese male. He was naked, hands tied and legs splayed underneath him. He had lost most of the skin from his back. 'This devil is Ahmad Musa, head of the SLM and responsible for hundreds of thousands of deaths. We dragged him all the way from Khartoum.'

The man whose name was Sam smiled and spread his arms in invitation.

'Come and see that these demons are dead. Believe that there is nothing more they can do to hurt you.'

Cautiously, the farmers came to the stage, staring wide-eyed at these people who had terrorised them for so long, scarcely believing that their torment might be over. Some spat on the bodies or struck them with sticks. One man brought in a large rock and started pulverising Musa's head with it.

The man whose name was Sam let them vent their fury. Let them remember this moment so that they might tell others what they saw. Presently, he had the cadavers removed and asked for calm.

'These dogs deserved your anger. Their bodies will be burnt and their souls condemned to eternal torment. We shall never forget what they did, but we must move on and establish a new order. And first we must revitalise the land.'

Ibrahim was as excited as he had ever been and could feel his head swimming. He had expected this to be his last day, but instead had witnessed the death of his country's enemies, and been given a lifeline for his family. The man whose name was Sam continued:

'Farmers of Darfur, you are the future. So you must learn the ways of the new. You will be shown crop spacing, crop diversification and crescent farming. These will seem strange, but will soon become second nature, and by using them you will flourish. You will be given machines that will help you plant seeds deeper, so that rodents can't eat them. You will be shown how to grow peanuts, hibiscus, lentils and watermelons abundantly. We have helped others like you, and like them, in time you can start to help others too.'

Now the Sudanese in the jalabiya robe, whose name was Ameen, began to speak.

'You know better than anyone that without water, nothing is possible. So you must unite with your neighbours to build dams to retain rain when it comes. We must build ways to divert water back to our lands. We must reforest to improve the soil.' He held up a tree sapling.

'First, you will be given three hundred trees to plant and nurture. For this you will be paid.'

Ibrahim suddenly thought this was too good to be true. He stood and interrupted these strange saviours who stood on the stage.

'Who is paying for this? God is great, but even this would be beyond him.'

The man whose name was Sam grinned, got down from the stage and patted Ibrahim on the shoulder.

'You're right Ibrahim Abdalla. This will take much money. But we have persuaded some people with plenty of it to part with some.' Now he became more serious.

'Dramatic changes are happening everywhere and there is to be a great rebalancing of the earth's resources and mankind's use of them. No more will Africa's people pay for the greed of others. In return, the continent must learn to end its own destructive cycle of civil wars, genocide and lawlessness.'

'These things are all I've ever known,' Ibrahim replied. 'Now if you can truly end those evils, my only battle will be with Mother Nature.'

He looked at Suliman, who stood proudly beside him, and smiled. 'And that is one fight I know we can win.'

4 December 2031, The Atlantic Ocean
Cull Day 295

The voice was deep and precise, the accent a mix of Finnish and Spanish. Captain Appel stood in the doorway, dressed in a black jacket and trousers.

'Reboot found out about our plan and arrested Helga. They offered us amnesty if I helped them. I talked to Sarah on the deck. Asked her to join us, but she would not co-operate. She was coming to warn you. I grabbed her and she fell overboard. It was an accident. I'm sorry Will.'

Jameson stood up and tried to lunge at Appel, but Waites and Beckley pushed him back down onto the bed.

'It was no accident, you threw her in the sea.'

Appel shrugged his shoulders. 'What would you have done? As long as I deliver you to Reboot in one piece, they have promised me a place in this new Eden they're creating.'

With Waites and Beckley holding him fast, Appel rolled up Jameson's sleeve and injected something into his arm. Darkness.

His subconscious mind registered a strange noise, but allowed his tired body to sleep on. He woke again, feeling parched and nauseous. Although his vision was foggy, he could make out a small square of light to his right. Engines droned; air whooshed. He was lying on a reclined chair inside a small, enclosed room. The room gently rising and falling.

It took another few minutes before Jameson had pieced the clues together. He was in a plane. He could move his arms freely; he was not tied to the chair.

What's going on?

He looked out of the window. The plane was flying over the sea about thirty-five thousand feet up. This was a commercial flight in a big jet and he was in a first class cabin.

Well, if I'm going to meet my maker, I'm going in style.

He tried to get up, but his legs weren't interested. Gulping down the contents of two small bottles of water, he waited for his strength to return and fell into another deep sleep.

The next time he woke, his vision was still blurred, but he could make out the outline of a face bending over him, really close. He could smell her perfume, her breath. A woman with long auburn hair and deep green eyes.

Smells familiar. Must be dreaming.

'Hello, Will. How are you feeling?'

'Sarah… Am I dead? Is…this the afterlife?'

'No, it's the executive cabin in an RAF Airbus A330. And my name's not Sarah, it's Ellie. I'm looking after you on the flight. Want anything to eat?'

His eyes finally cleared. Ellie had darker skin and her hair was brunette, but her eyes were the same striking green as Trevallion's.

'You look like someone I know...I knew. Where are we flying to?'

'We'll be landing on Ascension Island in forty minutes to refuel, then another eight and half hours to Brize Norton in Oxfordshire.'

'What do you want with me?'

Ellie smiled the shallow professional smile all flight attendants possess. The one they employ to reassure you there really is nothing wrong with the plane.

'I just want you to be comfortable Will. Now, how about some food?'

Jameson was still feeling sick; food was the last thing on his mind.

'Could you tell whoever is interested out there, that I'd appreciate a chat.'

She shook her head. 'Can't do that. I believe the people we're picking up on Ascension are the ones who are really anxious to talk to you. Just knock if you change your mind about food.'

After replacing the two water bottles, she left and locked the door.

Christ, what have I got caught up in?

Eventually the plane began to lose height. Jameson looked down at the vast expanse of the mid-Atlantic and saw a tiny dot of land in the distance.

Jameson had spent a day on Ascension Island a few years ago and discovered just what a curiosity it was. A tiny scrap of the British empire, about the size of Guernsey, it lay marooned in the tropical mid-Atlantic halfway between Brazil and Africa. Speaking to locals, he had learnt that bizarrely, officially nobody is actually 'from Ascension'. In 2006, as part of its plan to reduce its commitment to the island, the UK Government denied the right of abode, effectively turning Ascension's eight hundred citizens, into temporary visitors. Anyone who retired, or reached the age of eighteen without a job, had to leave.

As they circled the island, Jameson could see the airport which dominated its south-west corner. The runway was run by the US Air Force who had built it to accommodate the Space Shuttle; it used to be the longest in the world.

After a turbulent landing, the plane taxied to a berth near the small terminal building, and a fuel tanker quickly came alongside. Typically for Ascension, even though they had landed in sunshine, it was now raining hard.

When refuelling had finished, a jeep with US Air Force markings pulled up, carrying two well-built men and a woman in military uniform. They were greeted by a man in civilian clothes who briskly led them up into the plane – within minutes they were airborne. Looking down at Ascension, Jameson could see that most of the trees on the summits of its highest hills had been cleared to make way for aerials and satellite dishes. It was another reminder that not even in this remotest of places could nature escape a bludgeoning from humans.

As the plane soared above the clouds, so did his thoughts.

Perhaps Reboot had changed direction.

Perhaps they want me to help them with manufacturing the CDT-8.

Need to persuade Reboot that the gel still needed improvement and I'm the only person who can complete the work.

If I can, I have a chance.

One thing was clear to him, the knowledge locked in his head was the only thing keeping him alive. If they had that, then Waites could complete the rest of the work. He knew how to apply the gel and how much was needed. He could construct the hardware to make it all happen. If they tried beating the knowledge out of him, he knew he would cave-in sooner or later. And if he did, he would be as good as dead.

Feeling his panic rising, he looked around the cabin for a weapon. Perhaps with a knife he could escape, but there were no knives or sharp objects or anything that could intimidate an inattentive guard. Unless he could smother them with the tissues on the small table or knock them out with a small plastic water bottle. He laughed.

It's so hopeless it's funny. So funny I have to take a piss.

He stood and knocked hard on the door.

'Hey, out there. I need the toilet.' No response.

'OK, I'll do it on the floor.'

The bolt slid across and the door slowly opened.

A six-and-a-half-foot tall, man mountain dressed in a dull grey suit opened the door.

'You must be the evil boss's henchman.'

'You can use this.' The man's ruddy pockmarked face did not betray a flicker of connection, his black eyes remained dead. He simply pointed to a toilet in the walkway, where the door had been removed.

'Lucky for you, I don't need a crap then.'

A curtain was spread across the central aisle of the plane, separating first class from the rest. Through a small gap, Jameson could see that the plane was empty apart from a group sitting together near the middle. They included the three who boarded at Ascension and two others, one of whom he recognised as Appel. They were clearly not interested in talking to him while he was on the plane.

As he stood in the toilet, he caught sight of his face in the harsh light of the small mirror. His eyes were bloodshot and the bags underneath puffy, his skin a disconcerting pale yellow.

So much for the beneficial effects of having lots of sleep.

Despite his appearance, Jameson was becoming more sanguine about his immediate fate and resolved to conserve energy for the harder days that obviously lay ahead. On his way back to the cabin, he noticed Ellie making coffee in the kitchen galley.

'Could eat some food now, if you have any.'

'We've got a plane full on this trip,' she replied jovially. 'Chicken Kiev, meatballs or prawn salad?'

'I'll have the chicken.'

'White wine with that? I've got Sancerre.'

'Please. Probably won't get another for a while.'

Ten minutes later, the food arrived. Ellie laid it on the table and poured the wine.

'Join me in a glass?' Jameson enquired, eager to extract any information she might have.

'Sure. Not doing much out there.' She poured herself a glass and sat down. 'But don't ask me where you're going when you leave the plane. I haven't been told anything.'

'What have you been told?'

'That Reboot have chartered the plane to bring home an important person – which I assume is you.'

'That it?'

'I've been told not to tell anyone of course. Reboot like their secrets. Once you're taken away at Brize Norton, I forget you.'

Jameson felt that she was telling the truth, a view clouded by the fact he was warming to her. She was probably the last woman he would ever enjoy small talk with.

'This seems a pretty boring flight. Why did you choose it?'

She looked out of the window. It was early evening and the light was fading, but Jameson detected a sadness in her face. 'I was born on Ascension, flying over these waters is natural for me. My parents were originally from St Helena and settled on Ascension thirty years ago after being made promises by the

British Government. They were told the island would be opened up to tourism, and investment put in place to make it an attractive holiday destination. They promised more roads, hotels, shops, and even a casino. So my mother and father came over and started a small café and restaurant near the waterfront.'

'What happened?'

'There was no investment.' She sighed. 'The plans were put in but the Americans always made things too difficult. They didn't really want more people on Ascension. They just wanted an airfield and a place to put their satellites.'

'Where are your parents now?'

'Back on St Helena.' The airport was finally built there, and they felt that returning would offer them a better life.'

'They must have felt frustrated.'

'To put it mildly.' She rolled her eyes again and gave a rueful smile. 'It was especially hard because they had put everything into Ascension and couldn't make a penny back from their labours. They had to work their passage on the boat and then fall on the mercy of relatives in Jamestown when they returned.'

'Sounds hard.'

'Sixty-four is no age to be homeless.' She took another drink of her wine.

'I heard they called the St Helena airport "the most useless in the world".' Jameson was warming to this woman and wanted to hang on to her company.

She laughed bitterly. 'When I heard they were going to build the airfield on the east of the island, I thought it was a crazy idea. The wind generally comes in hardest there, the terrain is mountainous with deep valleys, but for whatever reason, that is what they decided. It meant levelling the landscape with millions of tons of rock to construct the runway. It took five years and a lot of tax payers' money.' She finished her wine and poured another.

'Two hundred and eighty-five million pounds, I heard.'

'More – there was corruption. Officials needed paying off too.'

'But for all that, it still didn't give St Helena an airport.'

'Building on that cliff meant the wind direction and speed were unpredictable. You know, the first jet took three attempts to land because of wind shear. The pilot had to sit alone with strong coffee and cigarettes for an hour after landing to settle himself. So the opening was put on hold until they found an airline prepared to make the trip. But the only plane they could use was not big enough to bring the three hundred and twenty people per flight the island wanted, just seventy. So you see once again my parents were sold a fantasy.' She looked out of the window again. Jameson could see tears welling in her eyes, but not enough to fall on her face.

'I'm sorry, Ellie.' It was a sad story, but he was hardly in a position to help. 'What have Reboot said about the island and its population?'

'Nothing. I assume they have too much on their plate to worry about four and a half thousand people stuck in the middle of the South Atlantic. My father has said that if the same rule did apply to the baby boomers there, it would reduce the numbers on St Helena by fifty per cent.'

'Including your parents?'

'No, they have escaped by three years – the one bit of luck they have had.'

'What do you think about what Reboot are doing?' He could sense she had doubts.

'If something radical isn't done, then it is obvious we have only a limited time left on this planet.'

'I sense there is a "but" coming.'

'But what they do is carried out with so little compassion and has no regard for love. The love we have for our family and for our friends. After all, isn't love the most precious thing our species has?' She impulsively put her hand on his.

'Yes of course,' Jameson replied.

'We are hardwired to protect those we love with our lives. To consider a rational debate about killing them so we can live better without them is absurd. After all, life isn't about simply surviving, is it Mr Jameson?'

She knows my name.

Knowing she had revealed too much she lifted her hand away.

'Better tidy up. We arrive in a couple of hours.'

'Sorry, I didn't mean to…'

She cleared the table without saying another word. Jameson cursed himself; he was enjoying the company of this articulate, intelligent woman and it was diverting him from his own dire situation. She paused by the door.

'It was nice to meet you. I am moving back to St Helena. You should visit, but I warn you, the roads are very steep and chicken is very expensive.'

'Thanks. I will if I get out of this, and I'll bring the family.'

'I hope they treat you well, although you look of an age that means they possibly won't.' She smiled one last professional smile, and then Ellie the flight attendant was gone forever.

He slept fitfully as the plane droned on through the night. Eventually the guard came in and put heavy cuffs on his wrists.

'We'll be landing in twenty minutes. Just relax and everything will be cool.'

19 June 2031, Cheltenham, England
Cull Day 128

'Before they passed the One for One decree, this facility was only operating at thirty per cent capacity. Now we're operating three shifts and getting through two thousand five hundred BBs a day. Minimum. We're very happy.'

Heidi Markram casually flicked her long brown hair back and smiled at the camera, holding the pose.

'Just stay there for two more seconds. Great, and that's a wrap Heidi.' Freelance film director Mark Lomas gave an exaggerated thumbs up from behind his camera.

'Thank goodness for that, my jaw was beginning to ache. I think we've earned a drink Mister Lomas.'

'The Reboot board should be happy with the film, and especially about how things are going here,' remarked Lomas as they sat together in the canteen. 'Whoever thought of that One for One scheme is a bloody genius.'

'Been a game changer for us,' Markram replied, as she sipped on her iced tea.

The scheme was the idea of Colonel Paolo Moschin, and was already proving devastatingly effective. After the initial success of the baby boomer cull over its first two months, the numbers coming forward had slowed. Millions of families were now hiding their condemned relatives and it was proving more difficult for the military and the police to hunt them down. So it was decided that a new 'incentive' was required to boost the numbers back up to the desired rate.

It was a simple concept. If a family had boomers who were not accounted for, then the remaining family members had to make up those numbers themselves, one for one. At first, people thought Reboot were bluffing until a series of live public broadcasts showed young men and women being led to their deaths. It had the desired effect – within ten days the flow of boomers was back to normal.

'As I'm here, any chance you could give me a tour of the place before I head off?' asked Lomas. He had heard about the dissolution centre which had been established in his hometown of Cheltenham, and how they were putting to death thousands of baby boomers in a painless 'almost serene' way.

His own mother, Magda, had been given up four weeks previously to another facility in the county and he had not been allowed to enter the building with her. They had said their goodbyes in a cold, sterile registration room in the car park. Resigned to her fate, she was composed and calm, unlike her son. He had held her tight to him, sobbing uncontrollably, not wanting to let her go. Gently pulling herself free, she had wiped his tears and kissed him on the forehead. Walking away, just as she was about to go through the door, she had looked back at her son for the last time, and said five words he would remember forever: 'See you when it rains.'

After her execution, there was no grave or plaque to commemorate her passing; all that Lomas and his family had received was a certificate sent that night by email. It bore the subject title: 'Given to the Earth 3,342,411' and simply recorded her name, place of birth, birth and death dates. He had cried for two days and hadn't thought about her since, until this moment. A tour of this place might help him understand what she would have seen and possibly felt in her last moments on earth.

Markram regarded the young bearded film director carefully. Tours were usually forbidden. Reboot were anxious about keeping their methods covert, but things were going well. Perhaps he might spread some positive news about how well her operation was run. It might filter through to her superiors at Reboot and could help her case in being given one of the UK's 'super centres' to manage. She knew one site in the Lake District could handle at least ten thousand boomers a day. Markram liked big numbers; it meant power and status. Just as in the old world, these things were worth having.

She nodded. 'But do not give details about what you saw here. Understand?'

'You can trust me.'

Markram led Lomas out of the canteen. 'Follow closely. Don't speak to anyone.'

The building had previously been home to the town's grammar school, one of the highest-achieving academies in the country. Now the pupils were gone and it had been repurposed as a killing station; the only bright young things walking the corridors this day were white-coated technicians and doctors.

They passed through a glass-covered walkway guarded by heavily armed, stone-faced soldiers and into a large sunlit hall.

'The boomer intake are brought in here alone. All relatives

have to say goodbye in the registration rooms.' Markram pointed outside to a row of wooden huts, each with a different large letter painted on its door. Lomas recognised them from his own traumatic experience with his mother.

'They are given five minutes together before we separate them. That can be tricky sometimes.' Markram rolled her eyes knowingly.

Lomas was beginning to be irritated by this woman, talking about people as if they were cattle and the building simply an abattoir. Working in this house of killing had totally inured her to the tragedy of the situation.

Lost in his thoughts, he followed Markram down a starkly lit corridor. The pale-blue walls were free of adornment except for a single small wooden cross halfway along its length. To Lomas, this nod to religion seemed incongruous in this house of pitiless killing.

Punching in a six-digit code, Markram led him through a heavy security door and into a circular reception area from which six more corridors led off in different directions. The air had a slightly antiseptic odour, reminding Lomas of the care home his father had died in. A strikingly beautiful woman with short black hair, and dressed in blue nurse's scrubs, stood behind a high desk in the centre. She looked up from her work and nodded in recognition at her boss. Markram responded with a thin smile before signing the visitor book.

'Morning, Elaine. Any dramas?'

'Just two screamers, Miss Markram. Both men, again. A shame because everyone else was very together. Spooked the whole group.' Elaine spoke in a clipped Cheltenham Ladies' College accent.

'We never have members of the same family together, Mr Lomas; it's a recipe for hysterics. When they get to this part of the building, they are all strangers.' Lomas again noticed the lack of compassion in her voice.

'Anyone still in the sedation rooms?'

'The last went through ten minutes ago, Miss Markram.'

'Shame. I would like to have shown our guest the procedure.'

Markram walked down the first corridor to their right and up to the first door. Peering through the reinforced glass window for a moment, she beckoned Lomas over to join her. The room was no larger than six-foot square with grey walls and no outside windows. Inside were two chairs, one fixed to the floor and fitted with wrist and ankle restraining straps. In the corner, stood a tall grey cabinet with both its doors open. Lomas could see that the boxes on its shelves all contained syringes.

'This is the sedation room. As you can imagine, once they've been through here it starts to calm down.' Markram smiled. Lomas felt nauseous as he imagined his mother being brought to a place like this.

Let me show you the really impressive part of the operation.'

Markram obviously enjoyed showing off the facility that she managed with such forensic efficiency. She walked briskly along the passageway humming to herself and stopped outside a set of large metal doors. Showing her pass to another straight-backed soldier, he unlocked one of them with a card key and she walked through.

This room was high-ceilinged and dominated by four large spherical tanks in its centre, rubberised pipes connected them all together. There was a gentle hissing noise as the pressure between each tank was constantly adjusted by an engineer sitting in an enclosed Perspex box next to them. He was transfixed by the changing numbers on the screen above him and seemed unaware of their presence.

'This is Cheltenham's pride and joy, Mr Lomas. Our very own PSA nitrogen generator plant, one of only three in the whole country. It allows production of high-purity nitrogen from air, up to 99.9995 per cent nitrogen. It works by the fractional distillation of liquid air which is held in here.'

She tapped one of the tanks, which made the engineer look up and give her a disapproving look.

'Nitrogen gas escaping from the liquid air is then captured in this tank, cooled, and then liquefied once more in this one. And then *voila*, it is ready to use.' She spread her arms in salute of this wonder of biochemical engineering.

'Normal membrane systems can't get near it.' She looked at Lomas, expectant of some adulation.

'I've heard about the theory. But what does that actually mean in practice?' was all he could offer in response.

Markram tutted. She disliked speaking to non-engineers.

'Two things. Number one, it means we are totally nitrogen self-sufficient. Number two, the boomers who come here are pretty lucky.'

'How?' Lomas was incredulous anyone could think anyone who came here were fortunate.

'Because they die quicker.' Markram was clearly getting agitated.

'Look, we know nitrogen hypoxia kills everyone eventually. So, as with every other dissolution centre around the world, for us that means putting a group of people in a sealed room and replacing the air inside with nitrogen. The method is normally super quick. Most lose consciousness within twenty seconds and have stopped breathing after another three seconds.' She stuck three fingers up in the air to accentuate the point.

'But our nitrogen is so pure, we're seeing these times almost halve. And because the body can't actually detect a lack of oxygen, it means it doesn't feel like suffocation. It's painless. It doesn't have any environmental impact either. It's the perfect solution.'

Despite Lomas being of the view that this woman was a

psychopath in the perfect job, knowing his mother hadn't suffered was a consolation.

'Why don't you have a go?' Markram enquired.

'A go? Are you mad?'

Markram was amused by his reaction. 'I've had exposure to it. We all have to spend time in the chambers to work here. It helps us understand any…issues. Five seconds is normally enough for me. I didn't have hallucinations, or pain, or confusion. I just felt weird. It wasn't like alcohol or any substance like that.'

'I've read it's not as quick as advertised,' replied Lomas. 'Research says some animals, like cats and dogs, are aware of their impending death before they lose consciousness. Apparently it can take seven minutes to euthanise a pig.'

Markram bridled at the comparison. 'Mr Lomas, we don't deal with animals, we deal with sophisticated, sentient beings. Of course they are well aware of their impending death. But we try to make sure that everything is as calm as possible.' She turned away and headed for the door.

'Aren't you going to show me where the gas is administered?' enquired Lomas, seeing she was eager to close down the conversation and the tour.

'We would need to put airtight suits on. I don't have time,' Markram replied curtly.

When they arrived back at the reception area, it was busy. A group of around fifty boomers were standing together in a registration line, barefooted and wearing pale-blue hospital gowns. Some chatted idly as if waiting to give lunch orders in a café queue, others waited quietly, shoulders hunched, heads down. One or two looked agitated, eyes darting, flinching at every unfamiliar sound. Perhaps these would be the screamers, thought Lomas.

Markram had been called over to the desk, so he went to collect his equipment from her office. He had just finished packing the lights and battery boxes when he heard a faint knock. A kindly looking elderly man was standing at the door. He was naked and holding his blue gown under his arm.

'Can I help you sir?' enquired Lomas.

'Just been to the toilet. Can't find reception.'

'Keep going to your right, it's not far.'

'Messed my gown.' He gave a pathetic whimper, hoping for reassurance he wouldn't be punished.

'Sure, they'll be fine about it.'

'But I won't be fine, will I?' His eyes bulged, as if the realisation of his imminent demise had just hit him. He threw the gown on the floor.

'I don't want to die. I have grandchildren I want to see grow up. We love taking them to school and having them at the weekends. It really helps our daughter out, you see. Perhaps they'll let me out to visit them, when all this nonsense is over?'

Lomas heard a shout and running footsteps from the corridor, causing the man to step inside the office. Two staff members ran past the door, obviously not spotting him. The elderly man waited, then dashed out again in the opposite direction. Lomas watched him lope away, as clumsy as a fleeing chicken. Within seconds he'd been caught by two nurses, each grabbing an arm.

'Come on Peter, let's get back in the line. We'll get you a new gown.' They reassured him as he walked by. The man looked desperately at Lomas, imploring him silently to intervene, to help somehow.

'Don't want to go. Don't…want…to…go…'

He struggled frantically but the women were stronger, and eventually the group disappeared down the corridor. Lomas did not move. He just picked up his camera.

Walking back to the reception area, he looked around for the elderly man. He had gone, led away to his fate, along with the line of new registrations. Within the hour, he and the other boomers would all be dead. Fifty more innocent souls 'given to the earth'.

Markram was still standing by the reception desk, signing paperwork.

'Thanks for the tour. I should have the first edit of your interview ready in the next couple of days.'

Markram looked up with the cool detachment of a very busy person. 'Remember, don't say a word about what you have seen today.'

'Of course.'

Markram put her papers down and looked coldly at Lomas.

'When it comes to execution, Mr Lomas, people need to understand that the death penalty is not a humane act, but this is as humane as it gets.'

Lomas looked at this woman, no older than forty, responsible for eradicating thousands of mothers, fathers, sons, daughters, sisters and brothers every week, yet clearly thinking no more of it than if she was swatting flies.

How does she sleep at night? How can she even feel connected to the human race?

'Have you lost your parents this way?' he asked.

Markram hesitated, taken off guard by the question, but understanding the reason it had been asked. She weighed up the value of telling some lie to cast her in a favourable light, to say her parents had willingly come forward to give their lives for the common good. She chose instead to tell the truth.

'My parents wanted to escape the cull. They begged me to help them, believing because of my position I could do something. Of course, it was precisely because of my position that I couldn't. One night, I drugged them and drove them here myself. They were put to death in this very building six weeks ago.'

'Weren't you upset? Even a little part of you?'

Markram looked down at her paper and signed her name.

'All dreams end. All hearts break. Caring won't change anything. We have to remove millions of people from the planet so it can survive. Surely you appreciate in the final analysis, that's all that matters. I look forward to seeing the film.'

Without saying another word, Lomas walked through the sliding double doors and left the building. As they hissed shut behind him, he took a large gulp of fresh air and immediately felt sick.

4 July 2031, Timbuktu, Mali
Cull Day 143

The man thrust his head into the open car window and smiled broadly. 'How much to have you in my bed all night?' His long Arabic face, deeply lined by the Saharan sun, was framed by a wispy grey flecked beard and a grubby cream head scarf. His left eye an unseeing milky opaque, his mouth host to a confusion of twisted, rotten and gold teeth, his breath a fetid mix of spiced meat and strong tobacco.

Sofia Müller recoiled from the unsolicited barrage on her senses. 'I am married. Here is my wedding ring. Go away, pig.'

The aberration cast her a withering look and spat on the ground as he walked away. 'Only whores travel alone in Mali. Why does your husband allow this, woman?'

Müller had been in Timbuktu just half an hour, but this

was the third proposition she had received. She was tired, dirty and annoyed with the unwanted attention. She was also angry at herself for the catalogue of bad decisions she had made prior to getting here.

She had refused the offer of an armed security guard despite the warnings. She had forgotten to disguise her long blonde hair, and worn a low-cut white T-shirt and denim shorts despite being told to play down her gender. She had insisted on driving a white Land Rover with huge Reboot identifiers all over it despite being told to keep a low profile. Now because of her arrogance, she stood out for all the wrong reasons in a place that was not used to any of those things.

Müller had driven non-stop from Bamako, a dusty and dangerous eighteen- hour journey across lawless desert roads. Earlier in the day, she crossed the Niger by ferry and carefully navigated the last twenty kilometres to the city along a broken paved road.

Despite the privations of her journey, she had made it to the rendezvous point outside the Hotel Bouctou exactly on time. Now to compound her misery, the Reboot representative she had arranged to meet in this city of prowling, predatory men was nowhere to be seen.

'Where is he?' she murmured to herself as she scanned the streets.

The famous Djinguereber Mosque was across the road to her right, and a steady stream of worshippers and tourists passed in and out of the huge building. Built from mud, straw, wood, clay and limestone blocks, Timbuktu's oldest place of worship had endured seven hundred years of blistering temperatures, ferocious sirocco winds and countless wars, yet still it stood and remained an important learning and cultural centre for Muslims.

The sun slowly descended behind the imposing, other-worldly

structure, silhouetting its numerous cone-shaped towers. In the crimson and orange half-light, its high vertical walls studded with bolstering logs looked impregnable, easily strong enough to stand for several centuries more.

Müller saw another man approaching the car from across the road. He was dressed in a Tuareg's yellow kaftan and a blue turban. Warily she leaned out of the window.

'I'm not going to suck your dick, so don't even ask.'

'It had not even crossed my mind, Sofia.'

The man, in his late thirties and the proud owner of a full dark brown beard and perfect white teeth, smiled and leaned on the car. Müller recognised him from the Zoom briefing call they had together four days previously.

'Jacob, you bastard. Where have you been?'

The man bowed theatrically. 'Apologies Frau Müller. I was making sure my people were ready for your visit. I would not have slept well, knowing we might not be prepared.'

Jacob Keita may have been a small man, just five feet tall in his sandals, but he was Reboot's most senior operator in Northwest Africa. Brought up in neighbouring Niger, and university-educated in the capital Niamey, he had been a radical all his life. While still a student, he had led a strike against the general deterioration of learning conditions at the university. He had been arrested and severely beaten by the police for the part he played in the uprising. Now, twenty years later, he was the man responsible for disposing of the bodies of some of those who had tortured him.

'Where am I staying tonight? I really need to wash and sleep,' said Müller.

'Here, of course,' replied Keita, pointing to the Hotel Bouctou. 'By all means use the shower, but do not drink the tap water – just from bottles.'

Müller rolled her eyes. 'If I've learnt anything in this

godforsaken place, it's that.'

'I'll come in and escort you to your room. If you don't want men knocking on your door tonight, it's best we appear as a contented and married couple.'

They collected her bags and walked together into the hotel's shabby central courtyard. Resting against a wall, a diseased and neglected yucca tree drooped sadly in its broken pot. Weeds and grasses grew freely through the cracked paving stones, and four broken chairs lay stacked together in one corner.

'Wait here. I'll check you in.'

As Keita walked off to the reception area, Müller warily tested a plastic chair and sat down at a small wooden table. The sound of scratching drew her attention to the far end of the yard; a rat scurried from an open drain and ran across the tiles before stopping to pick up a piece of discarded melon rind. The thin, mange ridden hotel dog, watched it disappear into a crack in the hotel's wall, before yawning and closing its eyes. Müller cursed her luck. Of all the burial projects she could have been chosen for across the world, why had she got the one in Shithole Central?

As she simmered, she recalled the briefing meeting in Oslo the week before, presided over by Erica Sandstrom and other senior Reboot members.

Sandstrom had introduced the meeting which was being beamed live to over forty-five countries.

'Welcome, everyone. I hope you can all hear me. Please indicate on the chatline if you can't.' Technical hitches in Mexico and Saudi Arabia were quickly remedied, and Sandstrom continued with her presentation.

The first slide was a picture of a simple church burial, black dressed mourners stood around the graveside as a coffin was lowered in.

'As you know, my friends, our carbon footprint doesn't

236

end in the grave. The wood, cushioning and metals used in traditional coffins continue to litter the earth. Thousands of litres of carcinogenic embalming fluids continue to leak into the surrounding soil and water.'

The next slide showed a diagram of a car.

'Difficult to believe perhaps, but even a single cremation uses as much gas and electricity as an eight-hundred-kilometre road trip. So finding an eco-friendly answer for the disposal of two billion large organisms was always going to be a big challenge. Well today, thanks to some remarkable work from our scientists, I can announce that we have chosen three separate burial methods that deliver to our key criteria of being both low energy and high volume.'

On the screen, a hollow plastic model of the number 'ONE' appeared and began to fill with water.

'The first is aquamation, also known as water cremation. Here the body is placed in a stainless-steel vessel filled with a solution of ninety-five per cent water and five per cent potassium hydroxide. Rushing alkaline waters at a temperature of one hundred and seventy-six degrees cause the body to dissolve in about twenty hours. All that's left is the skeleton, which can be ground up into a white powder for recycling as fertiliser. The process emits about a fifth of the carbon dioxide of traditional cremation. In participating countries, we believe we can build five aquamation centres every month. When fully operational, each should be able to process five thousand bodies a day.'

On the screen, a model of the number 'TWO' began to sink into a tank of water as Sandstrom continued.

'The second concept also involves water and has been practised for hundreds of years – sea burial. We will load ships with the bodies, each individually contained in a sealed biodegradable bag. These ships will then be sunk into the deepest parts of the oceans. The first three sites designated are the Mariana Trench in the western Pacific, the Galathea Depth in the Philippine Sea and the Puerto Rico Trench located between the Caribbean Sea and the Atlantic Ocean. There are approximately fifty-three thousand ships in the world's merchant fleets. We aim to commandeer at least one thousand of those for the task. With some of the biggest vessels able to carry over a million cadavers, this method will deliver high volume.'

On the screen, the number 'THREE' rotted into the ground in an animation sequence.

'The third method is recomposing. This is the process of transforming bodies into soil naturally. We have developed this with farmers who have practised livestock composting for decades. We lower the shrouded corpses into a simple recomposing vessel or hole and cover them with fast-acting decomposing agents. Sixty days later, each corpse is transformed into a cubic metre of nutrient rich soil which can be used to enrich the land. These recomposition sites will be constructed in sterile or low-fertility areas such as deserts. I am delighted to say that with this last method, we truly can prove that death can give life.'

Death can give life.

A catchy phrase, thought Müller, but as she waited for the keys to her room in this decrepit, vermin-infested guesthouse, life felt pretty grim.

She had been given the task of inspecting the new recomposition facility in the Sahara. The Reboot Council didn't want satellite images, they wanted a first-hand progress report, as soon as possible. So she had flown to Mali from Berlin, and then driven the thousand kilometres to this decrepit, vermin-infested guesthouse. She was not looking forward to the prospect of the night ahead or her second arduous day in a car.

Eventually, Keita appeared with a big grin and a huge brass key.

'You're in luck. They've given you the presidential suite.'

*

Müller rose at six the next morning, still feeling groggy after a night lying on a foam mattress on the floor in a room with nailed down windows, a broken fan and noisy plumbing. She managed just four hours' sleep, but knew they needed to get on their way before the heat of the day became unbearable.

The sprightly Keita, dressed in a long white cotton robe, headdress and heavy-soled sandals, was waiting in the hotel reception. He frowned at what Müller was wearing – white T-shirt, jeans and heavy army-type boots.

'Good morning, Sofia. Do you have anything to cover your arms? And perhaps a hat?'

'Forgot to pack them.' She shrugged.

'Just thirty minutes exposure to the Saharan sun could make you badly sick. We will give you something for protection.'

'Thanks,' she replied, painfully aware that it was another reminder of how much she had underestimated what she was coming into.

'We have fresh orange juice, bread, dates and honey for you in the car.'

'Coffee?'

'We have, with good beans and some cardamom. Perhaps a little thicker than you're used to, it will certainly clear your head.'

Müller followed the eager Keita out of the hotel. Outside, two huge Toyota Land Cruisers were parked either side of the Land Rover, making it look like a toy. Both cars were caked in dust and mud, yet the RB livery was still clearly visible.

'Come, travel with me. The air conditioning still works in this one,' said Keita smiling. 'Temperature at the site yesterday was forty-six degrees, so you'll thank me.'

'Do you have the drones?' Sandstrom enquired. She wanted

to make a film of her trip, getting above the site would be the best way to illustrate its scale.

'We have three, all travelling in the other car,' replied Keita.

Even at this early hour the city was bustling, with market stalls already doing good business in the narrow streets. As they drove out of the centre, mopeds weaved in and around the two vehicles, sounding their horns furiously. The riders doggedly intent on getting to their destinations quickly, regardless of the risks. A line of heavily laden donkeys laboured past, backs bending under the weight of overfilled fruit boxes. Three camels stood tethered to a palm, bellowing their annoyance at anyone who came near. A group of women walked by, each carrying a towering bundle of fabric on their head. Sharia law was still observed by many, and all the women wore black veils and loose-fitting clothing. Whatever their religious beliefs, no one was spared the choking, eye-stinging dust. The untarred roads around the inner city remained permanently caked in a layer of fine sand. It billowed in restless clouds as the huge cars disturbed the air, plastering the single-storey, mud-brick houses in an orange film that gathered in shifting piles outside each front door.

As she stared out at the sights from the back of the car, Müller could appreciate why people referred to 'going to Timbuktu' as like venturing to the very edge of the world. Its position on the edge of the Sahara, where roads were virtually non-existent or impassable, made it one of the most remote places on earth. Its climate also made it one of the most demanding too, now she could also understand why Reboot had chosen this particular part of Mali as the location for one of its super burial sites.

As they began to emerge from the suffocating grip of the urban sprawl and journey out into the desert, the roads deteriorated into deeply rutted trails barely distinguishable from the sand around them. After half an hour of watchful progress, the drivers halted at a small intersection to lower the tyre pressures.

Keita looked pleased. 'Good. We have finished with the roads and not ruined our Michelins. Now, this is where we travel across the dunes.'

'Where I assume things will get even rougher,' replied Müller grimly.

'A little, but the cars are up to it. We've only ever had one puncture on the sands…and a fan-belt breakage.' Keita put his hands together in prayer and looked skyward. 'We trust in Allah. It is his way sometimes to decide we must suffer, so we always make sure we carry plenty of spares.'

The cars set off again, picking their way around the sinkholes, the date trees, the cactus, the shrubs, the clusters of lovegrass, the rocks and the bleached bones. As they picked up speed, Müller clung to the hand grab, trying to prevent herself from smashing her head on the roof or crumpling down into the footwell. She thought the car must soon shake itself to pieces.

'How…far…away…is…the…site?'

'You only have to endure for another two hours.' Keita smiled on seeing her discomfort. 'We had to build the pits in a place where the only curious things were going to be camels or swallows.'

As they crashed along, Müller gritted her teeth and cursed her luck. In spite of her discomfort, gazing out at the monotony of the Sahara eventually became soporific, and within a few minutes she had fallen into a deep sleep.

'Wake up Sofia.'

Müller jumped awake and found she had slumped down in the bench seat and that her head was resting in Keita's lap. Appalled, she sprang up and slammed her head against the door window.

'We are nearly at the pit,' Keita shouted above the din.

Müller's head slowly cleared and she could make out a large, dusty smudge through the front windscreen about a kilometre away.

'Why is it here?' she asked.

'As I said it had to be far from prying eyes…'

'No, why this exact location? Why this particular place in the middle of nowhere?'

'We required a long seam of deep desert. The depth of sand varies widely in this part of the Sahara, from just a few centimetres to over forty metres. What we have found is around thirty metres. That is perfect for what we need.'

For all of her discomfort, Müller was beginning to admire the obvious planning and effort that was going into creating this project.

'So much bloody sand,' said Müller. 'Where does it all come from?'

'Nearly all sand in deserts comes from somewhere else, sometimes from hundreds of kilometres away. In distant times, this was once fertile grassland and the sand was washed in by rivers. When the area became arid, there was no longer any vegetation or water to hold the soil down. Eventually all that was left was this.' Keita wound down the window and swept his hand theatrically over the landscape. The blast of hot air caused Müller to involuntarily put her hand over her face. 'Sand is just finely ground rock material Sofia. And under the sand beneath our feet you will find more rocks.'

Müller had stopped listening; the car had halted at the top of a towering dune.

'We are here!' exclaimed the driver.

As she sat trying to settle her nausea, Müller looked down to where the man was pointing. Rising up from the desert floor she could hear a thunderous cacophony of engines, grinding axles and vehicle horns. But despite the obvious frenetic activity far below, she could see nothing of it through the dense cloud of sand and dust.

'Where is it?' she asked.

'It is nearly midday. They will answer the azan soon, then you will see the wonder,' Keita reassured her.

As they waited, from somewhere in the murk a beautiful lyrical wailing started up and cut through the clamour. It was a haunting sound, an unworldly melody that might be coming from some honey voiced, ethereal spirit of the desert.

'Allahu Akbar Allah is the greatest, Allahu Akbar Allah is the greatest…'

For a few moments, the chanting seemed to have had little impact, but gradually the noises subsided as engines were turned off and men downed their tools. After another minute, every other sound had ceased and the dust started to settle. Müller strained to peer through the gloom. Then, as if summoned by some magician's spell, it was there. She stared down, wide-eyed in amazement at the scale of the site of the 'cursed pit'.

Fifty metres below, for as far as she could see, the dunes had been levelled flat and through the middle of the huge man-made plain, a trench had been gouged. Müller estimated at least forty metres wide and two kilometres long. At the top of the earthworks at various points along its length, towering excavators, each with a huge bucket suspended from its arm, stood idle. They had bitten down into the full depth of the desert floor, exposing the solid rock at its base. As the cranes enlarged the trench, the sides had been fortified with reinforced concrete walls and steel plates to stabilise it among the shifting sands. At the near end of the massive chasm, a rolling ramp allowed lorries to enter and exit and collect their loads. Now with the dust fully settled and the sun penetrating the haze, Müller could finally appreciate the sheer scale of the geography.

She picked up her binoculars to see in more detail what appeared to be a small town about half a kilometre to the north. A number of large prefabricated administration buildings dominated its centre with dozens of pitch-roofed wooden huts of uniform size arranged in neat rows around them. She could also make out a supermarket, an oil station, a school, a sizeable solar panel plant, even a mosque, complete with minaret. Groups of palms and neat rows of mature shrubs had been planted around the complex to lend the scene a surreal normality.

To the west, two industrial buildings loomed large, one a concrete-mixing plant, the other a steel foundry. From the latter, two large chimney stacks belched dense trails of oily black smoke into the shimmering Saharan air.

Further to the east, something in the sky caught Müller's attention. She watched in amazement as a huge freight plane came in to land, touching down on a rubberised landing strip in a blizzard of sand. Near the airfield's makeshift observation tower, several other planes with nose cargo doors yawning, were having their cargoes of machines, material and supplies unloaded into a long line of slab-sided container lorries.

'Impressive, yes?' Keita asked, subtly imploring Müller to admire his work. 'Most of what you see has been brought in by air. At least fifty wide bodied planes in and out every day, coming from Europe, Asia and even America. They will help us build over twenty pits in this region alone, each capable of swallowing a million people.'

'It's...amazing, Jacob.' Müller put down her binoculars, reached out and shook his hand.

Keita felt a moment of elation. He had worked night and day for the last three months to make this logistic nightmare a reality. He was proud of what he had achieved but also knew that this woman's approval was essential if he was to continue as the man in charge.

'How many people work down there? I can't actually see any walking about.' Müller was beginning to take notes.

'Fifteen hundred, mostly engineers and construction workers. No one walks in the open at this hour if they can avoid it. With the modern equipment we have here, the men can remain in their air-conditioned vehicles and machinery and still be very productive. Everyone remains on site for four weeks, working twelve-hour shifts, and then takes two weeks off.'

'Where do they come from?'

'Locals, mainly from Kabara, Mopti, Goudam and of course Timbuktu. We also have people in from Niger, Algeria and Mauritania along with some specialists from America, Australia and Europe.'

'Do you have any trouble with Muslims…for what we are doing here?'

Keita looked quizzically at Müller, as if he had not understood the question.

'They have no problem with us making a few holes in the desert.'

'With the cull I mean, Jacob.'

'The cull presents a specific problem for Muslims because it is forbidden for followers of Islam to know the time of their own death in advance.'

'Can see that might be a problem,' she conceded.

'Some orthodox imams are not co-operating with us, but thankfully with a little persuasion…most are.' Keita winked at Müller. 'They still do not understand the need to eradicate baby boomers, but agree with the imperative to reduce overall numbers. We agree the quotas and they provide the numbers. They mainly come from the elderly, the mad or the sick.'

'Have the Reboot Council accepted this?' Müller was surprised at this concession.

'Not officially.' Keita removed his sunglasses and wiped some dust away with the folds of his robe. 'I have been given discretion in this matter, as have others across the Muslim world, all in the interests of keeping numbers moving. But in time it will change.'

Müller suddenly felt queasy again. 'Is it possible to get a drink?'

'Of course, of course. There is fresh water here, piped through from an underground lake. They even have icemakers in the town. Perhaps when you have recovered, I can show you more of what we created here.' Keita waved for the driver to continue into the site.

'And we must disguise the fact you are a woman. Some of these men haven't seen one for quite some time.'

Müller sighed at the privations and slights women suffer in this part of the world, but there was no question in her mind that this was a startling achievement, and her superiors would be pleased with her report. Now she wanted nothing more than to complete her tour as quickly as possible and travel far away from this place of stifling heat and the incessant attention of sex-starved males.

As the car travelled down off the crest of the dune, she turned to Keita.

'Any way you can get me on one of those transport planes tonight?'

15 August 2031, Waiheke Island, New Zealand
Cull day 185

Tom and Helen Hatfield gave each other a knowing look as they walked hand in hand from the car park and up the stone steps to the clinic. To a casual observer they would have looked like any normal loving couple, except for one obvious quirk. She was at least half his age.

'Good morning. It's the Hatfield's to see Dr Finch.'

The fresh-faced young man behind the desk looked up at the couple.

'Welcome. Could you fill out these while you're waiting? One for each of you, please.' Tom Hatfield took the forms and handed one to his wife.

'Here you go, dear.' Hatfield held the paper tight as his wife tried to take it from him. She gave a barely perceptible nod and he released his grip. Reaching into her bag for a pen, she worked her way through the questionnaire.

'Doctor Finch shouldn't be long.' The young man gave a professional smile and went back to staring intently into his laptop.

Within two minutes, Tom Hatfield had completed his form. Standing up, he walked over to the water cooler. 'Like one, Helen?'

Before she could reply, a door opened and a tall, athletically built man in a doctor's white coat breezed into the room. Without acknowledging the Hatfields, he passed the receptionist a large manilla envelope.

'Take these to the Army office in Victoria Road would you? Straight away, please.'

The young man looked slightly put out. 'Can't it wait until after lunch, Doctor?'

Finch waved his hand towards the door. 'Now, please, Kane. And get me a sandwich while you're out. Cheese salad.'

With a theatrical sigh, the young receptionist left the room. Finch shook his head as he watched him go, and finally turned to his new clients. 'Tom and Helen, nice to meet you. Come on through and bring your forms with you please.'

He led the couple into his office and ushered them to sit in the two green leather upright chairs in front of his desk. As he did so, Tom Hatfield scanned the room, looking for obvious signs of any recording equipment.

Finch sat down and took their forms. After giving the contents a cursory scan, he looked earnestly at the couple. 'Lovely to meet you both. Everything seems in order as far as your personal details go. Been on Waiheke long?'

Tom Hatfield replied, 'Came over from Auckland last week. We're renting a mate's apartment just a spit from the beach in Putiki Bay. Let us have it at a good rate.' He looked to his wife for affirmation. 'Love it here, don't we dear?'

Helen Hatfield smiled weakly. 'Yes, we like…the gentle pace.'

Finch sensed the tension between them. 'Waiheke is a special place. Obviously recent events have changed its personality somewhat. With the cull in full swing, we've lost quite a few of our…er…longer-term residents.'

'Yes, we've noticed the difference this time. Younger people are moving in. I like it. It's…more lively,' Helen Hatfield replied.

'Yes, it certainly is.' Finch looked out of the window briefly and then down to his desk. 'Now, the first thing I would like to do is ascertain why you are here. And I'd like to ask you individually in turn – if that's OK?'

Tom Hatfield shuffled uncomfortably in his chair. 'Why?'

'It's quite normal, Mister Hatfield. Sometimes a couple come in for an initial consultation, both believing that they are here for the same reason. But very often for one or other of them, that is not always the case. Just last week a young newly married couple came to see me and…'

'We are here for the same reason, Doctor Finch. We're simply having some issues with our sex life. You must see a lot of that in your job.'

'Is this true, Mrs Hatfield?' Finch asked.

Helen Hatfield looked down at the floor and did not answer.

Tom Hatfield slammed his hand on the desk and stood up to go. 'Jesus, we've only been here two minutes and already it feels like a police interview.'

'He won't fuck me anymore, OK,' she stammered, still looking at the floor. 'And it's killing us.'

She started to sob softly. Finch leaned forward and passed her a tissue from a dispenser on his desk. As she took it from him, he patted her hand gently.

'Sorry to cause distress, Mrs Hatfield, but if I can't get honesty, I can't help you.'

'No, of course not, doctor,' she replied, calmed by his understanding and empathy.

'Now please, Helen, can we start at the beginning?' Finch looked intently at her, then back at her husband. 'Mr Hatfield, I'll come to you in a few minutes.'

'Think I'll go get some fresh air.' Tom Hatfield glanced at his wife. 'OK with that, Helen?'

She looked away from the doctor, wiping away a tear. 'Sure Tom. See you in a few minutes.'

Hatfield walked out of the clinic and opened up his car. Reaching onto the back seat, he pulled on a baseball cap and a fur-lined puffa jacket, turning up the collar. After putting on his sunglasses and a thick red scarf, he felt ready for an anonymous walk through Ostend, Waiheke's busiest shopping area.

Going successfully incognito was not a game for sixty-eight-year-old Hatfield; for him, being a baby boomer meant it was a matter of life and death. He had managed to evade the attentions of Reboot because he was already well- practised at hiding his true identity and age. Working as a freelance landscape designer and gardener for the previous twenty-five years, Hatfield hadn't paid income tax, and regularly forged his driver's licence. In doing so, he had effectively lived off-grid, out of reach of the authorities. He had also kept moving, regularly changing his office and home address.

But all of his artful dodging ended the day he decided to marry a client.

In 2028, wealthy Auckland widower Helen Carlson hired Hatfield to landscape her two-acre garden near Herne Bay. Within a week, he had created designs for a fifty-thousand-dollar makeover; within another week they had fallen in love. Twenty-nine years younger than he, Helen was demanding in ways Hatfield had not anticipated. She wanted to put down roots, have lots of holidays and lots of sex. The reason they had come to see relationship specialist Doctor Finch was because Hatfield had only managed to accommodate two of her demands.

Hatfield strolled as nonchalantly as he could as he made his way past Ostend's numerous boutiques, art galleries and bars, inside he felt anything but calm. His wife's frustration at his lack of libido had shaken him. And even though he had walked down this promenade many times before, today he felt all eyes were upon him. Staring curiously at this old man with his stiff walk, sagging jowls and liver spots dotting the thinning skin on the back of his hands. He felt sure that at any moment someone would wrench off his cap and with it the dyed wig piece that sat precariously on his balding pate. As he passed the Hot Beach Café, three young men sitting outside stopped their chatter to gawp at him. Two young girls looked up from their phones and started to giggle, one took a picture as he shuffled past. In truth, it was a warm day and with most people in T-shirts and shorts, Hatfield simply looked oddly overdressed in his winter attire. They soon forgot him as he moved by.

At the end of the street, a group of soldiers stood around a tank parked at a crossroads checkpoint, idly watching a volleyball game on the adjacent beach. Hurriedly, he crossed the road to head in the opposite direction. Staring in the shop windows, Hadfield lamented that he couldn't go in. In normal times, he would have chatted with the owners but in his heightened anxiety he was simply too afraid of being questioned, of being exposed as a persona non grata. Since the persecution of his generation had begun, his young wife had done the lion's share of the shopping duties. Well, from this day he thought, she would have to do it all to keep him safe.

As he reached the end of the line of shops, he noticed a poster on a board. Its headline read: $10,000 REWARD FOR BOOMERS.

Hatfield could feel his panic rising again. What were they doing on this crappy little rich boys' playground? He and his wife had agreed that hiding in plain sight can sometimes work, but now Waiheke just felt too small, too close-knit. Worse still, it was to become a major destination for executions. He had heard of a dissolution centre being constructed in the old War World Two tunnels on the island's remote north-east corner. Is it any wonder, Hatfield mused, that he had lost his sex drive? How could any man get a hard-on when he was worrying there might be a knock on the door at any moment, announcing that he was about to be dragged out of his bed and executed?

Helen had been very understanding and he knew she loved him; he also realised that time was running out to improve matters. As he walked back to the clinic, he resolved to confront one of the major issues blighting his life and their marriage and put it right. Throwing his jacket, scarf and cap in the car, Hatfield strode purposefully back into the clinic. He had been gone for thirty minutes, but it appeared the receptionist still hadn't returned from his errand.

'Hello. Anybody here?' Hatfield called out with no response. He knocked on Finch's office door, but again was met with silence.

Irritated, he pushed open the door and entered the room. Waiting for him inside were three soldiers, two pointing their rifles directly at his chest. The third, an officer, smiled at him and held out a set of handcuffs. 'G'day, Mister Hatfield. We'd like you to come with us.'

For a second, he thought about running, but knew that he would be gunned down without mercy. 'How did you know I was here?' Hatfield asked as they twisted his arms behind his back and fastened his wrists.

'Your wife told Doctor Finch everything. He's very good at getting to the truth. You're the third boomer he's handed in this week.'

As they led Hatfield away to the army truck, he looked across the car park.

Finch was standing by his car with his wife. They were holding hands.

5 December 2031, United Kingdom
Cull Day 295

Cool was the last thing Jameson felt.

I'm finally going home, but what will I find there?

The sun had risen over the nation of his birth. He looked down on the patchwork fields, rolling hills, hedgerow-fringed roads, quarry lakes and creamy sandstone coloured villages that flagged, even at five thousand feet up, that this was England. Or more precisely, this was the Cotswolds, the part of England he loved most. But the country he had left over a year ago was very different now. Now he was a pariah, no longer needed or wanted, here or anywhere. So instead of the joy he should be feeling in the skies over this unique and familiar landscape, all he felt was a deep, gut-wrenching dread.

After the plane landed, he was led to the exit by his minder.

When they reached the plane door, he strained to adjust to the daylight. The clock on the control tower said It was eleven o'clock, but RAF Brize Norton looked deserted. Three huge grey transport planes were lined up over to his right, with no sign of the crews. There were no fuel tankers, no catering vans, no cars, no buses, no baggage handlers. It was as if this usually busy military airfield had been evacuated.

'Are we going through customs? You must have my passport.' Jameson smiled benignly at his sullen guard.

'Won't need one. You're a VIP.'

They stood together at the bottom of the steps like the oddest of odd couples. As he waited, Jameson was struck by the muscular bulk of his guard, who looked even more immense in the open air. He noticed a multicoloured tattoo, possibly a flying dragon poking out of his collar just below his ear.

'Get that in China?'

'Eh?'

'Your dragon, did you travel to China to get it?'

'Camden.'

Still they waited, still no sign of a reception party.

'What are we waiting for?' Jameson enquired after another five minutes which seemed like twenty to his still-weak legs. He didn't receive an answer this time and they continued to wait in silence. Behind them, the steps were removed and the plane taxied away. As it did, two cars approached from the direction of the terminal building. In front, a black Mercedes saloon with heavily-tinted windows; following behind, a dark brown box-shaped security van with small reinforced windows and a heavy door on each side.

The van stopped in front of them. A tall man in full riot gear and wearing a mirrored faceguard stepped out, a heavy baton swung menacingly from his heavy belt.

'Welcome home, Mr Jameson. We're taking you to your next destination.'

The guard grabbed Jameson's cuffs, led him to the door and pulled him up into the van's dark interior. The air was clammy and fetid – smelling of sweat, urine and fear. As his cuffs were attached to chains hanging from the roof, he could just discern the shapes of two people in orange overalls sitting silently together on a steel bench. At the rear, inside a floor-to-ceiling metal cage, a person lay prone on the floor.

He was about to enquire who it was when the guard put his finger in front of his faceguard to warn him not to speak. Stepping outside, he closed the door with a sharp metallic thud and the van moved off.

Jameson's eyes gradually adjusted to the gloom and he could make out more details of his travelling companions. The two opposite, a man and a woman, looked around his age. Each wore glasses and both looked pale and undernourished. The person in the cage was a larger man, also in orange overalls. He stirred and tried to sit up, but for some reason wasn't able to. For a few miles, no one spoke, then the man on the bench broke the silence.

'Welcome to the fun wagon. What's your name?' he asked in a dry, weary voice.

'Will Jameson. And you?'

'Steve Hamlin. This is my wife Sylvia.'

Jameson could see that one of the lenses in her glasses had broken and her hand was wrapped in a bloodied bandage. 'Looks like you've been in the wars, Sylvia.'

She rubbed her hand with a pained expression. 'Let's just say they don't make exceptions for ladies.'

'What's your story, Will?' Steve Hamlin asked.

'I'm a scientist, just back from Antarctica.'

'Yes, but what's your story? You must have a story they want from you, or you'd be dead already.'

'Dead?'

'Yes, they wouldn't have thought twice about it. So what's your story?'

'I've found a way of potentially stopping the ice melt.'

Hamlin's eyes widened. 'Well, they'll definitely want that.'

'What's your…er…story?' Jameson enquired.

'I work for Carbon Engineering, or I did until these Reboot bastards grabbed all our assets.' He shook his head. 'We've been developing a system to remove carbon dioxide pollution out of the atmosphere and convert it back into gasoline, diesel and jet fuel.'

Jameson was intrigued. He had heard of the theory but thought it was impossible. 'Sounds like science fiction.'

'Chemically, it is complicated, but the process doesn't rely on unprecedented science. All we've done is graft cooling towers onto a paper mill. The towers have large fans to pull in CO_2 from outside to come into contact with an alkaline liquid. The liquid undergoes a series of chemical reactions and is frozen into pellets, heated, and converted into a slurry. The carbon dioxide is then combined with hydrogen and converted into liquid fuels.' Hamlin's face brightened. 'So if you burn our gas in your car, you would release carbon dioxide pollution as normal, but as this carbon dioxide came from the air in the first place, the emissions would not introduce any new CO_2 into the atmosphere.'

The van suddenly came to an abrupt halt, thrusting them all violently forward. The driver cursed, before setting off again.

'It seems even in this Utopia, there are bad drivers,' Jameson quipped.

Hamlin continued, eager to relay his story to a fellow scientist.

'Our short-term focus was making carbon-neutral hydrocarbon fuels. Longer term, we saw this as a technology for decarbonising transportation forever…and then these savages came along.' He slumped back, seemingly defeated by the perverseness of the situation.

'So why do Reboot want you?'

'Perhaps, like you, I deigned not to write much of this down. They need me to explain the process and its various formulations to others. Others, of course, who were not born before 1964.' He threw Jameson a rueful look. 'I suspect they will use Sylvia to get me to co-operate.'

'Reduced to a bargaining chip,' Sylvia responded. 'What has this world become?'

'Screwed-up, big time.' The voice came from the man in the cage who had now managed to sit up. He was of African-Caribbean descent and no older than thirty. One of his eyes was swollen shut and his nose looked broken.

'What are you doing in there? You're no boomer,' Jameson asked.

'I'm not playing ball…and these guys don't like it.'

Jameson passed him a water bottle through the bars. The man greedily took a large drink. 'Thanks, I needed that.'

'What's your story?' asked Hamlin.

'My name is Clive Walsh. I am…I was a smart grid engineer.'

'We're none the wiser,' Sylvia replied.

Walsh took another gulp of water. 'I was helping to build the 6G future grid.'

'You're a phone engineer?'

Walsh shook his head. 'This wasn't for phones. I was producing a system which would have given Reboot full control of the national electricity and data grid.' He struggled to his feet and leaned forward against the bars to make sure he could be heard. 'The technology would enable smart grids to connect billions of data points. From wind turbines to rooftop solar panels, from electric vehicle batteries to dishwashers, all working on a demand-response basis. Processing all this data, alongside artificial-intelligence-led weather predictions would ensure that every watt of energy would be utilised as efficiently as possible at any given moment.'

'Well, that certainly would be a new tomorrow,' Hamlin said, whistling through his teeth.

'Their goal is to achieve net zero emissions all the time, and they believe the only way they can achieve that is to manage consumption.'

'So why are you here?' Jameson enquired again. 'You sound exactly the kind of person Reboot want. Smart and young.'

'I don't believe in their big idea. The Big Cull… Whatever you want to call it. I believe in what they want to achieve, but not how they're going about it. I helped my grandparents to escape…and they found out.'

'Yup, that would piss them off,' said Hamlin.

'The fuckers beat me up and threw me in here.'

It appeared to Jameson that Reboot had gone to another level of ruthlessness and brutality. They had decided that their enemies weren't simply just baby boomers any longer; it was anyone who stood in their way.

They drove on for several more hours, stopping numerous times at various check points where papers were signed and their identities verified by stern-faced security forces. At a service station, they were allowed out one by one for a toilet break and given a bottle of water each. Eventually, it started to become dark and Jameson could make out the familiar evenly spaced lighting of a motorway. The white flashes of the LEDs streamed through the high-set windows illuminating the sullen figures of his fellow prisoners, as if they were flickering images in an old black and white film. An old movie called *The Last Journey of the Damned,* he thought, suddenly feeling very depressed.

The van droned on monotonously through the night, Jameson

tried to sleep, but the bench was hard and the chains made his wrist ache. The one time he did manage to fall unconscious, he woke to find himself on the cold floor with his arms suspended above him. It was still dark when they finally arrived at their destination. He could hear voices and the mechanical sound of a large gate slowly opening.

Hamlin looked across at him plaintively, his wife leaning on his shoulder, still asleep. 'I guess this must be the end of the road.'

'Just as well. I need a drink,' Jameson replied.

'Meet you at the pool for a Peach Bellini.' Hamlin rolled his eyes.

The van continued slowly over a bumpy road for another four hundred metres then halted again. The door swung open and the tall guard in the mirror faceguard entered and unlocked Jameson's chains.

'This is your stop,' he barked.

Jameson rose stiffly to his feet and was pulled roughly through the door. After slamming it shut again, the guard returned to the van and drove off, leaving Jameson alone in the chill early morning air and in complete darkness. He heard a heavy click as two spotlights suddenly lit up shining their powerful beams directly on him. As his eyes adjusted, he realized he was standing in the middle of a cobbled courtyard, a large castellated building looming high above him to his left. It looked vaguely familiar, but he couldn't make out any details that might reveal more.

A grey-haired, stern-faced woman dressed in a British military uniform stepped out of the shadows directly in front of him.

'Welcome to Scotland, Mr Jameson. And welcome to Edinburgh Castle.'

3 September 2031, Western Pacific
Cull Day 204

By any measure, the *Pu Tuo San* was a big ship. At over three hundred metres in length and sixty metres across, equivalent to three football pitches laid end to end. In her day she was one of the world's largest super tankers, yet she still rolled like a toy in a bath on the bucking Pacific swell as she laboured along at her maximum speed of thirteen knots. In her prime, this giant of the sea would easily transport two million barrels of crude oil, but the ageing *Pu Tuo San* was carrying a very different cargo on this voyage – the last voyage she would ever make.

Over recent times, the ship had seen little use. Because of Reboot's paralysing grip on the oil industry, the tanker had remained anchored off Singapore for most of the year. Now for the first time in months, she was at sea again, and her new captain was enjoying the steady reassuring rumble of her enormous engines far below him.

Akhilesh Kumar had been in charge of many tankers over his career, most notably the *Oman Darya* in 2028 when he had been detained along with his ship in Gibraltar for transporting banned Iranian oil. After his release, he had vowed never to captain another vessel, but this was different. This was something he believed in.

Normally, there would be around twenty-five crew to help Kumar run a ship of this size, but on this trip he would have to manage with just six. He stood diligently on the bridge with his first mate, the experienced and avuncular Inesh Patel; both men stared out through the salt-sprayed windows at the foaming breakers. The enormous plate glass apertures wrapped themselves nearly one hundred and eighty degrees around the main operations bridge. Sited at over sixty metres above the waves, they gave Kumar and Patel a commanding view over the massive superstructure stretching ahead of them. From this lofty perch they could see ahead twenty nautical miles to the horizon, a big help when steering such an ungainly vessel.

Kumar was happy with their progress so far. 'It's been a good trip Inesh, much calmer than we might have expected at this time.'

Both sailors were well used to the vagaries and moods of the Pacific Ocean. Even fifty-foot waves did not overly concern them. Since they had left Jurong Island eight days previously and sailed south-west, through the South China Sea, past the Philippines and into the Philippine Sea, the going had been surprisingly good. It was a time of year and area well known for sudden and destructive typhoons, but none had come near them so far.

'Varuna has been kind indeed,' Patel replied cheerfully, evoking the name of the Hindu sea deity. 'Which is just as well. We do not want this cargo breaking loose, eh Captain?'

Kumar pursed his lips and nodded grimly, then picked up

the intercom phone to his officer in the sonar room. 'How goes it below?'

'All well sir, nothing to report,' came the reply.

'Good, I will be coming down to check the cargo shortly.'

'Aye aye sir.'

Kumar looked out to the starboard side. About a mile away a sleek grey ship was running a parallel course.

The RSS *Stalwart* had escorted them on the five-thousand-kilometre trip. French-built, the frigate was the pride of the Republic of Singapore's navy. Bristling with modern weaponry, she would have presented an imposing sight for any enemy, however today her mission was not about creating death, but burying it.

The *Pu Tuo San* was to be sunk into the cavernous depths of the Mariana Trench, along with her cargo of the bodies of over two million Asian men and women; boomers culled mainly in Malaysia and Indonesia, and brought to Singapore for processing and sea burial. The refrigerated holds of the ship had been crammed to the brim with the individually shrouded cadavers, then welded shut with metal plates.

Two days previously, the engine room crew reported a sickly sweet smell coming from the hold area. Kumar had assumed that some of the cooling units must have failed and decomposition of some bodies had accelerated. The stench attracted hundreds of black-browed albatrosses which circled over the ship night and day. With the smell starting to pervade the whole ship, he was glad they had almost reached their destination.

Now with just a few hundred miles to go, Kumar had decided to examine the holds one last time. Leaving the bridge to Patel, he made his way down the series of ladders leading to the main cargo hold platform fifteen metres below. There to meet him was a flame-haired, fresh-faced man dressed in an oil-stained boiler suit, and he looked concerned.

'Liam, what's wrong?'

Liam Thompson was Kumar's chief boiler room mechanic. Born in Dublin, Thompson had worked on ships like the *Pu Tuo San* for most of his twenty-year career. A big advocate of Reboot's mission, he volunteered for this trip and only arrived from Ireland two days before the ship sailed.

'Most of the fridges have failed, sir. The bodies are bloating and putting real pressure on the hold seams. They might split at any time.'

'Show me.'

'You'll be needing this.' Thompson handed Kumar a rubber dust mask. It had glass covers to protect the eyes and a large air filter. 'It'll take the worst of the stink away, but you still won't be able to stand it for long.'

Putting on the masks, they walked down another steep flight of steps, emerging onto a small murky corridor created by the towering holds on either side. Even through the thick activated charcoal filter, the sickly-sweet smell of decomposing bodies assailed Kumar's nostrils, instantly provoking a gag reflex. Thompson pointed to a seam line on the huge hold door nearest to them. Kumar shone a torch at the spot but didn't have to get too close to see the problem. Several of the iron rivets that held the structure together had started to pop which in turn was causing the plates around them to buckle and split. A thick brown liquid oozed through fractures in the metal, pooling in cloudy viscous puddles on the floor.

Kumar decided he had seen enough and they ascended the steps. Before removing their masks, they ducked through into a sealed compartment and slammed the door behind them.

Thompson looked gravely at his captain. 'That is pretty typical of all the holds in this area. We haven't got too long before the things in there will be swimming about with us out here.'

'We will have to dump the ship sooner than we thought.'

Kumar thanked Thompson and ran back up to the bridge, his first mate oblivious to the danger they were all in, was happily whistling to himself.

'Mister Patel, we must sink her now.'

Patel looked perplexed. 'But we are not over the deepest site. It will take another day before…'

Kumar interrupted him. 'We don't have another day. We are over the trench and that is good enough. Signal to the *Stalwart* that we will be slowing in ten minutes to begin the scuttle.

Scuttling was the controlled sinking of a ship by deliberately allowing water into the hull. Reboot's engineers wanted to ensure that the tanker stayed as intact as possible on its eleven-kilometre dive to the bottom, so no explosives would be used. The plan was to open up the seacocks and hatches to the sea at twenty-five adjacent points simultaneously so that it would settle evenly into the water.

While this was being carried out, Kumar would continue to steer at around five knots along the line of the trench. It might take six hours or more to fill the ship with enough water to eventually drag it down, but it would cause less stress on the hull. At a designated moment, the crew would be taken off by a recovery vessel from the *Stalwart*. They had all agreed it sounded feasible in theory, but it had never been attempted by Reboot or anyone else before. This was Sea Burial 001, and its success was crucial. There were many more trips planned for Kumar and his crew of body sinkers.

'All engines ahead slow. Crew to scuttling stations.' Kumar barked his order before realising that only he and his first mate were on the bridge. Patel smiled grimly as he relayed the captain's command to the *Stalwart*. The ship juddered as its engines started to slow, Kumar began to feel nervous, almost for the first time realising the magnitude of what he had been asked to do.

'This will be the last resting place for those poor souls. We had better do this right.' He knew that the bodies would ultimately provide a banquet for the sightless feeders at the bottom of the deepest oceanic trench on earth. He was also aware that despite their precautions, the ship could still break up on its journey to the depths.

At around nine hundred metres, the light would fade and the *Pu Tuo San* would continue her plummet in complete darkness. The water pressure would gradually rise to a crushing thousand times greater than that on the surface. As the increasing pressure overcame the ship's structural integrity, weak points would start to buckle, rivets would explode, brace bars bend and snap, seams would split. Over the course of the ten-minute dive, the cadavers would be crushed together into a mass of viscous mucus. Thank God, thought Kumar, that these horrors would happen out of the sight of any human.

'This will be more than just another ship at the bottom of the sea, it will be the deepest' Patel said. 'I know the record is held by the *Rio Grande*, a German ship sunk in the South Atlantic Ocean, during the war. She lies more than five and a half kilometres down. This could be twice that.'

A shout from the intercom interrupted their conversation.

'Scuttle procedure complete, sir. All seacocks and hatches locked open.'

'Diesel levels?' asked Kumar. To avoid pollution, they had deliberately only brought enough fuel to reach their destination.

'A little more than we had planned, sir.'

It couldn't be helped, Kumar thought. They had to act now or the whole trip could end in gory disaster.

'Thank you Liam. Report to the bridge.'

Five hours later, Kumar and his crew were aboard the *Stalwart*, standing on her bridge and staring out at the floundering bulk

266

of the *Pu Tuo San* about a kilometre away. They had turned off the engines and abandoned her twenty minutes previously. The tanker was sitting low in the water and the swell was washing freely over the decks. Under a blood-red sky, thick clouds and seabirds gathered overhead, and as if to complete the portentous significance of the scene, a fine drizzle began to fall..

A small fire had broken out on the bridge and a thin ribbon of grey smoke escaped through a shattered window. Nevertheless, all of the ship's one hundred and sixty-four thousand tons were sinking as evenly as they had hoped. Kumar had seen many ships sink aft first, which often caused the hull to rupture along the centre line, but there were no signs of that happening here.

The *Stalwart's* commander, Captain Zhong Kuirun patted Kumar on the shoulder. 'Congratulations, it looks like she's holding together.'

Kumar looked sadly at the floundering *Pu Tuo San*. He had only been in charge of her for a few days, but as with all his ships he had still grown fond of her.

'Could I say a prayer?' he asked.

The captain passed Kumar the ship intercom. He closed his eyes and began the Hindu prayer he remembered reciting as a boy as part of the last rites at his grandfather's funeral.

'Burn them not up, nor quite consume them, Agni: let not their body or skin be scattered. When they attain unto the life that waits, they shall become subject to the will of gods. The Sun receive thine eye, the Wind thy Prana; go, as thy merit is, to earth or heaven. Go, if it be thy lot, unto the waters; go, make thine home in plants with all thy members...'

Suddenly a shout went up from the sailors lining the guard rail.

'She's going!'

Kumar opened his eyes. All he could see of the great ship now were the tops of the two huge crane gantries, the red funnel and the communications tower. All around, the sea foamed in great fountains as it greedily grasped the ship to itself. Huge air bubbles formed, burst and formed again as the last pockets of air were squeezed out of rooms, corridors and cabins by the onrushing torrent. The water swirled in an agitated dance to the death throes of this giant of the seas. Even at this distance, he could hear the crashes and moans of steel under stress. Then, with one large, enormous gasp of resignation, the *Pu Tuo San* finally gave up the uneven struggle and slipped out of sight. All that remained to suggest the ship had even been there were dozens of small eddy pools and pieces of flotsam bobbing and swirling on the surface.

'Should we stay to see if anything returns to the surface?' asked Kumar.

'My orders were to return immediately. A reconnaissance plane will come later to check the location for debris.' Kuirun made a note of the exact co-ordinates of the sinking site which would be relayed to the Philippines Air Force.

'This is a grim business, Captain, but you have demonstrated this method as being feasible. May I offer you and your crew a drink in the mess?'

'I think we need one. Thank you.'

The *Stalwart* turned in the direction of the setting sun, and no one looked back. If they had, they would surely have noticed the white bullet-shaped objects exploding to the surface, leaping into the air and splashing down into the wake of the ship, as thousands of shrouded, gas-filled bodies escaped their metal tomb.

And they would have seen the black-browed albatrosses starting to circle lower in greedy anticipation of their unholy feast.

19 September 2031, South Korea
Cull Day 220

'Your journey has been remarkable, but are you the man to unite Korea?'

Hwang Sung-yueng surveyed this southern European in his expensive suit sitting opposite him with caution and a little disdain. For the last sixty minutes, he had put up with the man's disrespectful questioning and his stinking cigarette smoke. And he was getting angry.

How could this jumped-up army officer question his ability and desire to bring together his divided nation? What does this man know about his journey? He had not lived under slavery. His family were not imprisoned in the country of his birth.

Outraged though he was, Hwang was too experienced a diplomat to reveal his true thoughts and feelings. Ultimately, he knew he needed the approval of this man with the pale-blue eyes and scarred face.

'Colonel Moschin, I have both the skills and the motivation,' he replied calmly.

Hwang had been North Korea's deputy ambassador to the UK, but two years earlier, he had defected to the South with his wife and children. On learning of his 'treachery', the leadership in Pyongyang accused him of leaking secrets and swore savage revenge on 'this human scum' and his family.

He could have lived a quiet life in his new homeland, but decided instead to run for election to South Korea's National Assembly. A natural showman and wearing a bright-pink suit, Hwang cast a charismatic figure during the campaign and astounded everybody, including himself, by winning. Over the past year he had used his new political platform to denounce his old masters in North Korea. Now he was ready for the next step of retribution – to free his homeland from slavery and to release his family from persecution.

'Colonel, I have seen what you have achieved with Reboot. It has been truly remarkable. You have shown that any obstacle can be overcome and any decision, no matter how radical, can be justified and enacted for the common good.' A polite smile formed on Moschin's face, then quickly faded. Hwang continued.

'I myself have made choices and achieved things I would never have thought possible. Now I am ready to achieve my greatest dream. Will you give me the opportunity?'

Moschin's face gave nothing further away as he regarded this man he had met just two hours ago. In truth, despite the success Reboot had achieved over the past months, he was tiring of placating aggrieved citizens like Hwang Sung-yueng, wearying of racing around the world sitting in endless meetings, arguing semantics and power-sharing with politicians.

He was a frustrated military man operating in a world where armies were no longer used to fight, but to intimidate. He relished warfare, mano-a-mano confrontation; he lived to make mayhem. He had never felt so alive as when he was part of special forces operations in the second Gulf War back in 2003. Sleeping and fighting in the desert, destroying radar stations, laying road mines, evading capture for weeks on end. Moschin was a man who needed enemies, and now he had in his sights one of the biggest there was. In the shape of an obese, chain-smoking, gout-afflicted forty-one-year-old named Jae-Ho Kom, head of one of the last nations still untouched by Reboot.

'You will get your wish.'

Moschin brightened at the thought of taking out the world's number-one bogey man. 'We shall work together to remove this tyrant and unite the Korean peninsula and its islands. Welcome to the Reboot movement.' He stood up, walked over to Hwang and shook his hand.

'Thank you, Colonel.' Hwang was happy. It seemed he had convinced Moschin of his unique credentials to become the first leader of a united Korea since World War Two. But his moment of triumph was short-lived as Moschin quickly curtailed their handshake and invited him to sit.

'But first, I would like to hear about your plans to turn Korea green…'

Since the Korean War ended in 1953, South Korea had grown into one of the world's largest economies. During this time, the nation had become heavily reliant on fossil fuels. Efforts to decarbonise under incumbent President Moon Jae-in had been slow, too slow for Reboot; coal still supplied forty-four per cent of its power generation. Now Moschin wanted to know how his anointed successor intended to speed up the process.

As he listened intently, Hwang outlined his plans for reaching forty per cent renewable power by 2038. This included scaling up the use of liquefied natural gas, switching to electric and hydrogen vehicles along with the immediate introduction of a carbon tax. He spoke of his intentions to suspend any new coal-fired power stations not already under construction, and his pledge to shut older plants within five years. As he closed his presentation with the promise of a zero-carbon South Korea by 2050, he looked for approval from Moschin. His reward was another thin smile.

'It is a good plan. We are aware that you are starting from a poor position.' Hwang nodded, then Moschin delivered his hammer blow.

'We agree with everything except your timetable. You must achieve all these things in half the time.'

'It is impossible,' Hwang protested.

'It will be more impossible when Yellow Sea storms sweep away your coastal regions. More impossible when summer heatwaves kill thousands in Seoul, Busan and Daegu. More impossible when wildfires decimate your forests from Gangwon to Sokcho. We do not have the luxury of one more minute. Our forefathers have used all the time we may have had.'

Hwang could see it was hopeless to protest. He knew how difficult the task was and that compromises would have to be made. Best not to fight the battle here, he reasoned, best to start the work.

'Very well, we will adjust accordingly,' his inner diplomat replied.

'Good,' replied Moschin. 'Now, let's eat. Tomorrow we can plan how to kill your little fat guy.'

The next morning at 8 am, Hwang was back in his office at the National Assembly Building in central Seoul. It was a room he had chosen himself because of the view it gave of the Han River and the majestic arched Seogang Bridge whose roads opened up the city to the west. He drank strong black coffee, trying to clear his aching head after the alcohol-soaked night he had spent with Moschin. Nursing his third cup, he gazed out of the window at the swollen river below. After days. After days of heavy rains, the Han's normally benign clear waters had become a racing brown blur. Every few seconds, the shattered remnants of a tree would appear on the boiling surface, then splinter and leap as it slammed into the base of the forty-year-old bridge. The steady stream of cars and commuters passing over the structure seemed completely untroubled by the sights and sounds of the maelstrom just ten metres below. As he watched, captivated, he failed to notice that Moschin and another man had entered the room.

'Morning, Hwang, how's the head? That soju is pretty heavy shit.'

Soju was Korea's favourite alcoholic drink. Often drunk in long glasses like beer, it was nearly as strong as vodka.

'My head is fine, Colonel,' Hwang lied.

'Well, I admire your fortitude. I have a thumping headache.' Moschin poured himself a coffee and turned to the man standing by his side.

'This is Joe Evert, the Central Intelligence Agency's senior agent in Korea.'

Hwang hadn't needed the introduction, having already guessed who Evert worked for. He looked classic CIA – clean-shaven, crew-cut hair, black-framed glasses, white shirt, black tie, black trousers and patent leather shoes.

They have been using the same dress code manual since the 1950s.

He shook Evert's hand, and as the three of them sat down by the window, Moschin too spotted the raging torrent pushing hard against the bridge.

'Hope that isn't going to collapse. The airport is on the other side.'

'It will hold. It has been built well,' replied Hwang, keen to accentuate his faith in Korean engineering.

'Nice to hear. Now Evert is here to tell us how we might get to take out the bad guy from over the border.'

'Thank you, Colonel.'

Evert produced a picture of the North Korean leader and placed it on the table.

'Jae-Ho Kom. Ugly bastard, isn't he? The last time we had him in our cross hairs was in 2018. It was in the early hours of the fourth of July at the launch of his first intercontinental missile. We watched that porky bastard for a full seventy minutes, strolling around, smoking his western cigarettes, laughing at nothing and scaring the bejesus out of his generals.' Evert closed one eye and made a pistol shape with his hand.

'We knew we could destroy them and him with a precision fire, but we did nothing.'

'Because?' Hwang was amazed by this revelation.

Evert shrugged. 'Because…we were scared. Putting Kim six feet under might have triggered a crazy North Korean response which could have been massive. We just didn't know. So we held our fire. Instead, the next day we sent a message. The US Navy and the South Koreans put on a display of precision firepower showing we could have easily stopped the launch, and if the programme continued…' Evert sliced down his hand in a karate chop. '…we would blast it and buck-teeth boy into atoms.'

Moschin interrupted. 'But the fact remains that you have over thirty years of diplomacy, sanctions and military exercises under your belt, yet you have still failed to stop the North Korean nuclear programme.'

Evert looked slightly put out at the barbed remark. 'Assassinating a foreign leader used to be an integral part of America's national security toolkit, then Gerald Ford stopped the policy over fifty years ago. When President Jefferson was elected, he was all up for reinstating the policy until…'

'…until somebody assassinated him,' said Moschin, then lit himself his first Gauloises of the day.

Hwang instinctively stood to get away from the reeking smoke. 'So gentlemen, to cut to the chase. I assume that we are here to talk about finally wiping Jae-Ho Kom, his family and his government from the face of the earth. I must tell you that this is something South Korea and I are prepared to do unilaterally.'

Moschin sat back in his chair and took another large drag on his cigarette.

'Well, that's good to hear, because we have a plan that involves exactly that.'

22 September 2031
Cull Day 223
The Kom family palace, Wonsan, North Korea

Meeting between Jae-Ho Kom and Jang Chang, vice-director of the Workers' Party of Korea:

Jae-Ho Kom: 'You think I should meet this dog?'

Jang Chang: 'Could be a trap.'

Jae-Ho Kom: 'He says the South wants a new relationship. If we agree he will sever ties with the US and these Reboot madmen.'

Jang Chang: 'It could still be a trap.'

Jae-Ho Kom: 'He is prepared to meet on our side of the DM zone. We can seize him out of sight of the Western media.'

Jang Chang: 'It would send other deserting scum a strong message.'

Jae-Ho Kom: 'We can televise his execution.'

Jang Chang: 'With the anti-aircraft guns as with Hyong Yong Choi?'

Jae-Ho Kom: 'Too quick. Flame thrower.'

Jang Chang: 'Like O Sang Hon? He squealed like a pig for ten minutes.'

Jae-Ho Kom: 'Agreed then. I will meet the traitor. Will you attend?'

Jang Chang: 'I don't want to miss the look on his face as we welcome him back. I will dress as a soldier again.'

28 September 2031
Cull Day 229
Demilitarised zone, North and South Korean border.

The rendezvous between the Korean leaders was to be in the recently rebuilt liaison building just inside the North's border. North Korea had destroyed it for the fourth time, just two years previously during another period of political tension. The meeting was scheduled to last just thirty minutes, and had just two agenda items – the current status of South Korean, US and Reboot relations and date of the next meeting.

At five minutes to twelve, Hwang stepped out of the South Korean border building and started the walk to the liaison building just eight hundred metres away. Jae-Ho Kom had insisted that for the first exploratory meeting, Hwang should come alone. If these terms could not be met, he would pull out. South Korea's new president had agreed.

It was a typically humid day on the thirty-eighth Parallel, 38 degrees and no breeze. Despite the tensions in the air, the cherry trees on both sides of the border hung full and still. The mosquitoes, gnats and dragonflies happily buzzed between the two distrustful lands. Overhead, a grey heron flew north, blissfully unaware it had passed from democratic republic to dynastic dictatorship in the space of a few wing beats.

Hwang walked down the gravel pathway trying to look nonchalant, in reality his hands were shaking and his legs felt like lead. He quietly sang South Korea's national anthem to try to calm his nerves.

'Until that day when Mount Baekdu is worn away and the East Sea's waters run dry may God protect and preserve our country.'

He looked down at the ornamental pond that ran alongside the path. A fountain in its centre sprayed fine water across the surface, encouraging a bright orange koi carp to bob its mouth out of the water in hope of catching a bug. Scores of pink water lilies had opened and greedily soaked up the midday sun. The image reminded him of Huwon Secret Garden in Seoul where only diplomats and high-ranking officials were allowed to visit. Occasionally, he would go there to relax with his family at a weekend. Perhaps if the weather was kind and the air pollution tolerable they would lay a blanket on the lawn and enjoy a picnic of fruit, sandwiches and rolled omelette. His children often threw crumbs in the water, and the catfish would gather in great clusters and jostle furiously to get their share. Hwang felt sad that he would never see his wife, son or daughter again.

As he continued his painful walk, he passed generous stepped borders of pink lilacs and white and yellow magnolias in full bloom, their colourful display lent this most northerly strip of South Korea an open, gregarious and welcoming atmosphere. It was all in sharp contrast with the drab, joyless grey of its neighbour's land where a single solitary row of yellow dahlias along the edge of a wooden hut offered the only optimistic pop of colour. Hwang knew that the visual divergence was wholly deliberate.

As he approached his destination, a group of stern-faced soldiers emerged from inside the building and started to form up in two menacing lines either side of him. Their movements were robotic and disciplined, with every deliberate step their heavy black boots clattered on the concrete pavement. Startled by the unexpected flurry of activity, Hwang hesitated for a split second but managed to persuade his legs to keep walking.

Then suddenly, there he was. A squat, stout figure in a black suit walking briskly towards him, smiling broadly. Jae-Ho Kom. The man he had served but had never met, the man who had haunted his dreams for years, the man who had ordered his family to be taken from their homes. The man who had lined his family's pockets with gold and allowed his people to starve.

The person Hwang despised beyond imagining was now in front of him, wanting to shake his hand as if they were long-lost friends.

Hwang felt serene. He calmly regarded the face of this man who had enslaved his people. He registered his small black eyes, his pale, puffy skin, his yellowing teeth, the small flakes of dandruff on the collar. He didn't extend his hand, he didn't smile, he just delayed long enough to see the fear register in the dictator's eyes as he realised he had been tricked. Only then did Hwang reach inside his trouser pocket to press the switch that detonated the Semtex bomb strapped around his waist.

Colonel Moschin sipped a large whisky and drew on his cigar as Agent Evert strutted around the room in delight.

'We hit pay dirt and no mistake.' Evert took a large gulp from his can of Budweiser. 'We wiped out the evil king and his equally evil sister. Plus a few of the important minions too… Premier Kim Jae-Ryong, one vice-premier, four ministers and two generals. We even got Jang Chang, dressed as a fucking soldier for Christ's sakes. That's some headcount, right there.'

'They got sloppy,' replied Moschin. 'In war that costs lives.'

'And now everything's changed. After decades of being the biggest intelligence black hole in the world, every general, every politician, every citizen in North Korea wants to be our friend. Turns out they wanted rid of him as much as we did.' Evert finished his beer, crushed the can, threw it in a bin and reached for another.

'Remember, Evert, we owe it all to Hwang. He was a baby boomer who truly atoned for his sins.'

'Well, he knew we wouldn't let him live after we found out his age, and we gave him the chance to free his family. He got what he wanted and so did we. As far as his country is concerned, he died a big-time hero.'

Colonel Paolo Moschin ran his index finger along the scar on his cheek and allowed himself a smile. They had achieved another victory in the Reboot cause. They had freed one half of Korea from its nightmare and united it once again in a common cause.

Better still, he had a beautiful big Brazilian cigar to enjoy.

6 December 2031, Edinburgh
Cull Day 297

Lying on the floor eating rusks. The smell of wet laundry. Smell of dirty cotton nappies. German au pair. Waiting with Mum in the queue at the butcher's. Half a pound of butter. Four slices of bacon. Sloppy grandmother kiss. Smell of iodine. Visit to hospital. Cigarette smoke. Mum drunk. Dad drunk. Auntie drunk. Kicking ball through the window. Dad shouting. Pike hanging on garage handle. Mum laughing. Dad with a beard. Holiday in Weston. Candyfloss. Donkeys. War comics. Sunburn. Sprained arm. Brother dies. Dad crying. Sick in the car. Smell of bleach. First football match. Riding a bike without stabilisers. Grazed knees. Kissing Pamela Stoat. Passing eleven plus. Wearing glasses. Playing football. Smell of Germolene. Rain on a plastic roof. Wet grass. Wearing shorts on my first day of school. Queuing for the toilet and not holding it. Smell of foundation. Vapour trail in the sky. Scoring a goal. Skimming stones. Coach trip. Boat trip. Egg and cress sandwiches. Cotton dressing gown. Nylon sheets. Cod liver oil and malt. Pocket money for weeding the driveway. Swallowing seawater. First day at grammar school. Chemistry lab. Scoring a goal. Jumping the moat. Best mate Geoff Dyer. Woodstock triple album. Playing in the band. Losing my virginity. Passing my driving test. My first accident, wrecking the car. Passing exams. Going to Cambridge University. Pride of the family. Getting drunk in the Anchor, falling in the river. Appearing with the Footlights at the ADC, bricking myself. Summer in Brussels. Working in the Hard Rock Café. Falling in love with Emilia. She broke my heart. Getting an honours. More pride, resentment from Tom. Mum gets breast cancer, lying with her at the care home. Holding her hand. Dad crying. First job, first pay packet. Loving London. Loving life. Loving Soho. Getting robbed and beaten up in Stockwell. Trying cocaine. Loving cocaine. Every Friday and Saturday and Sunday. My first flat in Clapham. Meeting Bethany in Covent Garden. Falling in love again. Travelling across Europe. Getting married in Tetbury, my hometown. Beautiful day. So happy. Honeymoon in Nice. Patrick is born. Move to the Cotswolds. Start Jameson Hesketh. Company growing. Move office. Move house. Bella is born by caesarean. Just five pound two ounces. Dad diagnosed with Creutzfeldt-Jakob disease. Dad dies ten months later to the day. Start Eco division at Jameson Hesketh. Develop successful wave energy power system. Open offices in Singapore and San Francisco. Invent new plastic recycling method. Bethany says she wants to leave me. Take sabbatical, win back my wife. Three miscarriages. Fertility treatment. Failure. Depression. Counselling. Bethany starts health food business. Put off retirement again. Trial ice gel. Failure. Failure. Success. Plan Antarctica mission. Select team. Success. Fall in love again. Anger. Shock. Sorrow. Anger. Trapped in a van.

*

'Hello Ice Man.'

A voice cut through into Jameson's mind, waking him out of his slumber, cutting short his showreel of life memories.

'Enjoy your trip down memory lane? I assume it included the smell of Germolene, black and white TVs and summer trips to the seaside? English baby boomers seem to share remarkably similar experiences with chloral hydrate. It's rather charming.'

Although his mind wasn't tuned in and his vision was blurred, he recognised the Scandinavian accent. It was the voice of the lunatic he had heard on Sarah's phone in the helicopter. The voice of Erica the Mad. Erica Sandstrom.

The previous night he had been brought down into this dark, damp circular brick room beneath the castle and given dried biscuits and drugged water. Now he was lying strapped on a table, shivering in just his underpants with a crazy Norwegian woman looming over him, gibbering nonsense.

'I knew I would meet you one day Mr Jameson. The man with the secret of eternal ice.' She touched his brow. 'I must treat you like no other.'

'This is very melodramatic, isn't it? Have you got a laser beam to fry my balls?' Jameson was trying to put on a brave face. In reality he was totally terrified.

Sandstrom shrugged. 'I'm new to this, but our experts insist that if you want to unsettle someone, then first you have to put them in an unsettling place.'

The door opened, and a short, rotund man wearing a white lab coat entered pushing a trolley; a cloth covered the contents of the top tray.

'This must be Dr Fiendish,' Jameson joked again, then turned his head and violently vomited onto the floor.

Sandstrom stepped back from the mess. 'Nothing fiendish about Stefan, but he's ex-KGB so he does know his chemicals.'

'Stefan' pulled the cloth back to reveal three syringes, each with differing volumes of liquid in their barrels. Jameson could feel his fear and the vomit rising again. He pulled involuntarily against the leather straps which held his hands and feet.

Stefan picked up the first syringe.

Jameson tried to pull away. 'What the fuck is it?'

Sandstrom held her hand up, and Stefan put the syringe back on the table.

'Sodium thiopental of course. It won't hurt…as long as we don't give you too much.'

Sodium thiopental, the truth drug. It could be effective because it put people in the twilight zone between consciousness and unconsciousness. Normally it made them feel disinhibited and much less inclined to lie.

Sandstrom paced slowly around the room, clearly revelling in the power trip.

'So, Will, are you going to fill in the gaps about your formulation?'

'Why would I? If I do, I'm dead.' Though his head was swimming with panic and part of him wanted this ordeal over, enough of Jameson's mind remained in control to determine that he keep to his stonewalling strategy.

For now.

Sandstrom's face hardened. 'If you die, then at least your death would have been worth something. Your work will have helped the earth survive for at least another millennium.'

She pulled over a chair and sat at the end of the table, looking at him between his feet. 'You will be remembered forever as the man who stopped the ice melt. They might even put a blue plaque outside your house.'

He raised his head. 'I want to be part of this new world I'm creating.'

'But you're not welcome, Will.' She smiled coldly.

'Then you're not getting anything from me, you bitch.' He kicked his leg towards her face. Sandstrom jerked her head back in surprise then made a signal to Stefan for the proceedings to begin.

Stefan took a syringe off the tray and without care, plunged the contents into Jameson's arm. He winced from the pain then shivered at the sensation of the liquid flooding into his arm.

That hurt, the clumsy bastard. Just keep it together and you'll be fine Will.

Within moments Jameson began to feel light-headed. He could hear talking, they weren't talking to him. One voice belonged to Sandstrom the other sounded East European.

'How does this work?'

'The same way as alcohol. It will make it difficult for him to lie. Lying is complicated. If you suppress higher cortical functions as this does, you are more likely to tell the truth, simply because it's easier.'

Sandstrom smiled. '*In vino veritas* – in wine there is truth. If you want to know what your lover really thinks of you, get them drunk.'

Stefan stood over Jameson and shone a light into his eyes. 'He should be ready now.'

She turned on a voice recorder and held the microphone up to his mouth.

'So, Will, tell us a little about your amazing CDT-18. I heard from your colleagues that it can insulate melting ice. Most impressive.'

Jameson's head was swimming, but he still felt in control.

OK Will, just tell her enough to keep her interested. No more.

'It seemed to be effective in the field trials, but much more needs to be done.'

'What needs to be done?' Sandstrom asked. 'What exactly needs to be done?'

Lots of things need to be done. Lots of really complex things you Scandinavian harpy.

'Many things, many, many complicated things.'

'It sounds fascinating, Will. I'd love to know every detail.' She breathed into his face, so close that he could feel the warmth, smell the coffee she'd had that morning.

Smells like Colombian roast. I would kill for some Colombian roast. Better still Peruvian. 100% Arabica. Rich and intense with background tones of almond and chocolate. I would kill for some and I would die for some. With perhaps a fresh pain au chocolat to go with it. And a good book, perhaps a novel by…

'Will, Will, your CDT-18 is a brilliant idea. Please tell me more,' Sandstrom insisted.

Normally you can't shut me up on the topic. Just keep it vague. Make it appear that there's still much to do, many more trials required. Tell her about Tom.

'Ask my assistant, Tom Waites. He'll have more detail. He's a good lad, a little raw around the edges…'

'Tom has knowledge, but you know the really big stuff. You're the main man, the one with the brains. We want to hear it from you Will.'

More flattery – it was spearing through Jameson's defences like a sniper's bullet. There was a part of him that was dying to tell Sandstrom everything, itching to reveal every detail of the last five years of his life. To tell someone, anyone, even these Reboot psychopaths about the ways he had worked it out. To brag how he had proved the science community, with their conventions and cynicism, totally wrong.

Those naysaying bastards should give me the credit I deserve.

'I'd love to share it,' Jameson blurted out, almost in relief.

Sandstrom's face brightened as she moved the microphone nearer. 'Well, tell me now, Will. I'd love to hear everything.'

He started to talk but only gibberish came out. His mouth was moving, but he couldn't form the words or the coherent sentences he wanted.

'Ice melt. Ice melts. Melt ice. Crystals. Stop melting.'

'What is he saying?' Sandstrom exclaimed.

Stay solid. Protect crystals. Melt bad. Gel good.

'Wait, I'm trying to tell you. Just give me a minute.' Jameson hit the table with the back of his head to try to clear the fog in his brain.

'Slow down, take it easy Will.' She stroked his arm.

'OK, OK, OK. It's the ice. The ice is sinking. Sinking. The gel was good. Really good. Your hair is nice, you should grow it.' Jameson shut his eyes and began to laugh.

'I've seen this before,' said Stefan, shaking his head. 'Some people are susceptible to the drug and want to talk to their interrogator, but the drug causes the brain to lose its ability to recall detail. He could tell you he has a wife and children, but he might not be able to tell you their names.'

'How about another dose?'

Stefan shook his head. 'It won't work. He will simply be more eager to tell you what he knows, but even less able to do so.'

Sandstrom shrugged, turned off the recorder and walked to the door.

'OK, we'll try Plan B.'

Even in his soporific state, Jameson knew.

That sounds bad.

Twenty minutes later, his head began to clear. Pulling on his restraints to give him a better idea of self and his physical state, his thoughts went to what Plan B might actually entail.

Pain and mutilation.

He used to love war movies as a boy. Growing up in the 1960s that meant watching John Mills in *Ice Cold in Alex,* David Niven in *A Matter of Life and Death,* Gregory Peck in *The Guns of Navarone* and Jack Hawkins in *The Cruel Sea.* But the actor and film that stood out to him more than any other was George Chakiris in *633 Squadron.* Chakiris played a Norwegian resistance leader who had been captured and then sent to Gestapo headquarters to reveal his secrets. The British send a bomber to destroy the building and kill him before he breaks, which they do successfully. While the plot and the action gripped him, what really stuck in his young mind were the torture scenes. Chakiris had been tied to a table, and while they didn't show what the Nazi torturers were actually doing to him as he lay there helpless, Jameson easily could imagine them.

Fingernails ripped out by pliers, shin bones smashed with a hammer, testicles cut off with a razor blade.

Yet despite his agonies, Chakiris did not give the Germans what they wanted. He did not betray his comrades. As a ten-year-old boy, Jameson imagined too that he would somehow find the resolve to resist the sadistic torturers' worst horrors and emerge a hero. But now, as he lay on the table with his mind flushing itself of the truth drug, he began to doubt it.

So thirsty, so bloody parched. My throat is on fire. If they give me a drink, I'll tell them what they want. Just a nice long glass of water with some ice is all it would take. Where are they? Leaving me alone for a while? Probably just another convention in the interrogation playbook. Page one hundred and ten: let the victim stew.

Then the door swung open, pushed with such force it smashed into the wall. The sound of the impact reverberated around the bare brick cell. It was quickly replaced by the heavy metallic crunching of hobnailed boots on concrete as two grim-faced muscular men in army fatigues walked in. Jameson's spirits sank another degree as he recognised them as the duo who had boarded the plane at Ascension Island. Before he could even register their faces or a word being spoken, he felt a crushing blow to his ribs which forced the air out of his lungs. He tried to draw a breath and the pain was excruciating.

Can't breathe. I'm hurt. Should I call for Mother? We were never especially close, she would probably tell me to stop whinging. Insist I don't bleed on the carpet.

A face was above him, snarling. His breath smelling of beer. He spat as he talked.

'Tell us about formula.' Again the voice was Eastern European, Polish perhaps.

Christ. Why is it always Eastern Europeans?

'Go to hell.' A voice came out of Jameson's mouth; it wasn't his. It was George Chakiris.

He heard laughter, the cackling, unrestrained laugh of a sadist, of someone born to this pitiless work. A bang on the back of his head, then two pitiless blows to his face, the first probably breaking his nose, the second possibly fracturing a cheekbone. He was so stunned by their ferocity and speed, that there was no pain, just lots of blood from his shattered nose. It ran into his mouth and down his throat, and he started to cough.

Metal taste. Liquid in my nose. Watch the carpet William. Sorry Mum.

Seeing the potential for their victim to choke on his own blood, they untied his bonds and pushed him upright into a chair.

'Formula. Formula.' A slap across his face; it smarted a little, nothing more.

'Stop, it tickles,' his inner Chakiris declared. Jameson wanted the voice to shut up.

Stop goading these animals you prick. Perhaps they'll leave you alone.

They emptied the icy contents of a water bucket over his head. It didn't worry him; it revived him. He licked the dripping nectar off his lips, leaned his head to try to suck liquid off his shoulder. They stand him up and the second man buries the metal toecap of his boot into Jameson's groin who bends over and hits the stone floor with his temple.

Relief.

His next conscious thought.

Body sore, every breath painful. Face caked in something crusty. Mouth feels strange, swollen, numb, explore gums with my tongue, two teeth missing. Wearing an orange jumpsuit. I'm dying.

As he slowly recovered his senses, Jameson realised he was sitting tied to a metal chair that had been fixed to the floor. This was not the damp, circular room. This was not the torture chamber. The walls were polar-white, sterile. It smelt clean, antiseptic scrubbed. The room was oblong, modern. It had two large windows at one end; one he could see through, the other he couldn't. Then as his eyes finally focussed more clearly, through the clear window he could see people, men and women, boomers, and they were all naked. They didn't look in at him. They didn't look at each other. They didn't speak, they didn't acknowledge each other. They just looked down at their feet and shuffled slowly past. Then as he watched uncomprehending at what he was seeing, he recognised someone. A big man, with white hair and a white beard – Mike Appel.

'They're on their way to oblivion.' A female voice filled the room. 'But no one weeps for them, because they have lived like gods. And even gods must die eventually.'

The voice was distorted, synthesised, but he knew who it was. Then a door opened behind him.

'Hello, Dad.'

11 October 2031, Southern France
Cull Day 242

Sébastien Roussel was travelling at high speed and heading north on the A51, the famous 'road of holidays' that linked Aix-en-Provence, the French Alps and the Côte d'Azur. As the speedometer registered one hundred and thirty kilometres an hour, he gripped the thin Bakelite steering wheel of his ageing powder blue Citroën DS hard with both hands. Normally he drove his beloved classic car with care, but on this day he was angry.

Angry because this was a Saturday, and the one day he got to spend with his children was being disrupted. Angry because just three hours ago his boss told him he was being fired from the job that he loved.

Roussel squeezed the steering wheel harder as he recalled the moment Benoît Long, the assistant energy minister had phoned.

'Seb, it's Benoît.'

'Hello Benny, you sound worried. Everything OK at the plant?'

For a few seconds, there was silence, then an exaggerated sigh as Long finally blurted out his bad news.

'Reboot want to take over assembly and put in their own team. I'm afraid you're out.'

Silence.

'I'm sorry Seb. They've just told me.'

More silence.

'We will pay you the full term of your contract of course, every last euro.'

Roussel was stunned. It was of no comfort that his lucrative contract would be paid. He had just been sacked from his job as leader of the most ambitious scientific project in human history – the quest to harness the power that makes the stars shine.

He had been, until a few seconds earlier, director general of the International Thermonuclear Experimental Reactor Project (ITER), the reactor that when operational would establish the viability of clean-fusion energy.

The holy grail of carbon-neutral energy production – fusing, as opposed to splitting, atoms – had been chased for decades by scientists who saw its incredible potential. The project aimed to use hydrogen fusion via superconducting magnets to produce massive heat energy at temperatures ten times hotter than the sun. According to ITER's scientists, if they were successful, an amount of hydrogen the size of a pineapple could be used to produce as much energy as ten thousand tonnes of coal. Better still, the electricity it produced would be free from carbon emissions and could liberate mankind from burning fossil fuel altogether.

Roussel had been a prominent doctor of chemistry and physics at France's atomic energy commission when he was headhunted by his government to lead the project. Soon realising that the scale of the logistics and science were so daunting that no single country could make it alone, Roussel convinced the politicians he must look to engage the whole scientific community. His mastery of six languages and natural diplomacy helped him establish a network of physicists, engineers and chemists across thirty countries all willing to share their knowledge. Changing tariffs, intellectual property laws and xenophobia were constant early-day problems, often restricting the flow of materials, people and ideas across borders. But Roussel's energy, positivity and dedication kept things moving.

When it was eventually decided that the main reactor facility would be based in Cadarache in Southern France, Roussel had moved his family to nearby Manosque so that he could oversee construction. Now, nearly two decades later, and despite an overspend of three billion euros, he was confident power could be produced from the site in just another six months.

But that was still not fast enough for those Reboot bastards, thought Roussel.

So he had to cancel his precious time with his children and now he was speeding in his shuddering old car towards the site to confront them and to implore them to change their minds. As he saw the signs for his exit coming up, his mind turned back once more to his conversation with Long.

'This is madness Benoît. We are so close.'

'Not close enough it seems, Sébastien. You know this is not my doing. Reboot are running the European Union, the UK, Russia, the United States, Japan, China, India and South Korea, so they call all the shots now. I'm sorry.'

'These people are ruthless and crazy,' Roussel replied bitterly.

'You don't know how crazy Seb. They didn't kill the American president because he was a lunatic. No, no, no. It was because he was threatening to withdraw funding for ITER.'

'Look, I understand their impatience. Christ, they are impatient about everything. This just can't be progressed any faster. We are at a critical stage with the Tokamak.'

The Tokamak fusion reactor was at the very heart of the project. Designed to harness the energy of fusion, it would use the enormous heat generated by its magnets to produce steam, and then electricity by way of four of the world's most powerful turbines.

'We're at the point of installation. The cladding wall is finished and we are due to start lowering the cryostat base into the pit. As you know, it's the most complex component we'll be handling. It's essential I'm there to oversee the operation.'

'Sorry Seb, Smits will be overseeing it now.'

Robert Jan Smits was director general of Research at the European Commission in Brussels. He had been the leading candidate for the ITER director general job, but did not possess Roussel's physics knowledge or linguistic skills so he was rejected. But Smits was a powerful man who bore grudges. He had been constantly uncooperative and made life difficult for both Roussel and the project, especially when it started to run over budget.

'Smits?' Roussel could hardly believe his ears. 'Smits is a bean counter, a bureaucrat and a self-serving prick.'

'Well, someone at Reboot rates him.'

Roussel was quiet for a few moments as he considered his options.

'Benny, tell me as a friend. Is there anything I can do?'

'Nothing. Believe me, I've tried. If it's any consolation, they are promising limitless resources and manpower to accelerate the programme.'

'We are dealing with the unknown. You know as well as I do that it's not just a case of throwing money around.'

As he had put the phone down, Roussel suddenly felt very tired. Even though he had welcomed the intellectual challenge, the ITER project had been a huge burden for him to bear these last twenty years. It uprooted his family and cost him his marriage; he hardly saw his three children. His health had deteriorated and he rarely slept more than four hours a night.

Maybe this was a good thing. Perhaps the project needs new blood, drive and energy to complete the next phase. I'm still only forty-six. I could try something new. In the meantime, I could get to know my children.

He slumped back in his leather chair in his home office and looked out of the window. The sun was out, illuminating the tidy rows of olive trees, oaks and pines that grew on the slopes of Mont D'Or. Halfway towards the summit, he saw the small white house, with its low brick wall, surrounded by vineyards on all four sides. Often he gazed at it through binoculars and sometimes he would see the owner, an old man, sitting on the terrace sipping wine in the glow of an early evening, faithful German shepherd at his feet. It always looked to Roussel like a wonderful place to grow old, and he promised himself he would try to buy it when the project was finished. He reckoned he might take a walk up there later and put the proposition to the old man on his terrace. Right now he felt like a coffee.

He walked down the stone stairwell from his second-floor apartment, opened the ancient red oak door, with its assortment of unused locks and chains, and stepped out into the narrow Rue d'Aubette. The street was barely three metres across and typical of this compact medieval town. Even though the tightly-bunched four and five-storey stone buildings in the area were constructed in differing architectural styles, they were made coherent by the uniformity of their colourful wooden window shutters, painted in vibrant shades of yellow, red or blue. Like Roussel's own apartment, most buildings boasted extravagantly large wooden doors hung on oversized black hinges studded with iron insets and ornate metal plates, hefty iron door knockers set into their centres. Everywhere, hanging baskets and terracotta pots bulged with blowsy pink and lemon blooms, the food market overflowed with the rainbow bounty of a late summer harvest. The town's cobbled pavements had been cleaned overnight, their time-polished blue stones dazzled like jewels. On this morning, Manosque looked a picture of easy beauty and happy industry. Roussel was glad he had come out; he felt his spirits rising.

As he neared the centre, people greeted Roussel as he walked by. Although he was known locally as 'the ITER man', they didn't treat him differently to any other resident. Roussel liked the informality. It was a blessed relief from the rigid protocols and endless politics of his job. In fact, he decided as he strolled along, he didn't just like Manosque, he loved it and he especially loved its smells.

The smell of the freshly baked cream patisseries at Giraud's Boulangerie on the Rue des Sophoras which he liked to treat his team with on a Friday lunchtime. The scent of the orange blossom, jasmine and lilies from the flower seller on the corner of Place du Joubert that always filled his apartment with love and life. The mouth-watering waft of the suckling pig roast at the front of Becker's butcher's shop at boulevard Charles De Gaulle. And the exotic scented aromas from the Starlight Brothel at Rue L'Armistice which occasionally offered him comfort and diversion from his chaotic life.

He was not seeking out any of these pleasures today, Roussel was heading for the café in Saint-Sauveur Square where awaited his favourite smell of all – freshly-ground strong coffee. As he turned into the square, he was delighted to see that his usual table was vacant. It looked directly out at the beautiful bronze and marble fountain of Saint-Sauveur. The ornate Catholic church that stood opposite the fountain was one of the town's oldest, having welcomed worshippers for over six hundred years. Roussel loved the tableau – he had spent many hours at this busy intersection just watching the world go by, dreaming of saving the world with his fusion energy and of rescuing his marriage with promises of finding more time for his family.

No sooner had he sat down than the gangly long-boned, moon-faced café owner, Michel Laprade, was at his table. 'Bonjour monsieur Roussel, no children today?'

'Picking them up at midday. Their mother had the boyfriend over last night…so they're running late.'

Laprade smiled knowingly. 'Women, they always want control. Can I get you the usual?'

'Yes, and a small cognac.'

'Café au lait, croque-monsieur and a Martell on their way.'

'Make it a large one.'

With the merest hint of a raised eyebrow, Laprade turned on his heel.

Roussel pulled a packet of cigarettes out of his jacket pocket, lit one and took a deep drag.

Time to give these up.

Even though smoking was forbidden at the ITER site, he still managed to work his way through twenty every day.

The square was in shadow most of the time, the tall church saw to that, but on a clear day in the morning and evening the sun would make a brief appearance.

It was ten o'clock, and the clock on the town hall could be heard cheerfully announcing the fact. A mother, obviously late, hurried through at the far side of the square, her two excited young daughters followed in her wake, holding hands and giggling. An elderly man in a black beret sat on the cobbles in the shade of a young Aleppo pine, nursing a carafe of red wine, breaking bread onto a blue chequered cloth between his legs. On a narrow wrought iron balcony, a bare-chested man in his thirties read a book, wife or lover cutting his hair. A grey and white cat stretched out and yawned near Roussel's feet, under one paw the half-eaten hind legs of a small rodent.

He was about to rest his eyes for a few moments when a narrow brilliant beam of light fired into the square, shooting through a gap between the red clay-tiled rooftops.

As Roussel idly watched, the pure white ray hit the base of the fountain, momentarily highlighting the intricate filigree in the bronze. In the same instant, a two-metre-high jet of water exploded into the startled morning air as the fountain's water timer kicked it into spectacular life. The old man looked up from his bread and raised a glass to the sight. Briefly distracted from his book, the bare-chested man said something to his hairdresser and they both laughed. Even the lazy cat raised his head at the divine synchronicity of the display.

Roussel looked at this extraordinary scene and felt the hairs on the back of his neck stand up and his pulse quicken.

What am I thinking?

I can't just roll over and be pushed out of the project without a fight. I was the best man – the only man – to complete the job. No one could bring the right talent and ideas together like Sébastien Roussel could. We were so close to firing up the Tokamak, so close to proving all the doubters wrong. Why should someone else, especially that little shit Smits, get all the credit?

When Laprade came with Roussel's order just a minute later, his most famous customer had already disappeared.

Roussel's elderly Citroën had not appreciated the punishing high speed rush. Half a kilometre from his exit for Saint-Paul-lès-Durance, the exhaust had begun to spew out coughs of black smoke and he could smell burning oil. Even though this was a

Sunday, the roads were unusually quiet. In fact, he couldn't remember seeing another car on the motorway since joining it at the Manosque junction.

As he approached the autoroute toll, Roussel reached in his pocket for the electronic tag which normally allowed him straight through without stopping. As he neared his normal exit gate he had hardly slowed. When he finally realised that the gate wasn't moving, it was already too late. The Citroën nosedived into the steel barrier pole which smashed through the windscreen and into his skull.

'Sébastien Roussel was an extraordinary man. We would not be where we are if it was not for his fantastic determination and vision.'

Robert Jan Smits was slowly delivering his eulogy before the three hundred people who had crammed into Saint-Saveur church. Another six hundred stood in the square outside, listening through speakers.

'Thanks to him, the project he started twenty years ago is on track to reach first plasma in December.' He paused for dramatic effect. Half of the congregation murmured knowingly; the other half looked unmoved. 'Many of you will already appreciate the significance of that. For those of you not in the scientific community, it means we will be a giant step closer to saving our planet.' Smits solemnly walked down from the pulpit and touched the French tricolour flag draped over the wooden coffin.

'On behalf of future generations, I thank you, Sébastien.'

When the service was over, Smits walked slowly out of the church with Erica Sandstrom and Colonel Paolo Moschin.

'You were very generous in there,' said Sandstrom. 'I thought you hated the man.'

'I did. You will never hear me say anything good about that bastard again,' replied Smits. 'He was too soft, too democratic.

This project needs more ruthless governance. It's too important to be given to liberals.'

'I agree,' said Moschin. 'But a shame he had to die.'

They walked out into the small square and stood by the fountain.

'We just wanted to stop him getting to the site and causing a disruption. We didn't kill him – his damn car did.'

Moschin dipped his hand in the fountain basin and took a drink. 'You know, back in 1955, that Citroën was seen as the future, packed with new innovations. First mass-production car with disc brakes.'

'Well, things move on, things move on,' said Smits.

'Speaking of which, how is the schedule going? Is the Tokamak complete? When will the cryostat be closed?'

'All on track as far as I know.' Smits was taken aback by the level of knowledge Moschin seemed to have. The colonel lit a Gauloises, took a deep drag and pointed it accusingly at Smits.

'As far as you know? You need to be on top of this, Smits. We were going to replace Roussel because he didn't keep us in the loop. Don't fall into that trap yourself.'

'Of…of course,' Smits replied suddenly unnerved by the threat.

'To be clear…'

Moschin prodded Smits' shoulder to reinforce each point.

'We want the integrated commission phase started in 2032 not 2035. We want evidence of first plasma the following year. And we want the deuterium-tritium operation brought forward by at least five years.'

'If you get me the resources, I will deliver,' Smits replied, recovering some composure.

'Well, you two have lost me totally. I'm dying for a coffee. Surely this place can offer that?' Sandstrom walked off towards Michel Laprade's café.

Behind them, the fountain spurted into life again. It was ten o'clock, but there was no beam of light this time from Earth's nearest star.

4 November 2031, Texas, USA
Cull Day 266

'Let me get this straight, Bill…'

Christobel Hayes could hardly believe what she was being told by the caller on the other end of the phone.

'…as from midday tomorrow, Eastern Time. We can shoot to death – legally – any person we identify as a gen-u-ine baby boomer?'

'Not quite, Chrissy,' came the reply. 'We still gotta work alongside the FBI, the National Guard and the police department. They'll give us the names and last-known whereabouts of local boomers who have run. Where possible, they'll give identifiers like height, weight, colour and so on. If we have them cornered, and there are any doubts about who it is, you have to take a picture of their face and send it in to the state database. Is that clear Chrissy?'

'Clear as day, Bill.'

'They will let you know if you have the right person. Is that clear?'

'Crystal, Bill. Then we can blast them to kingdom come?'

'Yes, and only then. We'll know more details after the nine o'clock all-channel broadcast tomorrow morning.'

'Well, I'll be damned.' Hayes was thrilled with the news. 'This is exactly why the GOA exists – to serve our country by bearing arms. Bill, the members are going to be thrilled, real thrilled. See you tomorrow for the turkey shoot. Sleep well.'

'These ain't turkeys Chrissy, these are human beings...'

But Hayes wasn't listening. 'Yadda, yadda, yadda,' she muttered to herself as she put down the phone to her boss.

Christobel Hayes was the Texas director for the Gun Owners of America, a gun rights organisation with over two million members. She had been talking to the organisation's founder, Senator H.L. 'Wild Bill' Norgate. Like her, he was delighted that some of the 725,368 firearms in the Lone Star State would now be put to good use. Unlike her, Norgate didn't want it to turn into a bloodbath.

Hayes left her office and walked down the steps to her favourite place. Unlocking the heavy metal door, she flicked a switch and stepped into the gun room.

The strip lights flickered on and illuminated the red brick-walled, low-ceilinged space. The wall to her right was covered top to bottom with modern guns of all calibres, from heavy semi-automatic assault rifles to superlight pocket pistols. All had been mounted neatly to the brick work on bespoke matt-coated steel hanging frames. Without exception, the guns were constructed of dull carbon black metal and plastic.

The left-hand wall accommodated older weaponry, guns mainly of First and Second World Wars vintage. These had been produced from a greater variety of materials like chrome, stainless steel, hardwood and even white ivory. Towards the back of the room on the concrete floor, a number of belt-fed heavy machine guns stood on splayed tripod stands. Hayes smiled like a child in a candy store as she surveyed her formidable arsenal.

Hayes had lived a troubled life. An only child born into a blue- collar family in the middle of the mid-eighties economic boom. Living in Detroit, both parents enjoyed steady jobs with General Motors, but when the recession paralysed car production throughout the state, the family had to leave its comfortable home. Her father Wayne turned to drink and for the next six years took his frustrations out on his daughter. Unable to stand it any longer, Hayes left home at sixteen and worked her way south and away from her father. Finally settling in Oklahoma, she gained a degree in business management and started a career with a law firm. With her striking auburn hair, big bust and long legs Hayes soon began attracting men. She met a businessman at her local gun club, married him and gave birth to Madison the following year. Within another year, he had left them for a blonde lap dancer.

For the last ten years, she had worked hard to establish a better life for herself and her daughter in San Antonio. She was now a respected land estate manager and a director at the GOA. It had taken her that time and most of her spare cash to accumulate the collection of deadly firepower that was now her pride and joy. No one was going to push Christobel Hayes around again.

She walked slowly around the basement, surveying the room like a critic in an art gallery, admiring and considering each gun carefully in turn. As was her habit, she talked to herself quietly as she deliberated.

'OK, I'm only gonna take three or four weapons. First, I'll need a reliable long shot to pick 'em off at any range over three hundred feet…so that'll be the C15.'

Also known as the McMillan TAC50, the C15 had broken the world record for the longest rifle kill. A Canadian sniper operating in Iraq had scored a confirmed fatal shot with the weapon at over two miles. Hayes carefully took it off its mount and inserted it into the brushed black nylon GOA-branded field carrying case along with the rifle's high power telescopic sight and silencer muzzle.

'If I manage to flush out a group, I'll need a reliable semi. My standard AR-15 fits the bill there...no doubt about it.'

Known as America's most popular rifle, over eight million Americans owned an AR-15. It was also the mass murderer's weapon of choice. It had been used in shootings in Newtown, San Bernardino, Denver, Las Vegas and Sutherland Springs. Again, Hayes took it off the wall and placed it lovingly in its custom-built protective carry bag. She had just started to consider a third weapon when a young girl shouted down into the cellar.

'Momma. What you doing down there?'

It was the high-pitched voice of her twelve-year-old daughter. Hayes walked to the bottom of the steps and looked up. Standing above her was blonde, gangly, teeth-braced Madison, dressed in the gold and blue sequinned costume of San Antonio High School's marching band. She ran a silver-topped marching baton backwards and forwards skilfully between her fingers.

'Momma's just sorting out things for tomorrow, honey. Come down and help me.'

Madison put down her baton and joined her mother.

'I'm going to be doing something real important that'll need different kinds of guns. I've already picked out these.'

'What you doing that needs those heavies?' Madison enquired, recognising the two bulging carry bags laid on the floor.

'Wanna persuade some baby boomers to turn themselves in. The Reboot Council in Austin needs help rounding 'em up.'

'Sounds fun. Can I come with you?' She fluttered her large blue eyes. 'Promise not to get in the way.'

'No honey. Don't want you seeing nothin' that'll give you nightmares. You'll get your turn when you're of age.'

'Not fair. I hate those nasties as much as you for what they done.'

'Answer's still no. Now help me out here.' Hayes turned to her handgun collection. 'I'll need a pistol to finish them off. I could take this…'

She held up the dull-grey, polymer-finished Glock 17. Madison took it and dry-fired the weapon at the ceiling.

'It's light and the seventeen-round mag gives real confidence in a firefight, but I prefer this one because…it's pretty.' Madison handed the Glock back to her mother and picked up a pistol from the other wall.

'Well, I'd want to look good so this is the one I'd have, Momma. The Colt.'

The semi-automatic Colt M1911 had been a standard-issue sidearm for the US army for over seventy years. It was heavy but lethal. Hayes' gun was half-chrome with a white pearl grip engraved with her initials. Costing ten thousand dollars, it was also the most valuable gun she owned. She smiled at her daughter.

'Agreed – it's going to the party.'

Hayes slipped it carefully into its soft leather monogrammed holster, buttoned down the flap and placed it on the step.

'Now last – how about a heavy calibre? In case things get… unpredictable.'

'Might need to make some noise to intimidate those old folks,' said Madison. 'How about this? Always gives me goosebumps when you open it up.'

She pointed to a heavy-set gun standing on a splayed tripod that dominated the far end of the room. Its eighteen-inch barrel with air holes cut along its entire length, was connected to a twelve-inch oblong bullet chamber through which ran a belt of bullets fed from a large wooden ammunition box. A simple chrome pistol grip handle jutted from the back of the weapon. Despite its rough-and-ready appearance, the Browning .30 calibre was probably the most accurate belt-fed machine gun ever made – and it was certainly one of the loudest.

'Agreed. The .30 cal. is a great choice. So I'll need a couple of belt boxes.'

Satisfied with her choices, Hayes stroked her daughter's hair. 'How about some milk, cookies and Malcolm in the Middle before bed, honey?'

Madison kissed her mother on the cheek. 'Love, love, love it when you're in a good mood, Momma.'

Hayes brought up six boxes of empty cartridge cases and smiled at her daughter. 'Well you know how I like firing my guns.'

'Your favourite thing. That mean you'll be making bullets all night?'

'I need five hundred rounds of mixed calibre, but I'll keep the noise down, baby.'

'Promise you won't play Nirvana at full blast?'

'Don't worry, I'll wear headphones.'

An hour later, Hayes had performed her maternal duties, and finally got to enjoy two of her other favourite things – making hot lead and listening to Kurt Cobain and the boys. She always opted to make her own ammunition because it always proved more accurate in competitions. She also preferred subsonic rounds, believing that bullets that travelled just below the sound barrier gave better punch. So with the intention of giving every single round the care, love and killing power she felt they deserved, Hayes put on her headphones and her favourite Nirvana tracks on repeat. Five hours later, Hayes had finished. She slept like a baby.

Up at seven, she had breakfast and saw Madison onto the bus. Knowing the day could be unpredictable, Hayes had arranged for a friend to pick her up after school. By nine, she had loaded her pickup with the weapons and put on her camouflage fatigues. She was ready to go killing, but knew she still had to wait for the starting pistol, so turned on the TV to watch the broadcast.

Right on cue, the now familiar black Reboot symbol appeared on the screen, along with the usual wording 'Important Public Announcement'. Soon, the familiar face of Richard Macy appeared, sitting at a desk dressed in his usual plain white shirt and green tie. Macy had become a pre-eminent spokesman for Reboot's US council after the organisation had taken over running the country. Whenever there was something important to say, he was normally the person saying it.

He had informed the nation of the 'unfortunate, but necessary deaths' of President Jefferson and Vice-President Summers and the dissolution of both the Republican and Democratic parties. He had announced Reboot's plans to halt climate change and the decision to exterminate baby boomers. Throughout this extraordinary year he had kept the country up to date with the progress of those initiatives and the necessary introduction of the One for One plan. And now it fell to Macy again to tell the country with the highest gun ownership in the world that they could use their weapons to round up any citizen between the ages of sixty-seven and eighty-five and, if necessary, terminate them.

'Good morning, America.'

Macy smiled widely to reveal a set of teeth, that looked at least a size too big. In spite of the serious nature of his bulletins over the past few months, for many of the millions who watched them, the contents of his mouth had been a constant source of amusement. They remembered the first appearance of this strange man with his yellowing, tombstone teeth. Reboot had liked his reassuring performance in front of the camera, but not the poor state of his orthodontics. Macy had obviously spent a lot of time in the dentist's chair since then.

'Good morning, America,' he repeated. 'I know there has been a lot of anticipation about my announcement today. Let me be clear. Whatever you may previously have heard or think you understand, please disregard it. If it does not concur with what I am about to tell you, then it is false.' He looked hard at the camera and paused for dramatic effect.

'Here are the facts. When I told you many months ago of the need to reduce our nation's population count by removing the baby boomer generation, we knew it was going to be a big ask. After all, the US has over seventy-three million people who fall into that category.' His face brightened and he smiled his expensive smile.

'I am delighted to tell you that we are well on track and leading the world in this difficult yet crucial task.'

On the screen, a number of graphs appeared at the side of Macy's head.

'We are leading the world in baby boomers taken down as a proportion of population at twenty-two per cent. We lead the world on actual terminations at 34.5 million. Our kills-per-day numbers have held up fantastically, and we're now averaging a cull rate of around a hundred thousand BBs per day.' Macy folded his arms and became serious again.

'But folks, that still leaves 38.5 million to go. Although the One for One initiative has worked well, we're now seeing another slowdown in boomers coming forward. So that is why I am asking all loyal Americans today to assist us in our task in two ways…'

He held up his middle finger to the camera. To Hayes, it looked like he was insulting the viewers.

'Number one. To inform us about anyone in your family or

anyone you know born between 1946 and 1964 who is still at large.'

Now he held up two fingers, which to Hayes looked even worse.

'Number two. To actively assist the law enforcement agencies to locate and round up these people to be dealt with accordingly.' The Stars and Stripes flag appeared behind Macy; it billowed dramatically in front of a deep-blue sky.

'My fellow Americans, if you are interested in helping your nation in this vital endeavour, as I most sincerely hope you are, then you should contact your local police authorities to let them know that is your intention. They will enter your names on the new National Cull Enforcers Register and you will be assigned tasks in due course.' An image of a hand signing the register appeared behind Macy.

'Do not – I repeat, do not – take the law into your own hands. If you decide unilaterally to do so, then you run the risk of suffering the ultimate penalty yourself. We are a civilised country, and the United States must set an example to the world. This is not a turkey shoot.' Macy's face disappeared and was replaced by the Reboot logo and a contact number.

Hayes' eyes widened. 'The hell it ain't.'

Driving at speed towards downtown San Antonio, it took her just twenty minutes to reach the nearest police station on Jones Maltsberger Road. To her dismay, there was already a long queue of people outside waiting to sign up. Cursing, she headed for the FBI building three miles away on University Heights.

The scene here was so much quieter with no people or cars. Hayes reckoned it must be closed. Parking by the front door, she noticed activity inside and walked in. The bespectacled man at the reception desk looked up.

'You here for the turkey shoot?'

Just five minutes later, Hayes had signed the requisite paperwork and was being given rules of engagement by Agent James Terrell. Overweight and wearing a cheap synthetic suit, the balding Terrell sweated profusely in the stuffy, windowless interview room as he gave her the low-down on identifying suspects.

'Most important thing to remember, Temporary Agent Hayes, is…you gotta ascertain one hundred per cent who you got in front of you.'

Hayes nodded blankly. Terrell sighed and started reading from a piece of FBI-headed paper.

'We accept any of the following forms of ID: birth certificate; W-2. Prior year's state, federal, or tribal tax return; Social Security card; Certificate of Naturalization; Certificate of US Citizenship; Permanent resident card – unexpired; Permanent resident alien card – unexpired; US government, military, state, or tribal-issued ID – unexpired; Passport – unexpired; Military discharge documentation; Weapons permit – unexpired; Driver's license – unexpired; Government assistance program document – that includes proof of identity; Statement of benefits from a qualifying program – that includes proof of identity; Unemployment or worker's compensation statement of benefits.' He handed the list to Hayes.

'You got that, Temporary Agent Hayes?'

Hayes had stopped listening. She just wanted to get going. 'Got all that, Agent Terrell.'

'OK, your first assignment. We've been told that there may be a bunch of boomers holding out in Texas Hill Country near the Wildlife Ranch. We think they might have been killing some of the wildlife for food. Two bison have been shot and butchered.'

'Bison? Should keep 'em in meat for a while,' Hayes quipped. Terrell ignored the comment.

'I want you to go look, keeping it real low-key. Act like a tourist. See if you can spot anything. They were last seen near Enchanted Rock. You can park up there and scout around. DO NOT display or use your guns for this recce, Agent Hayes.'

Once again, Hayes wasn't paying attention. She had absent-mindedly fixated on two beads of sweat streaming down Terrell's expansive forehead. They had disappeared behind his ear and reappeared as a single rivulet running down the back of his collar.

Hearing her name, she snapped back to the present.

'Did you get that, Temporary Agent Hayes?'

'Yes, Agent Terrell. You riding with me?'

'You're a lone wolf today. Love to come, but got to file your papers.'

Hayes knew the reason Terrell wasn't coming – he was afraid. He was no shooter, just a pen-pusher. But that was fine; the boomers would have spotted him a mile away. She shook his clammy hand, and as she walked to the door, Terrell shouted after her.

'And for Chrissake be careful. They could be armed. Just because they're getting on in years doesn't mean they can't be dangerous.'

Natural Bridge Wildlife Ranch was an animal sanctuary designed as a drive-through African Safari where visitors could see zebras, ostriches, giraffes, buffalo, bison, and other African animals roaming about in the semi-wild. It was normally a half-hour drive straight down I-35 North from San Antonio, but Hayes didn't rush. She was mulling over tactics, muttering to herself as she drove.

'Hide the Colt inside my top. The flak jacket should disguise the shape. The rest can stay locked and loaded in the back. Hang the field glasses round your neck. Act like you're just checking out the animals. Don't stray too far from the car. If you spot them and they run, fire a warning shot. If they keep running, blast the motherfuckers.'

Satisfied with her strategy, she put on the radio. Bruce Springsteen was blasting out 'Born in the USA'. The tune was over fifty years old but it was still her favourite song from her second-favourite artist. She sang along, happy in the knowledge that no one could hear her. Hayes rated her shooting; she could not say the same for her singing.

'Got the time, Preston?'

'Just gone noon. Time we were getting some sleep. We want to be wide awake for the hunt tonight.'

'I've got a hankering for zebra steak.'

'Sure need something fresh. Bison's starting to stink.'

Preston Knodell and Joe Cantu stood at the mouth of the Natural Bridge Cavern looking down into the long meandering valley which contained the wildlife park. They had led their group of baby boomers here as a temporary refuge five days ago. Usually a popular attraction, the Cavern was closed due to a recent landslide, and its owners were still trying to raise finance to make it safe. It all meant that instead of being busy with tourists, they had the place to themselves.

The group of six boomers, which included Knodell's and Cantu's wives, had evaded capture without too many alarms or surprises. Their plan had been simple, only move at night, steal food, water and transport as they went. Be prepared to kill anyone who got in their way.

Keeping to this simple strategy, they had successfully travelled seven hundred and fifty miles from Topeka in Kansas and were closing in on the nearest place that could offer them sanctuary – Mexico.

In an extraordinary alliance of convenience, Mexico's President López Obrador and the powerful Sinaloa, Gulf and Knights Templar drug cartels had joined forces to resist Reboot and the Mexican Army's attempts to control the country. The situation was unresolved and dangerous, but still offered Knodell's fugitives a possibility of redemption from the madness. The border was just another hundred and fifty miles, they had agreed that this cavern was to be their last stop before a final push to Nuevo Laredo.

'How are the others? enquired Knodell.

'All good. The cave is damp but everyone feels safe here.'

Knodell was pleased that Cantu's mood had lightened over the last few days. He was a very different person to the trigger-happy paranoid that had started their journey two weeks ago and who had nearly ruined everything on the first night. At a gas station in Wichita, he had levelled his gun at a police officer quietly eating a doughnut in his patrol car, oblivious to their presence. While his wife had stopped him that time, he remained twitchy and ready to blast anything that got in his way.

Gradually, as they racked up the miles without incident, he relaxed. Now, his face looked less drawn, his grey eyes less bloodshot, his nervous tic almost gone. He had even shaved off his grey stubble. *A good sign* thought Knodell.

'Can you ask Marie and Libby to do the next watch Joe?'

Cantu nodded and walked into the limestone interior of the cave. Within moments he had disappeared into the inky black.

Knodell leaned back against the smooth boulder behind him, rested his eyes and reflected on his life. For the past forty-nine years, he had lived happily with his wife Sandy in their hometown of Topeka. They liked the town with its easy-going, hard-working, middle-class aspirations. They liked the fact it had a great zoo, its own racetrack and was home to the Evil Knievel museum. They liked that it wasn't too far from Kansas City and its theatres, and they loved that it was only a short flight from Lake Michigan and their beloved boat.

The Knodells adored the carefree life too, so while they had plenty of friends, they never had kids. They didn't like stress much either, so they both worked an undemanding nine-to-five at the local Internal Revenue Office. They drove the three miles to work together and drove the same miles back together every night. Life in Topeka had delivered a quiet, predictable monotony and that was how Preston Knodell wanted it, because of what had happened to him in back in 1974.

He had just turned twenty, and had graduated from college two months previously when he was drafted to serve in Vietnam. Marked out for his twenty-twenty vision he was selected to train as a sniper and reached the battle zone in early 1975. In just three months, he had racked up twenty-eight confirmed kills and won a Purple Heart and two other citations for his marksmanship. He was transferred to an elite unit to guard the American Embassy in Hanoi, just as the victorious Vietcong started to advance into the city.

On 29 April, the fall of the city was imminent and all US troops were ordered out. Knodell fought his way through panic-stricken crowds to reach the helipad on the top of the embassy building and just managed to get onboard the last helicopter to leave. Overladen and struggling to take off, he was forced to kick two women from the skids to prevent it crashing. As they sped low over the city towards the harbour where US warships waited, enemy troops fired at the craft, killing a trooper next to him.

His ordeal did not end there. The pilot hadn't been trained to land on the ships waiting for them. The helicopter crash-landed onto the deck of the USS. *Blue Ridge* and Knodell was thrown overboard. In the fall, he lost all his kit, including his beloved rifle. He was eventually picked up five hours later, exhausted and with a broken shoulder, clinging to a wooden raft.

These were the reasons Knodell liked a drama-free life. He'd had enough adventure during his time in Vietnam to last a lifetime. But even that had gone to hell, and here he was on the run, skulking in a damp cave, miles from home. A decorated veteran, fleeing from a country that he served and that no longer wanted him around or even breathing.

So right now, he was grateful for his army training from all those years ago. It had taught him how to function, how to hide and how to stay alive in a place where everyone wanted him dead. It had given him confidence that they could make it to Mexico because he knew he was better than his pursuers. Better still, he had an M21, the same semi-automatic sniper rifle as the one he lost in the South China Sea, and it rested, fully-loaded next to his right arm. Even in this craziness, that gave him comfort.

Knodell opened his eyes and looked down into the valley. Two giraffes lazily chomped on acacia leaves that had been hung for them in the top of a tree. A small flock of ostriches strutted around the edge of a waterhole like they owned the place. As he looked to the north, a spark of light caught his eye as the midday sun hit a window or a mirror. Grabbing his rifle he quickly focused the powerful telescopic sight on the source. A blue pickup truck travelling slowly through the park; its tinted windows preventing him making out the driver or any other occupants. As he watched, it turned up the dirt track that led towards the Cavern.

The truck entered the car park in a cloud of dust and drove into the shadows of a Texas ash tree. The vehicle was now just eight hundred metres away and twenty metres below Knodell's position.

As he watched intently, the dust slowly settled and a slim, big busted woman in camouflage overalls stepped down from the car. She had binoculars, and Knodell relaxed, thinking she was probably just an animal enthusiast wanting to get a better view. He continued to watch as she went to the back of the truck and reached under the tarpaulin sheet stretched over the tray. Knodell watched impassively as she pulled out the unmistakable shape of an AR-15, checked the safety and slid the weapon back out of sight.

Knodell dropped onto his stomach in an instant, took aim at her head and calmly squeezed the trigger. The woman's body snapped back against the truck and crumpled onto the tarmac. The report of the shot echoed down the valley.

'What the fuck?'

Marie and Libby had just appeared to take over guard duties. Knodell was already on his feet, rifle still smoking.

'Get everyone ready, we're leaving. Tell them we've got a pickup and some new guns.'

7 December 2031, Edinburgh
Cull Day 298

The ride down to Cramond from Edinburgh Old Town normally took twenty minutes on the number 41 bus. It was usually a pleasant journey too, if the weather was dry and you were lucky enough to get a seat on the open-top deck. Travelling down the gently sloping Dundas Street, framed on both sides by well-tended Victorian terraced houses. Passing over the Water of Leith Walkway, then skirting the Botanic Garden with its tantalising glimpses of exotic broadleaved trees and palms. Past the sprawling green spaces of Wardie Fields before eventually emerging onto West Shore Road, announcing the broad elegant majesty of the Firth of Forth estuary.

The sun was shining and Jameson was sitting at the front of the top deck of the bus, but he didn't pay heed to any of the sights on offer. He only had eyes for his daughter Bella who sat by his side. Her long dark hair blew freely in the warm breeze and her turquoise-blue eyes shone like glass. His little girl had grown into a beautiful woman and best of all, she looked pleased to see him.

'Sorry they hurt you, Dad. They weren't meant to.'

'You know me – stubborn old bastard.'

She put her hand softly over his. It felt good, it felt genuine, but Jameson was all too aware of the black plastic ties binding his hands and the two rogue interrogators sitting behind them. They were now dressed in T-shirts and jeans but looked no less intimidating.

'How have you been? Have they treated you well? Have you spoken to Mum?'

'Yes, and yes, and Mum's fine. She's been frantic about you, obviously.'

Suddenly he felt ashamed.

I've hardly thought of Bethany this past year. It's always been the same with my work. It came first, she and the kids a distant second. I have also betrayed her yet here I am, being told that she had been worrying about me.

'I wish I could see her. I wish you, Patrick and Mum could all be together and this nightmare was over,' he replied forlornly.

'Part of me does too, Dad. But I think you know that world is gone.'

'Which world is that? That one that showed compassion and respect for life? That one that was working hard to find answers to the same problems that Reboot are trying to tackle?'

'Your generation was never going to make the decisions that were necessary.' She flashed him a hard, embittered look, then turned away.

Jameson bit his lip, not wanting to fall out with his daughter again so soon.

She nudged his arm. 'Come on, this is where we get off.'

The bus came to a stop and she led him down the stairs with

the two heavies in attendance a few steps behind. Bella pulled gently on the ties to guide her father across the road, and after a short walk into the quaint beachside hamlet and whitewashed houses of Cramond.

It was twenty past nine and low tide, so the vast beach beyond the sea wall was fully exposed, which meant that the kilometre-long causeway leading to Cramond Island was open to walkers for the next four hours. A large noticeboard at the landward end of the causeway set out in bold red letters the times when it might be safely crossed, despite this every year dozens of visitors still found themselves stranded on the island by the incoming tide.

They walked down a short flight of algae-covered granite steps and onto the smooth concrete of the causeway. On the right-hand, a row of ten-feet-high pyramid shaped concrete pylons ran along its entire length. It was a striking sight, and Jameson tried to imagine what they were for. Bella noticed his quizzical look.

'They were built during the Second World War as a submarine defence boom.'

'Where are we going, Bella?'

'To meet someone I think you'll be interested to see.'

They walked on for a minute saying nothing. The sun continued to shine and the gentle shore winds regulated the temperature to a pleasant twenty two degrees. In different circumstances thought Jameson, this would be an agreeable stroll. Bella smiled, letting go of his ties.

'Remember when you took Patrick and me for mystery walks? It was always too tiring for my little feet and you had to carry me the final mile.'

'Yes, and the final mile always ended in some pub garden with a Coca-Cola for you and your brother and a beer for me.'

'Maybe some salt and vinegar crisps, if we were lucky.' She beamed.

God I love you.

For Jameson, it was a blessed reminder of happier times, a memory of long summer days, beautiful hill views and swimming in slow-flowing rivers like the Churn, Coln and Windrush which lazily meandered their way through the Cotswolds. Those were the times he remembered most fondly about family life. With his tribe and in the place he loved. Yet here he was, walking with a member of that tribe and in this place, he was a dead man walking.

He felt an urge to run, to escape this fate. He tensed to take flight and escape his captors, then just as quickly the urge passed. It would never succeed and he didn't want to get flattened again by those humourless apes following behind. So Jameson kept walking with his daughter and the apes towards this sinister low-lying island that lay in front of them, now curious to find out who or what waited for him. His cracked ribs were starting to ache.

Why did it have to be so far away?

'Whatever happens, I want you to know…I love you, Dad.' Bella touched him on the shoulder.

'That sounds ominous. Aren't I suppose to say that to you?'

'Yes, but I'm not the one who's tied up.'

'Why am I tied up? Boomers are too decrepit to run very far.'

They both laughed at the absurdity.

As the group approached the end of the causeway, Jameson could see that a barbed-wire perimeter fence had been erected along the entire shoreline, restricting access to the Island itself. They stopped a few paces in front of a heavy gate, and one of the po-faced heavies spoke into his phone. The gate slowly opened and they continued their journey on a cracked prefabricated concrete path. To their left on a small rise, an old gun emplacement rusted away in the salty air. Nearby, a pair of twisted searchlight housings were doing the same. As they continued along the path, the ground rose gently, and more wartime relics came into view around them.

Long abandoned concrete buildings, smothered in graffiti lined both sides of the path, their windows smashed or boarded up. Further on to their left, three neat rows of rectangular concrete bases scarred the ground, each punctuated with the blackened remains of fireplaces at either end. Bella again noticed her father's frown.

'That's all that remains of the wooden barracks buildings.'

Jameson raised his eyebrows, fascinated by this wartime ghost town. 'Must have been quite a garrison here.'

'At least two hundred, all Home Guard, all probably your age.' She smiled.

'Even old men made a contribution to the war effort.'

They walked for another five minutes before stopping at the entrance to a bunker with a curved moss-laden corrugated iron roof. Treacherously damp steps led down to an ivy-covered door. One of the bodyguards warily descended.

'Careful, steps are slippery.'

Jameson couldn't help but smirk at the irony.

Yesterday, this ape would have beaten me to death. Now he's worried I'll turn an ankle.

He descended the steps gingerly and followed his daughter through the heavy door which opened onto a wide metal gangway and into Cramond Island's greatest secret.

Oh my God.

Stretching out far below them was a vast brightly-lit circular space, its smooth grey concrete walls descending at least fifty metres underground. The gangway that Jameson stood on ran along the entire outer diameter, forming the top level. As he looked down into the dizzying chasm, he could see at various points more open metal stairwells running down to at least another four floors. Each punctuated by doors or other openings which seemed to lead off into more corridors. Peering down over the low side rails of the gangway into the cavernous void gave Jameson a tingle of vertigo. Far below, he could see heavy netting had been fixed to the sides of the bottom rail to catch anyone who might fall.

As he continued to process what he was seeing, a tall man in a light-grey fitted suit walked over to the group. He briefly spoke to Bella, before turning to Jameson.

'Good morning Mr Jameson, I am Stephen Cooper. Welcome to the place where exceptions are made for exceptional people.'

Three hours later, and Jameson was sitting in a small windowless office opposite Cooper who sat behind a desk looking into a laptop. They had removed his wrist ties and he nursed a mug of hot sweet tea. Bach's 'Air on the G String' was wafting through a speaker in the ceiling; on the surface, all was calm but Jameson's head was still swimming from what he had been told.

I am to be spared. I am to be allowed to live and will be reunited with Bethany, Patrick and Bella. But I'll have to remain on the island and continue my work.

'We anticipate perfecting the formulation, installation and manufacture of your gel will take at least two years, by which time, the boomer cull should have ceased,' Cooper had concluded.

This all seems too good to be true, so it probably is.

'Who will I be working with?' Jameson asked.

'It made sense to us to suggest you continue with your colleagues from your recent Antarctica expedition.'

He can't be serious. There is no way in the world…

Jameson's first impulse was to refuse to work with the duplicitous Waites and Beckley, but he wanted to find out the truth about Sarah. This would be his only chance to find out.

He smiled at Cooper. 'That makes sense. What facilities are here?'

'We can bring in any equipment and create whatever

laboratory conditions you desire. When the War Department created this bunker during World War Two, they even installed a 250,000-gallon swimming pool in the basement. We can fill it directly through pumps from the estuary for your tests.'

Jameson nodded, but said nothing for a few moments.

'Who else is here? Who else have you made exceptions for?'

Cooper stood and pressed a button on the wall. 'You've already met three of them – Steve Hamlin of Carbon Engineering, Sylvia his wife and Clive Walsh, the 6G grid engineer. Like you, they revealed nothing during their interrogation, so in one sense, like you, they too have earned their place here.'

Jameson was wondering if they too had suffered cracked ribs.

Cooper walked around the room enthusiastically extolling the virtues and ambitions of the Cramond Island project. 'There is an amazing community of scientists here. Pioneers in biomass burning, renewable electricity generation and modular floating wind farms. Innovators in new battery chemistries, green hydrogen and carbon-negative technologies.'

'Impressive. All brought here under their own free will?'

Cooper ignored the question. 'There is one scientist who is looking into broad-spectrum solar power which promises to be able to capture twice the amount of the sun's energy. Another is having amazing success with CO_2-trapping seaweed. I am sure you will enjoy getting to know them and their work.'

'Sure, I will. When can I see my wife?' Jameson asked wearily.

'All in good time. She knows you are here.'

The hairs on the back of his neck prickled. He felt nervous and excited at meeting his wife for the first time in over a year.

Cooper sat down again and leaned forward, a serious expression on his face. 'One last thing, Mr Jameson. Because of your unique situation you have not seen how the world has changed in your absence. Let me tell you, before you have romantic notions that this is some sort of aberration and things will return to what they were before; they will never go back. Look at this...'

Cooper turned his laptop to face Jameson. It was a map of the world, but like nothing Jameson had seen before. Most of the political borders were gone. France, Germany, Spain and the forty-one other countries that had made up Europe had all disappeared. The continent was now defined on the map by just one green colour. The same applied to Scandinavia, Russia, China, Turkey and all of the Middle East. Australia, New Zealand, all of North America had all been subsumed by a sea of green. Only Asia, Africa and South America were any different. With just six countries on those vast continents, Indonesia, Taiwan, Central African Republic, Somalia, Mexico and Venezuela still marked in red.

'There is no homeland anymore. No more best of British, no America first. Just Mother Earth.'

Jameson shook his head.

'Reboot's greatest triumph has been to change a belief. The belief that homo sapiens could do what they liked within their own borders, without first regarding the needs of nature and the planet. We are stopping the waste; we are helping people live within the limits of the resources available to them. We have given humanity a chance, that is all. It remains to be seen whether it is still enough to save us.'

Cooper snapped his laptop shut. 'Now I wish you all speed in your work. The decline of the Thwaites Glacier must be stopped or we will all be swimming.'

Jameson was led out into the main atrium by a young soldier whose hobnailed boots resounded noisily on the metal stairs as they walked down to the next floor. A luminous yellow sign on the wall proclaimed that they had arrived on level C. Another ten paces on, the soldier stopped at a door marked 9C.

'In you go,' he ordered.

Jameson entered, and the door was immediately closed and locked. The room was small, about four metres square with plain whitewashed walls, no outside windows and a slate-grey carpet.

So this is home for the next two years.

In one corner of the room stood a small desk and wooden chair, in another a tired looking beige coloured two-person settee and a black-painted coffee table. A pine wardrobe, empty bookcase and an unmade double bed completed the extent of the furnishings. There was just one other door which he assumed led to a bathroom.

He was about to have a look when a gentle knock on the door checked him.

'Come in. I'm not naked,' he shouted.

Bella walked in carrying a tray.

'Cup of tea and biscuits, Dad?'

Jameson smiled. His daughter might be hard work sometimes, but she always knew how to cheer him up.

'Going to drink with me?'

'Of course. What do you think of your room?'

'I think if I was paying more than forty pounds a night, I'd be pissed off.'

For ten minutes, father and daughter chatted amiably again about simpler, less troubled times. Then Bella moved to collect up the cups.

'Time to go, Dad.'

Jameson stood up, walked over to the space in front of the desk and lay down on the floor on his back.

'Come over here a minute.'

Bella looked confused. 'I've really got to go.'

'Five minutes. Please.'

Bella slowly walked over and settled down next to her father.

They lay there for a minute, saying nothing, looking up at the grey concrete ceiling above them. Jameson broke the silence.

'Remember this?'

'Yes.' Bella began to softly cry.

'We used to go into the garden, lie on the grass and look straight up at the sky and watch the clouds pass by.'

'Yes, I remember.'

'You were always amazed by how fast they appeared to be going.'

'I loved looking at the stars more.' Bella reached out and held her father's hand. 'I used to do it when you weren't around. That time staying on Dartmoor was the best. The dark sky was amazing. I thought I could see right back into the origins of creation. It was so good, even Patrick joined me once.'

Jameson smiled at the thought of his children flat on their backs on the damp grass in a garden in Devon. Then felt a pang of guilt as he recalled that it was yet another family holiday he didn't make because of his work.

I was such a selfish idiot.

'You were always a busy child, constantly on the move. Stargazing used to slow you down. Mum used to call it your comfort in the cosmos.'

Bella squeezed her father's hand. 'Do you think we can save our little part of it, Dad?'

'Perhaps, but not this way. You can't build the new Jerusalem on barbarism. It will devalue life forever. Who will they pick on next? Generation X? Men with limps, women with ginger hair?'

'At least we're trying something,' Bella snapped. She took her hand from his and they both stood up.

'Bella, I'm sorry. I know you believe in what Reboot are doing, but it goes against every moral code.'

'We'll just have to suspend morals while we do what must be done.'

She walked to the door, stopped and then turned. She reached into a pocket, pulled out her phone and showed Jameson the picture on the home screen.

'This is your granddaughter.'

Jameson looked at the baby smiling up at him and felt a giant lump in his throat.

She's beautiful.

'Her name is Sky. I'm doing this all for her now, and nothing is going to get in my way.' She put the phone back into her pocket.

Jameson grabbed her hand. 'Darling that's wonderful, I can't wait to meet her.'

'Thanks, she's adorable.'

This is crazy. It's still no world for my granddaughter to grow up in.

He squeezed her hand, suddenly desperate to convince his daughter of a different path. 'Bella, can you get hold of Mum and get us out of here? We could get a boat and work our way up the coast. Try to make contact with the resistance movement. There must be plenty in the countryside around here.'

Bella pulled her hand away and looked hard into her father's eyes.

'Please give this a try. Mum will be here tomorrow with Patrick. Reboot have given their word to me that we will all be safe – as long as you co-operate. Everything is in place here, the equipment and the people. If you can manufacture the gel and get it working, you will be a hero and we shall all be safe…'

Jameson could feel his resolve weaken. He hated what Reboot was doing, but now the grip they had on events seemed unbreakable, too advanced to stop.

Perhaps I am the only one who can save us. This really could be the only way I can be with my family, the last chance for me to be a grandad.

Jameson shrugged. 'OK, I'll give it a go. It's not as if I have a lot of options.'

Bella kissed her father on the cheek and left the room. The door automatically locked behind her with a heavy clank.

Like closing the cell door on a condemned man.

Suddenly feeling dog-tired, Jameson slumped on the bed and closed his eyes.

He is in the jungle, trees tower above him like supernatural giants. Through the jungle canopy he can see chinks of white light hundreds of feet up. The light spears down and hits the jungle floor in small pools, illuminating dried, curling leaves as he passes over them. He is running. Running like never before, flying over the ground like an Olympian at the peak of his powers. It feels joyous, intoxicating. He can keep this speed up for miles, forever. He yells in joy at the elation. Suddenly, he senses something behind him – there is a rumbling, like a wave gathering energy. He continues to run, now faster, sensing that he must to avoid this threat. The rumble is now a roar. He accelerates again, running so fast everything around is a chaotic, cascading blur.

He dare not look back, must keep going, must go quicker. But he is powerless. He senses that this 'force', this 'thing', this 'them' is overtaking him on both sides. Now they are in front, blocking his way, hemming him in, and he stops. They advance towards him, with jaws open and raised. They are coming to kill.

As he waits for them to rip him to pieces, he realises.

I will never leave this place.

When he has revealed his secrets, outlived his usefulness, he will be culled.

Because here as in nature, when it comes to protecting the greater good and demonstrating the absolute will to achieve it, there can be no exceptions.

There is a knock on the door, and he wakes. It is pitch black in the room, his room lights have been turned off. He hears a voice.

'Come on Ice Man we're leaving.'

Yes.

Printed in Great Britain
by Amazon

81833269R00192